From *BEYOND LICH GATE* . . .

A hero's descendant, Aitchley Corlaiys was chosen to restore the endangered land of Vedette to greatness . . .

To *THE CATHEDRAL OF THORNS* . . .

To complete his quest, Aitchley had to travel across Vedette—for love, for land, and for the Elixir of Life itself . . .

Now, the explosive conclusion to the captivating fantasy adventure . . .

A LEGEND REBORN

by the author of *The Wheel Trilogy*
STEVEN FRANKOS

D1572510

A LEGEND REBORN

STEVEN FRANKOS

ACE BOOKS, NEW YORK

This book is an Ace original edition,
and has never been previously published.

A LEGEND REBORN

An Ace Book / published by arrangement with
the author

PRINTING HISTORY
Ace edition / February 1997

The Putnam Berkley World Wide Web site address is
http://www.berkley.com/berkley

Make sure to check out *PB Plug,*
the science fiction/fantasy newsletter, at
http://www.pbplug.com

ISBN: 0-441-00419-9

ACE®
Ace Books are published by The Berkley Publishing Group,
200 Madison Avenue, New York, New York 10016.
ACE and the "A" design are trademarks
belonging to Charter Communications, Inc.

PRINTED IN THE UNITED STATES OF AMERICA

10 9 8 7 6 5 4 3 2 1

A LEGEND REBORN

Prologue
Fast Forward Search

TW-O: 114-84-1311825
102112-09-5

Multiple images flickered across the CRTs, accelerated footage that flashed hurriedly across the wall of monitors in a blur of colors and exaggerated motions. Fast-paced images of the town of Solsbury and a gathering within the Tridome, a sparse grouping of nobles from across Vedette sitting, bored and disinterested, while a young man and dwarf confront a quartet of lords. Images of sleek black animals, wolflike in nature, pursuing a group on horseback. Fast-forward pictures of a dark town—men and women in priestly robes standing sentry on each corner—while a young man and a diminutive blonde creep, hand in hand, through the streets without being seen. Images of a harsh, searing desert, league after league of nothing but sand heaped high in dunes of melted gold. Footage of a riot, people taking to the streets of Viveca while a badly mended fishing trawl hangs out a high castle window, three people dangling from its frayed netting. Images of thick trees and constant rainfall, the camera lens nearly fogging up at the unbearable humidity of the Bentwoods. Images of mushroom houses beside a waterfall nearly a mile high filling the valley with cloudbursts of prismatic spray. Accelerated images of gloomy basalt caves cutting a subterranean swath through volcanic rock, slender, blue-gray women in snakeskin loincloths acting as guides. And images of a place beyond that of the living . . . a vast plain of hard-baked blue earth where a line of silvery-white ghosts makes its way up an enormous staircase of marble and gold and fades into a sunlike orb of brilliant white Oblivion.

Irising into focus, cold gray lenses watched the fast-forward blurs across all forty screens, no trace of human emotion in its videocamera eyes. Articulated fingers of gray steel stood poised over the controls of its somber gray editing board as if hopeful that something had been overlooked . . . something that contradicted what the metallic construct standing before the wall of monitors already knew to be true.

The human-shaped mechanism nicknamed Tin William by its programmers stared impassively at the banks of color video display terminals lining the wall above its editing bay, fast-moving images reflecting eerily in its grayly tinted videocamera eyes. Behind the robot, half-crouched on fully extended tripod legs, the arachnid form of Camera 4 sat watching the man-shaped figure of metal, its single glass eye recording in full detail everything about the humanoid robot. It watched in a tight one-shot, focused primarily on the expressionless face of the creature called Tin William yet capturing the fast-forward movements of some of the screens as they gleamed off the robot's silvery-sheened surface. Although the robot's face was not articulated enough to express emotion—and its mouth was nothing more than a triangular speaker grid unequipped to show happiness or sorrow—there was still an air of troubled thoughtfulness about the construct, a tangible feeling that radiated from the silver figure as though the many scenes flashing across the wall of forty terminals sent an anxious barb through its digitized, inhuman heart.

Tin William paused the image in VDT 23, videocamera eyes irising as it inspected the scene frozen before it. The image was that of a young man—not more than seventeen years of age—looking puzzled and afraid as he plucked a bluish-green decanter off an altar formed of writhing, twisted red thorns, an undeniable question sparkling in his blue-green eyes. The brown clothes covering his lean yet muscular frame were dark and damp with arctic moisture, and there were scrapes and bruises across his face and arms, red and fresh in the high-resolution monitors of the editing-bay wall. His worn and tattered cloak was even more beraggled than before, and the pale, skeletal remains of a single gyrofalc feather slouched languidly across the wide brim of his hat, half shadowing the look of apprehension frozen on his videotaped features.

The construct called Tin William turned away from the bank of CRTs and stared blankly across the tiny white chamber that was its workstation. Aitchley Corlaiys, it concluded dourly, videocamera eyes staring but not seeing, does not understand. Despite the warnings, Aitchley Corlaiys has been unable to properly process the information he has received. Despite the helpful lore of the fungoid Rhagana gardener, Gjuki, and the curious questions posed by the human healer, Sprage, while journeying through the rain forests—or even the inexperienced translations of the preadolescent *Kwau*, Taci, while at the mysterious Canyon Between—Aitchley Corlaiys has remained unquestionably confused. He has not seen the subtle connections . . . remains unaware of the interrelationship of all things. He has misconstrued the meaning of my words to reflect his own insecurities and strengthen his lack of self-esteem, and—while any future actions taken by Aitchley Corlaiys will, in fact, have serious repercussions on himself, his people, and the very world he lives in, he remains ignorant of my main intent.

Assessment: Something must be done to steer Aitchley Corlaiys, once again, in the proper direction.

Although incapable of expressing emotion, the robotic TransWorld Observer threw what could have been a furtive glance at the chamber around it. Camera 4 stared back phlegmatically—what it saw transmitting live to VDT 37—and there might have been a moment of silent introspection as Tin William turned back to the forty screens hovering above the editing bay.

The robot's eyes glistened with reflections of videotaped images. Conclusion: the manlike machine computed, the only viable solution is . . . personal intervention.

Steel fingers flicked a single switch and sent the entire wall of monitors blinking off, forty screens consigned to an impenetrable blackness. Then, with a purposeful clank of metal feet across tile, the construct nicknamed Tin William turned on its silver heel, stepped through the sliding panel of its automated front door, and strode out into the burning sands and blistering heat of the Molten Dunes.

1

The Smell of Blood

Dark and unfathomable, the blackness was absolute, a voidlike sea of impenetrable ebony lapping at the distant shores of dreary blue rock. Arctic winds blew up from the depths of the darkness—tinged with frigid barbs of cold and laced with the breath of polar ice—howling and moaning in bodiless anguish. Strands and veils of ragged dark moss ringed the jagged rim of the pit, waving and fluttering as if beckoning in the unearthly winds, and a huge structure built entirely out of crimson brambles grew up out of the very center of the darkness like some thorny red heart in an ocean of lightlessness.

Aitchley Corlaiys stared down at the black emptiness beneath his feet, the uneasy twist and wrench of vertigo souring his innards. A glittering silver cable of braided spidersilk was all that stood between him and a fall into liquid blackness, and he shuffled nervously across the silken line, using a second strand of spider's silk stretched above his head to help steady him. His legs wobbled and trembled like the slender line beneath his feet, and sweat coated the palms of his hands, making his grip slick and untrustworthy. He tried to keep his attention on the solid ground at the edge of the pit, but it was increasingly difficult to ignore the yawning black chasm of infinite nothingness gaping hungrily below him.

Ahead of him—also trying to navigate the bob and sway of the spidersilk lines—shuffled Harris Blind-Eye, his lean and wiry body sagging as he inched across the twin ropes. A great smear of damp red slicked the left side of the brigand's body—starting at his left shoulder and soaking the entire left side of his tattered clothes with a gruesome, tacky scarlet—and there was no familiar glint of knavery or iniquity in his blue-black eyes. His face was slack and pale beneath his ragged black beard and mustache, and his movements were slow and difficult, although he tried to conceal his discomfort with a mask of bravado. A bulging saddlebag slung across the outlaw's good shoulder, and Aitchley feared the added weight of the pack might very well pull the lockpick off their silver tightrope and send him plunging into the inky darkness below.

Beyond them—still separated by some thirty feet of liquid blackness—Aitchley's blue-green eyes fixed longingly on the safety of the distant rim of the massive pit, wishing the somber blue stones were beneath his feet rather than this unsettling, weightless feeling that roiled in his belly as he stood suspended out over frigid air. He could see the fanglike stalagmites rising up out of the blue earth to probe at the featureless skies—could even see the intense white light of Oblivion shining brightly on the eastern horizon—but his eyes remained locked on the people waiting for him at the edge of the enormous pit.

Half-hidden behind the deep blue outcroppings of unearthly stones, Aitchley could just make out Calyx, the dwarf's large nose protruding from behind the rocks like a rosy gourd of flesh. The ruddy features of his face were scrunched up in a grim mien of sure disaster, and tiny eyes fixed rigidly on the young man and lockpick as they made their slow way across the infinite chasm. Pudgy hands gripped tightly to the heavy warhammer at his belt, and the dwarf's large sack sat behind him in a lump of dark tarpaulin almost as big as the smith himself.

Behind the dwarf—like three misplaced saplings in a world devoid of foliage—stood Gjuki, Gjalk, and Eyfura, three Rhagana from the humid interior of the Bentwoods. Both Gjalk and Eyfura were completely nude—their sticklike forms and leathery brown skins unhampered by clothing—but Gjuki wore ill-fitting human clothes over his plantlike frame. A thick leather apron covered the front of the fungoid gardener's body like a breastplate, and there could have been a look of mild worry on his otherwise impassive features as he watched the two men struggle their way across the tightrope of spidersilk. All three had hair that wavered in the cold winds like tangled mops of green moss, and each had frondlike sideburns that trailed like light green ferns down the sides of their cheeks, thicker and more pronounced on Gjuki and Gjalk than on Eyfura. Heavy, woolen blankets tried to keep out the otherworldly chill of the Outside, and their small, pearllike black eyes stared out over the gargantuan pit at the two men fighting to make their way back to them.

To the left of the three Rhagana, Sprage and Poinqart tried to remain concealed behind the dark blue stalagmites, the former doing a better job than the latter. A look of trollish determination and human worry contorted the olive-green features of the half troll's face, and his thick, spatulate fingers clenched the rocks in front of him with a bone-crushing strength of hybrid frustration. Poinqart understood that he had to stay hidden-unseen or else grave-deadly-danger might befall his friend, yet an almost overpowering urge to run out and help Aitchley screamed and yowled at the back of his brain. Even so, he forced himself to fight down the ever-increasing desire and wait, feeling Sprage's restraining hand resting upon his green and hunched shoulder.

Beside the half troll and healer—half-crouched behind a spear of blue rock—was Berlyn, a look of unfettered fear and worry etched on her beautiful face. Her long, platinum-blond hair streamed and billowed in the arctic gale of the pit-born winds—yellow-white strands blowing across her face—and the torn and tattered hem of her skirt fluttered about her legs, exposing soft pale flesh up to the hip because of a jagged tear up one seam. Her slim and delicate hands wrung together in apprehensive fits, and beautiful gray-green eyes stared out across the oceanlike expanse of blackness to where Aitchley made his careful way across the braided cables of spider's web.

Berlyn, Aitchley thought to himself, unable to stop the warm feeling that rose in his body at the sight of the diminutive young blonde, I did it! Can you believe it? I actually did it! Me! Aitchley! I actually succeeded at something!

Although suspended high above lightless nothingness, Aitchley felt a lopsided smile pull briefly across his lips. Even through the thick material Tin William had called nylon, the young farmer could feel the unnatural warmth of the magical elixir resting in his backpack. A sorcerous staff of blackened and gnarled wood—also radiating the unearthly heat of true magicks—was strapped to his back beneath the shoulder straps of his pack, and a magnificent new sword of gray-white steel rested in his sheath to replace the one shattered by the Eternal Guardian's many-limbed attack. All in all, it was still hard to believe that he had actually succeeded. That he, Aitchley Corlaiys—someone who couldn't even bring forth a decent harvest—had done something that no other living creature in all recorded history had ever done.

He had obtained the fabled Elixir of Life.

Aitchley was unable to stop the smug smile from stretching even more broadly across his lips. So much for typical Corlaiys luck, he chided his pessimism.

The smile unexpectedly fled Aitchley's face when Harris suddenly stopped in front of him, the brigand's slow progress halting entirely. The southern-city thief hung from the twin ropes, head bowed against his breast in a kind of exhausted slump. His eyes had closed and his face looked even paler than before.

A worm of worry twisted its way through Aitchley's stomach as he stared questioningly at the immobile thief. "Harris?" the young man quietly asked.

Head resting against his breastbone, Harris did not reply.

Aitchley took a tentative step forward, feeling the silken rope sag beneath his and Harris's combined weight. "Harris?" He risked another whisper.

A blue-black eye cracked open irately. "What?" came the gruff retort.

Despite the outlaw's infirmity, Aitchley was unable to meet the feral hatred that burned in that single-eyed glare and glanced down at the cold, black emptiness beneath his feet; starless pitch smiled back up at him. "I . . . um . . ." The young farmer faltered. "Are you all right?"

A grave smile that became an even graver sneer pinched the lockpick's mouth. "No, puck," he answered with derisive—albeit fatigued—sarcasm, "I am *not* all right. I'm a walkin' dead man. I've got a hole the size of me father's fist in my left shoulder, and I'm standin' out over the bungin' Daeminase Pits themselves! It's not what I'd call a day out in the Solsbury Hills!"

Regardless of the outlaw's treatment of him in the past, Aitchley felt a spear of concern drive through his innards. After all . . . Harris had saved him from the Eternal Guardian. "It's not much further," the young man observed. "You can do it."

Harris attempted another sardonic smirk but didn't have the strength. "You're not listening to me, puck," he replied, his single eye closing. "Might as well be a thousand leagues; I'm not gonna make it."

Worriedly, Aitchley reached out a helpful hand, leaving himself balanced with only one hand around the silken rope overhead. "Here," he said. "Why don't you get rid of that saddlebag? We've got enough supplies on—"

With a burst of unexpected strength, Harris jerked the leather pouch slung over his right shoulder away from Aitchley's fingers. "No way, scout," the bandit answered vehemently. "I've gotta have something to show for all this, don't I?"

The lockpick's abrupt move startled Aitchley into a sudden sway and rocking on the silver spidersilk underfoot. Once his equilibrium had been reestablished, the young man trained an inquisitive eye on the southern-city thief's bulging sack. "Are you trying to tell me you stole something from the cathedral?" he demanded.

Harris found the strength to stretch a faint grin beneath his beard. "I wouldn't call it so much stealing as I would assuring my self-sufficiency," he replied. "Besides . . . you took the elixir. What do you call that? Borrowing?"

The selfish revelation caused Aitchley to draw back his hand in shock. "Yeah, but . . . you could have brought back another incarnation of the Guardian by taking something," the young man declared. "That's how you conjured it up in the first place . . . by trying to take something from the cathedral!"

Harris's grin widened enough to show yellowed teeth. "That's why I grabbed the stuff while you were still busy fighting the first incarnation," he remarked. " 'A full share of anything of value,' remember?"

The realization that Harris had not come immediately to his aid filled Aitchley with an unexpected charge of anger-induced adrenaline. "You mean you let that thing throw me around the cathedral while you were robbing the place blind?"

Harris's exhaustion pulled the smile from his lips. "Robbing the place blind? Fah!" he responded glumly. "All I got was a couple of fancy rings, some dandy-ass cloak, and a few tiny vials of magical shim-sham. Hardly an impressive haul for going beyond Lich Gate. Shoulda gotten me something of real value." A blue-black eye opened just enough to give Aitchley a look of leering envy. "You wouldn't be thinking of selling that sword to me when this whole thing's over, would you?"

Aitchley placed an instinctive hand on the hilt of his newly acquired weapon, feeling his fingers curl almost supernaturally around its glittering golden handle.

Harris let his eye close again. "I didn't think so," he remarked.

Overwhelmed by the southern-city lockpick's blatant disregard for any life other than his own, Aitchley paused momentarily over the infinite darkness of the Daeminase Pits. I should let the son of a bungholer fall, he thought angrily to himself. All this time I thought he helped me defeat the Eternal Guardian, and he was off bunging around with magic rings and potions . . . with a bloody hole in his shoulder no less! Daeminase Pits! I could have been killed while he was stealing things! I'm surprised he didn't take the elixir itself and try and trade it for his stupid knives and necklace! I should have learned by now not to put anything past Harris Blind-Eye! He's worse scum than the filth in southern-city sewers!

Despite the angry shock flooding his thoughts, Aitchley managed to beat back his fury. Regardless of Harris's crimes, Aitchley would never have been able to get the Elixir of Life without the southern-city outlaw's aid, and for that, he was indebted to him. He couldn't let him fall into the chill emptiness of the Pits any more than he could drive a blade between the traitorous lockpick's shoulders himself. Harris had helped him, and Aitchley would do his part to help Harris.

Careful that the braided silk did not snap beneath their combined weight, Aitchley moved closer, entwining one arm around the thief's waist. "Come on, Harris," the young farmer said. "Give me your saddlebag; I'll put it in my backpack for you. We're getting out of here."

Face pale and left side slick with blood, Harris let him take his saddlebag, lifting his head weakly to look past Aitchley's shoulder at the crimson cathedral looming behind them. "Doesn't matter much anymore, scout," he said. "They know we're here."

Aitchley felt a cold fist close in about his heart as he threw a quick glance over his shoulder at the Cathedral of Thorns; his fear intensified when he saw the gangly, insectlike forms of the Daeminase rising up out of their deathlike sleep and come clambering down the walls after them.

*   *   *

Berlyn watched in wordless anticipation as Aitchley and Harris came to a stop over the vast expanse of the Daeminase Pits. The arctic wind played gleefully through her long, platinum-blond tresses—keening and howling around the face-carved outcroppings of dark blue rock—and despite the urge to run out and help him, Berlyn forced herself to remain behind her protective cover of unearthly blue stone, wrestling with the apprehension and anxiety swimming hotly through her veins.

When she had first seen Aitchley make his way out of the brierlike doors of the Cathedral of Thorns and begin across the double lines of spidersilk, the young blonde had been filled with a warm rush of relief, but all she could feel now was the stomach-churning fear that roiled through her innards like a torrent of warm, queasy waters. The fact that Aitchley had stopped halfway over the infinite blackness of the Pits seemed like a cruel joke to the young girl. What had happened to make them stop anyway? she worried frantically. What could be so important that they had to stop to talk about it? That they couldn't wait until Aitchley was safely back with her? Every second Aitchley stood out upon that rope only increased the danger of falling. So why had they even bothered to stop at all?

That was when she heard the distant snufflings.

The fear at Berlyn's breast suddenly dropped a thousand degrees, growing so cold that it hurt her chest. Her breath caught sharply in her throat with a sudden, high-pitched intake of air, and she hardly realized she had stopped breathing altogether as she stared out across the lightless expanse of the Pits at the grotesque structure of red thorns and twisted brambles rising up out of its depths. Sudden movements of red on red blurred the exterior of the cathedral, and the terror at her breast moved to encompass her mind, its numbing horror seeping past the young girl's eyes to penetrate her very brain.

They were moving, she realized with horrified shock. *They were moving!*

Slowly at first, then with renewed vigor, the gaunt, skeletal forms of the Daeminase moved across the crimson thorns of the cathedral, pulling themselves up out of their dreamless sleep with large, curious sniffs at the pluvial air. Huge, horselike nostrils at the end of their lean, equine-shaped heads twitched and quivered as they sampled the musty violet sky, and an eagerness and excitement seemed to radiate through their thin, insectlike bodies as they drew up out of their deathlike slumber, streams of viscous saliva drooling from around their silver-fanged mouths. Tight, shriveled red flesh puckered and sealed as the inhuman monstrosities pulled themselves off the giant thorns impaling them to the cathedral walls, and eyeless faces all turned with hideous expressions of ravenous hunger down to where Aitchley and Harris slowly resumed their trek across the spidersilk ropes.

Unrestrained horror turned her voice into a tiny, little-girl whisper as Berlyn squeaked, "They're moving."

Calyx gave her a cynical snort as he hunkered down behind his protective rock. " 'Bout time, too," he grunted. "Stupid place to stop and have a conversation anyway."

Berlyn blinked, yet her gaze remained riveted to the movement on the cathedral's walls. "No," she corrected, her voice still hushed with preternatural terror. *"They're moving."*

Frowning, Calyx caught the inflection in the scullery maid's words and turned beady eyes on the long, gangly shapes beginning to move with more and more rapidity down the thorny walls. A familiar look of dwarven despair crossed the smith's ruddy face, but he turned away from the distant cathedral long enough to flash Berlyn an unfelt, insincere smile. "Oh, well," the dwarf quipped gravely. "So much for getting out of here alive."

                    *   *   *

Stark, ancient horrors so primeval that they arose from the very farthest recesses of his mind shrieked and screamed through Aitchley's skull as he tried to navigate his way across the strands of spidersilk, trying desperately to keep one hand gripped to the rope above his head and the other wrapped around Harris's sagging middle. He tried to block out the curious sniffing and snufflings that filled the air behind him— tried not to listen to the sound of gaunt, bony forms scuttling and scurrying spiderlike down the sides of the red thorn walls— and keep his attention focused on the narrow cable beneath his feet, but nothing he could do could blot out the undeniable terrors skittering and scuttling with insectlike agility at his back.

"Come on, Harris," he coaxed, practically pushing the southern-city lockpick's limp form ahead of him. "Just a little further."

Harris's face was a ghastly white, rimed with beads of perspiration. "And then what, puck?" he queried darkly. "Where we gonna go?'' His head hung slack against his breastbone. ''They've got us. Can't outrun 'em. Can't hide from 'em. They're gonna drag us all . . . down. . . .''

The ancient fears rampaging through Aitchley's mind also brought with them a tremendous surge of adrenaline and self-righteous rage. ''What the Pits kind of talk is that?'' he shouted at the brigand. ''I thought you didn't even believe in the Daeminase!''

A faint smile tried to stretch Harris's pale lips. ''Kinda hard not to believe in something when it's chasin' you across the Pits,'' he said wryly. He forced his feet to move a few inches. ''No use, puck. They know I'm here. They can smell me.''

Aitchley practically lifted Harris off the ropes to keep him moving forward. ''What do you mean they can smell you?'' he wanted to know. ''What are you talking about?''

Harris found enough strength to look at the young farmer beside him. ''It's me they're after, puck,'' he said. ''They smell my blood . . . know what kind of a person I am. Makes me all the more desirable to them, doesn't it?''

Aitchley blinked a few times in his confusion. ''What?'' he asked again.

Struggling against looming unconsciousness, Harris offered Aitchley another weak grin. ''Doesn't seem . . . strange to you that they didn't wake up . . . what with all that noise we were makin' while inside?'' he asked, his voice beginning to slur. ''Only woke up . . . after . . . I started out across the rope. That's 'cause they smell my blood . . . know I belong with 'em. Daeminase . . . like my kind the best.''

''And what kind is that?'' Aitchley inquired, harshly skeptical.

Harris's smile grew. ''Murderer. Outlaw. Thief,'' he said with just a hint of pride. ''You know . . . typical southern-city scum.''

Despite the hurried sounds of inhuman activity behind him, Aitchley fought back the black pessimism taking root in his own mind. ''So what?'' he challenged the lockpick. ''Doesn't mean I'm going to give up now! I mean . . . we've actually got the elixir! I'll be damned if I'm not gonna use it!''

Harris's smile faltered. ''You'll be damned anyways . . . if . . . Daeminase . . . catch us. . . .''

All strength suddenly evaporated out of the rogue's wounded body as he succumbed to the unfeeling blackness of bloodless unconsciousness. The unexpected shift in weight threw Aitchley forward with alarming force, and the young farmer felt rather than saw Harris's limp form lurch out over the infinite blackness of the Pits and pitch forward off the ropes.

Harris's weight dragged Aitchley down after him.

2

Ghost of a Chance

With an agonizing wrench at his right shoulder, Aitchley was jerked forward, dragged down by the weight of Harris's limp form in his grasp. Limitless darkness smiled up at the young man as his center of gravity shifted, and the abrupt tug at his right hand ripped his left hand free of the spidersilk. A startled yelp was all he could muster before pitching helplessly forward, his thoughts short-circuited by the electric flood of vertigo and terror screaming through his mind. It was only by pure chance that he fell forward onto the lower strand of spider's silk, managing to catch himself on it by the crook of his left arm and left dangling above viscid blackness, Harris hanging from his right hand.

Berlyn shrieked when she saw Aitchley careen off the ropes, a cold, hollow emptiness piercing her breast. Despite the hungry scrabblings of the Daeminase, she jumped to her feet and stepped away from her protective covering of rocks, unconcerned that eyeless red faces turned hungrily in her direction.

A heavy grimace chiseled its way across Calyx's face as he tugged insistently at the tattered hemline of the scullery maid's skirt. "Would you get down?" the dwarf hissed at her, beady eyes tracking the spiderlike crawl of hundreds of red shapes. "It's bad enough they see them. They don't need to see us, too!"

Berlyn ignored the dwarf's warning, taking a worried step

closer to the edge of the Pits. Her eyes remained locked on the two forms dangling perilously over infinite nothingness, and she could feel the emptiness growing in her breast as she watched Aitchley trying to pull himself back up by one hand and unable to find the strength. "He's going to fall," the blonde realized, horror muting her voice.

Calyx gave up trying to pull the girl back down and stood up beside her, having to stand on tiptoe to see over the dark blue stalagmites. "He's not going to fall," the dwarf responded confidently, a trace of his misplaced optimism surfacing. "He'll probably get eaten first, but he's not going to fall."

Berlyn took another hesitant step forward, struggling with the fear and anxiety rampaging through her thoughts. "I've got to save him," she suddenly resolved.

Reacting quickly, Calyx latched back onto the scullery maid's worn and ragged shift, keeping her away from the edge of the Pits. "Whoa! Hold on, there!" he advised. "He's halfway out over the Daeminase Pits! You can't seriously expect to just waltz out there and pull him up all by your lonesome, can you?"

Berlyn swung imploring eyes on the smith. "Well, we've got to do something!" she demanded. "We can't just let him hang there!"

Poinqart was suddenly at her side, Sprage dragged along in his futile attempt to restrain the half troll. "Poinqart will go," the hybrid boldly declared. "Poinqart is Mister Aitch's protector-friend; Mister Calyx-dwarf said so. Poinqart can pull-save Mister Aitch to safety-ground, no problem!"

Calyx's dark mien deepened as the hybrid started a purposeful waddle toward the spidersilk ropes. "Poinqart, no!" he warned. "I told you before, the ropes might not support your weight. And they certainly won't support you, Aitchley, and Harris!"

Desperation flamed in Berlyn's gray-green eyes. "But we can't just leave him there!" she cried.

Calyx stared thoughtfully out across the expanse of blackness surrounding the Cathedral of Thorns like an ebon moat. "I'd go myself, but it's the same for me as it is for Poinqart," he mused out loud. "Only another human can safely walk across those ropes." He turned a questioning—albeit cynical—glance up at Sprage. "Sprage?" he queried.

The color drained rapidly from Sprage's face as he looked

out at the watery blackness of the Pits. "Not me!" he all but screeched. "I'm afraid of heights!"

Calyx shrugged with a sardonic grunt. "Somehow I had a feeling you'd say that," he mocked. A thoughtful gleam came to his gaze as he returned his attention to where Aitchley hung by one arm over virgin darkness. "If only the kid would let go of Blind-Butt, we'd be all right," he murmured, half-seriously, under his breath.

A deep, emotionless voice sounded behind Berlyn and the dwarf as crimson figures continued to scrabble about the cathedral walls. "I will go, Master Calyx," Gjuki announced. "Master Aitchley is my friend, and I will not see him come to any harm."

A look of surprise momentarily blanketed the dwarf's face. "What?" he retorted, flabbergasted. "You're joking, right? All three of you Rhagana can barely move!"

Face impassive, Gjuki only nodded once. "While it is true this unnatural cold is most disabling, I will not stand idly by while Master Aitchley's life hangs in the balance."

Gjalk offered an affirmative nod beside his brother. "I, too, will do whatever is in my power to aid the QuestLeader," he said.

Calyx held up a hand before Eyfura could voice her agreement. "Nice sentiment, guys," he replied, "but you know it's not possible. If we send you out there, we'll just have three more people in jeopardy." He returned his gaze to the twin strands of silver spidersilk. "I just don't see why the kid doesn't drop Harris."

Berlyn unexpectedly screamed as thin, sticklike fingers grabbed the lip of the pit near her feet, scarlet talons reaching up out of the darkness and digging deep furrows into the dark blue earth. The eyeless red face of a Daeminase rose up out of the liquid blackness of the Pits—thick streams of viscous saliva oozing from its lipless mouth—and an eager hiss seeped through row after row of silver, needlelike fangs as the creature lunged for where Berlyn had been standing.

Calyx tugged free his warhammer, a bleak frown drawn beneath his salt-and-pepper beard. "Great," he muttered darkly to himself. "Now who's gonna save *us*?"

Clinging desperately to the lower strand of spidersilk, Aitchley tried to ignore the red-hot ache throbbing through his left shoulder and the deadweight pulling at his right. He had tried, unsuccessfully, to grab the spidersilk with his left hand, but—every time he tried—he felt the rope start to slip away from under his arm and had to stop or else fear falling into the lightless infinity of the Pits. There was an unpleasant ache at his elbow as well as the soldered spider's silk dug painfully into his arm—pinching at his flesh and cutting off his circulation—and he could already feel the precarious tickling numbness of pins and needles starting to spread through his left hand.

Oh, this is just bunging great, the young man thought foully to himself. I come all this way—actually obtain the Elixir of Life—and then fall off a rope and get dragged down into the Pits for all eternity! Bloody typical! What I should do is just drop Harris. Be pretty pathetic to make it this far and then bung it all up trying to save someone who's tried to sabotage the quest. Daeminase Pits! The son of a bunghole tried to kill me twice! So why am I still hanging on to him? If I dropped him, I'd at least have a chance to save myself.

Aitchley scowled as the pins and needles started to creep up his arm. You can't drop him 'cause you're not a killer, his darker side answered with some disappointment. The only time you've taken a life is in a kill-or-be-killed situation, and dropping Harris would just be plain and simple murder. And—whatever else you may be—you are not a murderer!

Aitchley's frown deepened. Morality from my pessimism, he grumbled to himself. Can it get any worse than this?

The braided spidersilk anchored under the young man's arm began to bounce and shake with sudden agitation, and the young farmer managed to glance up beneath the brim of his hat to see four or five gangly red shapes drop down from the walls of the Cathedral of Thorns and start out nimbly across the ropes to where he dangled.

A freezing chunk of the polar winds seemed to solidify in Aitchley's gut. Great, he jeered himself. I had to ask. . . .

Berlyn yelped as she dodged the scythelike sweep of a gaunt red arm, feeling razor-sharp talons slice the pluvial air above her head. Wincing, she drove the blade of Aitchley's throwing ax into the cadaverous side of the Daeminase facing her—trying to ignore the abrupt clatter of its teeth and the brutal shock wave that ran up the length of her right arm—but shrieked a second time as the towering red monstrosity swiped at her again, scarlet claws catching and tearing the shoulder of her dress.

Calyx brought his warhammer up and around, shattering the arm reaching for Berlyn and sneering heavily as the limb almost instantly began to regenerate. "This is *not* going well!" he observed with dwarven cynicism. "Liahturetart said our weapons might not have an effect on 'em!"

Cowering behind an outcropping of face-carved rocks, Sprage poked his head up only long enough to see the Daeminase's eyeless face turn briefly in his direction. "How can our weapons have an effect on them when they impale themselves on giant thorns to sleep?" he screamed, all but hysterical.

Bloodlessly, Calyx smashed a taloned red foot, watching as splintered and fragmented bones knitted seamlessly back together beneath the tight, emaciated flesh. "There's got to be a way to stop 'em!" he concluded dourly. "If it moves, it can be made to stop moving!"

Berlyn screamed as the monster lunged for her again, slashing inches away from the tip of her nose. "But it doesn't even bleed!" she cried in her horror. "How can we stop it?"

A powerful green arm suddenly shot out over Berlyn's left shoulder with all the strength of a battering ram, catching the Daeminase with a four-fingered fist right in the middle of its featureless face. Silver teeth shattered as the crimson beast flipped forcibly backward—half its skull caved in—and it emitted a single hiss of perturbation as it tumbled off the edge of the Pits and disappeared back into the inky blackness below.

Poinqart watched the creature vanish with a mixed expression of human rage and trollish disgust on his hybrid face. "*Eperythr* nasty-no-good-things," the half troll declared, repulsed. "Poinqart does not like *Eperythr*-no-face."

Calyx slipped his weapon back into his belt. "That makes two of us," he quipped, returning his attention to the twin lines of spidersilk.

More deadly red claws appeared at the rim of the chasm as three more Daeminase pulled themselves free of the darkness, hungry slobber streaming from their jaws. A fourth clambered free near Sprage, and a fifth rose up some distance to the north.

With a resigned sigh, Calyx pulled his warhammer free a second time, tossing an annoyed glance at those behind him.

"Anytime anybody comes up with a brilliant idea, let me know," he remarked. "I'm fresh out."

Struggling to maintain his grip, Aitchley heard one of Berlyn's shrieks over the high-pitched keening of the wind and felt the lump of cold fear in his belly grow colder. All thoughts of the infinite blackness looming below him—or of the insectlike creatures scuttling crablike across the spidersilks toward him—fled the young man's mind. His only concern was for Berlyn, and he felt an invigorating surge of adrenaline course through his body as he hung there.

Berlyn! His brain reeled with the sudden realization. She's in danger! I've got to do something!

Kicking up his legs, Aitchley tried to hook a foot over the braided silver rope from which he hung. It was a move he had been quite good at as a child when he and Joub would climb trees over in what had once been the Grantham orchard, but nowadays the orchard was just another barren patch of lifeless ground in northern Solsbury, and Aitchley had never tried hanging from his feet with the weight of an unconscious lockpick pulling him down. Futilely, the young farmer continued to kick and thrash, but the spidersilk cut only deeper into his left arm and the abrupt surge of strength drained from his body as rapidly as all sense of hope.

Despondently, he tried to train worried blue-green eyes on the distant lip of the Pit. Berlyn . . . the young man mourned to himself. I'm sorry. I can't do it.

A sudden hand reached down before the young man's gaze, helpful fingers grabbing for the young farmer's arm. "Quickly, lad," a familiar voice said. "Take my hand."

So surprised by the unexpected aid, Aitchley slipped off the rope and plunged into inky blackness.

Cocking back an arm and swinging in a wide arc, Calyx caught a Daeminase as it lifted itself over the jagged edge of the Pits, smashing in its featureless face and taking little satisfaction as it tumbled back into absolute darkness. Beside him, Berlyn's throwing ax severed the gripping fingers of another crimson monstrosity, knocking it back into the blackness even as new fingers grew like scarlet buds from its maimed hand.

"Would I be stating the obvious if I said we're all going to die here?'' Calyx commented, spinning to face another surfacing creature.

''We are not going to die here,'' answered Eyfura, her spear dislodging another Daeminase before it could clamber free of the Pits. ''We have come too far to fail now.''

Calyx barely ducked a vicious swipe of scarlet claws before knocking his attacker back over the edge. ''Doesn't mean *gnaiss*-shavings to me, lady,'' he retorted grimly. ''Where I come from, there aren't any rules saying that how far you've come makes you immune to dying. If that were the case, Procursus would never have gotten killed and we wouldn't be here today!''

Knuckles white around the hilt of his *navaja,* Sprage remained safely hidden behind the rocks. ''Then what say we do the smart thing and run away?'' he whimpered fearfully. ''No sense in everyone dying.''

Perspiration trickling down her forehead despite the arctic chill, Berlyn slammed her throwing ax sideways into another eyeless head that crested the rim. *''No!''* she barked harshly. ''We're not leaving Aitchley!'' She violently ripped free her weapon and drove its pointed end through the hissing mouth of the injured Daeminase. ''He's never left anyone else behind; I'm not about to leave him!''

Calyx allowed a grave smile to stretch his lips. ''You heard her,'' he replied, a trace of conviction in his own voice. ''We're not leaving.'' He tried to push another creature away but only succeeded in slowing it down. ''We're all gonna die here today, but we're not leaving.''

Sudden claws unexpectedly slashed upward from the pit, catching Calyx across the face and spattering Berlyn with blood. With a weak groan, the dwarven smith crumpled to the blue earth, bright rivulets of warm life fluid cascading across his left cheek as bony red arms reached hungrily for his fallen body.

Ax blade flashing, Berlyn shuddered as her weapon caught Calyx's attacker across the forearm, chopping through red flesh and splintering thin, narrow bones. There was no blood as the limb fell away from the Daeminase—only an enraged splatter of thick spittle—and the severed arm continued to twitch and spasm, daggerlike claws flexing and clenching in a disembodied attempt to still reach Calyx.

Disgusted, Berlyn kicked the severed arm back into the Pits, swinging sideways with all her strength as the wounded Daeminase sprouted a new arm from its ragged, bloodless stump. "Sprage!" the blonde shouted tersely. "Get Calyx! Get him away from here!"

Regardless of the inhuman red horrors welling up over the lip of the jagged pit like frothing scarlet brew, Sprage jumped hurriedly to his feet and came to the scullery maid's side, his sack of herbs held tightly in one hand. Even though a roiling fear churned through the healer's stomach—even though cold sweat streamed down his face—Sprage sprinted swiftly to where Calyx lay motionless, his expertise overriding his irrational fears.

"Gjalk!" the long-haired physician cried. "Get me some gauze! And help me drag him out of here! He's heavier than the Cavalier's catafalque!"

Watching healer and Rhagana move Calyx to safety, Berlyn did not see the Daeminase rise up in front of her, a raking talon slashing at her legs. Murderous red claws caught in the hem of the young blonde's skirt, and she shrieked in her sudden surprise, jerked forward by the abrupt grab. Fabric tore and shredded—adding another ragged tear up the front of her dress—and Berlyn felt her center of gravity shift, her left leg pulled out from under her and over the edge of the Pits.

An olive-green hand snatched her away from liquid blackness, pulling her back up from the edge and setting her gently aside. The horror of what had nearly happened had hardly begun to register in the blonde's mind as she stared blankly down into the lightless void that had nearly claimed her life, and she wasn't even able to give Poinqart a grateful smile . . . her thoughts overwhelmed by the sudden nearness of her own death.

Picking up Calyx's dropped warhammer, Gjuki slammed the weapon into the featureless face of another Daeminase, his pearllike black eyes seeking out Berlyn's frightened face. "Forgive me for saying so," the Rhagana said with some trepidation, "but I am beginning to believe Master Calyx was right."

Berlyn could only blink back her wordless terror.

Squinting against the silvery light that radiated from the helpful hand clasping his own, Aitchley stared up into the face of the man who had saved him. Eyes wide, the young man was unable to find his voice as he was helped back up onto the lower strand of spider's silk, Harris drawn up after him and slung limply over the rope.

Awed stupefaction roiling through his brain, Aitchley blinked a few times at the eerily glowing man before him. "Ca . . . Ca . . . Captain d'Ane?" he finally made out.

Captain d'Ane smiled through the misty silver light that constituted his ethereal substance. A million glowing motes of unnatural energy made up the elderly captain's lambent form, and Aitchley wasn't sure, but when he looked at him a certain way, he could see straight through the old war hero to the dark blue rim of the Pits beyond.

Aitchley fought his wonderment for control of his voice. "I . . . I . . . I . . . I thought you were dead," he said, dumbstruck.

D'Ane offered the young farmer a pleasant smile of ghostly, semi-opaque lips. "I am, lad. I am. What else would I be doing beyond Lich Gate glowing like this?"

The good-natured words did little to still the disbelief storming through Aitchley's head. "But I . . . uh . . . I thought . . . um . . ." He stared hard at the unreal shape of his former companion. "Are you a ghost?"

D'Ane helped Aitchley find his footing on the ropes, lifting Harris easily in his semitransparent arms. "Well, yes, I suppose I am," the captain said humorously. "Don't rightly know how it works, but I believe LoilLan had a hand in all this. Only Fate could decree that I'd be on my way into the Uncreated and see you and the others in need of some dire assistance. Figured I was meant to help the quest beyond the walls of Lich Gate after all."

Throwing an uneasy glance over one shoulder at the pursuing Daeminase, Aitchley swung his gaze back to the way d'Ane effortlessly held Harris in his silvery grasp. "But how . . . I mean . . . I thought ghosts could walk through walls and stuff," the young man admitted. "How come you were able to pull me up? And how come you're able to hold on to Harris like that?"

The balding warrior flashed the young farmer a sincere smile. "I'm dead, lad," he said with a little too much merriment in his voice for Aitchley's liking. "Don't ask me how I'm doing it; I'm not even alive anymore. The rules aren't the same. Most I can figure out is that here—beyond Lich Gate—is the Land of the Dead, and since I'm dead, I can pretty much do the things I used to do while back in our world. I suppose if I came back out with you, I wouldn't have much of a body then, eh?''

A long-buried pang of guilt rose in Aitchley's breast as he began across the ropes after the silver-white form of his dead friend. ''So come with us!'' he suddenly declared. ''I have it! I've got the elixir! Come with us and I'll use it on your body back in Viveca!''

The captain's smile faded as he eyed the young man dubiously. ''Now, you can't be doing that, lad,'' he warmheartedly scolded the young farmer. ''The whole purpose of this quest was to use the elixir on your ancestor. I'd hate to think that *I* was the reason the Cavalier wasn't properly resurrected.''

''But Liahturetart said there might be enough for two uses,'' Aitchley argued, his guilt gnawing away at the corners of his mind. ''I mean . . . it's the least I can do for you. I'm the reason you died in the first place.''

A familiar look came to the balding warrior's diaphanous face, and Aitchley found that—even though he was glowing and semi-opaque—d'Ane could still make the young man feel like an incompetent little farm boy. ''I died because I was old, Aitchley,'' the captain replied, just the slightest reprimand in his voice. ''I didn't die because of you or because of the quest or even because of Paieon's guards. I died because it was my time to die.'' His hazy, ghostly eyes took on a faraway look. ''There's a scheme to all things, Aitchley,'' he went on. ''The old make way for the young, and the sick give way to the healthy. It's something so basic you practically forget all about it when you're alive. You remember so much once you've died. It's like a great weight's been lifted from your mind and you suddenly remember things you never even knew you knew.'' A ghostly hand clamped amicably on Aitchley's shoulder. ''Thanks for the offer, lad, but I kind of like being dead.''

A familiar buzzing voice filled Aitchley's head from his subconscious, and he heard the enigmatic words of Tin William echo over and over again in his brain at the similarities to d'Ane's remarks.

''What sort of things?'' he asked out loud.

Captain d'Ane blinked himself free of his thoughts. ''Hmm?'' he asked back. ''What was that?''

Aitchley nervously cleared his throat. ''I said, what sort of things do you remember?''

The smile returned to d'Ane's spectral face. ''Oh, all sorts of things,'' he answered cordially. ''The way the world works.

Our place in the overall scheme of things. What the gods expect of us. All the kinds of things we forget about while we're preoccupied by living."

Aitchley blanched as the words sounded frighteningly close to Tin William's. "Well, like what?" he pressed. "Would our place in the overall scheme of things have something to do with being wary of nature's scales?"

D'Ane looked at the young man with a hint of admiration in his ghostly eyes. "Well, yes, I suppose it could," he responded. "We do tend to forget that there are other races and creatures living on the same lands we live on. We tend to be somewhat arrogant when it comes to things like that."

"And . . . and what about the balance of all things?" Aitchley continued to question. "You know? Birth and death? Destruction and creation? Would they be thrown horribly out of balance if I used the elixir on you or the Cavalier?"

A thoughtful glisten came to d'Ane's apparitional eye. "Why, no, not that I'm aware of," he said. "The overall balance isn't infallible, lad. Sometimes people die before their time. Others outlive their usefulness by many years. Some even die and come back without the aid of any magical elixir. Using it shouldn't cause any major disruptions in the way things work. Why?"

Aitchley tried to shrug, but the ache in his shoulders—and the backpack and staff weighing him down—muted the gesture. "Oh, I don't know." He feigned ignorance. "Just something that I heard might happen if I tried to use the elixir."

D'Ane offered the young man another reassuring smile. "Nonsense, lad," he said. "If nature itself allowed the elixir to be created, then nature itself would be able to cope with it, right?"

Aitchley nodded thoughtfully to himself, a heavy feeling of misgiving that had been with him since the Molten Dunes easing from his mind. *D'Ane has a point,* he noted with some rare optimism. *If using the elixir did cause something bad to the natural order of things, it would never have been allowed to have been created in the first place. Even the most confusing motives of gods and men make at least that much sense. So what in the Pits was Tin William trying to say with all that "nature's scales" mulch? Or did he even know what he was saying? I mean . . . he's not even from this world let alone this universe! He's just a stupid machine that can break down as* easily as a plowshare or chain harrow. Who says he even has to make sense?

Feeling just the slightest bit better about the mysterious warning left to him by the otherworldly robot, Aitchley continued to make his hasty way across the twin strands of spider's silk. *Just because I feel better for the first time in months about the elixir doesn't mean I'm out of trouble yet,* the young man mused. *I've still got to get back to solid ground and make sure Berlyn's all right before I can do anything else.*

That was when a Daeminase pulled itself up onto the ropes in front of Aitchley, blocking his path with a murderous hiss and a mouth full of a thousand teeth.

3

The Dreamless Who Dream

Single eye unblinking, Camera 12 recorded the turmoil raging on around it. It closed in with a tight one-shot on the lithe form of the Berlyn/ scullery maid/heroine, taking in the look of determination and fear clouding her beautiful features before following the arc of her throwing ax as it loped off a groping red claw. Then, tracking the spiral of the severed hand, the camera panned across to the lean Gjuki/Rhagana, watching as he attacked with the Calyx/dwarf's heavy warhammer despite the visible ache the cold caused his fungoid form. Beyond that, Camera 12 could see where more and more crimson Daeminase/villains clambered up over the ragged edge of the enormous pit, barely kept at bay by the Eyfura/Rhagana and the Poinqart/half troll/sidekick. Nearby, the Sprage/healer and the Gjalk/Rhagana attempted to aid the wounded Calyx/dwarf so that the comic relief would not die.

Despite a proper brain in its metal shell, Camera 12 was aware that at least four other remotes were positioned somewhere off in the distance—each transmitting what they saw back to the desert workstation and TW-O: 114-84-1311825— and whatever exciting shots 12 missed would be picked up by one of the other cameras. Camera 12, however, had been the primary unit on the "A. Corlaiys/Lich Gate" shoot, and it continued to follow its original programming although such prerogatives had been rescinded due to its unprogrammed interference.

Gears whirring and servos humming, Camera 12 turned in what was almost a questioning manner, sweeping its single eye out across the stretch of liquid blackness that was the Daeminase Pits. The Aitchley/hero was no longer where he had been—and a number of Daeminase were steadily making their way across the spidersilk ropes in his place—and 12 made a curious pan of the surrounding area before finding the Aitchley/hero nearly free of the chasm, the final few feet blocked by a hissing, slavoring Daeminase/villain.

There was a disgruntled squawk from atop the camera as it started a purposeful scuttle toward the Pits. "What you do?" an irate Trianglehead wanted to know from his perch atop the camera's steel-mesh saddle. "Why you move?"

If the Aitchley/hero is in danger, then go to his assistance, the spiderlike camera instructed itself.

Trianglehead clutched tightly to the tungsten steel beneath his talons, ruffling agitated feathers as the arachnid machine sprinted forward. "Awk! Zstupid kamera!" the fledgling voiced his consternation. "Zstay where isz zsafe. What you think? You zstupid human or zsomething?"

Aitchley/hero in peril, the construct continued to prompt itself. Go to his assistance.

With a final aggravated yawp, Trianglehead flapped clumsily off the moving camera and hopped to where Sprage and Gjalk tended the wounded Calyx. The bird's milky-blue eyes glowered after the hurrying camera, but a sudden wall of gaunt red forms blocked the arachnid machine's way, causing Trianglehead to instinctively duck behind a dark blue stalagmite and continue watching from behind the safety of the indigo stones.

A powerful steel leg telescoped out from Camera 12's rounded body before any of the Daeminase blocking its way could react. There was no blood as the metal leg speared effortlessly through the solar plexus of the nearest creature— ripping through red, leathery flesh and splintering brittle, inhuman ribs—but a vengeful hiss escaped the beast's many-fanged mouth as it pulled itself off the leg impaling it, its injured midriff healing almost instantaneously.

Another spiderlike limb of cold metal slammed into the Daeminase's skull, fracturing bone and compressing brains so that the creature sprawled over the edge of the pit and into the blackness below, its hind leg twitching spasmodically.

Berlyn flinched when a sprinkling of cerebrospinal fluid tickled her arms, and she turned to see another of Camera 12's tripodlike legs shoot out and crush the skull of a nearby Daeminase, dropping the creature where it stood. Convulsions racked the lean, skeletal form of the injured monster, and a tiny stream of red-brown liquid dribbled out from its shattered skull, joining the messy cascade of thick, viscous saliva from its mouth.

Teeth clenched, Berlyn returned her attention to the creatures facing her, redirecting her attack for the eyeless heads that crested the rim of the pit. "Aim for their heads!" she yelled to the others around her.

An eerie ululation of inhuman agony sounded on the blonde's right as Eyfura drove her barbed spear straight through the eyeless face of one of the Daeminase, the scarlet creature doing a macabre dance at the end of her spear as it twitched and convulsed into lifelessness.

A brief flicker of emotion crossed Eyfura's leathery face. "You are correct, Berlyn GoldenHair," the SpearWielder observed, jerking her weapon free and turning to face another beast. "The Dreamless who Dream are unable to survive a blow to the head. Strike quickly and strike true and perhaps the words of the MetalShaper shall not come to pass."

Berlyn could barely keep the frown off her lips as she spun about to face another eyeless monstrosity, already feeling the painful throbbing at her shoulders and in her arms. There was no way that she'd be able to keep this up, the young girl knew. She wasn't a fighter any more than she was a duchess, and if something didn't happen soon, she was either going to lose her already tenuous grip on Aitchley's throwing ax or simply fall down dead from exhaustion.

Gray-green eyes swept out across the pitch-black expanse of the Daeminase Pits at where the spidersilk ropes swayed and twisted in the polar breeze; of Aitchley and Harris, there was no sight. . . .

Gripping the overhead rope with one hand, Aitchley jerked free his new sword, momentarily startled at how easily the weapon flowed into his grasp. It was almost as if the sword leapt out of its sheath of its own accord, and Aitchley hardly used any strength to direct the silver-gray blade in a precise arc out in front of him, catching the Daeminase blocking his path squarely in the neck.

Bone, muscle, and sinew parted as easily as water as Aitchley's new sword cleaved through the throat of the eyeless monster before him, littering the air with a sparse drizzle of reddish-brown fluid. Still hissing, the decapitated head spiraled back into the darkness of the Pits—teeth bared and saliva spraying—while the headless body teetered in a moment of reluctant bewilderment before pitching off in the opposite direction, long, deadly talons still flexing and clenching.

Aitchley's new sword slipped back into its sheath with almost as much ease as it had come out.

Captain d'Ane threw a nervous look over one semitransparent shoulder, "Quickly, lad," the deceased soldier coaxed the young man, "they're gaining on us."

Squinting through the captain's opalescent midsection, Aitchley could see the dozen or so Daeminase scuttling across the ropes behind them, their lean, gangly arms and legs moving with an almost spiderlike grace across the silken cables. Gelatinous tendrils of saliva oozed from around silver-fanged maws, and hungry nostrils opened and closed on their otherwise featureless faces as they savored the scent of fresh blood tainting the pluvial air.

"This is not going well," Aitchley muttered gloomily to himself, trying to hurry the rest of the way across and nearly losing his footing.

A familiar feeling of despair and self-pity began to surface in the young farmer's thoughts, and he turned weary blue-green eyes to the edge of the massive chasm. It was closer now than ever before—hardly ten feet separating him from solid ground and getting closer with every step—but it was hardly the safe haven it had been. Numerous red shapes kept rising up out of the Pits to form a knot of red flesh between Aitchley and unearthly blue soil, and more gaunt, bony figures climbed onto the ropes behind him, scrabbling hungrily over one another in their eagerness to reach the young man first. Even more continued to dart and scurry across the crimson thorns of the distant cathedral, and the hope that had once burned in Aitchley's breast was quickly doused by an all-too-familiar pessimism.

There's too many of them, the young man realized with growing despondency. They're coming from everywhere! Like rats in a storehouse! There must be thousands of them! We should have known better than to try this! Nobody goes beyond Lich Gate and lives! Nobody!

Blue-green eyes suddenly locked with gray-green eyes, and Aitchley felt an unexpected surge of determination burn through his chest. Even though droplets of reddish-brown gore dotted her face and arms, Berlyn remained as beautiful as ever, and Aitchley felt the look of relief that crossed her face give him an added boost of much-needed strength.

No! the young man resolved emphatically to himself. We've come this far! I'm not going to fail now! Berlyn's counting on me! Everybody's counting on me! Daeminase Pits! I've got the bloody Elixir of Life! The whole world's counting on me!

Swinging himself forward from the rope overhead, Aitchley jumped the last few feet of spidersilk and landed back on the hard, lifeless soil of the Outside. His strength and determination flowed through his veins like molten lead, and he flashed a reassuring, lopsided grin at the young blonde nearby, moving to join her in the press of hissing, eyeless monsters. Unexpectedly, more creatures rose up between the two teenagers, and—as if sensing the magical potency of the items on Aitchley's back—all the surrounding Daeminase turned on the young man, eager slaver drooling from their horselike jaws.

"*Aitchley!*" Berlyn screamed as the monsters blocked him from her view.

Aitchley's newfound strength faltered. "Oh, mulch," he cursed.

Hearing the screaming-cry of Missy Berlyn, Poinqart tried to peek-see through the impenetrable wall of nasty-no-face-*Eperythr*. More and more of the nasty-no-faces were clamber-climbing up the sides of the darkness-Pits, and there was very little poor Poinqart could do to keep them back-away. For every ugly-*Eperythr*-no-face poor Poinqart hit-smacked away, three more would hurry-rise out of the blackness, stinky-smelly-breath blowing in Poinqart's face. Poinqart did not like-see such slimy-ugliness—Poinqart liked ugly-no-face-*Eperythrs* even less than he did nasty-bad-brown-trolls—and there were so many of them, the half-troll could no longer even see his companions.

Mister Aitch and Missy Berlyn are Poinqart's friends, the hybrid concluded earnestly. Mister Calyx-dwarf had made Poinqart their protector-friend, but Poinqart was not doing a very good job-task of it, was he? Too many ugly-no-faces blocked-obscured poor Poinqart's vision-sight. Poinqart would have to do something about that in order to rescue-save his friends.

Grabbing the nearest Daeminase in powerful, four-fingered hands, Poinqart lifted the creature effortlessly off its feet and hurled it into the ever-expanding horde of monsters. Perturbed hissing—like a nest of disturbed serpents—knifed the air as Daeminase crashed into Daeminase, and a number of the lean, spidery creatures went spilling back into the emptiness of the Pits, spindly arms and legs flailing. But there were still too many of them. Poinqart was still unable to see his friends among the eight-foot-high monstrosities, and a sudden hand of wicked red talons swiped across the half troll's shoulder blade, drawing a stream of blood to his olive-green flesh.

Ouchy-ouch! Poinqart thought to himself, a mixed mien of trollish anguish and human surprise registering across his features. Must be careful-care. Poinqart will be no good to his friends if ugly-no-faces make him alive-no-more-dead.

Large, gaping nostrils—relishing the taste of freshly spilled blood—opened and closed in wordless excitation on the empty faces of the Daeminase, eager heads staring without eyes in the direction of the wounded half troll.

Poinqart felt a momentary burst of panic fill his half-breed thoughts. Uh, oh, he thought grimly to himself. Poinqart has a bad-no-good-feeling about this. . . .

Lost in the press the crimson bodies, Aitchley blindly swung his newly acquired sword, loping off arms and legs in a swath of bloodless carnage. Behind him, still gripped in Captain d'Ane's spectral arms, Harris Blind-Eye remained blissfully unconscious, the left side of his body a gruesome smear of vivid red dampness. Horselike nostrils sniffed and tasted the air all about the wounded thief—hungry, eyeless glares fixed rigidly in the lockpick's direction—and Aitchley hacked and slashed at the cadaverous red forms closing in around him in a vain attempt to cut a path to freedom.

"Aitchley!" Captain d'Ane called from behind the young farmer. "Behind us!"

Practically guided by his new sword, Aitchley spun nimbly on his heel and faced the black emptiness of the Pits, spotting the horde of scarlet creatures that scuttled ever nearer across

the twin strands of spidersilk. Silver-gray steel sang through
the thick, unnatural air, severing the tough, braided silk as easily as Aitchley's old sword might have cut through twine. No
longer anchored to solid ground, the silver cables dropped out
from beneath the mass of red creatures scurrying out over voidlike nothingness. Hissing and snarling, over a dozen Daeminase
fell back into the darkness, falling—Aitchley hoped—a million
leagues to the unfathomable bottom below.

Wheeling back around, sword slicing through bone and flesh
as easily as through empty air, Aitchley continued to fight his
way through the confusion of talons and silver fangs. "Berlyn!" he shouted through the chaos. "Where are you?"

The scullery maid's voice sounded from somewhere on
Aitchley's right. "Aitchley!" she cried back. "I'm—" The
abrupt pause in the girl's words caused Aitchley's stomach to
knot painfully. "I'm over here!"

Catching what he hoped was a glimpse of the blonde's yellow-white hair, Aitchley struggled to her aid. "Hold on!" he
yelled back. "I'm coming!"

Mucid, thick saliva suddenly splashed the young man as a
Daeminase launched itself on top of him, knocking him back
and throwing him to the ground. Aitchley hardly felt his head
hit the dark blue rocks—all but ignoring the sudden display of
lights and colors flashing behind his eyelids—yet his new
sword plunged itself through the emaciated breast of his attacker, ripping through to the back of the eight-foot-tall monstrosity with the crunch of broken bones and the dried
parchmentlike rip of shredded flesh.

Despite the blade piercing its chest, silver fangs snapped shut
perilously close to Aitchley's face, a portion of his hat brim
lost forever down the gullet of an inhuman throat.

A solid steel leg unexpectedly slammed into the side of the
Daeminase's head, punching out the opposite side in a grotesque rainfall of brains and cerebral fluid. Aitchley had to blink
a few times before he recognized the single-eyed stare of Camera 12 peering down at him, and he had to fight a sudden bout
of dizziness and vertigo as he clambered hastily back to his
feet.

"Twelve!" the young man commanded, the harshness of his
own voice hurting his head. "Get me to Berlyn! Now!"

Obediently, the spiderlike camera whipped about, catching
two Daeminase with an extended leg and knocking them back

into the Pits. Slinging the Cavalier's shield onto his left fore-arm, Aitchley grabbed hold of one of the leather saddlebags strapped to the camera's metallic abdomen and let it lead him through the crush of cadaverous red bodies, powerful legs knocking aside any would be attackers.

A wry chuckle sounded behind the young farmer as Captain d'Ane shadowed him through the chaos. "So I wasn't going senile, eh?" quipped the soldier's ghost, eyes trained on the arachnid machine leading their way. "Glad to know I died with all my faculties intact."

Aitchley did not respond as he forged his way through the ever-increasing horde of Daeminase; his thoughts were too concerned with Berlyn and her immediate safety. He could barely see her through the tall, gaunt figures that swarmed about them like giant, humanoid insects, and he was constantly ducking vicious claws and hungry teeth that seemed to lash out at him from every conceivable direction.

As another Daeminase fell—a steel leg plunging through the back of its enlongated skull—Aitchley felt a great rush of relief wash over him. Wearily, Berlyn met the young man's gaze, a similar look of relief crossing her features. Her face and hair were bespattered by reddish-brown ichor—and the left shoulder of her dress had been ripped away to reveal the pale, tender flesh beneath—but she was unharmed. Complete exhaustion etched itself onto her expression, and she gripped Aitchley's throwing ax with both hands, hardly able to bring the weapon up past her knees.

Before he was hardly aware of it, Aitchley had launched himself at the young blonde and held her tightly in a warm embrace.

Worry and anxiety swirled in the scullery maid's beautiful gray-green eyes as she searched the young man's face. "You're all right?" she fretted.

Aitchley allowed himself another lopsided smile. "I'm fine," he replied. "You?"

Berlyn nodded curtly, her long hair momentarily spilling into her face. "I'm all right," she answered.

Aitchley was unexpectedly jerked around as the Cavalier's shield saved him from a murderous sweep of scarlet talons on his left; the Daeminase's own momentum was magically hurled back at it. "I've got the elixir," he said, turning back to face Berlyn. "Where's Calyx?"

A look of deep concern drew heavy lines across the young girl's face. "I don't know," she replied. "He got hurt. Sprage and Gjalk took him over there someplace."

Aitchley followed the scullery maid's ambiguous pointing finger with a lump of dread riming his heart. Calyx? the young farmer anxiously asked himself. Hurt? Maybe dead? No!

Urgently, the young man swung his gaze back to Camera 12. "Twelve," he instructed the machine. "Get us to Calyx. Then get us the Pits out of here!"

A barbed spear drove through a nearby Daeminase as Eyfura cleared a path behind the two teenagers. "No need, kid," a gruff voice sounded down near the Rhagana's knees. "I'm right here."

Wheeling, Aitchley spun to see Calyx behind him, flanked on either side by Gjalk and Eyfura. Sprage stood nervously behind the three, Trianglehead perching comfortably on the healer's shoulder. Blood smeared the dwarf's black-and-silver beard and soaked through the bandages about his cheek, yet a glimmer of dark mirth continued to spark in his tiny eyes.

Aitchley narrowed his eyebrows at the unhealthy pallor of the smith's skin. "Are you all right?" he asked in his concern. "What happened?"

The dwarf gave the young farmer a cynical smirk beneath his blood-streaked beard. "What do you think happened, kid?" he asked back with typical dwarven sarcasm. "I wasn't paying attention. Now can we get the forge out of here?" He turned sharply on his heel, just the slightest hint of unsteadiness in his compact, stubby frame. "Oh, and nice to have you back, Captain," he added without turning back around.

Despite the dwarf's air of strained indifference, Aitchley was finding it harder and harder to wrestle with the fear churning inside him. Even as he ran from the Pits with Berlyn beside him, he couldn't shake the sense of impending doom that rattled about his skull. Now was the time for something to go really bad, the young man couldn't help thinking to himself. Now that we're all back together. Now that we've actually succeeded in our quest for the Elixir of Life and are on our way back to the safety and sanctuary of Vedette.

Aitchley threw an anxious glance over one shoulder as he wound his way through the dark blue stones and indigo stalagmites lining the lifeless surface of the Outside. The Daeminase scrambled after them, eyeless faces locked on their back and hungry saliva streaming from their jaws. Hundreds of them continued to clamber up from the jagged edge of the Pits, and Aitchley could still see inhuman shapes and silhouettes scuttling across the distant walls of the Cathedral of Thorns in their frenzied search for a way across.

How many of them are there? he wondered frantically to himself. They just keep coming! Look at them all! There must be at least a thousand on the cathedral alone! So how many were down in the Pits just waiting for us to come across?

The cold, lifeless earth gradually sloped downward as the young man ran through the glacial trough back toward the small hole in the icy stone that would lead them back into the ice caves of the unearthly columbarium. He wondered fleetingly if the Daeminase would follow them through, but then remembered what Taci had told them back at the Canyon Between. "The *reu'dheu* will awake if they are disturbed," the young girl had informed them gravely, "and they will not return to their rest until you are dead."

Oh, that's nice, Aitchley's pessimism snorted with black humor.

Aitchley threw another look over his shoulder as they sprinted through the sloping valley of dark blue stone and cold gray ice, the pulsating warmth of the Oblivion obscured by the hanging valleys and unscalable cliffs of the glacial gorge. The Daeminase had fallen farther behind, he noted with some relief. So maybe they would give up. Maybe they weren't going to chase them forever. Maybe Taci had been wrong.

Poinqart unexpectedly halted before the young man, almost causing the farmer to crash into him. Berlyn skidded to an equally ungraceful stop beside the young man, half sliding in the pebbles and polished till of the rock-strewn ground. The other six also came to clumsy halts.

A momentary flare of anger shot through Aitchley's breast as he glared down at the hybrid. "Poinqart!" he barked harshly. "What in the Pits are you stopping for?"

The half troll turned apologetic yellow-black eyes on the young man. "Poinqart is forgiveful-sorry, Mister Aitch," he said, "but Poinqart has a question-query."

Fear boiled up in the young man's stomach to countermand the anger. "Poinqart, there isn't time!" he shouted, throwing another worried glance over his shoulder. "The Daeminase are right behind us!"

A familiar frown creased Calyx's bandaged face. "Yeah? Well, we'd better make time," he remarked, " 'cause I've got a question, too."

Aitchley turned impatient eyes on the wounded dwarf.

Beady eyes fixed on the valley ahead of them, Calyx did not meet the young man's gaze. "Look," was all he said.

The fear in Aitchley's gut turned to scalding horror as he swung his gaze forward. Leathery banners of dissected flesh flapped in the arctic winds, and dried, brittle bones and cordlike strands of flayed muscle and sinew intertwined with one another to form a grotesque meshwork of mummified viscera.

Someone, the young man realized, had closed Lich Gate!

4

Gate-Crashers

"Okay." Calyx pursed unhappy lips. "Who's the wise guy?"

Deep rumblings of apprehension and fear repeated a similar question in Aitchley's thoughts, and he stared up at the massive portals of bone and sinew with a growing sense of foreboding. Dried and withered entrails intertwined with fossilized femurs and humeri. Ribbons of coagulated blood linked with strands of desiccated veins and mummified ligaments, creating a latticework of intestines and thoracic vertebrae. Ropy tendrils of brownish-red moss helped bind some of the bones and bowels together, and two eyeless skulls grinned down from atop each fifteen-foot-high portcullis, mocking the ten standing below with their fleshless, lifeless smiles.

Berlyn wrapped her fingers timorously around Aitchley's arm. "Why would anyone want to close Lich Gate?" she wanted to know, the quaver in her voice betraying her fear. "It doesn't make sense."

"Maybe one of the Daeminase did it," Sprage suggested, throwing a worried glance over one shoulder at the oncoming horde of crimson monsters. "It's stuck us in here with them."

"That could very well be, Healer Sprage," answered Gjuki, "yet none of the Daeminase were able to get past us. And even if one had, wouldn't we now confront that creature at the gate?"

"The Daeminase didn't close Lich Gate," Captain d'Ane declared. "Lich Gate's never been opened."

The confidence in the captain's voice threw a tumult of bed-fuddled shock swirling about Aitchley's brain, yet Calyx swung a dark look at the dead soldier, a skeptical frown on his bandaged features. "Excuse me, Captain," he answered snidely. "I don't know how it is for dead people, but those gates were open when we first walked through 'em."

D'Ane offered the dwarf a fleeting smile of spectral lips. "Of course they looked open," he agreed. "They're open for anyone who wants to pass through Lich Gate. It's just that you can't leave once you do."

Calyx's frown deepened. "Well, there's an interesting little tidbit of information," he sarcastically announced. "You can pass through Lich Gate, but you can't leave Lich Gate." He swung accusing eyes on the wraithlike soldier. "Don't you think you should have told us this before, Captain? I mean, trying to get an elixir from someplace where you're not allowed to leave is kind of like pumping the bellows after the fire has gone out, isn't it?"

A look of apparitional chagrin creased the warrior's face. "I'm sorry, Calyx," he apologized, "but I just didn't know while I was alive. It's something you remember once you die."

"But what about Yzan the Supramundane?" Aitchley queried. "What about all those books Liahturetart was reading from?"

"Yzan visited the Outside by means of a vision," Captain d'Ane explained. "He was never here physically."

"So what about you ghosts?" Calyx demanded. "You guys all walked through a solid wall to get here. How's a closed gate supposed to keep you in?"

D'Ane looked down at the unconscious lockpick in his translucent arms. "The closer we get to Lich Gate, the more substantial we become," he answered. "Right now I'm probably as real as you are. I suppose the further away from Lich Gate I go, the less tangible I'll become."

"So so long as we're on this side of Lich Gate, it's always gonna be closed?" Aitchley questioned. He gave the gates a perplexed grimace. "So what are we going to do?"

"Would it help if we all walked backward?" Sprage quipped.

"Get serious, Sprage," Calyx barked back.

"I *am* being serious," the healer jeered, heavy cynicism tainting his voice. "If you walk up to Lich Gate and it's always open, maybe we can fool 'em into thinking we're entering in reverse."

Holding a withering gaze on the long-haired physician, Calyx slowly turned back to face d'Ane. "Witling healers aside," he scoffed, "is there any way to get Lich Gate open from this side?"

D'Ane shook his head sadly. "Not that I know of," he said. "And that's alive or dead."

With an almost imperceptible hiss of steel against leather, Aitchley's new sword slid smoothly out of its sheath. "Well, we haven't got time to argue about it," the young man declared, able to hear the eager scrabblings of the nearing Daeminase. "We'll just have to chop our way through."

As glittering metal swung at the meshwork of shriveled arteries and preserved internal organs, Calyx shook his head despairingly. Steel bit easily into brittle bones and dried viscera, but Aitchley's next swing faltered when he saw the damaged gate instantly begin to re-form, dead tissues and shattered ossicle knitting and melding seamlessly back together. Even before the young man's shock had worn off, the damage to Lich Gate was undone.

"Forget about it, kid," Calyx advised the young farmer. "Looks like Daeminase guts if you ask me, and we've already seen how quickly those little buggers can heal. Even with all of us hacking and slashing, I doubt we'd make a dent big enough in the damn thing before their living buddies caught up with us."

"So what are we going to do?" Berlyn demanded, the fear in her voice growing as the Daeminase raced closer.

"Perhaps we could scale the gates to freedom?" Eyfura mused out loud, tiny, button-black eyes trained on the grisly portals.

"Fifteen feet high with a horde of Daeminase on our asses?" Calyx asked back. "We wouldn't get halfway up before we got dragged back down. And besides, Poinqart and I are both wounded. Not to mention Blind-Butt's dead on his feet."

None of his earlier jesting apparent, Sprage threw an anxious glance over his shoulder. "Well, we'd better come up with something 'cause we've got about ten seconds before we're all in some deep Entamoebae slime!" he declared.

Yellow-black eyes narrowing under bony protrusions, Poinqart gave the nine behind him a look of human timidity and trollish uncertainty. "Poinqart thinks he knows a way out-around ugly-slimy-Lich-Gate," the half troll said.

Warhammer in his grasp, Calyx turned to face the approaching Daeminase. "Sure," he replied with a shrug. "Why not? I'm open to suggestions."

Poinqart turned back to the twin gates. "Something Poinqart peeked-saw when Mister Aitch hack-slashed the portal-gate." Spatulate fingers drew aside an inhuman draping of esophagi to reveal a dull and rusted plate of metal; a cross-shaped indentation was cut into the metal. "Poinqart thinks it might-be-maybe a keyhole-way-out."

Glowering, Calyx shot an unfriendly glance over his shoulder at the rusted lock. "Figures," he grumbled. "Any other time Blind-Ass suffered a mortal wound, I'd be happy." He turned back to the oncoming Daeminase. "Sprage, see if you can do something for Harris. Yank his beard. Jerk his parbuckle. Do something to keep him alive long enough to pick that lock. Kid, you and the troll are with me."

Swallowing hard, Aitchley moved to the back of the group, his fingers curling tightly around the hilt of his new sword. He didn't like the fact that Berlyn stepped up beside him—throwing ax resting against her bared shoulder—but the advancing tide of insectlike figures silenced any protests he might have had. Even he wasn't stupid enough to think that he, Calyx, and Poinqart were enough to stop such an army of regenerative monsters. But all that was kind of pointless unless Sprage could help Harris, wasn't it? Aitchley knew there had to have been a reason why he hadn't let the southern-city bungholer fall.

A misplaced grin tugging his blood-dotted beard, Calyx swung beady eyes up at the young man. "Nice sword, kid," he complimented. "Where'd you get it?"

Alleviating some of the raw horror flowing through his veins, Aitchley briefly shifted his attention to the wonderous new blade in his hands. Although nervous sweat moistened his palm, his grip was firm and confident around its golden hilt. "Hmm? Oh. I got it inside the cathedral," he answered. " 'The greatest treasures of all mankind and beyond,' remember? Guess this was one of 'em." He didn't mention the fact that his first sword had been shattered by the Eternal Guardian . . . in no mood to get a lecture on the proper technique of defense and swordplay from the dwarf.

Calyx was in no mood to give lectures. "Hmmph," he responded. "Never would have thought it would have wound up beyond Lich Gate."

Aitchley fixed a questioning eye on the dwarf. "Why?" he asked. "Do you recognize it?"

Calyx laughed. "Recognize it?" He chortled. "Hammer and anvil, kid! I forged the damn thing!"

Startled, Aitchley turned his new sword over in his grasp. "You?" he sputtered. "How could you . . . ? I mean . . . You forged this?"

"Belonged to Procursus," the dwarven smith said with an emphatic nod. "Best damn sword in all QuinTyna's Creation." He gave another nod toward the magnificent blade. "That's the weapon that took down Myxomycetes. 'Course, I thought they sealed it in Procursus's tomb with him, but . . . hey! I guess I should be proud to have my sword in the Cathedral of Thorns."

Shock momentarily clogged Aitchley's throat. "But . . . but . . ." he sputtered. "How can I be holding the Cavalier's sword when it's buried with him up at the Dragon's Lair?"

Calyx shrugged, returning his attention to the nearing Daeminase. "Who knows?" he replied. "Magic? Sorcery? The fact that this whole place doesn't operate by the same laws of nature that we're used to? You've got to remember, kid, the Cathedral of Thorns holds the greatest treasures ever: those that were, that are, and that will be. You know, typical religious paradox stuff."

The astonishment almost proved too much for the young man. "But how is that possible?" he wanted to know. "I thought . . ."

Calyx smirked beneath his beard. "One thing you've got to remember when dealing with magic," he said. "Anything's possible."

Aitchley slowly turned away from the dwarf, his blue-green eyes locked on his ancestor's sword. No rules. No laws, he reminded himself with a pessimistic frown. Whatever happens, happens.

The Cavalier's sword glinting in his hands, Aitchley turned to face the army of eyeless creatures almost on top of him. And what's going to happen now is that we're all going to die! his darker side gravely predicted.

Dark brown eyes narrowed, Sprage inspected the limp form
in Captain d'Ane's diaphanous hold, a disapproving frown tugging at his lips. A fresh shellacking of red coated the left side
of Harris's body, and the brigand's face was an unhealthy, mottled gray. Frown deepening, Sprage placed a questioning hand
at the lockpick's throat, barely able to detect the faint, weak-
ening throb of a pulse, and the shallow, hurried breathing that
came from the thief's colorless lips only hardened the healer's
scowl.

"He's in shock," he mused out loud. "Captain, lie him
down and find something to prop up his feet. Gjalk, I need the
bundle of lady's mantle from my bag. It's the long-stalked plant
with palmately lobed leaves. Kind of hairy. I'll need you to
start making a poultice with it. It'll stop the bleeding and aid
in the healing. I don't have time to boil up some *kalreif* shoots
right now. Gjuki, I need you to press right here at his shoulder.
Right above the bone. Should help slow the bleeding."

As the two Rhagana and soldier's ghost did as instructed,
Sprage tore away a section of the lockpick's sleeve with Calyx's *navaja* and inspected the wound. A perfectly rounded hole
punched through the brigand's left shoulder just below the clav-
icle, leaving a gaping red maw in the outlaw's body. Sprage
couldn't tell if the scapula had been broken or chipped as well,
yet he could tell just by looking that—if the bandit survived—
the arm was going to be useless. Too many muscles had been
severed—both superficial and deep—and the lockpick had been
fortunate the giant thorn hadn't been just a bit lower or else it
would have punctured a lung. Still, the physician mused, there
might be a broken rib or two that could cause complications.

"Is there a chance that we can save Harris Blind-Eye?"
Gjalk inquired, handing Sprage the poultice of lady's mantle.

Sprage placed the moist cloth over Harris's gaping wound,
screwing up his nose at the unpleasant stench of the plant. "I
don't know," he answered truthfully. "Even if he does pull
through, he won't be able to use this arm. Think he can pick
the lock with only one hand?"

There was no glint of respect in Gjuki's tiny pearl-black eyes
as he looked down at the unconscious rogue. "Harris's tal-
ents—while not admirable—are varied and resourceful. Since
the Daeminase threaten his life as well as ours, I believe it
would be in his best interest to find a way to open the gates."

A weak, febrile voice sounded from Harris's direction. "Ah, you're just still mad at me 'cause I poked you in the guts a few months back, plant-man," the outlaw taunted groggily.

A look of shock registered across Sprage's face; if only all of his patients had constitutions like Harris Blind-Eye! "How are you feeling?" he queried. "Light-headed? Cold? Thirsty?"

Irritated contempt scrawled Harris's pale features. "Quit asking me so many damn questions!" he snapped back. "I feel like I just got a bunging thorn punched through my arm! How the Pits else am I supposed to feel?"

"Damn lucky is one," Sprage countered. "You're fortunate you didn't sever an artery. You would have bled to death by now."

Harris's contempt grew to outright hostility. "Oh, yeah, right." He sneered. "I'm just so damn happy I can barely restrain myself. Stand back, scout. I think I feel like dancing."

"All jesting aside," Captain d'Ane interrupted, "are you well enough to pick a lock?"

Harris had to blink a few times before he was able to focus on the silvery image of the deceased captain. "Well, Yram's bunghole," he swore. "Look who's decided to come back from the dead." A cruel smile played briefly across the lockpick's lips. "Can't say I've missed your self-righteous soliloquies, Captain."

D'Ane returned the lockpick's smirk. "I haven't come back from the dead," he argued. "I'm still dead. And if you're not able to do something about Lich Gate, you're going to be joining me soon enough."

Blue-black eyes glared at the twin portals of sinew and bone, the grim smile growing. "Suppose I could," he muttered. "But Harris Blind-Eye don't come cheap." He looked toward the rusted rectangle of metal half-hidden behind Daeminase offal. "I unlock this gate, my services to you are over. I mean completely. I want Mandy back and the necklace that controls this damn bracelet. Got that?"

Sprage threw up impotent hands. "Hey, I'm not in any position to—"

"Such things will be as you ask, Harris Blind-Eye," Gjuki interrupted, a look of grim necessity on his otherwise stoic features. "But remember, you will need our services to safely navigate your way back through the Bentwoods and the Mountains of Solid Blackness. It would, therefore, be unwise to attempt any southern-city knavery."

Harris clambered unsteadily to his feet with the help of Captain d'Ane. "Deal, plant-man," he responded. "Now step aside. I work alone."

Sprage tossed a glance of growing apprehension at the advancing Daeminase. "Tell that to them," he muttered under his breath.

Perched on the healer's shoulder, Trianglehead ruffled redviolet feathers. "You koward," the bird admonished. It nestled its head under one wing. "That good."

Wrestling with the gnawing unease in his belly, Aitchley tightened his grip on his ancestor's sword and readied himself for the oncoming Daeminase. Everything that had taken place had happened in mere seconds, he realized. Seconds that had felt like days. Nomion's Halberd! It had felt like an eternity hanging out over the Daeminase Pits! And now they were locked in and facing an army of inhuman monstrosities.

The Cavalier's shield draped the young man's left forearm, yet the mass of silver fangs and scarlet talons coming at him brought a sense of doom to his thoughts. Why hadn't they bothered to ask the *Kwau* how they had returned from Lich Gate? Or why hadn't the blue-gray women volunteered the information? But that was the trouble with limited communication, wasn't it? Only a few of the *Kwau* understood their language—passed down from generation to generation since the time of the Pilgrimage of Folly—and Taci had told them that the *Kwau* had stopped such journeys to Lich Gate long ago. Maybe the information had just been lost in time . . . a solution long since forgotten since it was no longer needed.

Aitchley again tightened his grip around his sword. Fat lotta good that does us now, he grumbled pessimistically to himself.

Crimson claws scrabbled on somber blue rock as the Daeminase loped closer, eager drool streaming from their jaws. Daggerlike fangs glittered with saliva-slicked splendor as the beasts charged nearer, featureless faces seemingly able to see the ten quest-members without the use of eyes. The dire cold in Aitchley's stomach grew, and he threw one last look at the young girl standing beside him before stancing himself for battle.

This is it, his darker side mused. Been nice knowing you.

Something unexpectedly pushed its way past the young man, almost knocking him to his knees. Startled, Aitchley barely caught a glimpse of the arachnid silver form that shoved its way through their line of defense and launched itself at the oncoming demons. A look of similar surprise was on Berlyn's face as she watched Camera 12 move to the front of their little group and spin about on spiderlike legs, its rounded back end directed at the hundreds of thousands of red creatures sprinting down the glacial valley toward them.

With a high-pitched whine, Camera 12's rocket ignited, catching the front line of Daeminase in an explosive discharge of blue-white flame. Rodentlike squeals and inhuman cries of agony erupted from the eyeless monstrosities, regenerative flesh burning, healing, then burning again. Noxious smoke spiraled up into the empty violet sky of the Outside, its foul, stomach-churning stench bringing tears to Aitchley's eyes, and charred and disfigured bodies crumpled in great heaps to the ground, their skeletal remains twisted and fused even as their regenerative abilities tried to return life that had already been extinguished.

Calyx let out a sudden whoop of a warcry. "Don't just stand there, kid!" the dwarf shouted at Aitchley. "The camera's buying us some time! Let's use it!"

Still wrapped in a blanket of surprise, Aitchley took a robotic step forward, the Cavalier's sword sweeping out before him. Glistening steel caught a Daeminase trying to clamber over the cindered remains of its brethren—scuttling out of range of the blue-white inferno issuing from Camera 12's abdomen—only to have its head lopped off in a silent swing of silver-gray metal. A startled hiss was all the creature could get out before its body tumbled lifelessly to the dirt, gangly arms and legs twitching and flailing in convulsive mimicry of life.

Arm and shoulder still aching, Berlyn lashed out with Aitchley's throwing ax, catching a Daeminase trying to come at them from around the far side of the ravine. Brownish-red fluid splashed the rock walls as the creature's head was pinned between unearthly blue stone and Berlyn's blade, and the monster snapped vicious silver teeth at the diminutive scullery maid before having enough common sense to fall over, dead.

Sword taking the top off a Daeminase's enlongated skull like the top off a soft-boiled egg, Aitchley squinted in the heat and fury of Camera 12's powerful, gimballed rocket, feeling the hairs on his arms burning and singing even though he stood safely at the front of the spiderlike camera. Regardless, for every dozen of Daeminase destroyed in the wash of blue-white flame, another twelve would rise up behind them, clambering over the smoldering remains of their dead brethren and gaining precious inches on the trapped quest-members. *If we don't get Lich Gate opened pretty soon, all of this is a waste of time,* Aitchley thought despondently to himself, trying to throw a worried glance over his shoulder but too caught up with what was going on in front of him to really see anything. *With more and more Daeminase pouring down the sloping rock of the glacial ravine, our only chance is to escape. Just run and keep running until the Daeminase give up . . . and hope Taci was wrong.*

There was an unexpected screech the likes of which Aitchley had never heard before, and he turned to see a demonic claw sweep past Camera 12's fiery defense, scarlet talons catching at the joint of one of its spiderlike legs. Wires and circuitry sparked and flared, filling the empty sky with a sudden fireworks of blue-and-white pyrotechnics, and Camera 12 lurched sickeningly to one side, one of its back legs almost completely severed from its arachnid body.

The horde of Daeminase instantly swarmed over the injured camera, scrambling over the damaged construct like a tide of living red water.

More sparks popped and flashed as inhuman claws tore and dismantled the intricate joints of Camera 12's many legs.

"No!" Aitchley screamed, diving blindly forward to help the downed machine.

Overtaken by a berserkerlike rage he had not felt since outside Solsbury, Aitchley waded straight into the heart of the oncoming Daeminase, the Cavalier's sword singing in a deadly arc about his head. Insectlike monsters hissed and snapped as silver-gray steel ended their deathless existence, painting the walls of the glacial trough with brackish red fluid. Yet for every arm he chopped off or every demon he beheaded, more and more of the gaunt red forms swarmed down upon him, threatening to overwhelm him the same way they had overwhelmed Camera 12.

Angry tears welled in the young man's eyes as he tried to fight his way through to the damaged camera, teeth clenched so hard that his jaw began to hurt.

Scarlet talons unexpectedly sliced the air near Aitchley's ear, cutting into the nylon strap of Tin William's backpack and nearly passing all the way through to the young man's shoulder. Saliva-smeared jaws clacked shut so close to Aitchley's face that he could smell the stale, mummified breath that came from inhuman lungs, and although he slammed the Cavalier's sword straight through the silver teeth before him, the Daeminase continued to fight and struggle until the blade pierced its brain and exited out the back of its skull in a grotesque spray of cerebral fluid.

Sword flailing, Aitchley spun on his left and caught another beast through the breastbone, cleaving his newly acquired sword violently downward and disemboweling the creature. Inhuman intestines spilled to the ground with a wet splunk, horrid, warm odors of death and decay filling the air even as the Daeminase gathered up its fallen entrails and shoved them back in its rapidly healing body.

The ravine completely filled with demonic figures, Aitchley was no longer even able to see Camera 12.

Urgent hands were suddenly on Aitchley's shoulders, trying to pull him back from his berserker fury.

Bloodlust in his eyes, Aitchley turned an ichor-stained face on Berlyn, trying unsuccessfully to blink back the rage that consumed him.

"Aitchley, come on!" the blonde was yelling at him furiously. "Harris has the gates open! Let's go!"

The words hardly held any meaning to the young farmer, and he swung back around to continue his relentless slaughter of crimson bodies. Somewhere . . . his enraged mind convinced him. Somewhere under all these bungholers, Camera 12's still alive. It's got to be!

The hands remained on Aitchley's shoulders. "Aitchley," Berlyn called again, and this time the softness in her voice cut a deep furrow through his anger. "It's too late. We've got to go."

Mindless vengeance suddenly jumbled by abrupt remorse, Aitchley paused, his ire faltering. Most of their group was already running through Lich Gate and back into the tiny cavern that led into the icy depths of the columbarium, and only Berlyn and Calyx remained beside the young man, trying to help hold off the Daeminase before the monsters overran them.

Aitchley swung his confused gaze on Berlyn; there were

tears in her eyes as well. "It's too late, Aitchley," she repeated. "Let's go."

Suddenly snapped free of his intense rage, Aitchley's instincts kicked in and he ran, grabbing Berlyn by the hand and pulling her along behind him. *What was I doing?* the rational side of his brain finally managed to shriek. *I could have been killed!*

Calyx looked up at the young man as he ran alongside the two teenagers. "If it's any consolation, kid," he said, "your machine bought us the time we needed to get the gates open."

Some of the vindictive fury remained burning in Aitchley's breast. "No, it isn't," he retorted, grinding his teeth together. "Camera 12 saved my life out in the desert, and this is how I repay it? By letting the Daeminase rip it apart?"

Calyx's ruddy face was grim with dwarven wisdom. "Hey," he quipped, flashing the young man a sincere grimace, "you knew the job was dangerous when you took it."

Angrily—right hand strangling the hilt of the Cavalier's sword—Aitchley ran for the circular opening in the lifeless blue rock of the Outside, hurriedly helping Berlyn down into the columbarium's arctic darkness before following. Yet even as they dropped down the tiered levels of the frozen waterfall and back through the icy corridors of the gray-white glacier, Aitchley was unable to purge himself of the undying anger and guilt. *Why did people have to die at all?* he wanted to know bitterly. *It isn't fair! And why am I always blaming myself? Camera 12 knew what it was doing. It's not like I told it to move to the very front of our line!*

Despite the desperate rationale surging through his thoughts, the tears returned to sting Aitchley's eyes. *Bloody, bunging typical,* he thought morosely to himself.

The chill of the columbarium helped take Aitchley's mind off some of the anger and sorrow rampaging through his cranium, but nothing short of freezing to death could free the young man of the conflicting emotions churning through his thoughts. Grief, regret, and intense flare-ups of rage pitted themselves against one another inside Aitchley's head, and he fell into one of his dark moods as they ran, hardly feeling the polar cold numbing his feet and stinging his face.

Worriedly, Berlyn ran beside the young man, her own concern helping distract her from the exhaustion of her own body.

The half-melted ice of the columbarium splashed up against the bare flesh of her legs—bringing goose bumps to her pale limbs—and her arms and shoulders still ached from repeatedly swinging Aitchley's throwing ax at the never-ending horde of Daeminase. Thankfully, the monstrosities had dropped out of sight somewhere behind them, but she could still hear them now and again, their scarlet claws scrabbling and skittering across the cold gray floor . . . their hungry snarls filling the corridors with vents of white mist and ominous, bestial echoes.

It was too bad what had happened to Camera 12—Berlyn didn't think she'd ever be able to forget the grating scream of metal and wiring torn asunder by inhuman claws—but what had been even worse for the young girl was seeing Aitchley almost meet a similar fate. So caught up in his own rage, the young farmer had had no idea how close the Daeminase had come to overpowering him, and Berlyn just didn't know what she'd do if she lost Aitchley now. He had been willing to go beyond Lich Gate for her . . . what was she prepared to do for him?

The young scullery maid risked a quick glimpse at the young man running beside her, their hands locked even as they ran. She could tell he was in another one of his moods, but at least this time she knew the reason. She knew the young man felt helpless—knew he blamed himself for what had happened to Camera 12—but she also knew it was better not to say anything. Sooner or later Aitchley would pull himself out of his funk, but anything she said now might redirect the young man's anger and melancholy out onto her. Aitchley would just have to deal with it himself.

The cold continued to seep in past her shoes and leech the feeling away from her toes as Berlyn hurried through the icy gray caverns of the columbarium, her breathing coming in heavy, labored gasps. Ahead of her—lighting the path with Tin William's magical lightstick—Calyx led the group back through the urn-lined halls of the unearthly glacier, twisting and turning down the numerous corridors as if he knew which way to go. Sprage and Captain d'Ane followed behind the dwarf—the latter floating more than running—and they were followed, in turn, by Poinqart, helping carry the deathly pale Harris. Even though Sprage had bandaged the lockpick's shoulder, Berlyn could tell the outlaw was not faring well and surmised he probably wouldn't last much longer . . . not unless Sprage could do a more thorough job . . . or, at least, until the Daeminase caught up with them.

The young blonde frowned heavily. Listen to me, she scolded herself. I'm starting to sound like Calyx!

Trying to push the dark thoughts out of her head, Berlyn raced down the slightly sloping floor and around another corner, trying not to slip in the rimy puddles of half-frozen water. Icicles stabbed down from the ceiling—transparent mockeries of limestone deposits—littering the ground with more puddles of arctic liquid, and Berlyn did her best to keep up with Aitchley while trying to sprint around or leap over these cold, gray wallows of half-frozen slush.

Silvery light suddenly struck the young girl's eyes, and she nearly halted in bewilderment as they ran free of the columbarium and back out onto the unnatural fog of the Bridge of Mists. A million stars filled the velvety sky overhead—and a million more filled the sky below—and despite the cold wind that still blew from the mouth of the infinitely high glacier, Berlyn was never more grateful to be outside.

Pausing only long enough to shove Tin William's lightstick into his belt, Calyx bolted out across the mist-formed bridge, practically disappearing into the gossamer clouds kicked up by his boots.

Sprage wasn't quite so sure of himself. "Uh . . . Are you sure this is a good idea?" he asked, stopping at the edge of the bridge. "I mean . . . it's not sunrise yet."

Calyx didn't bother to stop or look back. "So?"

"I believe what Healer Sprage is trying to say is that daybreak will cause the bridge to dissipate," Gjuki explained. "And since we cannot be sure what time it is—"

"I know what Sprage was trying to say, Gjuki," Calyx interrupted, "and I'm well aware of the dangers, but if you want to stay behind and play with the Daeminase, you go right ahead. I'll take my chances with the bridge."

Gjuki threw a curious glance over his shoulder at the columbarium; the first of the Daeminase came scuttling insectlike around an icy corner and out toward the bridge. "Your point is taken, Master Calyx," he replied, then hurried out after the dwarf.

Keeping her eyes on the brumous structure beneath her, Berlyn struggled with the vertigo and fear inspired by the unnatural Bridge of Mists. Many times on their first journey across she had made the mistake of looking out over its misty rails, yet even the deepest chasm wasn't as infinite as the Canyon Between. Empty space beckoned beneath her feet as black and as enormous as the canopy of stars overhead, and there was something about looking down into the heavens that sent conflicting signals rampaging through Berlyn's brain. It was almost as if her instincts were trying to tell her that the sky was always supposed to be above you, and the sight of dark heavens and silver stars below threw her equilibrium into turmoil.

"We spent an inordinate amount of time beyond Lich Gate," Gjalk DarkTraveler remarked as he ran, moss-green ponytail billowing behind him. "It would be safe to assume that we will not complete the crossing before sunrise."

Calyx scowled beneath his bandages. "Less talk. More running," he advised.

Gjalk turned button-black eyes toward the dwarf. "I was only stating what I know to be true," he said.

"I don't need you to tell me the obvious," Calyx shot back. "I'm a dwarf. You don't think I've considered the possibility of the bridge fading out from underneath and all of us dropping into the sun? Believe me, I've considered the possibility!"

"If we quick-fast run, Poinqart thinks-believe we will reach the other-safety-side before the burning-bright-sun comes up," Poinqart stated with hybrid optimism.

Practically carried in the half troll's gorillalike arms, Harris released another weak bark of laughter. "Hah! You hear that?" he jeered. "The stupid troll says we're gonna make it. So I guess we're gonna make it, huh?"

"Keep flappin' your lips, Blind-Butt," Calyx retorted. "Poinqart can just as easily toss you over the side like so much *gnaiss* shavings. We don't need you slowing us down anymore. You've done your part."

"Yeah, and I expect to be paid handsomely for it," the lockpick proclaimed. "Because of you lot, I've lost the use of my arm. Not only do I want that bungin' necklace and both me girls, but your Lord Tampenteire better be ready to pay me a whore's money pouch of gold!"

"Can't speak for Tampenteire," Calyx said, "but I'm afraid we can't give you back your necklace."

A momentary fluster of anger added a little color to Harris's pale features. "What?" he growled. "You'd better be able to give me that necklace or else I'll cut your heart out, dwarf!"

Calyx smirked despite himself. "Love to, Blind-Butt," he mocked, "but we ain't got it anymore."

Harris's anger intensified. "What?" he insisted. "If you're jerking my bung-rod, dwarf . . ."

Calyx's smirk grew. "No joke, Blind-Ass," he replied. "See, Poinqart was in possession of your precious little necklace back when we were attacked in the Bentwoods. Had it in his *meion*'s saddlebag." His smirk blossomed to a full smile. "And you all know what happened to his *meion*. I'd say your precious little necklace is either lying somewhere in a big clump of leaves or maybe a brown troll's got it. Who knows? You'd just better hope that a *stupid* troll doesn't figure out how to set that thing off. I can see it now. One minute you're sitting around with some friends playing Jackstones and Spilikins, the next . . . *boom!* Sorry, guys. No right hand!"

A murderous sneer twisted beneath Harris's ragged beard, returning some of the glimmer to his blue-black eyes. "You'd better be lying, dwarf," he threatened in a menacing snarl, "or else you die first."

"You know I'm not lying, Blind-Butt," Calyx answered, relishing the lockpick's fear, "or can't you read me anymore? You remember. Your special 'knack' for reading people?"

Berlyn didn't think it altogether intelligent to be provoking someone as ruthless as Harris Blind-Eye—after all, out of the ten quest-members, she had had the misfortune to spend an entire month alone with the brigand—but she also knew Calyx's immense dislike for the outlaw. Harris had made it perfectly clear that he didn't want to be there—had tried on numerous occasions to sabotage the quest and kill the people involved—but it still didn't make it right for the dwarven smith to taunt him like that. Even half-dead, Harris Blind-Eye was still a serious threat. Berlyn only hoped Calyx realized that.

As the strain of breathing got harder and harder—and as the muscles in her thighs and legs melted into rubbery, useless things—Berlyn tried to keep her pace consistent, attempting to match Aitchley stride for stride. The young man still hadn't said anything—his face fixed in a tense mask of self-loathing and seething anger—and Berlyn could just imagine the thoughts going through his head. *Probably still blaming himself for everything that's happened to us,* the young blonde surmised. *Probably thinking how we're all going to die and it'll all be his fault.*

Ironically, the petite scullery maid wasn't far off in predicting Aitchley's self-incriminating thoughts. Bleak pessimism ran rampant through the young farmer's head as he raced across the unreal surface of the Bridge of Mists, his boots landing on floorboards that were neither wood nor misty air, and he struggled with self-doubt that they still had a chance to make it across before the inevitable rise of the sun. We walked across before, he told himself, trying to drown out the pessimistic foretellings echoing through his skull. And we don't know what time it is. We might still make it.

Yeah, right, the young man's pessimism snorted its reply. You reached the columbarium at moonrise. You spent at least half the night beyond Lich Gate. It took you an entire day to walk across the bridge before. Figure it out: you're dead.

Moonrise does not necessarily mean it was nightfall, the young man answered back. There are days when I've seen the moon up in the sky long before the sun has set. Maybe it wasn't as late as we thought.

You're only fooling yourself, the young man's pessimism chided. Typical Corlaiys luck. You know you're not going to make it.

Teeth clenched and jaw set, Aitchley continued running across the solidified vapor of the Bridge of Mists, trying to keep his own dark musings from slowing him down. At any moment he expected the bridge to just drop out from beneath him. Fear and doubt flowed like great torrents through his bloodstream, and occasionally, a powerful bout of remorse would rise up from his conscience, almost forcing him to stop.

Camera 12 is dead and it's all your fault, it seemed to say. You should die, too.

The warmth of Berlyn's hand in his, however, kept him going.

Unexpectedly, Sprage's voice broke through the burbling mists ahead of them. "I can see them! The Shadow Crags!" he abruptly cheered. "We're going to make it!"

Calyx snorted. "I told you so," he grunted, unimpressed.

Eyebrows raised, Aitchley directed his own gaze westward, spotting the dark wall of blue-gray stone that rose up out of the unnatural mists. Like a mountain range of basaltic stalagmites, the Shadow Crags stabbed at the night sky, its ensiform peaks rising up like the spines of some subterranean behemoth. Misty curls and hazy spirals continued to obscure most of the peaks—weaving and coiling like cloudy serpents—but Aitchley could even see the cavern where Taci stood waiting for them, a look of shock on the adolescent girl's blue-gray features as she watched the ten sprint across the unreal mists of the bridge.

"Hurry!" Captain d'Ane suddenly shouted. "I think it's getting lighter!"

"No problem," Calyx replied. "We'll make it across in plenty of time."

Golden-yellow light began to fill the void beneath Aitchley's feet, and—despite the nearness of the Shadow Crags—he felt a pang of anxiety pierce his breast. Unlike the moon, the Bridge of Mists did not need to be in close proximity to the sun before it started to disperse. The heat of the rising sun caused the bridge to dissipate, and Aitchley had no idea how soon that heat would affect the bridge. Maybe the first rays of sunlight were enough to alter the substantiality of the floorboards . . . maybe the next step they took would be their last. . . .

Aitchley looked ahead of him at the nearing mountain range. No, he suddenly realized in a surge of disbelief. We're going to make it! We're really going to make it!

He gave a last glance at the horde of Daeminase charging across the bridge after them. And they're going to get fried! he continued to cheer himself. So long, bungholers!

Unexpectedly—damaged in the earlier scuffle—Tin William's backpack suddenly slipped from Aitchley's shoulders, its frayed shoulder strap tearing clean through and dropping it into the thick vapors of the bridge. Berlyn nearly fell over backward as Aitchley abruptly stopped, spinning around in wild-eyed panic and rushing insanely back at the approaching Daeminase.

Agape, Berlyn could only stand where she was, watching the young man run back toward the oncoming Daeminase. "Aitchley!" she shrieked.

Aitchley tried to block out his own horror as he sprinted to where the backpack had fallen from his shoulders, making a frenzied search through the thick, endoplasmic tendrils of mist and fog for the missing knapsack. If you had to drop something, why'd it have to be the elixir? His pessimism sneered at him from inside his head. Stupid!

The yellow-gold light from below began to intensify as Aitchley's hand accidentally came across the unbroken shoulder strap of Tin William's backpack, and he snatched the maroon-colored bag back up into his grasp and wheeled around. He could see Berlyn standing in shocked surprise behind him, not knowing whether to continue westward or wait for him, and he motioned her forward with a frantic wave of his hand, hearing the nearby hiss and ravenous growls of the pursuing monsters.

Calyx stepped onto the bluish-gray rocks of the Shadow Crags and looked back out over the Canyon Between. "What in the forge . . . ?" he muttered out loud. "Kid! What do you think you're doing?"

Aitchley ignored the question, running for all he was worth back toward Berlyn. He held the backpack's unbroken strap in his right hand—its maroon-colored pouch banging against his knee—and he clutched the staff of blackened oak in the other, determined not to lose the staff until he found out what it did. Behind him, snarling and slavering, the mass of Daeminase scuttled over the misty bridgework, spidery legs taking great leaping strides after the young man and his girlfriend.

Aitchley reached Berlyn and unceremoniously pushed her forward, forcing her back into a run. "Go! *Go!*" he screamed at her.

Still cocooned in her earlier astonishment, Berlyn hesitated before pivoting back around and sprinting westward. She reached down with her right hand and pulled the torn and tattered hem of her skirt away from her knees to help her run, but she could still hear the incessant hissing and sissing of the Daeminase behind her.

That was when she realized it wasn't the Daeminase.

Berlyn looked down as the bridge beneath her feet started to lose opacity. "Aitchley!" she cried.

Hearing the hiss and sizzle of evaporating mist, Aitchley continued to push the young girl forward. "Keep going!" was all he said. "We can make it!"

The bright warming rays of the rising sun blossomed up out of the Canyon Between like the radiant petals of some solar flower, and Berlyn screamed when her foot unexpectedly passed through endoplasmic mist and into the void beyond. A dissonant harmony of crackling fog and writhing haze filled the young girl's ears as she fell, and she was hardly aware of Aitchley's hands trying to help her up without releasing his hold on his backpack and staff.

Only a few feet from where the two teenagers still struggled across the fading bridge, Calyx looked out at the dissipating mists with an expression of complete and utter helplessness. "Run, kid! Run!" he yelled. "You can still make it! *Run!*"

Helping Berlyn back onto a more substantial portion of the bridge, Aitchley lunged for the edge of the cliff, shoving the young blonde before him in an effort to save her life. Tendrils and trestles of mist dispersed into the ever-brightening sky, and—like some cloud-forged dandelion—the Bridge of Mists simply ceased to be.

Aitchley and Berlyn fell toward the rising sun.

5

The Power to Heal

Surrounded by swirling chunks of fog and fragments of solid mist, Aitchley Corlaiys felt gravity grip him about the ankles and pull. Desperately, the young man reached out for anything of substance, but all around him were spiraling twists and streamers of haze that coiled and writhed into even greater insubstantiality. The hissing, crackling destruction of the unnatural floorboards beneath his feet resounded loudly in his ears, and blinding golden light came at him from below, searing through the Bridge of Mists like yellow-orange knives of radiant sunshine.

A single curse spilled from Aitchley's lips as he passed through the evaporating trestles of fog and mist and dropped toward the sun below.

You know, the young farmer thought sardonically, I'm really getting tired of falling. Falling off cliffs. Falling into giant spiderwebs. Almost falling into the Pits. I'm really getting tired of it.

Something unexpectedly caught the young man in midair, wrenching his right arm above his head and halting his fall. Dazedly—trying to force the shock out of his eyes as quickly as possible—Aitchley craned his neck upward to see Tin William's backpack hovering above his head like some maroon-colored balloon, holding him aloft by its single, unbroken strap. He hardly had a chance to react before his fingers were almost ripped away from the floating backpack when Berlyn suddenly grabbed onto his legs, stopping her own plunge into the enormous golden inferno that rose up out of the canyon. Behind them—snarling and hissing their inhuman rage—the dark, gangly tide of Daeminase pursuing them dropped into the sun, spindly arms and legs flailing as they disappeared into brilliant sunlight.

Her grip around Aitchley's legs tenuous—her fingers and arms still sore from their earlier battles—Berlyn stared down at the red-gold effulgence rising up to meet them. "What . . . why aren't we falling?" she managed to stutter.

Aitchley gave another befuddled glance at the backpack hovering above his head. "I . . . I . . . I'm not sure," he answered. "Maybe the backpack's magic or something. . . ."

"But . . . but you had it on when we fell into the spider's web and it never did anything like this," the blonde pointed out.

Aitchley felt his mouth working but no sounds were coming out. "Well . . . um . . . I . . . uh . . . I don't know!" he finally admitted. "Maybe—"

A sudden shout pulled the young farmer from his speculations. "Kid!" Calyx yelled at him from across the chasm. "Quit flapping your gums and give me your hand! There's not much time!"

Apprehensively, Aitchley looked down into the infinite gap beneath his feet. An enormous sea of churning, roiling fire continued to rise up toward him, and he could see Berlyn's feet dangling precariously close to the unearthly flames. Constricting fear replaced some of his bafflement, and he returned his attention to the dark blue cliff where the other quest-members stood safely out of harm's way.

Stanced on the blue-gray rocks of the Shadow Crags, Calyx tried to reach an arm out to the young man. "Come on," he instructed. "Reach!"

Despite the ache in his shoulder and the bewilderment still running through his brain, Aitchley made a determined grab for Calyx's hand. The fear knotting in his stomach grew when he discovered there was still about ten feet between him and the cliff. "I can't!" he realized, a trace of panic twinging his voice. "It's too far!"

Berlyn choked off a scream as Aitchley's movements caused them to spin from the backpack's unbroken strap, turning them lazily through the thick, unnatural air. Far beyond being terrified, the young blonde just shut her eyes and held on as tightly as she could, trying to ignore the growing warmth playing upon her bare legs.

Calyx frowned heavily at the distance separating him from the two teenagers. "Your staff, kid," he suggested. "Reach out with your staff!"

The increasing panic caused a momentary mental block in Aitchley's thoughts, and he had to look down at his left hand before remembering the twisted length of blackened wood in his grip. Yes! he heard himself urgently think. The staff! Use the staff! You can reach Calyx with the staff!

Desperately—squinting against the glare of the rising sun— Aitchley reached out with the mysterious stave he had taken from off the altar of thorns, barely holding on to its silver-capped knob with his fingertips. The weight of the staff threatened to pull it downward and out of the young man's grasp, yet Aitchley made sure his grip was firm as he stretched out toward the blue-gray cliff and Calyx's waiting hand.

Dwarven fingers and carbonized wood remained separated by thick, pluvial air.

Almost leaning too far forward and plunging over the edge himself, Calyx straightened himself back up. "It's no good, kid," he said. He swung a dark look on those behind him. "Sprage, quick! Your rope!"

Openmouthed, Sprage forced himself to look away from the hovering teenagers. "Huh?" He gaped. "What?"

"Your rope! Your rope!" Calyx demanded impatiently. "Give me your rope!"

Even as the healer went to grab the coil of rope he had brought with them from Baroness Desireah's castle, the aston-ishment remained bright in his dark brown eyes. "But how can they *do* that?" he wanted to know.

Calyx snatched the rope out of the physician's hands. "Who cares?" he retorted. "It's not going to make much difference in a couple of seconds anyways!"

Feeling the throb of his wrenched shoulder and the growing heat of the rising sun, Aitchley also felt the dwarf's growing anxiety take hold somewhere in his bowels. How his backpack was defying the laws of gravity, he didn't know either, but the young man was fully aware of how little time they had left. The Bridge of Mists had completely dispersed around them— its solid beams of fog and haze scattered and dispelled before the heat of the rising sun—and Aitchley knew it was only a matter of time before he and Berlyn met the same fate as the Daeminase. *Just hanging here from my backpack isn't enough,* the young farmer knew. *We have to figure out a way to get out of here before it's too late!*

Calyx finished tying Sprage's rope into a loose loop, beady eyes narrowing through the brightening aurora of morning sunlight. "Okay," he said, "we're only going to get one shot at this." He stepped to the edge of the cliff. "Hold your staff up, kid. I'll try and hook the knob. Then hang on for all your worth 'cause I'm gonna jerk you out of there as quick as I can. Got that?"

Aitchley barely found the courage to nod, let alone answer, and he could feel Berlyn trembling down at his legs. Too afraid to even nod, the young scullery maid just tightened her grip and prayed. She could feel faint whispers of smoke billowing up from around her shoes—and some of the ragged and frayed threads of her skirt began to smolder and singe like burning hairs—but she held on. Memories of her time in the Molten Dunes came back to plague her as she felt the heat growing unpleasantly against her naked flesh, and she hoped Calyx would just stop talking and pull them to safety before both her legs got burned off in the sun.

Calyx spun his impromptu lasso above his head.

"Hurry-quick, Mister Calyx-dwarf!" Poinqart urged, human fear and trollish helplessness swirling in yellow-black eyes. "Nasty-burning-hot-sun is getting too nearby-close! Hurry-quick!"

Calyx shot the half troll a foul glance. "Don't push me," he warned. "I don't work well under pressure."

Berlyn cringed when something that felt like naked flames licked questioningly at her toes, causing her to pull her legs up to her chest in sudden fright. The air was heavy with dense heat haze—pervading the young blonde's nostrils and clogging her throat worse than any desert—and she didn't need to look down to know that the sun was nearly upon them.

Feeling Berlyn's unexpected move—and fearing she was losing her grip—Aitchley instinctively reached down with his left hand to help her, watching in a kind of slow-motion horror as Calyx's rope sailed out over where the staff used to be and lassoed empty space. Shock and ironic sniggering echoed inside the young man's mind as he watched the rope drop away from him and fall into the ocean of golden light below, vanishing in a quick burst of bright yellow fire like a moth flying into a taper.

Aitchley felt all hope drain from his system. We're dead, he concluded dourly.

There was an unexpected roar that gradually rose in pitch and something suddenly came screaming down from the heavens, scooping up Berlyn from behind and carrying her, meteorically, toward the Shadow Crags. Hugging Aitchley's legs and afraid to look, a startled yelp escaped the young girl's lips as something cold and metallic touched her bare legs, and she felt her foot snag something strong yet resilient . . . like a fishing net made out of steel. Aitchley was dragged along above the girl, pulled forward by his legs and almost losing his hat in the sudden burst of speed. He barely retained his grip on the mysteriously hovering backpack above him as they were carried up out of danger and deposited in a clumsy heap back on solid ground.

Eyes stinging from the intense heat—throat still dry from inhaling burning air—Berlyn clambered groggily to her hands and knees, trying to shake the sudden dizziness and confusion from her gray-green eyes.

Blinking, she stared up into the single eye of Camera 12.

Aitchley was on his feet before her. "Twelve!" the young man exclaimed. "You're all right! I mean . . . you're not dead!"

The arachnid construct swung its solitary eye on the young farmer and bobbed up and down on its remaining legs, agreeing enthusiastically without speaking. Torn and shredded steel showed where numerous claws had ripped through metal and wires—and half of its spidery legs had been severed or damaged in some way that made the machine have difficulty standing upright—but by using its gimballed rocket, Camera 12 managed to remain erect despite all the clawed steel and damaged circuitry exposed on its glittering abdomen.

Calyx finished coiling what was left of Sprage's smoldering rope and handed it back to the physician; Sprage accepted it somewhat reluctantly. "Seems your camera's a lot tougher than we gave it credit," the dwarf told Aitchley. He gave the rising sun a backward glance. "Now what say we get out of here before something else comes rising up out of there?"

Nodding, Aitchley helped Berlyn to her feet, slinging Tin

William's backpack over his shoulder now that he was back on level ground. Camera 12 wasn't dead, he cheered mentally, and neither was he or Berlyn! There was still the mystery of why Tin William's backpack had chosen that moment to defy gravity—it was acting normal now—but that could wait until later. Right now Aitchley wanted nothing more than to find a dark, quiet place to lie down and sleep off all the various aches and pains he had accumulated while beyond Lich Gate. Maybe a few hours of slumber would help dampen some of his discomfort and numb his mind of such nightmarish visions as eyeless demons and cathedrals of bloody red thorns.

One thing I know for certain, the young man concluded, stepping back into the darkness of the Shadow Crags behind Taci, I'm never going to be able to look at a sunrise the same way again!

They slept for nearly half the day camped just inside the Shadow Crags, still in view of the cloudless expanse of sky that stretched above and below the ethereal Bridge of Mists. It wasn't until the heavens began to fade into a mixture of deep blues and vibrant pinks that Calyx roused the group and forced them to move on.

Still feeling tired from previous nights of lost sleep—and feeling even more weary now that he has tasted a few tantalizing moments of real rest—Aitchley struggled to his feet and gathered his things together. It wasn't easy to push the weariness out of his muscles or ignore the wobble in his legs, but the young man forced himself up and about, feeling a little better after a quick meal prepared by Gjuki. He even found the strength to help Sprage clean and rebandage Harris's wound.

As early evening grew even more dominant over the sky, Aitchley draped the remaining strap of Tin William's backpack over one shoulder and shadowed Taci back into the twisting, volcanic tunnels of the Shadow Crags. Poinqart and Berlyn walked on either side of the young man—tired but smiling—and a sense of growing accomplishment helped fuel Aitchley's overtaxed legs. Tingles of unnatural energy coursed through his left hand and up the length of his arm from the staff of blackened oak in his grasp, and the Cavalier's sword rested comfortably in his old and worn sheath. Not only that, the most sought-after and written-about magical artifact in the entire world rested securely in his backpack, throbbing with a sorcerous life all its own. When they returned to Solsbury, he'd be hailed a hero, the young man realized with some astonishment. And he could probably sell both staff and sword for a king's ransom. He'd be wealthy as well as famous! What would Berlyn have to think about that?

Grinning lopsidedly at daydreams of riches and fabulous wealth, Aitchley made his way through the murky, claustrophobic tunnels of the Shadow Crags and back into the ancient *Kwau perbru*. It was actually kind of heartening to walk back into the enormous cavern, already familiar with its glistening underground pool and its high, columned walls. The dark blue hexagonal patterns of scored and fractured basalt running across the rocky floor reminded Aitchley of the tiles in the Tampenteire estate back home, and a wistful smile played upon his lips as he spied the tall ebony pillar of volcanic rock where he and Berlyn had spent a pleasant afternoon deciphering crude glyphs. Arched ceilings and elevated walkways natural in their construct all but disappeared in the musty gloom of the cave— vaguely highlighted by the rippling glow of the subterranean waters—and the small family of albino bats chittered and squeaked a greeting to the eleven quest-members as they returned to the *perbru*.

With a heavy sigh, Calyx unslung his burden of saddlebags and sank to the rough, basalt floor. "That's it for today," he announced. "We stay here for the night."

Eager groans and deep exhalations met the dwarf's words, and Aitchley collapsed to the ground in an exhausted heap, shrugging himself free of backpack, shield, and sword. They had only walked for a few hours since awakening—not more than three or four leagues from the Canyon Between—but there was already a painful ache at the back of Aitchley's knees and a soreness in his feet he had not felt since the Molten Dunes. Tendrils of discomfort continued to throb from his wrenched shoulder muscles, and the cuts and abrasions he had received by plowing through a couple of rows of pews back in the Cathedral of Thorns continued to chafe and gall like a bad case of poison ivy.

With a weary moan, Berlyn settled herself down on the ground beside the young man, offering him a small smile of cheerful encouragment. "How are you feeling?" she queried.

Aitchley lay back against his supplies, using Tin William's

backpack as a pillow. "Sore," he answered. "I could probably sleep for a week."

Berlyn's smile widened. "Me, too," she agreed. "Is there anything I can get you?"

Aitchley settled his hat down over his eyes, taking in a deep, relaxing breath. "No, I'm okay," he responded. "I'm just surprised Calyx is actually letting us stop so soon."

Berlyn turned to give the dwarven smith a concerned glance. "I think he's hurting more than he's letting on," she remarked. She lightly fingered the ragged tear of fabric at her shoulder. "None of us got out of there completely unscathed," she added.

Aitchley poked tentatively at a cut above his left eyebrow. "Tell me about it," he said. "The damn Guardian was throwing me around the cathedral like we were playing battledore and shuttlecock . . . and I was the shuttlecock!"

Gently, Berlyn moved in closer to the young man, draping a delicate arm across his chest. Aitchley winced as the cuts and bruises all along his body momentarily protested, but then the warming closeness of Berlyn overrode any discomfort and they slept like that, arm in arm, through the entire night.

Aitchley awoke the next morning to the pungent aroma of boiling *kalreif* shoots, the powerful stench filling the great cavern around him. Nostrils twitching, the young man propped himself up on one arm and turned to see Sprage squatting nearby, hunched over a small fire and a pot of water. Noticing the young man's grimace, the healer offered a wry grin as he stirred the contents of his foul-smelling brew.

"Not my idea," the physician declared, looking down into the thickening paste of *kalreif* and liquid. "Calyx wants to make sure everyone's okay before we start off again. Says the last thing he needs is for someone's arm to drop off from infection."

Aitchley screwed up his face at the putrid stink. "Oh, I don't know," the young man quipped. "Even a festering sore wouldn't smell so bad."

"Not at first, no," Sprage agreed cynically, "but even *kalreif* shoots pale in comparison to the stink caused by gangrene. Now take your shirt off. I haven't got all day."

Obediently, Aitchley removed his shirt—wincing as the fabric brushed fleetingly against the myriad cuts and sores crisscrossing his chest—and reluctantly let Sprage dab on the foul-smelling paste of herbs and hot water. He flinched as the healer rubbed the balm on some of his more sensitive wounds—hissing through clenched teeth at the sudden sting of salve against flesh—yet the warm touch of the herb helped relieve some of Aitchley's deeper aches almost instantly. If only the mixture didn't smell so Gaal-damned offensive . . .

Curiously, Aitchley turned to look at the empty ground beside him. "So where's Berlyn?" he asked.

"She's over there somewhere helping Gjuki with breakfast," replied Sprage. "Don't worry. She's already had her dose of stink."

A momentary flash of jealously sparked through Aitchley's mind at the thought of Berlyn sitting—topless like him—in front of the long-haired healer, but he quickly pushed the image out of his head. There was no reason why Berlyn had to remove anything anyway, the young man tried to console himself. And besides, Sprage's a doctor. I'm sure he doesn't get some kind of preverse thrill by having young women disrobe in front of him. At least . . . he'd better not!

Gently, Sprage dabbed some more *kalreif* above the young man's left eyebrow. "You know," he said for conversation's sake, "Calyx was telling me that around the time of the Cavalier and before, people didn't have to worry about serious infection. Or birth defects, for that matter."

Aitchley winced as Sprage painted over a sore on his left arm. "Well, how's that possible?" he wondered. "I always thought those were just natural things."

Sprage shrugged slouched shoulders. "They are," he replied, "but did you know there wasn't a recorded case of plague until one hundred and twenty years ago? Not once. And no one got boils or carbuncles before that. Or gout. Or even cleft palates. Things were as close to perfect as they could get."

"So what happened?" Aitchley inquired.

Sprage offered another noncommittal shrug. "Who knows?" he replied. "Things change. Damn Cavalier dies and everything goes to the Pits." He finished wiping *kalreif* across Aitchley's chest and flicked the remaining salve clinging to his fingers back into the pot. "Well, that's it for you," he declared, getting to his feet with a weary groan. "I have to go see to Harris now."

A twinge of concern came, unbidden, from the back of the young farmer's mind. "How is he?" he asked.

"Not so good," the healer answered honestly, "but you'd never know it to talk to him. All he does is complain about getting his stupid knife back and how many ways he can kill Calyx for losing the necklace. You'd never suspect that he had a great big bloody hole in his shoulder. I've met rabid xlves with better dispositions!"

Aitchley started to pull his shirt back on. "Need any help?" he offered.

Sprage flashed the young man a sincere smile. "Naw," he said, "I can manage. Besides, Gjalk's been helping me whenever I need it. Seems he's fascinated by human physiology. You just lie there and rest. Next to Harris, you got banged up the most."

As he finished pulling on his shirt Aitchley winced as something in his rib cage jabbed a painful reminder into his nerves. "You're telling me," he said with a grimace.

While Sprage gathered up his pot of herbs Berlyn returned to her spot next to Aitchley, carrying a small plate of food for the young man. Smiling, she sat down beside him—her nose momentarily crinkling at the overpowering stench of *kalreif* shoots—but Aitchley noticed a few pasty-white splotches on her shapely legs and one just above her right breast before he got too self-conscious.

"I brought you some breakfast," the blonde declared, handing Aitchley the plate. "It's not much, but Gjuki says we're starting to run kind of low. We'll have to ration ourselves more carefully until we get back to Viveca."

Aitchley tore at a piece of what was supposed to be cured meat; it tasted like cardboard. "Great," he remarked sarcastically. "Just don't tell Calyx or life will be totally miserable."

Berlyn's lips pulled back in a beautiful smile. "Oh, I don't think that's worth worrying about," she said. "Right now Calyx is too concerned about getting the elixir back to the Cavalier's Tomb without anything happening. To hear him tell it, everybody but Yram the Chaste herself will be out after us now that we have it."

Aitchley tugged off another piece of jerky and chewed forcifully on the dried meat. "I don't know what he's so worried about," he said. "Hardly anybody knows what we're doing. A couple of lords. A few dukes. A baron or two. What's the big deal?''

Berlyn smoothed out her skirt as she leaned back beside the young man. ''Well, that's one of the reasons Calyx is so worried,'' she said. ''It seems a lot of people do know about us. The whole town of Viveca for one. Rumors about the quest have been spreading for months now.''

Trying to wash the salty, bland taste of cured meat out of his mouth, Aitchley took a sip of water from his flask. ''So?'' he answered nonchalantly. ''People still don't know what we look like. I mean . . . do we even *look* like some fantastic quest going beyond Lich Gate? Gaal, no! We look more like some ragged band of southern-city misfits. Lord Tampenteire said so himself. I just think Calyx worries just to worry.''

Still smiling, Berlyn leaned farther back on her hands, watching the young man as he ate the breakfast she had prepared for him. There was a moment of awkward silence as Aitchley sensed the young blonde's adoring gaze—he hated it when people watched him eat—and he forced himself to throw her a crooked grin, hoping he didn't have any food stuck between his teeth.

As the young farmer finished nibbling on a piece of dried fruit, Berlyn removed the empty plate from his lap and asked, ''So . . . can I see it?''

A hot flash of embarrassment filled Aitchley's cheeks, and he sputtered a few feigned coughs into a clenched fist in order to hide his face. ''I . . . um . . . What?'' he flustered.

There was a mischievous twinkle in Berlyn's gray-green stare. ''The elixir,'' she said. ''Can I see it?'' Trim eyebrows narrowed questioningly above her eyes. ''What did you think I meant?''

Hoping the color in his face was not as vivid as the brambles on the Cathedral of Thorns, Aitchley turned shyly away from the young blonde and busied himself rummaging through his backpack. He had to remove the heavy leather saddlebag taken from Harris Blind-Eye at the Daeminase Pits—and set aside the mysterious thermos and Envirochamber given to him by Tin William—to get at the elixir, but he could feel the vibrant, almost sentient energies that radiated outward from the magical potion almost as soon as he opened his backpack. Like the gnarled and twisted staff at his side, the Elixir of Life pulsed with an almost living heartbeat of sorcerous emanations, send-

ing invisible tendrils of true magic arcing up Aitchley's hands
and scurrying into his arms as he freed it from his sack.

Berlyn's eyes widened as the eldritch glow of the elixir filled
the surrounding cavern. "Gaal," she breathed her awe. "It's
beautiful."

Reverently, Aitchley turned the decanter over in his hands,
blue-green eyes staring through blue-green glass. A thick black
stopper sealed the narrow neck of the bottle—ringed with a
heavy coating of yellow-white wax—and the glass was as
smooth as polished stone. No, not glass, Aitchley recalled, but
jaded-sapphire. The glass *was* stone.

Tiny bubbles of what might have been fermentation or glob-
ules of virginal light leapt and percolated in the miniature ed-
dies of the elixir, their effervescent activity mirroring the
delightful sensations that ran through Aitchley's hands, and a
rhythmic pulse of pure white light softly beat from the glittering
liquid depths of the potion, sending out a faint corona of magic
that washed over both Aitchley and Berlyn and chased away
their aches and pains.

Berlyn held out tentative hands. "Can I hold it?" she asked.

Cautiously, Aitchley transferred the decanter to the blonde's
arms. "Be careful," he advised. "Liahturetart said that any
undue shaking might make the magic circumcised. Uh . . . I
mean . . . circumspect."

Berlyn didn't even notice the young man's face go red with
embarrassment, her eyes locked on the bubbling, twinkling potion in her hands. The pleasing warmth of the Elixir of Life
seemed to leak through the container and scamper playfully up
her arms, wriggling through her body just beneath the skin. She
could feel invigorating energies flow through her shoulders—
banishing any ache or strain still plaguing her muscles—and
then pass through her breast, filling her heart with a revitalized
feeling of youth and vigor. Then the tingles and gooseflesh
moved down through her belly and over her hips, sparking a
pleasurable heat inbetween her thighs before creeping down the
length of her legs and centering delightfully in her toes like
some kind of genial form of pins and needles.

Berlyn shuddered at the fingerless caress of the elixir. "Oh!"
she gasped. "It tickles!"

Experimentally, Aitchley poked at the drying splotch of *kalreif* above his left eyebrow; there was no pain from the cut. "It
also heals minor wounds," the young man discovered, screw-

ing up his nose at the stink that surrounded him. "I wish I had known that before letting Sprage dump all this mulch all over me!"

Inquisitively, Berlyn noticed all her own cuts and abrasions no longer assailed her nerves, but she handed the elixir back to Aitchley before the soothing, gratifying euphoria made her start giggling like a little girl or built to something not quite so innocent between her legs.

A sudden voice behind the two startled them out of their experimentation. "So that's it, huh? Always thought it would be bigger."

Taken by surprise, the two teenagers turned to find the other quest-members gathered behind them, all drawn to the elixir's panacean glow. Suffused heaviest in the glimmer, Aitchley could see some of the color return to Calyx's face, the wounds across his cheek healing into pink-white scars beneath their coating of bandages and *kalreif* shoots. Even Captain d'Ane looked a bit more solid when bathed in the blue-green sparkle of the potion, his ghostly form taking on additional substance from the light itself. Only Harris was unable to join the group, lying, semiconscious, near the underground pond.

"It's incredible," Captain d'Ane said, spectral eyes going wide. "If the elixir is this potent while still in its container, imagine what it must be capable of once it's opened."

Sprage reached out an apprehensive hand and took the blue-green decanter from Aitchley. Immediately, the tingle of healing sorceries streaked through his body and imbued him with its energies. "Inconceivable," he breathed. He turned dark brown eyes on Aitchley. "Do you think I can use this a moment?" he asked. "It might help Harris."

A flurry of panic momentarily shot through Aitchley's brain. "Don't open it!" he cried. "We're not supposed to open it till we get to the Dragon's Lair."

Sprage pried his gaze away from the jaded-sapphire in his hands long enough to console Aitchley with his eyes. "I'm not going to open it," he promised. "I was just going to let Harris hold it awhile."

"There's something I never thought I'd hear," Calyx snorted sardonically. "We're actually going to let Harris Blind-Ass hold the Elixir of Life? While we're at it, why don't we just give him Berlyn and let him stab Gjuki again?"

Sprage didn't wait for Aitchley's agreement, moving quickly

to where the southern-city lockpick lay motionless. "Despite its powers, I doubt even the elixir can do anything for him at this stage," the healer remarked. "I don't think he'll last the week."

Out of curiosity, Aitchley pulled himself to his feet and followed Sprage to where Harris lay, pale and sickly in the rippling glow of the underground waters. Clean bandages and *kalreif* covered the brigand's wounded shoulder, but the dark red stain of fresh blood was already discoloring the wrappings. Harris's eyes were closed and a fine line of sweat bespotted his brow, but his eyelids fluttered weakly open as the pulsing nimbus of healing light first washed over him.

"Huh? Wuzzat?" the outlaw mumbled incoherently.

Delicately, Sprage placed the decanter of blue-green stone up against the bloody gauze wrapping the rogue's shoulder, ignoring the sudden curse and protest from Harris himself. Eyes wide, the lockpick could only lie there helplessly as the powerful magicks of the Elixir of Life flowed through his body through the gaping wound in his shoulder and eased and caressed his damaged nerves. Severed muscles made the attempt to knit back together, and even chipped bone started to re-form, helping relieve some of the bandit's pain. The wound itself did not completely heal, but at least there were the beginnings of scarring beneath the outlaw's bandages, helping him on his way to recovery.

As magically induced strength intensified in his weakened body, Harris smacked the aquamarine bottle away from his shoulder. "Get that bunging thing away from me!" he demanded. "Harris Blind-Eye doesn't need any stinking sorcery to get better!"

Dumbstruck, Sprage returned the elixir to Aitchley, staring in wide-eyed wonder at the healthy pallor slowly returning to Harris's face. "Inconceivable," he murmured again, placing an inquiring hand at the lockpick's throat. He turned a bewildered gaze back to those behind him. "His pulse is almost back to normal," he announced. "Color's good. No signs of infection." He ran a shocked hand through his graying hair. "I think he's going to live."

Calyx unraveled the bandages from his own face, lightly tracing the tender lines of scar tissue streaking his cheek. "Oh, goody, goody," he retorted. "You hear that, everybody? Harris Blind-Ass is going to live. I'm so happy I could kiss a muggwort.'' He stomped off to go rummage through his enormous sack. ''Why don't you tell me something real cheerful like we've got enough provisions to make it to Viveca. Or maybe that our horses will be waiting for us outside the Shadow Crags. Or maybe that we can take a shortcut around the Bentwoods or . . .''

Snickering, Aitchley stepped away from where Calyx dwarvenly ranted, returning to his backpack and sitting down. The others all went on about their business—only Berlyn and Poinqart accompanying the young man back to his spot—and Aitchley let Poinqart hold the elixir to his own wounded shoulder before returning it to the safety of Tin William's backpack.

''Tingle-itches, Mister Aitch,'' the half troll said, offering a crooked smile of hybrid friendship. ''Makes Poinqart's hurtfulouches go away.''

''That's just what it does, Poinqart,'' Aitchley said with a small shrug. ''If it's powerful enough to bring anyone back from the dead no matter how long they've been dead, I guess the power to heal is just a secondary benefit.''

''Handy-good-thing to have,'' Poinqart agreed with a nod. ''No more splinter-cuts or scratchy-scrapes. Poinqart does not like such nasty-no-good-things.''

Aitchley slid the canvas Envirochamber back into his backpack, making sure it helped hold the elixir stationary. ''Me either,'' he answered the half troll with a lopsided smile. ''I'm just glad—''

A sudden gasp from Berlyn almost caused Aitchley to drop the thermos as he was returning it to his knapsack, and he turned in sudden fright to look at the young girl beside him. A look of amazement marred the blonde's beautiful features, and she stared with wide eyes at something lying on the floor nearby.

A burst of adrenaline-mingled panic raced through Aitchley's system. ''What?'' he nearly shouted. ''What is it?''

Mouth agape, Berlyn jabbed an accusatory finger at the hard basalt ground, indicating the thick leather saddlebag belonging to Harris Blind-Eye. ''Aitchley!'' she squeaked. ''Look!''

Befuddled, Aitchley drew his eyes downward to stare at the saddlebag, not noticing anything out of the ordinary. He was about to look back at Berlyn and ask her what her problem was when he suddenly realized the leather pouch was hovering a few inches off the ground, enigmatically suspended above the dark blue hexagonal rocks.

Aitchley blinked mutely in awed stupefaction.

6

Bag o' Goodies

Aitchley caught Berlyn's hand as she reached tentatively for the levitating saddlebag. "Don't touch it!" he warned.

Berlyn flinched, jerking back her hand as if bitten. "Why?" she wanted to know. "What's in it?"

A deep mistrust lit in Aitchley's gaze as he stared at the floating saddlebag. "I don't know," he admitted, his voice hushed.

Berlyn pursed questioning lips. "Then why shouldn't I touch it?"

The uncertainty remained in Aitchley's eyes as he swung a cursory glance on the scullery maid. "Because whatever's in there was stolen by Harris Blind-Eye from the Cathedral of Thorns. There could be anything in there."

Despite Aitchley's misgivings, Berlyn reached out again for the pouch, carefully taking the worn leather into her hands. "I think it's safe to assume that Harris didn't bring the Guardian back with him," she quipped. Curious fingers undid the cracked leather tie holding the saddlebag shut. "Whatever's in here saved our lives," she added, "and I want to know what that was."

A million protests and arguments swelled in the back of Aitchley's throat, but none succeeded in escaping the young man's mouth, caught somewhere between his tongue and his larynx. He watched in a kind of inquisitive dread—curious yet fearful at what might be in the pouch—and tensed instinctively as Berlyn's fingers pulled free the knot at the saddlebag's flap and casually flipped it open. He didn't know what he expected to come out of the bag—maybe just a blinding flash of magic and a single thunderclap of energy that disintegrated them all on the spot—but it felt as if a million butterflies had suddenly taken up residence in his stomach, fluttering and bumping into one another as Berlyn reached a questioning hand inside the sack.

An admiring gasp came from deep within the girl's breast as she pulled free a magnificent cloak of charcoal-gray fabric, unceremoniously shoved into the cramped interior of the saddlebag. Even so, no wrinkles or folds creased the luxurious material, and Berlyn was unable to tell if the cloak was made of samite, wool, or of the rarer, dwarven fabric *affea*. Thin filaments of gold and silver thread interwove with the dark gray silk—creating serpentine waves and decorative fringe around the hemline—and huge, voluminous sleeves hung down like great silken tunnels. A large hood hung limp over the shoulders of the charcoal robe, and a beautiful clasp of garnets and diamonds drew the cloak together at the throat, sparkling with gemlike grandeur in the light of the campfire.

Despite the fact that the cloak appeared too large for the young girl, Berlyn climbed to her feet and slipped her arms into the gaping sleeves and the robe over her slim shoulders, snapping the brocaded clasp shut about her neck.

The quaver of anxiety continued to gnaw at Aitchley's innards. "I wouldn't do that if I were you," he cautioned.

Berlyn pulled the monklike hood over her head, her face practically disappearing into the shadows. "Oh, poo!" she jeered. "What did I tell you about getting a sense of adventure?" She pointed with a finger lost within the folds of the great robe's sleeves at the twisted, gnarled wood by Aitchley's side. "Only you would take a staff from the altar of thorns itself and not try and figure out what it does, Aitchley Corlaiys," she teased him.

At the mention of his mysterious stave, Aitchley glanced down and touched the carbonized oak beside him. The warm pins-and-needles sensation of true magic went crawling up his arm—almost as powerful as the elixir but with a different twinge to it—and Aitchley felt a curiosity build up inside him. Berlyn was right, he decided. Objects on the altar of thorns are supposed to be the most powerful artifacts of all time. I didn't even stop to think about it when I grabbed it, but . . . Daeminase Pits! This staff is probably as powerful as the Elixir of Life! I'd just have to figure out what it did.

A sudden flurry of panic erupted beside the young man as Poinqart jumped hurriedly to his feet, yellow-black eyes going wide as he jerked a finger at Berlyn. "Mister Aitch! Mister Aitch!" screeched the half troll. "Missy Berlyn! She's vanished-gone! Oh, help, Mister Aitch! Missy Berlyn is not there no-more-longer!"

Eyebrows knitting quizzically together, Aitchley glanced back up at where Berlyn was standing. A jolt of surprise shot through his system when he realized the half troll spoke the truth.

"What are you talking about?" Berlyn's voice suddenly came from directly in front of them. "I didn't go anywhere. I'm right here."

The surprise flooding Aitchley's brain grew to a mind-numbing shock as he gaped at the dark blue basalt in front of him, squinting blue-green eyes through the cavernous gloom of the *perbru*. The spot where Berlyn had been standing was now empty, but the young man didn't put it past the young girl to have hidden herself nearby in her youthful exuberance. It was one of the things about Berlyn he really liked: she had an almost childlike playfulness. Trouble was . . . there wasn't anything nearby to hide behind. No stalagmites. No wall to duck behind. Not even a big rock. It was almost as if she had completely disappeared.

Eyes narrowed, Aitchley got to one knee, staring intently at the empty space confronting him. Through the gloom of the massive *Kwau perbru*, he could just barely see a ripple of misplaced air standing about as high as Berlyn, wavering and bending the air about it like heat rising off the desert sands. Questioningly, he reached out a hand to touch the shimmering veil of heat haze and felt the crinkle of samite and the touch of warm flesh meet his fingers.

A hand from nowhere slapped his away. "Aitchley!" Berlyn's voice scolded. "Watch where you're grabbing! Poinqart's watching us!"

Aitchley blinked blankly at where Berlyn's face should have been, the feel of an invisible breast still warm on his palm. "Uh . . ." he stammered his bewilderment. "Where are you?"

Berlyn set her hands on her hips, staring down at the young man in front of her with heavy suspicion. "I'm right in front of you," she responded testily. "What's the matter? Have you suddenly gone blind?"

The young farmer blinked a few more times. "Uh . . ." was all he could say.

A curious cross of human confusion and trollish fright on his olive-green features, Poinqart took a cautious step forward. "Poinqart can no longer speak-see you either, Missy Berlyn," he said. "Disappeared-vanished, you have."

Berlyn pursed her lips at the two standing before her, wondering if, maybe, they weren't trying to pull some elaborate prank on her . . . some kind of perverse Corlaiys practical joke to teach her a lesson for wanting to go through Harris's saddlebag. "I have not disappeared," she protested, taking a threatening step forward. "I'm right he—"

The words died in the blonde's throat. As she went to step forward she automatically looked down to make sure no rock or pebble or fracture of dark blue basalt obstructed the path of her foot. The only problem was that her foot was no longer there. Rough, hexagonal stone was all that lurked beneath her— no cloak, no feet, no legs . . . not even a shadow!—and she threw a fearful look at her arms and the rest of her body only to find that they, too, had faded out of existence. Even though she couldn't see them, she could feel her toes wiggling in her shoes and feel the cold, silken caress of the heavy cloak about her bare legs, yet the idea of not having a body terrified her. Panicked, the young girl reached up with frantic hands and touched her face, invisible fingers searching across invisible features, and the feeling of terror rose in her invisible breast as she fumbled desperately for the clasp around her neck and jerked it open even though she couldn't see it.

The dark gray cloak crumpled into a charcoal puddle around the young girl's feet as she popped back into sight, the rippling, wavelike effect of distorted light dispersing on an unfelt breeze.

Berlyn gave the robe about her now visible feet a wary glance. "Brrrr," she said with a shiver. "That was weird."

Settling back down on the ground, Aitchley gave the cloak a sideways glance. "I told you not to play with it," he rebuked her.

A trace of self-righteous indignation forced its way past the young girl's apprehension, propelling her youthful curiosity back to the forefront of her mind. "Well, at least I figured out what it does now," she retorted. Her mouth twisted into a heartless smile. "What does your staff do?"

Aitchley gave the staff next to him a quick glimpse. "Causes the destruction of all life as we know it?" he offered as a sarcastic suggestion. There was a look of real fear in his face as he pushed the length of wood away from him. "Look, I'm not going to be the one to find out," he went on. "This staff is probably as powerful as the Elixir of Life, and I'm not gonna go bunging around with something taken off the altar of thorns itself!"

Her indignation helping to replenish some of her assurance, Berlyn gathered up the samite cloak pooling about her feet. "Then how are you ever going to find out what it does?" she asked.

Aitchley took the cloak out of the young girl's grasp and started to shove it back into Harris's saddlebag. "Maybe I'm not," he simply replied. "Maybe I'm just gonna bring it back with me and sell it to some intellectually bloated scient. Let it blow up in his face."

Berlyn grabbed the robe back, holding it protectively to her chest. "Hey!" she protested. "What do you think you're doing? We still haven't found out whatever it is making the saddlebag float."

Aitchley vehemently shook his head, trying to pull the cloak out of her hands. "And we're not going to," he replied authoritatively. "This is magic we're fooling around with here. *Real* magic. Not that second-rate legerdemain enchantment that passes for it nowadays. You could have gotten seriously hurt with that cloak."

Berlyn fixed the young man with a challenging gaze. "I didn't, though," she countered. She frowned heavily. "You're acting like somebody's parent."

Aitchley tried not to show the flinch of pain that stabbed through his breast at the remark. "I am not acting like somebody's parent," he shot back. "I'm just trying to be careful."

Berlyn placed adamant hands on shapely hips. "Well, where's the fun in that?" she asked. "Aitchley, you're seventeen years old. Why don't you act like it once in a while? You didn't want to go through Tin William's backpack either and look at all the neat stuff we found in there. If we hadn't, we'd have never have found the Envirochamber or the lightstick Calyx used in the columbarium. Those things made a huge difference in our journey.''

Aitchley felt the beginnings of doubt creep through his reluctance. "Yeah, but none of them are magic," he argued.

"How do you know?" replied Berlyn. "You said yourself they weren't magic as we know it, but it was still a kind of magic.''

"Yeah, but . . ."

Berlyn took the saddlebag out of Aitchley's protective grasp, delving a hand into the leather pouch and pulling out a pair of rings. Both rings glittered the yellow-white of pure gold in the light of the campfire, and each had a single stone set in the center. One was dark and a kind of muddy brown—glinting with hidden traces of red—while the other was a pale blue, flickering with a kind of spectral intangibility. Aitchley recognized neither stone—although the blue one could have been the biggest, roundest, smoothest turquoise he had ever seen—and he involuntarily flinched when Berlyn handed it to him, dropping the ring with the light blue gem into his hand.

"Here," the young blonde said. "Put it on."

Swallowing hard, Aitchley stared down at the gold-and-blue piece of jewelry, feeling the faint tingling emanations of its magic go scrabbling through his fingers. "Huh? What?" he answered, flabbergasted. "Are you crazy?"

Berlyn held up the gold-and-brown ring in her own hand, positioning it just before her left ring finger. "Go on," she taunted. "I dare you." There was a devilish twinkle in her gray-green eyes. "You put on yours, and I'll put on mine."

Pure horror began to discolor Aitchley's face. "What if they explode? What if they take our fingers off?" he worried. "This is stupid!"

Berlyn traced her finger around her ring's golden band. "Why would someone forge a ring that took your finger off?" Her smile grew. "Come on, Aitchley," she urged. "Sense of adventure.''

Hesitation ran like lava through the young farmer's thoughts, yet it was difficult not to enjoy the look of curiosity on Berlyn's beautiful features. She's enjoying herself and I'm standing here like some cowardly little muggwort, the young man thought dourly to himself. Some hero I am, huh? Afraid to even try on a little ring. But this is magic we're talking about here. Nobody knows what it can do anymore. The last of the Wizards died off over four hundred years ago and the only magical artifacts left were those beyond Lich Gate. Now we've actually got a few of them . . . but should we use them? Tin William said to be wary of Nature's scales. Was this what he meant? Did he know that we'd bring magical artifacts back with us and was he trying to tell me not to use them? Or was Captain d'Ane right when he said that nature wouldn't create anything it couldn't cope with? And is magic a force of nature or not?

Pondering the millions of questions suddenly forming in his head—and struggling with the apprehension and uncertainty fluttering about his belly—Aitchley looked down at the golden circlet in his hand, feeling the faint pulse of its magical essence. It's just a ring, he heard a portion of his mind remark. You don't want Berlyn to think her own personal Cavalier was a coward, now, do you?

Anxiously, Aitchley picked up the ring and slipped it over his finger, throwing a furtive glance at Berlyn.

Smiling, Berlyn fit her own ring onto her hand, feeling the faint tickling sensation of its magic flow through her skin and speed up the length of her arm. A gentle itch of pins and needles—nowhere nearly as strong as the elixir's—streaked like lightning up the young girl's limb and through her bloodstream, filling her head with a harsh, abrupt buzzing. Wincing, Berlyn squeezed her eyes shut, trying to block out the grating mental cacophony that had suddenly erupted in her head, but—as the pain faded and she opened her eyes—she was startled to find the *perbru* magnificently lit with ethereal spotlights of yellow-white light . . . all its murky, basaltic darkness banished by the ring around her finger.

Immediately noticing the look of discomfort that washed over Berlyn's face, Aitchley moved forward to help her and, at the same time, went to remove his own ring. He had hardly felt the shudder of electriclike sorcery go scurrying through his nervous system and fill his body with a kind of light-headed vertigo, but a startled curse broke through his lips when he tried to step forward and found his feet had left the ground, hovering a few inches above the basalt floor. Without anything solid underneath to propel him forward, Aitchley's boots dangled helplessly in midair, his feet kicking and thrashing wildly as he continued to rise off the ground. All thoughts of Berlyn or the ring around his finger fled his mind as he watched the tiled rock below drift away from him, the buoyancy churning within his body lifting him farther up into the air.

"Uh . . . help!" the young man cried.

Using eyes no longer obscured by the natural darkness of the cavern, Berlyn watched the young man levitate, a delighted smile on her lips. "Oh, Aitchley!" she exclaimed. "This is fantastic! I can see everything as if it were daytime!"

Aitchley kicked ineffectually at empty space, floating higher and higher above the hexagonal patterns of the stone floor. "Yeah . . . great," he agreed nervously. A look of worry scrawled across his face. "Uh . . . What do I do now?"

His face a combination of human amazement and trollish envy, Poinqart watched as Aitchley rose higher into the *perbru*'s vaulted ceiling. "Mister Aitch!" the half troll shouted. "Fly-high, you do!" The hybrid clapped excitedly. "Poinqart wants to do next! Oh, yes! Poinqart wants to fly-high, too!"

The sensation of weightlessness continued to pervade the young man's body, and his arms and legs felt as light as the musty air about him. "Uh . . . That's great, Poinqart," he replied anxiously. "But . . . um . . . how do I get down?"

A gruff voice suddenly sounded from somewhere down below him. "Kid!" Calyx yelled up into the shadows. "What do you think you're doing? Don't you know any better than to play around with magic? Now get your butt down here before I yank you back by the ears!"

Aitchley flailed weightless arms. "It wasn't my idea!" he yelled back. "Berlyn was the one who wanted to go through Harris's saddlebag!"

Another voice echoed from far below the young man. "Hey, puck!" Harris's snide tone cut through the gloom. "That's my bag o' goodies you're bunging around with! You break anything, you're paying for it!"

"But this is incredible!" Berlyn said. "I can see everything! Calyx, here! Try this on! It lets you see in the dark!"

Still floating higher and higher above the basalt tiles of the *Kwau perbru*, it was getting harder for Aitchley to make out his friends below. Their campfire was an orange-red flare somewhere behind him, and he had already passed a few of the elevated walkways that crisscrossed the upper stories of the *perbru* itself. He had tried to reach out and grab at the stone to try to stop his uncontrolled levitation, but it felt as if his airy fingers had no substance of their own, leaving him completely unable to stop his upward progression.

Well, the cynical side of his brain thought, there's always one way to stop this.

Without considering the consequences, Aitchley jerked the ring off his finger, feeling the weight return to his body. A curt scream tore the young man's lips as he suddenly plummeted like a rock—caught once again in the grip of gravity—and he made a frenzied attempt to replace the ring upon his finger before he made a rather unpleasant red splotch upon the basalt floor.

That was real smart, the young man's pessimism grunted. Let's try to think these things through before acting upon them!

A bewildered "whoof!" of escaping air fled the young farmer as he was suddenly caught in midfall, and he looked down between his legs to find himself seated on the back of Camera 12, its gimballed rocket cutting a bright blue-white swath through the gloom. The others all watched with astonished expressions on their faces as the silver construct slowly lowered itself back down, letting Aitchley slide clumsily off its back and regain his footing on solid ground.

From atop Sprage's shoulder, Trianglehead ruffled amused feathers. "Zstupid human," the fledgling squawked. "Flying isz for the birdsz!"

Aitchley acrimoniously threw the blue-white ring back into Harris's saddlebag, still feeling the lingering sensations of magical buoyancy swimming throughout his body. "You said it," he answered the gyrofalc, tying the saddlebag shut and tossing it back into his knapsack.

He swung a rankled glance at the others in the hopes to conceal his embarrassment. "Can we go now?" he demanded.

As the others began to gather up their things, Aitchley turned his impatient gaze on Calyx; the dwarf was too busy staring at his surroundings with the aid of Berlyn's magical ring.

"Whoa, Aitchley. Check it out," the smith declared. "You really *can* see in the dark!"

Shuffling his feet through the musty corridors of the Shadow Crags, Aitchley tried not to let his continuing embarrassment show as Berlyn took playful little skipping steps all around him. Calyx followed the young man with like enthusiasm, and— even though he was restricted by having to help the healing

Harris Blind-Eye—Poinqart tried to keep pace with the farmer, the mix of trollish yearning and human wonder still glowing in his eyes.

Berlyn hopped in front of the young man's path like some platinum-haired damselfly. "Oh, come on, Aitchley," she implored. "Let's see what else is in there."

"Yes, yes!" Poinqart agreed. "Poinqart thinks magic-lights are pretty-bright. He would not mind seeing many-much-more such things."

Aitchley tugged his backpack's single strap closer to his shoulder. "I said no," he snapped back. "I almost got killed fooling around with that ring."

"Camera 12 caught you," Berlyn reminded him. She flashed a gorgeous smile. "Come on, Aitchley. There were more things in there."

"Listen to the puck, sweetcheeks," Harris growled from beside Poinqart. "It's not his to be playing with. They belong to me, got that?"

Berlyn acted as if she didn't even hear the wounded brigand, and there was even a glint of enthusiasm in Calyx's beady eyes as he turned to look at the young farmer. "There's obviously a very subtle connection between your thoughts and the ring's capabilities," he mused out loud. "It stopped you from falling into the sun even though you weren't wearing it but just because you were thinking about not falling, yet it didn't stop you over the Pits because you weren't thinking about—"

"I wasn't thinking about not falling," Aitchley argued, eyes downcast. "I was thinking about being tired of falling, that's all."

Calyx shrugged curtly. "Same difference," he retorted. "You were thinking; the ring responded. I bet it probably would have stopped your fall back in the *perbru* even after you had taken it off." He stroked his beard thoughtfully. "I remember my grandfather telling me magic worked best when you didn't even realize it was working at all."

"*Magh* can be most *deme*," Taci said from the front of the group. "Most dangerous. But, at other times, it can be *kelb*. Helpful. More often than not, however, great *magh* is untrustworthy. Even the most *kelb* can easily become *deme*."

Berlyn gave the reddish-brown ring she still wore a curious glance. "I don't see how a ring that helps you see in the dark can be dangerous," she thought out loud.

"Listen to Taci," Captain d'Ane advised her from the back of the group. "Never trust magic. It's like trusting a thunderstrike."

Aitchley hardly heard the ghostly captain's words, shuffling down the musty corridors of volcanic rock in his own private embarrassment. It was getting pretty easy to make a fool of himself in front of Berlyn, and while the young girl didn't seem to mind, it only gave Aitchley's nagging self-doubt a powerful handhold. He hadn't felt this stupid since he thought Berlyn might actually pick him to fight the *Kwau* warrior during the rite of *battu* and picked Camera 12 instead. He should have known better than to play around with magic. True magic! He was just lucky something didn't just blow up in his face. Or maybe he wasn't. Maybe it would have been better if something did blow up in his face. At least that way he wouldn't be walking back to the *Kwau*'s cavernous home feeling like a complete and utter warthead.

Shouldn't play around with magic anyway, his pessimism jeered from the back of his mind. It doesn't belong in this world anymore.

An unexpected memory surfaced from somewhere deep within Aitchley's subconscious, sending a whirlwind of sudden questions running through his brain. Or maybe it does, he mused.

The populace of Sphere have long had an infatuation and interest in the natural phenomenon many worlds behold as magic. Now—while your world has long depleted its natural resource known as such—there still remained a form of natural phenomenon that required detailed study.

Still remained a form of natural phenomenon? Aitchley repeated to himself, the droning, buzzing words of the robotic Tin William resonating over and over again in his skull. So what in the Pits did that mean? Is magic dead or isn't it? And does this have something to do with all that "nature's scales" mulch?

Old, unsolved memories rising up to plague his already wounded ego, Aitchley made most of the trek back in silence, distancing himself from his friends by his quiet. He could sense Berlyn's concerned eyes on him now and again, but—like almost everyone else in the group—she was too excited about the magical knickknacks pilfered by Harris Blind-Eye from the

Cathedral of Thorns to really care. And that only made the young man's depression worse.

They walked at a leisurely pace for another four hours before Calyx called for a stop, plopping down on the basalt and going through his nightly routine of rummaging about his enormous sack. Aitchley settled himself down off to one side, lingering in the shadows where the light of their campfire barely reached him. He was still deep in his youthful melancholy but grateful for the early rest, and he felt even more of his pessimistic resolve crumble as Berlyn made her way over to where he was sitting and sat down beside him.

Gray-green eyes searched the young farmer's face, a small smile stretching across pink lips. "What's wrong?" the blonde queried. "Are you mad at me or something?"

The idea that he could be upset with the beautiful young scullery maid brought a chortle of laughter to the young man's throat. "No, I'm not mad at you," he replied.

"Then what's the matter?"

Aitchley unslung the Cavalier's shield from across his back and reclined against the dark, pockmarked wall. "I don't know," he admitted sheepishly. "I guess I'm just mad at myself." He couldn't bring himself to look her in the eye. "I made a fool out of myself back at the *perbru*."

Berlyn's smile grew even more beautiful. "You didn't make a fool out of yourself," she admonished him. "We were having fun. You can't look foolish having fun."

Absentmindedly, Aitchley pitched a few scattered pebbles into the darkness. "I seem to do a pretty good job of it," he answered sourly. "I almost got killed playing with that ring."

Berlyn's hand reached out and touched the young man's arm, the physical contact practically sending magiclike tingles through his flesh. "No, you didn't," she corrected him. "Camera 12 was there. And Poinqart could have caught you if Camera 12 hadn't." There was an inner light of youthful enthusiasm glittering behind the gray-green beauty of her gaze. "Come on, Aitchley," she said. "We're young. We're supposed to have fun. We're supposed to act foolish. Haven't you ever had an adult tell you to stop acting like some no-account muggwort?"

A ten-year-old memory of angry adults yelling at him and Joub as they chased a squealing, squalling group of escaped pigs through the streets of northern Solsbury came fleetingly to mind, bringing a small, one-sided smile to the young man's face.

"Well . . ." he began.

"And haven't you ever just done something stupid just because you felt like doing it?" Berlyn insisted.

Another childhood memory of him and Joub and a few other children playing in the creek near the Ilinot family's fields replayed itself in his brain . . . that and something to do with a handful of gollywoggles and the back of Olisa Rathne's dress.

Berlyn could read the humor in the young man's mien even without his reply. "See," she chided him. "There's nothing wrong with acting silly once in a while. And I think that after all we've been through, we deserve it."

Still snickering over the gollywoggle incident, Aitchley trained blue-green eyes on the girl before him. "Yeah, but this is still magic," he protested, although not as vehemently as before. "It's not like playing Tom Tiddler's ground. You heard what Captain d'Ane said. Never trust magic. And he should know; he's dead."

Purposefully, Berlyn removed the ring from her left hand, placing the magical trinket in Aitchley's. "Here," she said. "Try it on."

Aitchley could almost feel the color drain out of his face as he stared down at the ring, its ivylike strands of sorcery burrowing their invisible roots up into his arm. Just his growing familiarity to the unnatural pins and needles almost made the young man drop the ring and cower away like it was some poisonous snake, but then he looked up into the gray-green eyes confronting him and felt some of the old self-doubt come raging down at him from above.

Berlyn only smiled at the young farmer's reluctance. "It only lets you see in the dark," she explained. "It can't hurt you."

Struggling with the emotions and fears boiling inside of him, Aitchley swallowed hard and slipped the ring around his finger, feeling an instantaneous burst of discomfort explode at the center of his forehead. It felt as if someone had driven a white-hot dagger between his eyes—and he momentarily toyed with the thought of jerking the ring free of his finger and tossing it the length of the cave—but he left it on and slowly opened his eyes, squinting against the buzzing that, even now, was starting to fade.

An awed intake of air managed to escape the young man

even through his uncertainty, and he hardly noticed Berlyn's triumphant smirk. The cave they camped in was as bright and as detailed as if whitewashed in afternoon sunlight, their campfire a blazing bonfire of intense white light that hurt the young man's magically aided eyes. He could see every nook and every little cranny that riddled the rough, soriaceous walls of the basalt caverns, all murk and shadows banished by the red-brown stone upon his finger.

Aitchley stared at Berlyn through the brilliant, unearthly aura of sorcerously enhanced sight. "It's . . . it's incredible," he admitted breathlessly.

Berlyn's smirk stretched into a knowing smile. "And completely harmless," she added. "There's no way to get killed by having better vision."

Removing the ring from his finger, Aitchley had to blink a few times to reacquaint himself with normal vision. "Yeah, but . . ." he replied hesitantly. "It *is* still magic."

Berlyn took back her ring, throwing the young man a playful grin. "And I'm still curious," she answered. "Let me see your staff."

A surge of anxiety shattered the young man's brief amazement. "Oh, no!" he said. "I took this staff off the altar of thorns itself! It's way too powerful to bung around with! There's no telling what it might do!"

"All the more reason to find out," Berlyn replied. She snatched up the length of gnarled and blackened wood before Aitchley had a chance to stop her, turning away so he couldn't grab it back out of her hands. "Calyx said that magic works best when you don't even realize it's working at all," she remembered. "What I want to find out is if your staff is as sensitive to thought as the rings."

Dire apprehension wormed its way through Aitchley's guts as he watched the diminutive blonde sitting next to him lift the staff up and point it at the opposite wall of their campsite. They had stopped in one of the many caves along their route for the night—one of the many places where the narrow, labyrinthine tunnels of the Shadow Crags widened out into small grottoes and hollows—but it was nowhere as large as the *Kwau perbru*. It was only a few feet wide, narrowing and widening in waves of dark blue stone like frozen rock tides. Most of the others sat gathered around the light of the campfire; only Aitchley and

Berlyn sat apart from them, drawn to the shadows by the young man's earlier depression.

Aitchley reached out a worried hand to try and take the staff back. "Come on, Berlyn," he implored. "Give it back."

Berlyn shifted slightly, brushing off the young man's fingers. "Wait," she said. "I think I felt something."

The worry and trepidation began to increase as Aitchley forced himself to watch without comment, and at any moment he expected the staff to suddenly explode with blinding white light and engulf them all in its dazzling, uncontrollable fury. What happened instead startled him even more.

Come on. Do something!

Aitchley raised an eyebrow. "What'd you say?"

"Hmm? What?" Berlyn glanced back at him. "I didn't say anything."

"Yes, you did," the young man responded. "You said to do something."

Berlyn blinked back. "No, I didn't," she replied. "I didn't say anything at all."

"Yes, you did," Aitchley argued. "I heard you clear as day. You said to do something."

Nomion's Halberd! He can hear my thoughts!

"I heard that, too!" Aitchley exclaimed, almost scrabbling to his feet in his surprise. "Is that what it is? Am I hearing your thoughts?"

A red flush started to wash over Berlyn's face. "I . . ." she started.

The silver-capped tip of the oaken staff unexpectedly exploded with a blue-white blossom of energy, illuminating the cavern with a powerful glow of frigid magicks. Stale, musty air crackled and popped as a shaft of freezing cold lanced out from the head of the staff, arcing across the chamber and striking the far wall in a bellowing clap of sorcery and snow. Particles of ice torn from the moisture in the air skittered across the rocky floor, and a huge chunk of basalt cumbled to the ground, blasted free of the opposing wall by an overwhelming spear of sheer cold and powerful magicks.

Berlyn dropped the staff in her abrupt shock, not needing it to transmit her thoughts of utter stupefaction. "Uh . . . maybe you're right," she sheepishly told the young man. "Maybe the staff is too powerful."

7

Legends and Celebrations

"*I* seem to recall a legend a couple of thousand years old," Calyx was saying as they marched through the narrow tunnels beneath the Shadow Crags. "Long before the Cavalier, all of Vedette's human heroes were Wizards, and there were a lot of stories about good Wizards battling bad Wizards, about great wars fought over magical items, and fantastic adventures concerning the fate of the entire known universe resting on a single man's shoulders. The most famous of these was a fellow named Adal. Adal the Blue, they called him. Now, I don't know whether or not he actually existed, but the big thing with him is that he was supposed to have completely destroyed a conclave of evil Wizards somewhere north of where Karst was to be. Big deal for one guy to take on forty-six other Wizards, and these just weren't any kind of Wizards. They were Reds."

Aitchley blinked a few times at the gnarled staff in his left hand then shifted his confusion to the dwarf. "Reds?" he repeated. "Adal the Blue? What's with all the colors?"

"Colors were how people used to identify magicks," Calyx explained. "Green Wizards were those who used primarily natural magicks. Guys who could ride big vines like horses or pass into one tree and exit out another tree some hundred leagues away. Blues used the more powerful elemental magicks. Lightning bolts. Fireballs. Walls of ice. Whites were the most powerful 'cause they tapped into the Oblivion itself—the

Elixir of Life is a source of White magic—but they were kind
of religious in their dealings. Never interfere was their mantra.
Powers the like you've never seen before—able to switch your
ass with your face and you'd never know the difference—but
they hardly used their magic 'cause of some man-made religious restrictions. Reds, though, were the worst. Reds got their
powers by killing other people. Necromancy and bloodcraft,
they called it. Used to snatch people right off the roads and use
'em for their rituals. Real nasty stuff, too. Stake you to a tree
with your intestines draped all over the branches and you
wouldn't die for months. Or they'd flay your skin right off you
and then take your place by wearing it. And they had a real
nasty bunch of servants they made by killing young girls and
impregnating the corpses. Stillborns, they called 'em.''

Berlyn shuddered at the grotesque images brought to mind
by Calyx's words. ''So what does any of this have to do with
Aitchley's staff?'' she wondered.

''Adal the Blue had a magic staff,'' the dwarf went on. ''I
think it was supposed to be some present from his mentor . . .
or his mistress . . . or maybe his mentor was his mistress . . . I
don't remember the full story. Anyway, he had this really powerful weapon that could do all sorts of things. Spit fire. Call
down lightning. Shoot bolts of cold. Paralyze enemies. Even
project thoughts. He used it all the time . . . kind of an ancient-
day Cavalier. Ran around doing good deeds in the northern
territories of Vedette. Finally took it upon himself to wipe out
the conclave of Reds plaguing his area and used the staff to do
it.''

''How'd he do that?'' asked Aitchley.

Calyx gave the farmer a wry grin. ''Marched right up to the
gates of the Reds, let 'em take him prisoner, then broke the
staff. Legends have it the blast actually changed the course of
the Uriisa River.''

''So you think this Adal's staff is the one Aitchley has?''
Sprage queried.

Calyx shrugged. ''Makes sense,'' he replied. ''It has the ability to project thoughts *and* it expelled a bolt of cold. That's
two of the staff's powers.''

''Yet I thought you said Adal the Blue shattered his staff in
his confrontation with the Red Wizards,'' Eyfura pointed out.

''So?'' the dwarven smith grunted. ''Aitchley's wearing the
Cavalier's sword around his waist and I happen to know for a

fact that it's still lying with Procursus in the Cavalier's Tomb.''
He fixed a dark look on those around him. ''You have to understand something, people,'' he said. ''We've just come back
from a place where contradiction and coincidence don't mean
diddly-squat. Magic works the way magic wants to work. And
if the altar of thorns holds the 'greatest treasures of mankind
and beyond,' well, then, so be it. Adal may have broken his
staff, but that doesn't mean it has to remain broken beyond
Lich Gate.''

Aitchley gave the length of carbonized oak in his grasp a
wary glance, finding it hard to believe that it did the things
Calyx said . . . that Vedette was even once a place of powerful
magic and great Wizards. It's like something from a child's
bedtime story, the young man mused skeptically to himself.
With damselflies in their see-through gowns and gossamer
wings dancing from toadstool to toadstool. Cloaks of invisibility . . . Magic staffs . . . If I hadn't have seen it with my own
eyes, I'd never have believed it!

''So how can we tell?'' he wanted to know. ''I don't think
calling down lightning would be such a good idea.''

''There was a lesser power of the staff,'' Captain d'Ane said,
passing briefly through a wall the others had to walk around.
''Adal's Staff had the ability to cast continual light about his
surroundings. See if you can get it to do that.''

The thought of trying purposefully to summon up energies
long dead left Aitchley with a dry feeling in his mouth and a
queasy rumbling in his belly. ''Well, how am I supposed to do
that?'' he demanded. ''I'm no Wizard!''

''Magic allows itself to be controlled,'' Calyx replied. ''It
reacts the same way your body reacts. You don't think about
how you're going to move your arm, do you?''

Aitchley glared at the staff in his hand. ''Well, no . . .''

Calyx offered a single nod. ''Magic works the same way,''
he went on. ''Just think about lighting the place up and see
what happens.''

''A bloody big fireball large enough to blast us all into tiny
little bits!'' the young man retorted.

A familiar look of exasperation lit in the dwarf's beady eyes.
''The staff will know that's not what you want,'' he said.
''Look, if you don't want to try it, give it to Berlyn. She seems
to have a knack for using magic.''

The thought of giving the staff to Berlyn caused the churning in his stomach to become full-fledged nausea, and Aitchley's fingers tightened instinctively around the old wood. The tickle and itch of its magicks continued to pass through the palm of his hand and seep into his body—coursing over his nerves and filling him with a warm, fuzzy kind of feeling—but it did nothing to quell the uneasiness roiling about his innards. In what feeble attempts he had made to read, all Aitchley had ever learned about was how dangerous and unpredictable magic had been—how only a fool or a desperate man would resort to sorcery—and now he was trying to ignite a staff some two thousand years old without any proper training? But if two thousand years ago using magic had been as common as, say, taking a piss, what was so desperate or foolhardy about that? Aitchley had never read any books as old as Adal's Staff.

From somewhere deep within the farmer's brain, something arose to answer the questioning tingle of the staff, matching its pulse and rhythm with a tingle of its own. A strange kind of warmth seemed to strengthen just beneath the young man's skin—growing warmer and warmer but never becoming unpleasantly hot—and he felt powerful vibrations go scurrying down the length of his brain stem, shiver down his left arm, and go streaming into the twisted, blackened oak of the staff itself.

A vague, pale halo of silver-white light slowly formed around the metal knob atop the oaken stave, gradually filling the chamber with its sorcerous glow. Darkness and shadows fled before the increasing nimbus of eldritch illumination, and Berlyn had to remove her magical ring as the aura of magical brilliance fanned out from the head of the staff and filled the musty caverns with a blazing, unearthly light.

Aitchley squinted at the unnatural white fire that burned about the top of his staff. "I . . . I did it," he realized, amazed.

Gruffly, Calyx shielded his eyes from the overpowering corona of magic. "Can you turn it down a bit, kid?" he inquired. "Continual light isn't going to do anybody any good if it blinds you!"

A quaver of uncertainty and doubt returned to quench the young man's unexpected triumph, and he was going to say he didn't know how when the staff—as if acting on his thoughts alone—automatically adjusted its brightness, fading back down to a pale, silver-white lambency that illuminated more efficiently than Taci's flickering torch.

"Most astonishing," Gjalk DarkTraveler remarked, tiny, pearl-black eyes fixed on the staff's auroral knob. "Light without combustible materials." He reached out a leathery hand. "There is no heat?"

Aitchley blinked through the gloriole of silvery light. "None that I can feel," he replied.

Taci's midnight-blue eyes were wide with wonder. "*Bheidh* Aitchley," she said, "I did not know you were a *maghu*. A user of *magh*."

"I'm not," Aitchley answered, staring at the staff in like wonder. "I just . . ." He shook his head, words failing him. "I'm not."

So what do you think you're doing playing around with magic, then? the voice of the young man's darker side asked snidely. One wrong move . . . one small misstep . . . and you kill everybody else in the cave. You know it's true. You know you're capable of it. Bloody typical Corlaiys luck.

As if answering some unspoken desire, the silver light around Adal's Staff winked out, drawn back into the wood like a turtle draws its head into its shell. The unexpected disappearance of the light startled even Aitchley, and it took him a moment to realize it was his own thoughts and insecurities that had caused the light to go out. It *does* do what I want! he thought with some surprise. I got nervous, wanted it to stop, and it stopped! Without me even having to say anything! It just stopped!

Calyx smirked at the young man. "I told you so," the dwarf remarked.

Aitchley turned a deep shade of red; the staff, he realized belatedly, was transmitting thoughts again.

Without a sky above them or a sun to guide their steps, Berlyn wasn't sure but she guessed they arrived back at the *Kwau* caverns sometime around midafternoon. An excited call went out when the ten quest-members were spotted, and an ever-increasing cluster of young, blue-gray women pressed in about the group, faces aglow with amazement. Even though she didn't understand their language, Berlyn could sense the surprise in their voices, and she followed them to the huge cavern throne room of Queen Winema.

Like some graceful animal, the beautiful ruler of the *Kwau* slid off her glossy basalt throne and approached the group, her black-gray cloak of shed snakeskin flowing about her slender body. Berlyn tried not to let her eyes wander over the smooth, perfect curves of the queen's youthful figure or the flawless flare of her blue-gray hips—feeling the gentle prod of envy stab at the back of her thoughts—and forced herself to look Winema in the eye as she came nearer.

"Welcome, *Gwenn* Berlyn," the queen greeted her, smiling warmly. "I trust your pilgrimage was successful."

Berlyn cast her eyes down, offering a clumsy curtsy in an attempt to show respect. "Oh, yes," she replied. "We did very well, thank you."

Winema nodded, her crown of gefjun feathers bobbing around her pitch-black hair. "Good," she said. "I congratulate your success." She took Berlyn by the arm, drawing her closer to the throne. "You have done much since you have arrived here, *Gwenn* Berlyn," she went on. "You have lifted the *ta* on the ancient *Kwau* passageways and you have gone into the *Kad* and returned. You have found the sacred *Kwau perbru* and faced the undying threat of the Red Death. For this, *Gwenn* Berlyn, you must be honored." She turned to face the growing crowd of blue-gray women gathered throughout the amphitheater of stone, raising slim arms above her head with the jingle of beads and bone necklaces. "Henceforth, *Gwenn* Berlyn, you are *bhreus*."

Berlyn tried not to let her confusion show as she glanced anxiously at the beautiful ruler. *"Bhreus?"* she worried, eyebrows knotted. "That isn't anything like *battu*, is it?"

Winema let out a gentle laugh like the tinkling a crystal chimes. "Oh, no, *Gwenn* Berlyn," she answered good-naturedly. "It is the greatest of all celebrations." She faced the crowd again. "Tonight, you become *Kwau*!"

Sitting on a cushion of moss and gefjun down, Aitchley greedily shoved food into his mouth by the light of an enormous bonfire. Platters of fresh greens the like Aitchley had never tasted before were heaped like hay in front of him, and the *Kwau* caverns filled with the mouthwatering aroma of roasted gefjun. Despite its larger size, gefjun tasted as much as it looked like chicken, and Aitchley eagerly wolfed down all the meat set in front of him. Smiling, youthful blue-gray women constantly refilled the young man's plate—bare-breasted and beautiful in their servitude—and a crudely formed jug of a *Kwau* beverage similar to ale sat beside the young man. The drink, called *werg,* was nowhere near as potent as the Rhagana's nectarwine—nor was it even as strong as human ale—but Aitchley didn't mind. It was cool and sweet and tasted good alongside the cooked meat in a belly that had gone a long time without a proper hot meal.

Mouth full, Aitchley threw a happy glance at those around him. To his left—catered to by a number of *Kwau*—Calyx and Sprage sat side by side, eating as voraciously as the young man while having a heated discussion about ghosts, magic, and the physical and metaphysical makeup of Oblivion itself. Beyond them sat the three Rhagana, poking tentatively at the feast and limiting themselves mostly to the unusual greens and blue-hued tubers. To Aitchley's right sat Poinqart, his chin smeared with the juices of tender meat and his hamhock hands ready to shove more into his mouth. The half troll ate with a disquieting amount of slobbering and lip-smacking, but, Aitchley thought with half a smile, he probably wasn't making much more noise than the farmer himself. Behind Poinqart stood Captain d'Ane, watching the great feast with an amused look on his semitransparent features. The farther west he went from Lich Gate, the more spectral and intangible he had become, and a number of *Kwau* gaped at him with open astonishment, many of the younger women taking great joy in poking inquisitive fingers through the dead soldier's vaporous form.

At the end of their little line—surrounded by a bevy of half-naked *Kwau*—reclined Harris Blind-Eye, a smirk of yellowed teeth drawn across his features. His face remained an unhealthy hue—and Sprage had immobilized his left arm in a tight sling—but the look of cocky self-assurance helped return some of the familiar smugness to his scarred and dirty mien. Grinning, he lay back on a cloud of gefjun pillows and moss, letting an amply endowed young *Kwau* kneel above him and hand-feed him steaming pieces of roasted meat.

Catching the young farmer's glance, the southern-city lock-pick tossed back a smile of his own. "Some Carnival of the Twins, eh, puck?" he asked. He grabbed at a bare breast. "Can't remember when I've had such a good time."

Although the familiar misgivings about the bandit rose in Aitchley's thoughts, he allowed himself to return a sincere smile. "Mmmmff," he agreed, ravenously shoving another piece of meat into his mouth.

Harris took a hearty swig from his own jug of *werg,* offering some to the attentive *Kwau* kneeling beside him. "Haven't seen your little blonde slice of jam tart around," he observed lecherously. "Where's she at?"

Aitchley shrugged. "She's around somewhere," he answered around large bites. "Said something about some *Kwau* ritual they wanted her to be in. Some big ceremony."

With his good arm, Harris pulled his serving girl down on top of him, chortling as amber-colored *werg* spilled about him and the *Kwau.* "Too bad," he remarked, planting a sloppy kiss on gray lips. "She don't know what she's missing."

Aitchley turned away as Harris and the young girl grew a bit more adventurous, and he tried not to listen to the giggles and throaty sniggers of the drunken *Kwau* as she wrestled playfully with the wounded brigand. Disgusting, was all the young man could think. There are people trying to eat.

Starting in on another platter of meat, Aitchley felt the inevitable twinge of curiosity invade his system, making a quick survey of the surrounding cave. Harris was right, he realized. This was some of the best food he had ever tasted—it hadn't been since Tampenteire's estate that Aitchley had been so well taken care of—and Berlyn was missing out. He didn't know what this ceremony was—come to think of it, Berlyn wasn't too sure about it either—but he missed not having her there . . . especially now that the *werg* was beginning to nibble at the fringes of his sobriety.

Scanning the wide cavern, Aitchley looked across the great roaring bonfire and saw Queen Winema seated across from him, her slim, blue-gray legs tucked under her as she ate. Taci sat beside her, talking animatedly about something, and they were both served by obedient *Kwau.* Other high-ranking members of the *Kwau's kel* sat around their queen—Aitchley recognized the older matron who had first taken them to the queen, the somber-faced captain of the guards, Cilka, and even the attractive young Alaqua whom Aitchley had befriended back on the OceanGrass. All were caught up in the revelry of the feast, and the celebration lasted well into the night.

As the platefuls of food were finally cleared away—and more jugs of *werg* were brought out—Winema stood up, the light of the great bonfire sparkling with an almost metallic splendor off her blue-gray skin. She raised her arms above her head to get the attention of the tribe around her, and—as the noise and celebration gradually diminished—she spoke.

"*Ser,*" she said in her native tongue, and Aitchley had no idea what she was saying. "*Nekwt gwa an en bru. Nekwt gau en quaere oino eik. Nekwt acies oino nu'bhreus. Oino ghreu ka Luyan, gwenn skewja i' reg mei. Nekwt mag ya oino eik. Nekwt, sya Kwau . . . nu i' aiw!*"

The chant "*Sya Kwau*" began to reverberate around the room, and all the *Kwau,* young and old alike, began to slap their hands against the naked flesh of their thighs, starting a rhythmic clapping that echoed throughout the caverns. A heavy drumbeat answered from inside one of the neighboring corridors—growing in speed and intensity—and the jangling of some bell-like instruments took up the frenzied beat. Then, drawn out by the ever-increasing music, a cadre of dancers came running out from a number of adjoining caves, encircling the massive flames of the bonfire and beginning an exhilarating dance. Each *Kwau* was completely nude, and Aitchley felt a warm flash go all the way down to his big toe at the sight, aided, in part, by the effects of the *werg.* Only an array of gefjun feathers decorated the dancers' hair, and sparkling, silver-gray bands hung about their throats. Tiny bracelets forged from some sort of volcanic glass jingled and chimed about their wrists and ankles like miniature bells, and they whirled and gyrated in an intoxicating, frenzied pace, caught up in the rapture of their dance. Long strands of pitch-black hair flailed and cracked like ebony whips as the dancers spun and twirled in euphoric delight, and Aitchley found himself transfixed by the sight, not because of the nudity but, rather, because of the dervishlike spins and erotically charged movements of the dancers themselves.

As the music built to a deafening crescendo the *Kwau* dancers all fell to the floor on the final drumbeat, prostrating themselves before the opening to a narrow tunnel. Only a steady, thrumming beat remained as a small procession of blue-gray women stepped free of the corridor and into the massive amphitheater, their way led by two spear-wielding guards. Women in snakeskin shawls and gefjun-feather decorations strode out in regal fashion—like some primitive coronation procession—and a young girl of perhaps seven or eight littered their path with flower petals and water, an offering that Aitchley did not completely understand.

The young man's breath caught in his throat when he laid eyes on the last figure in the procession.

Flanked on either side by young *Kwau* wearing only snake-skin loincloths, Berlyn stepped out of the rocky corridor and into the light of the bonfire. Her long, platinum-blond hair spilled down her back in cascades of yellow-white tresses, intertwined with the iridescent green-and-blue feathers of a male gefjun, and a necklace of polished basalt and glittering obsidian draped between the valley of her bare breasts. A long, flowing cloak of gray-black snakeskin hung about her unclothed shoulders—and she made the attempt to hold the front of the cape shut over her naked chest, but there wasn't enough snakeskin—and a plume of gefjun feathers stood out around the collar of the robe, fanned out in eye-catching, peacock style. A triangular thatch of golden-brown biarki fur was all that she wore below her waist, nestled snugly between her pale thighs, and the firelight and shadows played lovingly off the tight musculature of her naked legs. A band of silver-gray spidersilk clung garterlike high about her right thigh, and she walked, barefoot, across the great chamber to stand before them all, a look of embarrassment scrawled on her beautiful features.

Aitchley felt a telltale bulge grow in his pants as he stared in a wordless stupor at the gorgeous young blonde standing—practically naked—before him.

Queen Winema stepped down off her cushions of moss and gefjun down and approached the blonde, undoing the strap to Berlyn's cloak and letting it fall to the basalt floor. "Tonight, *Gwenn* Berlyn," the queen declared, "you become one of us. You become *Kwau*."

Dotting Berlyn's forehead with some of the flower-petal water, Winema took another cloak offered to her by a nearby *Kwau* and draped it ceremoniously over the scullery maid's naked shoulders, tying it securely about the blonde's throat. This cloak was made completely of biarki fur, and—even as crudely stitched together as it was—it was still more beautiful or elegant than anything even Winema wore.

"You are *bhreus*, *Gwenn* Berlyn," the queen went on. "You are legend." She clamped a shining armlet of silver-gray spider's silk still warm from the fire around Berlyn's right arm, watching as the metallike silk fused into a solid piece. "This signifies you as *Kwau*," Winema declared. "You and your *bru* are always welcome here."

Her cheeks still flushed with embarrassment—fidgeting from one bare foot to the other—Berlyn dropped to one knee before Winema, lowering her chin to her breast as she had earlier been instructed. "I am *rivu*," she said.

Gently, Winema helped the blonde back to her feet, turning her around to face the cave full of *Kwau*. "Rejoice, *Gwenn* Berlyn," she proclaimed proudly. "*Nu sya Kwau!* You are now *Kwau!*"

A great cheer went up from the cavernful of women—echoing and resounding a thousandfold through the winding, twisting tunnels all about them. Cheeks red, Berlyn stood before the cheering throngs of *Kwau*, trying not to feel too awkward in her biarki-fur loincloth and little else. As soon as the applause and acclaim began to fade, Berlyn made a quick bow and strode over quickly to where the quest-members sat, wedging herself between Poinqart and Aitchley and not looking at either. The celebration immediately resumed with great heaping platters of fruit and even more *werg,* but Aitchley was hardly aware of the food, his mouth still gaping at the gorgeous creature sitting next to him.

Face flushed, Berlyn tried to adjust her biarki cloak so that it covered her small breasts; she only succeeded in drawing more attention to them. "I feel like an idiot," she grumbled under her breath, her face still bright red.

Aitchley gawked at the way the triangle of golden-brown biarki fur fell strategically between Berlyn's crossed legs.

Berlyn tugged embarrassedly at one of the feathers in her hair. "If I had known they were going to ask me to dress up like this, I would have never agreed to do it!" she continued to complain.

Firelight danced and frolicked across pink, pert nipples.

"At least I'm not cold," the scullery maid went on, rambling. "It's too warm in here for that. My feet hurt, though. I don't know how they walk without shoes. Must have some heavy calluses on their feet to walk over rock like this." She fidgeted from side to side, sliding her hands beneath her practically naked rear end. "Hurts to sit, too," she added.

For the first time since sitting down, Berlyn turned to face the young man beside her, realizing that, for all her talking, the young man wasn't paying a bit of attention to what she was saying. "I'm rambling, aren't I?" she asked, red-faced.

Firm thighs glowed a pale white in the light of the massive bonfire.

The red turned a deep crimson in Berlyn's cheeks when she noticed the young man's intent stare. "Aitchley!" she scolded, smacking him sharply across the shoulder. "My face is up here!"

Dumbfounded—his surprise doubled by the alcoholic *werg* coursing through his blood—Aitchley shifted his attention to the scullery maid's face. "You look incredible." He breathed his awe.

The heat intensified in Berlyn's face. "I look like a Gaaldamned fool," she muttered.

Aitchley's gaze wandered down the slim, naked curves of her body before being forced to return to her face. "No," he said breathlessly. "You look gorgeous."

Despite her embarrassment, Berlyn felt a shiver of delight rush through her. "Really?" she asked back. "I mean . . . you're not just saying that."

Unblinking, Aitchley just gawked at the blonde. "No," he answered, dazed. "I . . . you . . . that . . . uh . . . You look absolutely beautiful."

A coy smile drew across Berlyn's lips. "Really?" she asked again.

Aitchley practically forgot to breathe. "Really," he answered back.

As the red of Berlyn's cheeks lightened to a rosy blush, she had to look away or else feel the embarrassment all over again. "You know," she told the young man once she had her composure back, "I'm *Kwau* now." A tiny little smile creased her face. "And as a *Kwau*, I'm allowed to do anything I want . . . including first pick of any man I want to begin my *bru* with."

Aitchley stared into gray-green eyes. "Yeah?" he queried. "So?"

Berlyn kissed him lightly on the lips. "So I pick you, Aitchley Corlaiys," she replied.

In a swirl of biarki fur and golden hair, the diminutive scullery maid got to her feet, taking Aitchley by the hand. "Come on," she said with a knowing smile. "There's a lot of caves around here that need exploring." She led the young man away from the great celebration, tossing a seductive glance over one shoulder. "My sense of adventure needs appeasing."

This time Aitchley knew she wasn't being literal.

*   *   *

Aitchley awoke the next morning on a carpet of gefjun down and blanketed by Berlyn's biarki fur cape, his arms wrapped lovingly around the scullery maid's naked body. A few feathers still entwined the girl's hair, but a lecherous smile crossed the young farmer's face as he recalled the passion from the night before. They had clawed and wrestled with one another with an even greater ferocity than the first time, and—Aitchley had to admit—just the sight of Berlyn wearing nothing but a skimpy loincloth of fur and a jumble of beads and stones had practically sprained his bung rod. She was absolutely, positively, the most gorgeous female he had ever laid eyes on, and believe it or not, she was his!

Cracking open one gray-green eye, Berlyn let out a contented sigh as Aitchley pulled himself out of their downy bed. "What time is it?" she asked sleepily.

Slipping into his pants, Aitchley gave her a curt shrug. "I don't know," he admitted. "Feels early."

The scullery maid propped herself up on one arm, letting the biarki cloak that served as their blanket fall away from her body; she was gloriously naked underneath. "Then where are you going?" she wanted to know.

Aitchley began to lace up his boots, plopping his hat down atop his uncombed tousle of hair. "I was just going to go out and see if Calyx needed a hand gathering supplies," he said. "Winema said we could take whatever was left over from last night's feast."

Berlyn pursed pink lips, running a hand through her rumpled hair. "Let Calyx worry about the supplies," she teased. "Gjuki and Gjalk will be more than willing to help out."

A pang of guilt raced through the young man. "Yeah, but—" he started to protest.

Berlyn lifted up the biarki fur covering their bed, motioning for the young man to rejoin her. "Besides," she said slyly, "your *gwenn* demands your presence."

Grinning lopsidedly, Aitchley clambered back across the mat of down serving as their bed and slid back beside Berlyn, their lips melding in a passionate kiss. He could feel the blood pounding through his temples on its thunderous way to his crotch, and he could feel Berlyn's heartbeat quickening beneath the warm flesh of her naked breast.

Berlyn was right anyway . . . let Calyx worry about the supplies!

Left hand gripped about the haft of Adal's Staff, Aitchley stepped out of his tiny cavern quarters and back into the bustling activity of the *Kwau* caves, a grin on his face and a bounce to his step. He greeted everyone around him with a friendly smile, and even the warm mustiness of the volcanic tunnels did little to dampen his mood. Perhaps, he thought as he walked, much of his life had been bad, hurtful, and sad, but being with Berlyn had made up for it all. He was in love and that was all that really mattered. Berlyn was his, and he belonged to her.

Considering the possibilities of Berlyn's suggestions of using either the ring of levitation or the telepathic abilities of Adal's Staff next time they made love, Aitchley wound his way through the confusing network of tunnels and corridors to find the other members of the quest packing their bags with generous offerings of meat, vegetables, and even some flasks of *werg*. Harris and his overly friendly *Kwau* were the only ones not there—not having been seen since last night—and Sprage was busy examining an assortment of unfamiliar herbs and lathes shown to him by a young *Kwau* healer. Captain d'Ane stood nearby overseeing all the activity, and Berlyn had been right: Calyx was doing very nicely on the supplies without Aitchley's help.

Suddenly sensing someone standing next to him, Aitchley turned to find Taci at his side, a shy smile on her gray lips. "Greetings, *bheidh* Aitchley," she said. "I hope you slept well."

There was just a trace too much innuendo in her smirk, causing Aitchley's cheeks to redden momentarily. "Oh . . . uh . . . yeah. Fine," he responded.

Taci nodded. "Good," she said. "You are *Kwau* now just as surely as *Gwenn* Berlyn. It does us good to know our *gwa* . . . our . . . how do you say it? Our hospitality was well met." She took Aitchley's hand in hers and led him through a narrow branch of uneven basalt, stepping daintily over the jutting formations of solidified lava. "Please," she said, "come with me."

The tunnel they entered was far narrower than any Aitchley had been in before, and he had to fight off an abrupt bout of claustrophobia as his confusion mounted.

"Um . . ." he flustered. "Where are we going?"

"I wanted you to meet someone, *bheidh* Aitchley," his young guide said. "I promised you she might be able to answer your questions."

Led by Taci, Aitchley stepped through the narrow larynx of stone and into a small chamber filled with a carpeting of moss. Small clusters of bluish-green lichen lit the rocky cubicle with just enough light, and there was a small washbasin carved out of dark blue basalt. The only other object in the room was a slumped and gnarled figure, its pitch-black hair gone mostly white with age. Its blue-gray flesh was soured and puckered by countless wrinkles, and its bare breasts were shrunken and pear-shaped, distended as if by too much suckling. It wore a loin-cloth of snakeskin between its skeletal legs, and a circlet of silver-gray spider's silk crowned its forehead.

Despite the deterioration of the elderly *Kwau*'s body, there remained a bright spark of vitality in its midnight-blue eyes.

Taci offered a formal bow before the geriatric *Kwau*. "This is Kirima," she announced reverently. "She is our *weid*. Our wise one." Deep blue eyes flicked momentarily to Aitchley. "Perhaps she can answer your questions."

A flicker of befuddlement clouded the young farmer's mind as he stared at the ancient and decrepit woman. "Questions?" he repeated unsteadily. "I didn't have any questions."

"Back at the *Kwau perbru*, *bheidh* Aitchley," Taci reminded him. "The glyphs and symbols you saw prompted many *aerere*. Many questions."

The dim remembrance of darkly carved pictographs returned from somewhere deep within the young man's cranium: twin triangles that resembled a scale; a detailed picture of the Dragon, wings unfurled and flames zigzagging from its mouth. Also came a sharp barb of embarrassment as Aitchley recalled his misinterpretation of the scalelike symbol and how Taci had been obligated to correct him.

Aitchley shrugged in his awkwardness. "Oh, no," he finally answered. "I didn't have any other questions."

Taci lowered herself onto the carpet of moss, pulling Aitchley down by his hand. "But you had questions I was unable to answer, *bheidh* Aitchley," she said. "Questions of the great Mother Snake and how she was seen flying in the skies east of your world."

The memories grew stronger as Aitchley remembered his

brief bafflement over the Dragon glyph, wondering how the ancient *Kwau* had been able to render it so painstakingly detailed when it supposedly never left Vedette. "Well . . . uh . . . yeah . . . I guess." He fumbled to make some sense. "But it wasn't really anything important, though. . . ."

Taci held up a hand to silence the young man and asked the older woman a question in her strange, lilting tongue. A smile completely lacking teeth drew across the shriveled and ancient face of the woman called Kirima, and she answered the young *Kwau* in a voice as dry and as rough as the basalt walls around them.

"Kirima says there is no such thing as an unimportant question," Taci translated for the farmer. "Everything has its importance; ask your question."

Feeling kind of foolish, Aitchley gave the wisened old *Kwau* a lopsided grin. "It wasn't any big deal," he mumbled. "I was just wondering about the Dragon."

Another exchange of alien words passed between the two women.

" 'Just as the strange creatures you call Rhagana walk the woods like men made of trees, or the *Kwau* who live deep within the heart of mountains that once burned red with fiery rock, the Mother Snake ruled your skies like the great thunderstorm,' " Taci translated. " 'Just as the ground that shakes beneath our feet or the great tree that dies and falls only to be reborn, so, too, did the Mother Snake fulfill its purpose.' "

Aitchley scrunched up his face at the enigmatic words. Great! Just what I need! his pessimism groused. Another bunch of riddles!

A sudden idea popped into the young farmer's head. "So what's this purpose?" he asked, turning to Taci. "You said something like that at the Bridge of Mists. Something about having an influence."

"All things have their purpose and influence, *bheidh* Aitchley," Taci said after a brief trade of words with Kirima. "You and I. The rocks above our heads. The dirt beneath our feet. All these things have a purpose. A task. A place in the natural order."

Aitchley blinked questioningly. "You mean like a natural balance?" he queried. "Like being wary of nature's scales?"

It was Taci's turn to make a confused face. "Do you mean the scales of the Mother Snake?" she asked back.

"No, no," corrected Aitchley. "I mean the balance of the world. The regenerative cycle. Birth and death. Growth and decay. Destruction and creation. Forces that only nature should control."

A look of admiration glinted in Kirima's eyes as Taci translated the young man's memory of Tin William's warning, and a clawlike hand of gaunt, wrinkled flesh reached out and clutched the farmer around the wrist.

"Kirima says you are *weid* like her, *bheidh* Aitchley," Taci said, and the older woman agreed with a palsied nod of her head. "She says you understand much of the *oinowrios*. Much of the one world."

Aitchley pursed sardonic lips, staring down at the ground. "That's just the trouble," he grumbled under his breath. "I don't understand a bit of this."

Not hearing the young man's murmurings, Taci continued, "Kirima says that it is good you have the *dhreglei*. The Elixir of Life. She is certain you will do what is right by it."

At the mention of the fabled elixir—and with the words of Tin William still buzzing in his ears—Aitchley turned a puzzled eye on the shriveled old *Kwau* before him. "But should I use the elixir or not?" he agonized. "I mean . . . aren't there some things that shouldn't be tampered with?"

"You must use it, and use it wisely, *bheidh* Aitchley," Taci said once the exchange of words was made. "Kirima says in your heart of hearts you will know what to do."

The bewildering statement only made the young man's confusion grow. "But . . . " he sputtered. "I don't . . . I mean . . . I'm only supposed to revive my ancestor with it. What's that got to do with using it wisely? I mean . . . it's not gonna cause some horrible natural catastrophe if I do, will it?"

A sudden commotion sounded from outside Kirima's narrow cave, interrupting Taci's translation of Aitchley's words, and the young *Kwau* got to her feet to see what was going on outside. Aitchley moved to follow along behind her, but a sudden tug from the gnarled old hand still grasping his wrist prevented him. Questioningly, he looked down at the old wisewoman, perplexity swirling in his blue-green gaze. Kirima reassuringly offered the young man a toothless smile and picked up a nearby rock, drawing its pointed tip toward Aitchley's arm.

Anxiously—the noises outside the cave no longer important—Aitchley tried to jerk his hand out of the ancient woman's grasp, but found an incredible strength in those talonlike fingers. He could only watch in mute horror as the knifelike point of black rock came toward his flesh and pressed against his arm, and his relief was only slight when he realized it felt more like charcoal than sharpened basalt.

With shaking, quivering hands, Kirima sketched a crude lightning bolt across the young man's forearm in heavy black charcoal, ending in what might have been a reptilian mouth of great fangs. Dumbly, Aitchley could only stare at the childlike scrawl of the Dragon's face drawn sloppily on his arm as Kirima put down her drawing utensil and gripped his arm with both hands.

"*Tak gar, bheidh* Aitchley," the old woman said in her alien language. "*U'ghabh riht ghreu wer. Ser u'uti weid.*"

Puzzlement running like electricity through his brain, Aitchley could only stare back at the old woman, the crude sketch of the Dragon already smearing across his right arm.

Taci suddenly ran back into the cavern, a look of unrestrained terror on her youthful features. "*Bheidh* Aitchley!" she screamed. "Come, quickly! The *reu'dheu* attack our home! They kill many *Kwau* and we are powerless to stop them!" She grabbed the young man urgently by the arm, erasing what was left of Kirima's crude tattoo. "You must come quickly, *bheidh* Aitchley!" the young *Kwau* implored. "The *reu'dheu* have followed you!"

She pulled him to his feet. "The Daeminase are here!"

8

The Evil and the Red

The caves had become a sea of chaos and confusion, a chorus of echoing screams and shrieks and a tide of fleeing women, all threatening to swamp Aitchley with an overload of sensory perception. Befuddlement veiled the young farmer's mind—and he momentarily lost all sense of direction as he was buffeted and jostled by the horde of panicking *Kwau*—yet he fought to hold his ground and tried to make some sense of the disorder and turmoil, turning in what he hoped was the direction where he and Berlyn had spent the night. Shrill screams and cries of pure terror resonated all around him, and the green-blue glow of the phosphorescent lichen was all but blotted out by the mass of running figures, hurling an imbroglio of shadows and unnatural darkness flickering across the corridors.

He was still trying to collect his thoughts, when a familiar-sounding snarl came from somewhere on his right, and Aitchley spun to see something red and cadaverous rise up before a cowering *Kwau* guard. A high-pitched shriek tore from the girl's throat, and Aitchley felt something warm and wet spatter his face and arms, his nostrils filling with the coppery stench of fresh blood. His stomach twisted in revulsion as he dodged to one side, yet his thoughts remained primarily on Berlyn. Where was she? Was she all right? Had the Daeminase already killed her and the others? Would he be too late to save her?

A gaunt, skeletal red form suddenly materialized out of the

gloom directly in Aitchley's path, its lipless mouth pulling back in a slavering, hungry grin. Silver teeth glinted in the green-blue flicker of the lichen, and long bony fingers reached out for Aitchley, blood-smeared talons clacking eagerly against one another like scarlet knives.

Aitchley took a step back, his right hand going instinctively to his sword. It took a moment of grasping at empty air before the young man realized he didn't have it with him.

Daeminase Pits! he swore to himself, a sudden flare of panic igniting in his breast. My sword! I left it behind with Berlyn along with Tin William's backpack and the Cavalier's shield! I'm dead!

Drawing back a spidery arm to swipe at the young man's throat, the Daeminase lunged, thick, mucoid saliva spraying. Clumsily, Aitchley retreated, his feet stumbling over the body of the dead *Kwau* guard, her naked chest split down the front by inhuman claws and her splintered rib cage awash in a pool of red fluid. With a startled curse, he felt his center of gravity shift, and he started to fall backward, catching a last glimpse as the Daeminase swung at his neck.

Something red orange and explosively powerful volcanoed between the two of them, punching a bloodless hole through the Daeminase's skeletal chest and blasting the creature clear across the cavern. Stunned, Aitchley fell over backward, trying to blink the purple-and-blue afterimages out of his eyes. The deafening explosion continued to echo and reverberate up and down the length of the *Kwau* tunnels, and Aitchley turned a frightened and bewildered look at the staff in his left hand, hardly believing the telltale trails of gray-white smoke that curled and snaked from its silver-crafted knob.

What in the Pits was that? the young man thought, dazed. A fireball?

Hissing its annoyance, the Daeminase pulled itself to its feet, the gaping hole burned through its chest slowly drawing back together. Aitchley scrambled back to his own feet, forcing himself free of the amazement and glancing frantically around him. Fearful *Kwau* still clogged the corridors—screaming and shrieking as they ran past the wounded Daeminase—and all the tunnels suddenly looked frighteningly the same, blue basalt wormholes dimly lit by greenish-blue lichen. If he couldn't find his way back to Berlyn and his sword, he was dead! the young man concluded dourly. There was no way he could beat this thing with his staff. He didn't even know how the damn thing had worked!

A sudden figure running along with the *Kwau* caught Aitchley's eye, and the young man made a desperate lunge at the fleeing form. "Sprage!" he screamed. "Get over here!"

Sprage threw a single glance over one shoulder at the young man chasing him. "What? Are you crazy?" he screamed back. "There are Daeminase all over this place! Run!"

One eye on the recovering Daeminase, Aitchley dove after the healer, catching him by the arm and dragging him to a stop. Wild fear filled the physician's dark brown eyes as he came to a reluctant halt, and he stared in open terror over Aitchley's shoulder at the crimson monster slowly healing.

"What do you think you're doing?" the long-haired doctor cried, trying to pull his arm free. "Are you trying to get us both killed?"

Aitchley stood his ground despite the fear boiling through his own system. "I forgot to bring my sword," he explained urgently, "and I need to get back to Berlyn. Let me have your *navaja*!"

Fumbling nervously, Sprage withdrew his dwarven knife and handed it over to the young farmer, finally succeeding in tearing his arm away. "Here!" he shrieked. "Fat lot of good it's gonna do you!" He took off running again.

Looking down at the ebony blade in his hand—and suddenly realizing how small and ineffectual it would be against the Daeminase—Aitchley glanced back up. "Sprage!" he shouted after the fleeing doctor. "I could use some help over here!"

There was no reply; the healer had already disappeared down a dark basaltic corridor.

A ravenous growl split the gloom behind the young man, and Aitchley spun to find the Daeminase completely healed, long, insectlike legs launching it straight for him.

Aitchley gave one last despairing look at the *navaja*. "Uh-oh," he muttered with grim pessimism.

Drawn out of her gefjun down bed by the commotion outside, Berlyn slithered into her dress and snatched up her throwing ax. A spear of worry stabbed through her breast when she noticed Aitchley's swordbelt, shield, and backpack lying uselessly on the floor beside their bed, and she hurriedly gathered all the items up herself, slinging the backpack over one shoulder, the shield over her left arm, and the belt about her waist. The added weight almost immediately slowed her down—and the swordbelt chaffed something horrid against her hip—but she pushed herself forward just on the strength of her concern, hurrying through the narrow passageway of their private quarters and back out toward the *Kwau* caverns.

Something large and silver blocked the mouth of the corridor, and Berlyn stared down at the damaged and torn abdomen of Camera 12, unable to squeeze past the silver construct. Purposefully, the machine stood its ground—half in and half out of the hallway—its single eye facing away from the young girl, and Trianglehead perched comfortably on its meshlike saddle, combing a copper beak through red-violet feathers.

Berlyn tried to wedge herself between Camera 12 and the wall to no avail. "What's going on?" she wanted to know, having to raise her voice to be heard over the chaos.

Red flesh and eyeless features suddenly leapt out from around a blind corner, lunging toward the sound of her voice. An involuntary shriek tore through Berlyn's lips as the Daeminase pounced, yet powerful silver legs caught the beast across the side of the head and sent it tumbling back into the gloom.

"Red thingsz," Trianglehead said nonchalantly. "Kome back, they have."

Berlyn tried to stop the rapid triphammer beat of her heart as she attempted to push her way past Camera 12 again. "Red things?" she echoed fearfully. She shoved futilely at the metallic bulk blocking her path. "Twelve," she scolded, "let me by."

Trianglehead ruffled newly preened feathers. "Zsmart thisz time," remarked the bird. "No wantsz to go. Zstay here. Protect girl."

The pandemonium and clamor going on outside in the *Kwau* caves resounded and reverberated through Berlyn's ears like thunder, and she felt her fear and anxiety growing with each second. "Come on, Twelve," she begged the stubborn machine. "Aitchley's still out there."

As if suddenly prodded by something sharp, Camera 12 turned around to face Berlyn with its single glass eye. The scullery maid could almost read the alarmed question in the construct's gaze as it spun its damaged bulk around and launched itself down a nearby corridor, blue-white flame flickering from its rear.

Her knuckles white around her throwing ax, Berlyn trailed. She had no trouble navigating the dark corridors and gloomy caverns—her vision magically enhanced by the brown-red ring upon her finger—yet she could do nothing to quell the ever-increasing knot of fear in her bowels. Blood splashed the walls and floor a brilliant, sparkling red in the light of her sorcerously aided eyesight, and panicked *Kwau* continued to clog the tunnels and catacombs, trying to flee the advancing press of deadly red figures.

Avian anxiety flashing in his milky-blue eyes, Trianglehead clutched desperately to Camera 12's saddle as the construct barreled straight into the heart of the ensuing chaos. "Oooooh, zshit!" the fledgling cursed.

In the split second he had before the Daeminase was upon him, Aitchley redirected his gaze away from Sprage's *navaja* to the length of carbonized oak in his left hand, a worried look scrawling across his face. It would be nice, he thought pessimistically to himself, staring at the staff, but I still don't know how to use it. I don't know what made it go off before, and I don't think I could get it to do it again without—

Foul, fetid breath struck the young farmer in the face, and he jerked his head up to see claws and red flesh nearly overwhelm him. He had just enough time to let out a pitiful yelp of distracted fear and duck as murderous talons tore through the air where his head had just been. Thick, warm gobs of saliva dotted the young man's face as he scrambled frantically to one side—fighting the urge to block with a shield he did not have—and he tried to duck and run as the Daeminase spun to follow him, blank and eyeless features unerringly tracking him through the gloom.

Snarling vengefully, the Daeminase leapt again, silver teeth glistening in the green-blue glow of the phosphorescent lichen. Mind-numbing panic froze Aitchley in midrun, and he could only blink in petrified awe at the insectlike monster launching toward him, deadly claws and fangs filling his line of sight. Stupid, misplaced thoughts like never having to explain to Calyx why he had forgotten to bring his sword and shield in the first place went strolling through his mind in a kind of slow-motion horror, and the thought that he was going to die seemed secondary to never getting to say good-bye to Berlyn.

An unexpected hand landed on Aitchley's right shoulder and pulled the young man backward, nearly tugging him off his feet and drawing him into a narrow opening in the basalt. Hissing, the Daeminase flew past him, slamming face-first into the dark stone and landing in a crumpled heap at the base of the wall, dazed. Confused himself, Aitchley threw a wild-eyed glance behind him to see Taci clutching fearfully to his shoulder, her dark blue eyes aswirl with fear. He didn't know how he had managed it—he must have been more disoriented than he thought—but somehow he had wound up back outside the narrow passageway leading to Kirima's chambers, and Taci had saved his life by jerking him back inside.

"*Bheidh* Aitchley," cried the young girl. "What are we going to do? The *reu'dheu* are relentless in their hunger. They will destroy everything in their path!"

Still trying to shake the confusion and fear out of his skull, Aitchley violently shook his head. "Don't worry about it," he said, and he realized it was kind of a dumb thing to say. "I don't think they're mad at you. It's us they're following."

Throwing an apprehensive glance at the tunnel opening, Aitchley prodded Taci farther down the corridor, returning to Kirima's cramped quarters. Usually the touch of his hand against bare flesh would make him flustered and embarrassed, but right now he was too concerned with great scarlet talons tearing through the opening of the cave after them to care about what part of Taci's naked anatomy he might accidentally have touched.

Half running, half staggering, the two emerged back in the older *Kwau*'s rocky chamber. "Is there another way out of here?" Aitchley hoped, throwing a frantic look about the tiny alcove.

Eyes still bright with fear, Taci shook her head. "There is only one opening, *bheidh* Aitchley," she replied. She trembled nervously. "What are we to do?"

An angry snarl behind them caused Aitchley to spin on his heel, the taste of warm bile rising in his throat as he spotted the gangly red shape squeezing its way through the narrow larynx of dark blue rock.

Desperately, Aitchley surveyed his surroundings, searching for anything that could serve as a weapon; nothing came readily to hand.

The young man scowled. "Bloody, typical Corlaiys luck . . ." he murmured.

As the Daeminase forced its way through the narrow tunnel, Taci grabbed anxiously at the young man's arm and even the ancient Kirima pulled herself to her rickety knees. What might have been a look of triumph crossed the featureless face of the lean, insectlike monster, and—somehow knowing that it had cornered its prey—it stopped at the cavern entrance and let out a victorious, wolflike howl.

A spear point suddenly rammed out of the Daeminase's open mouth in a splatter of slobber and reddish-brown fluid, breaking teeth and shattering bone. Its triumphant howl became a garbled scream of agony, and it fell lifelessly to the floor, its spinal cord severed and its brain destroyed by the spear lodged in the back of its skull.

Half expecting to see a *Kwau* guard, Aitchley was slightly surprised to discover the tall, gaunt shape of Eyfura Spear-Wielder standing in the corridor. "Quickly, QuestLeader," the female Rhagana said. "Come with me. We must leave this place."

Taking a moment to blink the shock out of his eyes—and to feel a momentary flash of embarrassment at the ridiculous thoughts he had been prepared to use as his last—Aitchley hopped over the dead monster in the doorway and hurried after Eyfura, Taci still clutching his arm.

"How . . . how did you know where I was?" he wondered out loud.

Eyfura strode swiftly down the narrow passage. "The Metal-Shaper sent me to find you, and when I heard the discharge of your staff, I knew it could be the only thing to make such a noise in these caverns." She emerged back in the communal caves of the *Kwau* and took a wider tunnel to their right. "Hurry now," she added. "The Beasts of Nowhere overrun these caves even as we speak. We must be quick."

Hearing bone-chilling screams echoing through the many tunnels of the Shadow Crags, Aitchley needed no prompting as he followed the lean Rhagana through the maze of rock and gloom. Hordes of frightened *Kwau* continued to push their way past them, and Aitchley could hear snarls and growls of inhuman hunger resound up and down the dark passageways.

As he ran, more and more of his initial confusion and fear began to fade. "But . . . but this is impossible," the young man suddenly protested. "The Daeminase all got burned up in the sun. There shouldn't've been any left to follow us!"

"Calyx MetalShaper believes that not all had crossed the Bridge of Mists," Eyfura emotionlessly replied. "Those farthest behind had not yet stepped on before the bridge evaporated beneath Pahoe GoldenOrb's fiery touch."

"But . . . but . . ." Aitchley sputtered his astonishment. "That's . . . I mean . . . The Bridge of Mists was some ten or fifteen leagues long! It took us almost a whole day to cross the damn thing! Are you trying to tell me that Calyx believes that not all of the Daeminase were even on it when it faded? That there were some still in the columbarium?"

Eyfura offered a simple nod. "It is what the MetalShaper believes," she said.

Aitchley could only shake his head in disbelief. "Then there'd have to have been millions of Daeminase," he argued. "Hundreds of millions! Thirty miles' worth!"

"The Beasts of Nowhere are infinite, QuestLeader," the Rhagana remarked. "Even those that have fallen before our weapons will rise back up out of the Desolation which is the Pits. They are the Evil and the Red. That is their purpose. It is what they are."

"So what are you saying?" Aitchley challenged. "That a hundred million Daeminase are still chasing us?"

"No, no," Eyfura corrected, taking a quick turn to the left. "There only appears to be a hundred or more after us now. The others perished at the Canyon Between. But we must get away from here before those who follow us still destroy the *Kwau* who have honored us with their hospitality. Their primitive weapons are no match for the ancient evil of the Dreamless who Dream."

Mulling over what the female Rhagana had told him, Aitchley followed without comment, his thoughts a jumble of wonder and worry. If there had been that many Daeminase after them, he mused, it had just been sheer good fortune that they had mostly been destroyed at the Canyon Between. But if these last remaining beasts had been pursuing them ever since, why hadn't they caught up with them before? Why hadn't they attacked the very next day? Surely they could have caught up with them. Why had they waited until now? And where was Berlyn? Was she all right or was she dead or dying somewhere within the dark labyrinth of the *Kwau* passageways?

Unexpectedly, a snarling, hissing form came leaping out of an adjoining cavern, slamming brutally into both Taci and Aitchley. The adolescent *Kwau* screamed once in the young man's ear, and then his head hit hard stone.

Unconsciousness welcomed him into its ebon embrace.

Sprinting despite the added weight, Berlyn hurried after the arachnid Camera 12, trying to use the brief path the construct cut through the panicking *Kwau* and clusters of red figures. Some Daeminase lay dead at her feet. Most were in varying stages of regeneration, ragged spear wounds slowly healing in their bloodless chests. As she moved, Berlyn sent her ax blade cutting sideways into any downed monster, taking little satisfaction in the fleshy *thwunk* of steel severing flesh and bone. Foul ichor splashed her bare legs—and a familiar ache had already started to set in her shoulders—yet she kept Camera 12 in sight, praying to LoilLan that Aitchley was still alive in all this mess. How the camera knew where to go, she didn't know. She just hoped she got to the young farmer before any harm befell him. After all . . . the stupid warthead had gone and forgotten to take all his weapons with him!

A sudden figure blocked Berlyn's route, and she was forced to stop, staring in perplexity at the *Kwau* who stood before her. An angry, accusatory mien was chiseled across Cilka's blue-gray features, and the *Kwau* captain of the guards gripped the haft of her spear in a white-knuckled stranglehold, a bloody gash leaking scarlet over her bare breast.

"To al ar!" the *Kwau* shouted at Berlyn, and the scullery maid had no idea what she was saying. *"Bher dheu i ster dhuno bru! Gwel al lei ko! Na bhreus! Upo! Na kadh wer, i nu al dheu!"*

Sensing the accusation in the guard's words, Berlyn tried to push her way past. "I . . . I'm sorry," she stammered. "I . . . I have to go."

Cilka pushed back, straight-arming the young blonde with the shaft of her weapon. *"Na!"* she continued to shout. *"U'med kwei! Kwau dheu i u'wes ar! U'med pag ledde wi u'eik!"*

Momentarily startled by the *Kwau*'s shove, Berlyn took an unbalanced step backward to regain her footing, steadying herself on spread legs. She threw an anxious glance past the guard's shoulder at Camera 12, and she could just barely see the construct rocket down a distant corridor and vanish around dark stone.

Eyebrows narrowing, Berlyn trained impatient eyes on the *Kwau*. "Look," she said tersely, "I don't know what you want, but I don't have time for this. I have to go."

Cilka took a threatening step forward. *"Eg del u'sek kel,"* she yelled in her strange language, *"ib na kadh! Nu eg tak ag kwo del—"*

Berlyn's fist abruptly smashed into the *Kwau*'s jaw, immediately shutting her up and dropping her to the floor. Then, hurriedly, the diminutive scullery maid hopped over the stunned guard and made her way after Camera 12, shaking the pain out of her right hand. She really hadn't wanted to hit the woman— Berlyn had never struck another person in all her life (with the exception of Harris Blind-Eye)—but Cilka had been riding her ever since they had arrived at the Shadow Crags, calling her dangerous and a risk—and maybe that had been what she had been saying—but Berlyn didn't have time for apologies or I-told-you-sos. She needed to find Aitchley and the others and hoped that the young man had fared all right without his supplies.

Using the infravision of the magical ring, Berlyn rounded another corner and came face-to-face with an eight-foot-tall monstrosity, an abrupt shriek tearing involuntarily from her throat. Eyeless, the Daeminase turned on her, saliva spraying from its lipless mouth, and it bared row upon row of silver fangs, scarlet talons lashing out for the young girl's face.

Olive-green hands caught the Daeminase's head in a viselike grip, twisting effortlessly with inhuman strength and snapping its neck with an audible crack. Twitching, the demon dropped to the ground, spasming and convulsing as its regenerative abilities tried to repair its severed spinal cord.

The friendly face of Poinqart replaced the eyeless red beast that had earlier blocked her way, and Berlyn felt the pounding beat of her heart return to normal behind her breast.

"Missy Berlyn is okay-all-right?" asked the hybrid. "Mister Calyx-dwarf sent Poinqart out to search-find Missy Berlyn and Mister Aitch since Poinqart is their protector-friend." A belated look of half-breed confusion crossed the half troll's ugly features. "Mister Aitch is not-here-with-you-gone?"

The worry continued to gnaw at Berlyn's stomach. "No,"

she answered, "and I haven't seen him since this morning. He's not with you?"

A mingled expression of human grief and trollish vexation marred the hybrid's countenance. "Poinqart has been working-busy helping-assist Mister Calyx-dwarf with the yummy-food-supplies," he responded. "He has not seen Mister Aitch all early-morning-long."

With hardly a second thought, Berlyn chopped her ax blade down on the skull of the Daeminase slowly regenerating at her feet, cleaving its head in half. Then—a look of deep concern on her face—she swung her magically aided vision across the maze of tunnels and corridors and started forward, taking Poinqart's four-fingered hand in hers.

"I think Camera 12 went this way," she said, but there was doubt in her voice. "Maybe it knows where Aitchley went."

Waddling on stumplike legs, the half troll lumbered behind the blonde. "Poinqart hopes so, Missy Berlyn," he said. "Too many nasty-no-face-*Eperythr* around. Poinqart worry-fears Mister Aitch may be alive-no-more-dead if we do not find him quickly-soon."

Feeling the additional weight of Aitchley's backpack and weapons upon her, Berlyn silently feared the same as she ran through the darkened tunnels.

Blackness and vertigo assailed the young man's senses, and the rush of his own blood in his ears sounded like the crash of an angry sea. Dizzily, Aitchley lifted his head off the rough, volcanic rock of the *Kwau* tunnels and tried to chase the disorienting buzz out of his skull, his thoughts muddled and his senses dulled. He heard noises from a million leagues away—a struggle of some sort: screams, growls, the sounds of combat—and he made a hurried attempt to sit up, battling with the dizziness that threatened to knock him back down.

Something red and insectlike collapsed to the stones beside him, brownish-red fluid dribbling from its shattered skull. Its eyeless face was only inches from the young man's own, and a shot of fear-induced adrenaline helped purge the young man of his last vestiges of confusion and bewilderment.

Blinking rapidly, Aitchley gaped at an offered hand of leathery brown skin, wincing as the vertigo in his skull centralized around a single lump.

"QuestLeader"—Eyfura's voice broke through the incessant buzzing—"you are unhurt?"

Aitchley touched tentatively at the goose egg forming on his forehead. "I'll . . . I'll be all right," he stuttered. He clambered unsteadily to his feet, helping Taci rise beside him. "I . . . uh . . . What happened?"

"We were attacked," Eyfura explained. "Ambushed by one of the Daeminase." Tiny, pearl-black eyes inspected the young farmer's face. "You are certain you are well enough to continue?"

Despite the painful buzzing in his cranium, Aitchley gave the Rhagana a quick nod. "I've had worse," he responded truthfully. "Let's get—"

There was another hiss of inhuman rage from a connecting corridor, and Aitchley caught a fleeting glimpse of crimson flesh and silver teeth come launching out of the darkness. The dizziness running rampant through the young man's brain threatened to upset his equilibrium, and Taci's subsequent scream reverberated in his ear, almost making him lose his tenuous hold on consciousness.

Raw, blue-white electricity came forking out of the knob of Adal's Staff, crackling and arcing about the darkened tunnel in a cacophony of flaring tendrils and sparkling cobwebs of energy. The attacking Daeminase was stopped in midleap, its scrawny arms and legs flailing and thrashing as blistering magicks coursed through its cadaverous body, punching bloodless holes through withered, crimson skin. Blue-white sorcery spat and popped in a thunderous release of lightning, and the caverns were momentarily lit up by a macabre light show of aquamarine force and electrically charged particles.

Smoking and lifeless, the Daeminase crashed to the floor, the smell of charred flesh hanging heavy in the musty air.

"Your staff demonstrates its capabilities well, Quest-Leader," Eyfura commented, stepping gingerly over the electrocuted corpse. "It is, indeed, a powerful tool of nature."

Face white with shock, Aitchley could only gawk at the length of carbonized wood in his left hand. "Yeah . . ." he breathed in his awe. "Powerful tool . . . Right."

Still wrestling with the dizziness in his head—and now practically overwhelmed by the sheer destructive force grasped in his hand—Aitchley followed Eyfura through the twisting passageways beneath the Shadow Crags. That's twice the staff had acted of its own accord, the young man mused, and each time it had discharged a blast more powerful than the last. But why? And how in the Pits am I supposed to control this thing? Calyx said something about thinking about it and the staff reacts. But I don't even remember thinking about stuff! Or does my head hurt too much to remember? I don't know! All I want to know is what happens if I get mad at Berlyn or something and I'm holding the staff? Is it suddenly gonna go shooting fireballs and lightning bolts at her? Daeminase Pits! This thing might be more trouble than it's worth!

Staff in one hand, *navaja* in the other, Aitchley made a quick turn to the left and scrambled through a rough-cut hole in one wall, stepping into the eerie lava tube that led back to the surface of the volcanic mountain range. A number of *Kwau* stood guard at the opening, Queen Winema among them, and Aitchley was relieved to see others of the quest waiting for him, some of the fear and worry diminishing at the sight of his friends. His anxiety didn't completely disperse when he realized Berlyn was not among them.

Calyx greeted the young farmer with a nasty scowl. "It's about time you showed up," he quipped. "We're being overrun by Daeminase . . . or haven't you noticed?"

A ghostly shape drifted close to where Aitchley stood. "Dwarven sarcasm aside," Captain d'Ane responded, "are you all right, lad? You look a bit shaken."

Aitchley tried to wipe the look of stupefied fear off his face. "I . . . I'm fine." He threw a quick scan across the lava tube. "Where's Berlyn?"

Calyx smacked his warhammer impatiently into the palm of his left hand, dark eyes fixed on the circular opening to the funnel. "She's not here yet," he said, "but don't worry. I sent Poinqart out in the opposite direction from Eyfura. He'll find her." He paced farther down the tunnel. "Harris and Sprage aren't here either," he added.

"I saw Sprage," replied Aitchley, making a feeble attempt to point. "I think I saw him going in that direction."

Calyx gave a dismal grunt. "Hmmph," he answered. "That tells us a lot." He stroked at his salt-and-pepper beard. "Maybe he'll get lucky and find his way here on his own."

Aitchley shuffled his feet apprehensively, feeling guilty now that he had demanded the healer's only weapon. "I . . . uh . . . think he was going in the wrong direction," he said sheepishly.

Calyx only grunted a second time. "Sounds like Sprage," he remarked. "Doesn't matter, though. I'm just hopin' Blind-Butt finds his way here."

As the dwarven smith spoke, the glinting, spiderlike form of Camera 12 stepped clumsily through the cavern opening, having difficulty navigating the cut stone with its damaged legs. Behind it followed Poinqart and Berlyn, a look of relief crossing their faces upon seeing the others. Immediately, Aitchley and Berlyn locked in a tight embrace, holding one another tightly as if afraid to ever let go.

Calyx watched the reunion with a cold, wry expression. "Not good enough," he snorted. "Where's Blind-Ass?"

"I fail to see why the presence of Harris Blind-Eye is of such great importance to our departure," Gjuki remarked, a hint of perplexity in his usually stoic voice. "All he has done is cause us great strife and calamity. It would serve our quest better to leave him behind and journey on without him."

"I couldn't agree with you more, Gjuki," Calyx replied sardonically, "but I promised Winema here we wouldn't just run off and leave them to fight the Daeminase alone. We brought the bastards back with us, it's only fair we take care of 'em."

"But there must be one or two hundred Daeminase filling the halls behind us," Gjuki protested. "I do not see how waiting for Harris Blind-Eye will—"

"No, of course you don't," Calyx interrupted. "That's 'cause you don't think like me." A vague smile suddenly creased the dwarf's face. "Ah!" he exclaimed. "Speak of the Daeminase!"

Questioningly—still holding Berlyn tightly to his chest—Aitchley turned to see Harris Blind-Eye step casually into the dark tube, a wry grin beneath his ragged beard. At his side was the large-breasted *Kwau* he had spent the night with, and—if not for the look of absolute horror on the girl's face—Aitchley would have never have guessed that Harris had just fought his way through a mountain full of Daeminase.

Harris's grin turned to a malicious smirk as he stared at the waiting nine. "Now ain't that quaint." The southern-city lockpick sneered. "You waited for me. How nice."

Calyx took a determined step toward the brigand. "Yeah," he replied, "and look what else I've got for you." He extracted the outlaw's other stiletto. "Want her?"

Harris's smirk grew. "Yram's tits, I do!" he declared. "You

know how hard it is killin' Daeminase with just one knife?''

Calyx offered the blade to the thief. ''Here, then.''

A strained hiss of surprise escaped the lockpick's lips as Mandy's blade cut lengthwise into his extended palm, bringing a stripe of bright scarlet to the rogue's hand. ''What in the bungin' Pits did you go and do that for?'' Harris roared, snatching the stiletto away with his uninjured hand. ''You gone balmy?''

''It's a promise I intend to keep,'' Calyx responded, taking the outlaw's cut hand and smearing his blood across the lava tube's uneven walls. He watched with grim satisfaction as more blood welled up around the brigand's cut palm. ''There,'' he concluded. ''That should be enough.''

''That should be enough what?'' Harris barked angrily. ''You cut me in the bunging hand and don't expect me to do anything about it? You stupid ragworm! You've just made me a walkin' target for the Daeminase!''

Calyx started nonchalantly down the length of the lava tube, heading for the opening that would take them back out onto the surface. ''Exactly,'' the dwarf responded, ''and if we hurry, we might be able to put some distance between us and them before they catch your scent.''

Worriedly, Aitchley trailed behind the dwarf. ''But what about Sprage?'' he wanted to know.

''Leave him,'' the smith coldly replied. ''I'm sure he'll be all right. He's got great survival instincts . . . so long as he can find a bush to hide under. The Daeminase'll be after Harris once they catch a whiff of him. It's his kind of blood they like best.''

Barely restrained fury colored the look of surprise still on the lockpick's face. ''You're dead, dwarf!'' he swore. ''If the Daeminase don't get you, I sure as Pits will!''

Clambering up the stone-carved ladder and back out into natural sunlight, Calyx tossed the angry brigand a sarcastic smirk. ''If it's all right by you,'' he jeered, ''I'll take my chances with you any day.'' He offered the rogue a helpful hand up. ''Now, come on, Blind-Butt. They're gonna be after us any minute.''

Aitchley threw a final look over his shoulder at the dark caverns and passageways beneath the Shadow Crags before climbing the ladder and stepping back out into bright, warm daylight.

9

In the Tangle of the EverDark

Rain fell with machine-gun-like rapidity over the dense canopy of the Bentwoods, filling the jungle with the rat-a-tat-tapping of heavy droplets on broad leaves. A fine, white mist churned and roiled through the tree-strewn galleries like steam, and distant thunder rumbled through the leaf-obscured heavens. A multitude of birds and canopy-dwelling animals continued to hoot and gabble and roar despite the morning rain, and a chorus of happy frogs chirped and buzzed like insects. Crickets sang from their bromeliad apartments, and rainwater spilled in a million tiny cataracts from waxy leaf drip-tip to drip-tip, never quite reaching the rainforest floor.

General Ongenhroth Fain pushed his way past ariel roots and dangling lianas, spattering himself with pooled rainwater and soaking his already saturated clothes. A disgusted frown carved deep into the Patrolman's features, and he staggered and lurched through the lush curtain of vegetation, stumbling from the uneven carpeting of dead leaves beneath his feet and his own growing weakness.

Absentmindedly, the general scratched at the spreading black rash darkening across his right hand, trying not to think about the disease ravaging his body. He could feel the black buboes swelling beneath his arms and upon his neck, and others at his groin chaffed and itched as he staggered through the foliage. The blazing heat and overwhelming humidity of the Bentwoods did nothing for the high fever burning through him, and he could feel the gentle touch of delirium nibbling hungrily at the fringes of his mind. The coughing fits had grown worse—but he was fortunate not to have started coughing up blood yet—and his eyesight faded in and out, transporting him to a bleary, hellish world of impenetrable green and sweltering temperatures.

Sweating profusely, General Fain stared down at the leafy debris all about his feet, the smell of his own unwashed body rank in his nostrils. It had been days since he had found any trace of Corlaiys's little band of bung-ups, he thought gravely, and even longer since he had had any idea which direction he was going. His legs hurt and his feet were blistered, and the sickness churning through his body stole away any strength he might possibly muster to follow after the farmer. Food had not been a problem for him—even after he had used up the supplies he had stolen from Ilietis, he had been able to find a rabbit or two along the way—yet it was getting harder and harder to keep anything down, and his supply of water was limited to one cracked and leaky flask. It wouldn't have been so bad if his stupid horse hadn't gone and died out from under him, but he had pushed the animal at breakneck speeds for days without rest. And while it may have gotten him to the Bentwoods sooner, it left him without a mount and forced to rely on his own, plague-weakened legs.

Fain threw a last look about the jumble of greens and browns that made up the rain forest, despair filling his thoughts. This is futile, he was forced to conclude. There was no way he'd be able to pick up the trail with so much debris on the ground: constant rains washed away any tracks that might still exist; falling leaves concealed the rest. It was an impossibility to track anybody through the Bentwoods. Fain would have to find some other way to catch the Cavalier's little bastard.

Glowering, the Patrolman glanced over one shoulder at the veil of dense foliage lurking behind him; it looked almost identical to the greenery before him. His best bet, the general mused, starting, he hoped, back in what was a westerly direction, was to leave the Bentwoods. Wait until Corlaiys and his little band returned from Lich Gate and amubush them somewhere between here and the Dragon's Lair. Maybe outside Viveca? It was a good guess that they would journey back to the town for supplies. But now the only question was, could Fain get there before they did without a horse? Or would they unknowingly pass him up, leaving him to die—alone and forgotten—from the Black Worm's Touch?

Fain swung angrily at an overhanging leaf. More importantly, he thought darkly to himself, am I ever going to be able to find my way out of this bunging mess?

Something unexpectedly caught the Patrolman's eye, and he stopped abruptly, fixing an intense stare on a patch of greenery slightly to his right. The fever coursing through his bloodstream caused his vision to blur, and he had to blink several times before his brain would confirm what his eyes were truly seeing.

Slowly—as if afraid moving too quickly might make it vanish like some heat-induced mirage—Fain stepped over a large root of a buttressed tree trunk and knelt in the mulching of dead leaves, staring down at something brownish black and out of place. He couldn't be certain even from this close, but it appeared to be the body of some animal . . . maybe a small horse or calf. There wasn't much left of the corpse—a leathery flap of skin half-fused to the forest floor was all—and a few saddlebags, empty and rotting in the overpowering humidity of the Bentwoods. Nonetheless, Fain grabbed eagerly for the discarded pouches, desperately searching through the rotting leather for anything of value. Whatever may have been inside them, however, had been plundered long ago . . . if not by greedy brown trolls then by the inhospitable climate of the rain forest itself.

Slumping back against a tree trunk, Fain felt his hopes die as suddenly as they had come. Was this, then, to be his fate? he grimly wondered. To die out here? In the Bentwoods? What would kill him first? The heat or the plague?

As the rains began gradually to diminish from above, bright white sunlight poked its timid way through the canopy, driving the mist before it in a swirl of voiceless, evaporative anguish. Fain could already feel the heat intensifying even before the last of the rains had fallen on the highest branches of the canopy, and he settled back against the tree trunk, gravely accepting his dismal fate.

Silver twinkled flirtatiously from beneath a litter of leaves and flowering ginger, drawing Fain out of his despondency. Curiously, the Patrolman pushed himself forward and crawled over the dead horse's remains, inquisitive hands scrabbling at the jungle debris. Could they have carelessly left behind a weapon or some piece of equipment that might help him survive? he mused. Something that could at least help him get free of the Bentwoods' deadly hold?

A small smile came to his lips as Fain uncovered an item overlooked by hungry brown trolls and unaffected by the heat and humidity of the rain forest. A familiar feeling of projected triumph surged through his breast—highlighted by the delirium feasting on his fever—and the general forced himself back to his feet, holding tightly to his newfound treasure as he did to his renewed perseverance.

LoilLan has so decreed, the Patrolman thought deliriously, turning westward and stalking through the jungle. Only Fate would be so kind as to offer me such a boon, and I would surely be recalcitrant were I not to accept it. I am not meant to die here, nor am I meant to die at all. The elixir will be mine, and then all shall bow down before the might of General Ongenhroth Fain. Fate has so decreed it!

Grinning vilely, Fain shoved his way through the undergrowth with a newfound strength, clasping tightly to the delicate silver chain he had found in the leaves. And if not Corlaiys, he continued to think, then surely one of my foes shall fall!

Brilliant sunlight played red gold off the alchemical pendant in the general's fist as he forged his way out of the Bentwoods.

Positive he was going to trip and break his ankle in one of the millions of troublesome biarki burrows dotting the ground, Aitchley Corlaiys ran through the OceanGrass as quickly as he could, eyes downcast to watch his footing. He wished there was enough room for him on Camera 12 behind Berlyn, but he didn't want to overburden the construct, uncertain how it would handle his added weight with its crippled and damaged limbs. The only positive thing about the whole experience was that they were, at least, running downhill, the slight grade of the grassy plains assisting their desperate flight. Only trouble with that was that it helped the Daeminase gain speed as well....

Trying to ignore the burning ache in his shins and thighs—and cursing foully as his right foot narrowly missed falling into a biarki hole—Aitchley swung an irate gaze on those running beside him. Berlyn—her long platinum-blond hair splaying out behind her—rode on Camera 12, her torn skirt billowing in the rush of the wind, Trianglehead on her shoulder. Gjuki and Gjalk ran on either side of her, their long, lanky legs carrying them across the plains with inhuman ease. Eyfura ran alongside Aitchley, sprinting with great, long-legged strides that seemed to carry the Rhagana effortlessly through the tall grasses. In stark contrast, Poinqart thundered like a bull rhinoceros through the wildflowers, head down and shoulders squared, forcing a weary and pale-faced Harris Blind-Eye ahead of him. Aitchley could tell the southern-city lockpick was on the verge of exhaustion—he had stopped cursing and swearing sometime around noon and now only had the strength to run. His left arm was still strapped to his chest in a sling now dirty yellow with dust and sweat, and a fresh stain of reddish-brown blood seeped through the bandages at his shoulder.

Bringing up the rear—accompanied by a floating Captain d'Ane—Calyx's stumpy legs carried him as quickly as they could through the high, dry grass. "They still behind us?" the dwarf wanted to know.

Hovering, Captain d'Ane turned ghostly eyes on the black mountain range behind them. "They're almost free of the Shadow Crags," he reported, his intangible body rustling through the grasses like a semitransparent breeze. "We've got a pretty good head start."

"Pretty good but not good enough," grunted Calyx, his ruddy complexion deepening to a dark burgundy. "Unlike us, the Daeminase don't have to stop to eat or rest. They're tireless, and they will not stop until we're all dead." He threw a weary—albeit sarcastic—grin at those running ahead of him. "Anybody want to stop now and just let 'em eat us?"

Berlyn tossed an anxious glance over one shoulder, blond hair streaming into her face. "No," she retorted. "And there's got to be some way to lose them. They can't possibly follow us through the Bentwoods!" A look of uncertainty creased her beautiful features. "Can they?"

"I am hopeful that they cannot," replied Gjalk, "yet little is known of the Beasts of Nowhere. The constant rains within the Halls of the Living Mist may help to drown out our scent, yet, perhaps, the Dreamless who Dream use more than just conventional senses."

"So why'd it take so long for them to find us in the Shadow

Crags then?'' Aitchley asked; still puzzled by that fact. ''They should've attacked us the very next day.''

''Contrary to what Gjalk believes, I think the Daeminase rely primarily on their sense of smell,'' Calyx said. ''They didn't catch up with us right away 'cause one of the first things I had us do was have Sprage treat everybody's cuts with *kalreif* shoots, and—when you have to trust your nose 'cause you ain't got eyes—I think the stench really knocked 'em for a loop. A complete nasal smoke screen. The stink of the *kalreif* shoots disoriented them and they took a few wrong turns, completely blinded to our whereabouts. It wasn't until we were ready to leave the *Kwau* that they caught up with us again.''

Glancing down at the band of metallic spidersilk encircling her upper arm, Berlyn felt a pang of worry course through her. ''Do you think they're all right?'' she asked. ''The *Kwau*, I mean. You don't think the Daeminase killed them all, do you?''

''Winema said they had places to hide,'' answered the dwarf, ''and you could probably stash three whole armies in those tunnels and they'd never run into one another. So long as the Daeminase keep following us, the *Kwau* will be all right.''

''But we won't be,'' Aitchley grumbled, one hand on his hat to keep it from flying off.

Calyx didn't bother to answer such a dwarvenly obvious statement, and little else was said for the rest of the day.

They ran straight on through to nightfall—never stopping—only slowing to the occasional jog. By the time the moon rose high enough to cast silver-white light down upon the OceanGrass, Aitchley's feet hurt so badly he could hardly feel them, and he had aches and pains running up the length of his legs like tiny little invisible animals that had latched onto his limbs by their teeth. His face and arms felt sunburned—an uncomfortable reminder of his time in the Molten Dunes—and rivulets of perspiration wound down his face and soaked his clothing. No one else in their group seemed to be as weary as he was—with the obvious exception of Harris Blind-Eye—and Aitchley wondered fleetingly if he even had the strength to outrun the Daeminase. Regardless of how far they ran, they'd need to sleep sometime!

Grimacing, the young man wished he had the comforting aura of the Elixir of Life slung against his back—yearning for the soothing tingle of its magical properties—yet he had let

Berlyn keep the knapsack, afraid the bouncing and jostling of his running might disrupt the elixir's sorcerous abilities. At this point he even wished his stupid staff did something. Anything to relieve the soreness in his muscles.

Gradually, a great wall of solid blackness took shape before them through the darkness, running the entire length of the OceanGrass's western border. Squinting, Aitchley could hardly make out any detail—it looked like a single line of impenetrable darkness stretched across the horizon—and it wasn't until a few filtered moonbeams struck the towering crown of an emergent that Aitchley realized they were almost back to the Bentwoods.

In the darkness, the trees looked like one great mass of solid night.

A frown formed on Calyx's face as he spied the ebony-cloaked jungle. "Didn't want to get here at night," the smith muttered bleakly to himself. "Might cause problems." He turned beady eyes on the three Rhagana. "Any chance we can find Thiazi and Baugi in the dark?"

A faint expression of uncertainty furrowed Gjuki's features. "It will be difficult, Master Calyx," the fungoid gardener answered truthfully. "Certain features and landmarks will be hard to distinguish without sunlight." He offered what could have been an apologetic smile. "You must remember, this is the first time any of my people have ever come *back* from the Shadow Crags. Most of our explorations have been *toward* them."

"No apologies necessary," Calyx said. "It's the first time any of *my* people have come back from the Shadow Crags as well." He gave a dwarven look over one shoulder. "Probably be the last time, too . . ."

Sitting up attentively on the back of Camera 12, Berlyn pointed a slender arm through the night's blackness. "I think they're over there," she said. "I can't be certain till we get a little closer."

Exhausted and irritable, Aitchley was going to make a snide remark about how in the Pits could the petite scullery maid even pretend she saw them when he abruptly remembered the brown-red stone encircling the girl's finger. To her, the OceanGrass was as well lit as midafternoon—maybe even brighter since the ring had fully illuminated the caves under the Shadow Crags with only the aid of phosphorescent lichen and here she had the moonlight to increase her magically enhanced vision—so Berlyn wasn't hampered by the darkness.

Aitchley felt a thoughtful grin slide halfway across his face. Hmm, he mused. Maybe there is something to this magic after all. . . .

"Yes, I'm sure of it now," Berlyn went on. "They're just a bit to our right. Camped right outside the Bentwoods."

Under Berlyn's directions, the nine quest-members rejoined with their two Rhagana guides on the fringes of the Bentwoods and quickly explained the situation. Quietly, the two Rhagana listened, casting pearl-black eyes eastward where dark silhouettes of distant Daeminase still loped and sprinted through the tall, dark grasses.

"The tangle of the EverDark will help to slow them down," Baugi PathFinder remarked, "but our own path through will make it easier for them to follow. Perhaps we need to confuse them. You said the Beasts of Nowhere got lost in the tunnels beneath the Mountains of Solid Blackness?"

"As near as we can tell," replied Calyx. "Why?"

"Perhaps two trails will help to further befuddle them," Baugi continued. "Thiazi can take you back to the Valley of the Diamond Rains through the shortest route possible while I will make a second trail further to the south. It does not guarantee that the Dreamless who Dream will not pick up your scent again, but it might slow them down."

"Sounds plausible," Calyx agreed, slowly nodding. "You know this place better than I do." He turned questioning eyes on the PathFinder. "You're sure you can keep ahead of them? I don't want anybody getting ripped to shreds on our account."

Baugi offered the dwarf a faint smile. "Rhagana can be as one with the early-morning mist, MetalShaper," he replied. "I will be all right, but your concern is touching."

Tiny black eyes glinting in the moonlight, Gjalk Dark-Traveler turned to face the dwarven smith. "I, however, will not accompany you," the ponytailed Rhagana declared. "I must ask your permission to stay behind and wait for Sprage HerbMaster to arrive. It upset me greatly to leave him."

Calyx threw a disapproving glance at the Rhagana. "Sprage'll be all right," he countered. "He doesn't have an army of Daeminase on his ass!"

"Nonetheless," Gjalk stocially responded, "I had come to consider the HerbMaster a friend, and—if he does attempt to follow after us—he would never make it through the Halls of the Living Mist alone. I will wait for him here.''

Aitchley recognized the look of impatience scrawling across Calyx's features. ''Maybe you're not aware of it, Gjalk,'' the dwarven smith sarcastically said, ''but there's gonna be a whole lotta Daeminase running through this immediate area in the near future. If you wait around here, you might not be in enough pieces to help Sprage go anywhere!''

Gjalk flashed a brief smile. ''Have faith, MetalShaper,'' he answered. ''If you can trust Baugi not to get caught, please believe that I can remain here and not be seen. After all, this place is our home.''

Calyx just grunted and turned away. ''Fine. Great. You have permission,'' he snorted. ''Your funeral.''

Despite the dwarf's pessimism, Gjuki took a step forward, clasping a hand to his brother's forearm. ''You do me honor, SporeKin,'' the gardener said proudly. ''Leaving Healer Sprage behind did not sit well with me either, and I am glad you have taken it upon yourself to correct this error. Await him here and repay him with the kindness he offered me when I was brought into his care.''

Gjalk clamped his own hand on Gjuki's arm. ''So it shall be done,'' he answered. ''Now go as one with All That Is, WorldDweller. You do us all honor by your own actions.''

Impatiently, Calyx started to fight his way through the tangle of dark foliage without the aid of Thiazi's machete. ''Yeah, yeah,'' he grumbled acerbatedly. ''Do us all a little honor and let's get the forge out of here. I've had enough of dealing with dreamless, eyeless rotgrubs for one day!''

Wordlessly, Aitchley agreed, ducking an overhanging jumble of vines and entering back into the claustrophobic humidity of the EverDark. Behind him, Gjalk DarkTraveler offered a single wave of farewell.

The rain didn't so much fall as tumble from plant to plant, dribbling down onto Aitchley's hat from a million tiny water-falls. The musty air around him was filled with the muted thrum of raindrops on heavy foliage, and Aitchley muttered and cursed as cascades of warm liquid trickled down his shoulders, soaked through his already perspiration-slick shirt, and left the brim of his hat droopy and waterlogged.

I've forgotten how much I hate this place, the young man grumbled to himself, brushing past a huge leaf and getting

splashed by accumulated rainwater. I think even the Molten
Dunes weren't as bad as this. At least the Dunes got cold at
night . . . this place is just one huge furnace. You'd think taking
off your shirt or rolling up your pant legs would make some
sort of difference, but here the heat goes beyond that. It's stifling! Ugh! I hate humidity!

Wiping rain and sweat out of his eyes, the young man continued to push his way through the EverDark, trying to ignore
the fatigue gnawing at his muscles. Every part of his body
ached and—while he was grateful the tangle of vegetation
made running an impossibility—he wished they'd stop to rest
before he fell flat on his face. They hadn't even bothered to
stop for breakfast, eating a quick snack while still moving, and
Aitchley could feel the lack of sleep starting to fester at the
back of his mind. It wasn't good, he knew, to go too long
without sleep. You started seeing things in the bushes that
weren't really there and, sometimes, got really giddy . . . which
wouldn't be any help at all if the Daeminase should catch up
with them. Hopefully, Calyx would understand that and let
them sleep . . . if only for a little while.

It wasn't until some time around midafternoon—or so Aitchley guessed since the EverDark barely let in any sunshine anyway—that Calyx called for a stop. Wearily, the young farmer
dropped to the leaf-strewn ground, weakly propped up against
a tree trunk. His clothes were still damp from rain and perspiration, and his chest hurt as a familiar feeling of being waterlogged twisted in his lungs. Groaning, he tugged off his boots
and meticulously dried off his feet, remembering Sprage's
warnings of certain fungi that could thrive between the young
man's toes if he wasn't careful.

Dead leaves crinkled and crunched as Berlyn dismounted
from Camera 12 and joined the young man, offering him a
beautiful smile as she approached. Aitchley could barely find
the strength to smile back and just consigned himself to a single
nod to acknowledge her presence.

Groaning from the stiffness in her own legs and the tender-
ness in her shapely rump, Berlyn lowered herself onto the
ground beside Aitchley, the smile still on her lips. She had tied
her hair back in a loose ponytail to keep it off her neck and
shoulders, and—even though sweat slicked her platinum
tresses—she was still as beautiful as ever to the young farmer.

"I'm beat," the blonde declared, resting comfortably on the

jungle floor. ''I can't imagine how you must feel.''

Aitchley just grunted, unable to find the strength to reply.

Unslinging the maroon-colored backpack from off her right shoulder, Berlyn handed the sack to the young man. ''Here,'' she said, ''hold on to this for a while. It might make you feel better.''

Aitchley only grunted again, but he felt the intoxicating tingle of the elixir's powerful magicks seep through the fabric of the backpack almost instantly. Even muted as it was through the nylon, it chased away most of the aches prodding Aitchley's joints, and even some of the strain and fatigue cramping his muscles began to fade before its healing powers.

As the elixir slowly exorcised the weariness out of Aitchley's limbs, Berlyn settled back beside him and stared up at the foliage-obscured heavens, peering up through level after level of vegetation highways and catwalks. ''Do you think Sprage's all right?'' she worried. ''I mean . . . do you think Gjalk can find him?''

''Who says he has to follow after us anyway?'' Aitchley remarked, feeling more and more strength return to his sore and weary body. ''He's all by himself in a mountain full of blue-gray, half-naked females. I know *I* wouldn't want to leave.''

Berlyn gave the young man a playful smack across the shoulder, just a hint of jealousy sparking in her gray-green eyes. ''Aitchley Corlaiys!'' she scolded him. ''If blue-gray, half-naked females are more to your liking, then you go right ahead and go back there!''

Aitchley felt a warmth spread through his cheeks. He had to be careful, he reminded himself. The elixir had a habit of stimulating things besides weary muscles.

''I . . . uh . . . um . . . er . . . I mean . . .'' he sputtered helplessly. ''What I meant to say is that *you* were my favorite half-naked female out of an entire mountainful.'' He managed a lopsided smirk of lechery. ''Did you keep the outfit they gave you?''

It was Berlyn's turn to turn a deep shade of pink. ''I might have,'' she coyly responded, averting her eyes.

There was a momentary silence between the two, interrupted only by the raucous jungle noises from above. Then, tenderly—forgiving the young man the transgression of his elixir-riled hormones—Berlyn moved in closer, sharing the tickle of magic that passed through him as she draped her arms around him. "So when this is all over, do you think we'll have made a difference?" she wondered, snuggling up contentedly. "Do you think the Cavalier can do what Lord Tampenteire hopes?"

Aitchley gave a weak shrug, hearing a familiar robotic voice drone on and on in his skull. "I don't know," he replied uneasily. "I hope so."

There are some things that were not meant to be tampered with, Aitchley Corlaiys. Be wary of nature's scales.

Berlyn nestled in closer. "Well," she said positively, "I know it's made a difference to me." She gently kissed the young man on the cheek. "*I* still believe in heroes."

You must use it, and use it wisely, bheidh *Aitchley. In your heart of hearts you will know what to do.*

Aitchley could only stare blankly at the walls of green surrounding him. "Yeah," he murmured to himself. "Heroes. Right."

Sleep soon replaced any worries that might still be wrestling inside the young man's head and he slept, embraced by the woman he loved.

Urgent hands and urgent voices tried to pull Aitchley out of the peacefulness of slumber, drawing him violently back into the hot and humid confines of the Bentwoods. Groggily, the young man cracked open one eye, blinking rapidly at the blond blur and treelike silhouette hovering over him.

"QuestLeader! QuestLeader!" the dry, deep voice of Thiazi BladeWalker cut through his bewilderment. "Rouse yourself!"

Other hands shook his shoulders. "Aitchley! Wake up!" Berlyn demanded. "We've overslept! Get up!"

Still half-asleep, Aitchley rubbed at sleep-encrusted eyes and started to pull himself reluctantly to his feet. The rain forest about him was heavy with night—abuzz with the crackle, chirrup and whir of tree-hidden insects—and the insulating canopy overhead completely blotted out the night sky. The heat and humidity remained thick in the air, yet a few streamers of silver-white moonlight managed to creep in through some gaps in the treetops.

Berlyn hurried over to Camera 12, clambering astride the construct in a swirl of torn skirt and blond hair. "Hurry!" she coaxed the young farmer. "It's almost morning! The Daeminase might be right behind us!"

Finally realizing the importance of the young girl's words—
and sparked awake by the frantic actions of the others around
him—Aitchley helped gather together a few supplies and
jogged briskly to the scullery maid's side.

"What . . . what happened?" he wanted to know.

Camera 12 started through the tangle of greenery, not even
waiting for Thiazi to cut a path. "We overslept," Berlyn said
again. "Thiazi tried waking Calyx but I guess we were all just
too tired."

"Okay. Okay," Calyx grunted, embarrassed, from somewhere behind them, "so the Daeminase aren't the only ones
who can sleep the Sleep of the Dead. I was bushed. Give me
a break!"

"But what about Captain d'Ane?" Aitchley asked. "Why
didn't he try and wake us up? I thought he didn't need to
sleep."

"I don't," d'Ane replied sheepishly from the back of the
group, "but I guess I was sort of dozing. I didn't realize how
late it was until Thiazi woke up and made me aware of it.
And—as for waking up Calyx—I yelled as loudly as I could
but I'm completely useless when it comes to things physical.
I'm even more intangible than before."

"Not your fault, Captain," Calyx responded. "The blame
lies entirely with me. I shouldn't have slept at all. We should
have just kept going." He threw a quick glance over one shoulder. "Now the Daeminase are going to catch us and we're all
gonna die. Sorry."

Pearl black eyes glistening, Gjuki made a brief scan on the
thick vegetation behind them. "I believe we are still safe for
the moment," the Rhagana declared. "I hear nothing that resembles the sounds of pursuit."

"How can you hear anything at all?" Harris grumbled
spleenfully, the color of his face waning in the inhospitable
temperature of the Bentwoods. "Alls I can hear is that mish-
mash of noise up above!"

"The Rhagana are as one with the Bentwoods," Gjuki answered. "Just as you have learned to block out the sounds of
carts and horses and vendors selling their wares on your streets,
we have learned to fine-tune our senses as well. Although I
must say, it has been quite some time since I have had to do
this."

"It's been quite some time since Solsbury's been full of carts and horses and vendors selling their wares, too!'' Calyx quipped cynically. ''Maybe you're not as out of practice as you thought.''

Jogging clumsily behind Camera 12, Aitchley listened with half an ear to the others behind him, still trying to shake the lingering sleepiness out of his head. He had been in the middle of a dream when Berlyn had awakened him—he couldn't quite remember it now . . . something to do with cathedrals made out of rainforest foliage and a tribe of *Kwau*-clad Berlyns—but it had made it all the more difficult to wake up. He was just now beginning to regain full control of his faculties, and with it came the muted aches and pains from the last twenty-four hours of running.

I guess, he mused glumly to himself, there were some aches that not even the Elixir of Life could get rid of without drinking it.

Tired eyes fixed on the silver abdomen of the camera before him, Aitchley hardly paid any attention to the profusion of vines, trees, and shrubs engulfing him. There were times he had literally to push his way through a wall of vegetation—ignoring the sharp scratch of branches and the cruel jab of jagged fan palms—and he could barely see the ground beneath his feet, lost in a mulching of fallen leaves and squat growing ferns. Sweat already dribbled in great rivers down his face, and he blindly staggered after Camera 12, his chest aching and his legs burning.

''Try and stay together, please,'' he heard Thiazi Blade-Walker call out from behind him. ''Do not get separated.''

Not knowing if she was talking to him or somebody else of the group, Aitchley tossed a cursory glance over one shoulder, taking his eyes away from the tangle of greenery in front of him. It was all the jungle needed to snag the young man's foot in a looping of vine and send him stumbling sideways, leaving him desperately trying to regain his balance before falling face-first into the foliage.

A sharp incline suddenly materialized on his left, and Aitchley lost all sense of balance, somersaulting and tumbling down the plant-choked slope. He landed—more surprised than hurt—only a foot or two down on level dirt in a clump of rusty-hued maidenhair ferns, shaking the sudden confusion out of his head. He heard someone clamber noisily down the incline behind him—felt rather than saw Poinqart effortlessly lift him back to his feet—then turned his attention to the slight grade in the jungle floor where he had fallen.

Try and stay together, please, he thought foully to himself, a self-loathing scowl painted across his lips. Do not get separated. . . . Bloody, typical, Corlaiys luck!

An unexpected fetor of decaying flesh filled the young man's nostrils and he swung back around to the left, curious eyes sweeping the debris of the forest floor. ''Phew!'' he exclaimed. ''What stinks?''

''Deathly-dead-smell,'' Poinqart replied, a hybrid look of consternation marring his face. ''Something rotting-foul has died near here.''

Questioningly—the warm, fetid odor of decay strong in his nostrils—Aitchley took a tentative step forward, blue-green eyes fixed on the ground. A small stream gurgled a few feet to his left—swollen almost to brook size by yesterday's rains—and a huge, dark red flower grew near the water's edge. The flower itself was enormous—three feet across with great, leathery red petals—and a large, gaping hole stretched the center of the plant where most had stamens or pistils. Ugly, pale, wartlike lumps peppered the leatherlike petals like hideous freckles, and the stink seemed to be coming from the flower's gaping orifice.

''Whew!'' Aitchley remarked, pinching his nose shut against the stench. ''I've never known a flower to smell like that!''

Poinqart tugged persistently at the farmer's sleeve. ''Quickly-come, Mister Aitch,'' the half troll advised. ''Poinqart has a no-good-nasty feeling about this place.''

Aitchley took another questioning step toward the foul-smelling flower. ''Aw, come on, Poinqart,'' he said. ''I'm just gonna look at—''

Two white, pearllike eyes suddenly blinked into existence on the enormous flower's topmost petals, and a wiry, vinelike body slowly pulled itself out of the leaf litter, rising to a height of nearly six feet. Wicked black thorns covered the twisted, gnarled length of its impossibly thin, vinelike form—it wasn't much thicker than Aitchley's staff!—and fingerless, handless arms snaked out toward Aitchley like vegetable tentacles, ebony thorns glinting with a razorlike sharpness in the dim moonlight.

The giant flower took a clumsy, slithering step forward on serpentine appendages, reaching out for Aitchley with coiling green limbs. The smell of death hung heavy in the humid air.

10

Subterfuge and Mimicry

"Where do you think you're going?"

Gjuki stopped at the edge of the incline and threw a cursory glance at the disgruntled dwarf behind him. "I am going to make sure Master Aitchley is unhurt," the gardener replied.

Calyx scowled. "What for?" he wanted to know. "The half troll went with him."

Gjuki resumed down the slope, navigating through the sedges, begonias, and ferns as easily as someone descending a staircase. "That may very well be true, Master Calyx," he answered, "but Thiazi's warning to stay together as not just idle words. Even the smallest of distances can seem like many leagues to someone lost in the Bentwoods."

"He's not lost," Calyx argued with a heavy frown. "He just slipped down a little hill. He'll be back up in a couple of seconds."

"A little hill which we cannot see from here," Gjuki pointed out emotionlessly. "And if we cannot see him, than he cannot see us. That is how people get separated and, subsequently, lost."

Calyx waved the Rhagana off. "Okay. Fine," he grunted. "Go. Ignore the dwarf. Don't pay any attention to what I say. What's to stop *you* from getting separated from the rest of us?"

Gjuki couldn't help the tiny smile that drew across his bark-like features. "I will no sooner get lost in the Halls of the

Living Mist than you would in the mines of Solsbury,'' he said resolutely. He ducked into thicker vegetation. ''Go on ahead. I shall rejoin you shortly.''

Picking back up his pace, Calyx pressed on through the dense foliage, trying to ignore the unsettling cold that formed in his gut. Maybe it was just typical dwarven pessimism, but the smith couldn't help thinking that things were starting to go all wrong. Sprage getting left behind and Gjalk wanting to stay behind to find him. Baugi risking his life by trying to lead the Daeminase away from them. Oversleeping and giving the Daeminase a chance to catch up. These were things that sparked dark and dreary thoughts in the dwarf's head—let's face it. We have the elixir. It only makes sense we all get killed before we can use it!—and now Aitchley, Poinqart, and Gjuki had all branched off from the main party. Doom and gloom! They'd be lucky if they weren't all dead by sunup tomorrow!

Stumbling over vines and staggering over huge tree roots, Calyx hurried to keep up, trying not to think about the young man, half troll, and Rhagana he was leaving farther and farther behind.

Metal flickered in the dim moonlight, and the Cavalier's sword practically leapt into Aitchley's right hand, his fingers drawn almost magnetically around its hilt. All the weariness and fatigue riddling his body became a distant memory as he stared at the bizarre, pseudo-human plant confronting him, and the familiar weight of the Cavalier's shield flowed like water across his left forearm.

''What . . . what in the Pits is this thing?'' he wondered out loud, taking a cautious step backward.

Yellow-black eyes filling with a hybrid mix of fear and revulsion, Poinqart gaped at the approaching plant. ''Evil-bad flower, Mister Aitch!'' the half troll exclaimed. ''Run away! Run away!''

Warily, Aitchley took another step backward, blue-green eyes narrowing at the grotesque mockery of flora facing him. He could hardly bring himself to believe the sight that met his eyes, blinking a number of times to prove to himself that he was not dreaming. There was no way he could see how this creature could move, let alone be alive. Its entire body was no thicker than the young man's leg—nothing more than a human-shaped grouping of binelike creepers crested by an enormous flower for a head—and its arms weren't so much arms as plant-like tentacles. It had no hands . . . no fingers . . . no room in its narrow, ivylike body for any kind of internal organs or skeleton. Daeminase Pits! The damn thing didn't even have any feet! It just had two vinelike extensions that curled back underneath it when it stood—like a snake rearing back to strike—and even then, its legs didn't end. Its vine trailed back through the leaf litter like a twisting, writhing coil of green rope before coming to a stop near the base of a large tree, fine, reddish-brown roots digging into the soil and anchoring the plant to the forest floor.

Aitchley suddenly felt inexplicably guilty for all the weeds he had dug up back home in his family's fields.

Shrubbery unexpectedly parted on the farmer's right, and Aitchley swung a frenzied look at the jungle, fearful another one of the giant flowers had found him. A wave of relief washed over him as he spied the gaunt, treelike form of Gjuki slip past a curtain of ariel roots and step into the clearing beside him.

"Gjuki!" the young farmer exclaimed. "Gaal, am I glad to see you!"

Gjuki's tiny black eyes surveyed the clearing. "Quickly, Master Aitchley," he ordered, a trace of urgency tinging his usually steady voice, "come this way. It would appear as if we have accidentally stumbled upon a portion of the Rafflesia's hunting ground. We must be quick."

His shock and fear dampened by the reassuring presence of Gjuki, Aitchley moved to join the Rhagana, ignoring the slow-moving, clumsy flower before him. Suddenly vinelike limbs shot out with lightninglike speed, black thorns glistening in the moonlight, and—if not for the near-magical deflection of the blue-and-gold shield on his left arm—Aitchley realized those limbs may very well have entwined murderously about his throat!

"Whoa!" the young man shouted involuntarily, making a wild jump back while, at the same time, spinning to face the gigantic flower.

As light as the feather in Aitchley's hat, the Cavalier's sword drew the young man's arm up and around. Steel sliced through tough, plantlike fiber, and a thick, white, saplike ichor splattered the rainforest floor. Twitching, the Rafflesia's arm dropped away from its body, squirming and thrashing through the leaf litter like some giant green worm accidentally pulled from the earth.

Gjuki grabbed Aitchley by one arm, pulling him back toward the incline. "Quickly, Master Aitchley!" he urged. "Where there is one Rafflesia, there will be others. If we do not leave now, that may never be possible!"

Nodding, Aitchley followed, keeping one wary eye on the injured creature behind him. The Rafflesia continued to shuffle slowly through the clutter of fallen leaves and ferns—the thick, sticky paste coagulating at its severed limb—and it hardly seemed aware of its own amputated arm. Determinedly, it lumbered forward, its remaining limb flailing through the air. The smell of decomposition soured the humid air, and Aitchley thought the stench was beginning to get stronger . . . as if more of the giant flowers might be approaching.

Finding footholds and niches where there only appeared to be solid green, Gjuki made his way back up the sharp incline, his lean body barely rustling the heavy press of shrubbery. Trailing, Aitchley could only scowl as he and Poinqart staggered and lurched clumsily through saplings and lianas. The foul stench of Rafflesia continued to taint the air, and Aitchley felt a cold tingle of apprehension prick the back of his neck when he realized the smell was coming from somewhere ahead of him.

"Uh . . ." He tried to warn Gjuki, ungracefully stumbling.

Typical Corlaiys luck, snorted his pessimism. Can't even walk and talk at the same time!

Clambering back to his feet, Aitchley managed to lurch up the last few steps to level ground. "Um . . . I think I smell more of them," he said.

Gjuki had already started down the narrow pathway cleared by Thiazi's blade and Camera 12's bulk. "Yes," he replied. "There will be more. Many more. If we do not reach the others quickly, we will all be completely surrounded."

A sudden pang of worry—not for himself but for Berlyn— gave Aitchley an added boost of adrenaline. "But . . . but why do they smell so bad?" he wanted to know. "I mean . . . is there something wrong with them?"

Gjuki pushed his way through dense foliage. "It is the way the Rafflesia attract their prey, Master Aitchley," he explained. "By mimicking the smell of death, they lead unsuspecting scavengers into their hunting grounds and devour them." A

grim look momentarily creased the gardener's usually impassive face. "And if that does not work, they overpower anyone
foolish enough to enter their domain by sheer numbers." He
brushed aside an overhanging heliconia leaf. "Quickly, now.
The others may be in even greater danger than we—"

Vines of black thorn unexpectedly exploded out of the shrubbery, snapping and cracking toward Gjuki's head like green
whips. The Rhagana had a split second to blink his surprise
before the creepers entwined about his throat and pulled, jerking him clear off his feet and back into the jumble of rainforest
greenery.

Aitchley screamed. "Gjuki!"

Thunder rumbled across the canopy-hidden heavens, strafing
the night with a low-pitched resonance. Agitated foliage added
to the clamor, and Berlyn could barely hear herself think over
the noise of snapping branches and crackling, rustling leaves.
A white-hot pit of anxiety burned hotly in her stomach—sending a tingling, wild shiver of adrenaline rushing through her
petite frame—and she clung tightly to Camera 12's wire-mesh
reins, afraid the lumbering gallop of the damaged machine
might pitch her right off its cold metallic back.

A bandaged wing flapped against the young girl's head to
get her attention, and she felt copper talons dig a little harder
into her flesh.

She turned a questioning eye on the gyrofalc fledgling
perched on her shoulder.

"Gone again, he isz," Trianglehead remarked, a sardonic
gleam in his milky-blue eyes.

Berlyn blinked her confusion. "What?" she asked. "Who's
gone?"

"Aitchley," the bird responded. "Gone again. Klumszy.
Klumszy. Klumszy."

The white-hot anxiety melded into a seething panic as Berlyn
turned to scan the jungle behind her. "Aitchley?" she all but
shrieked. "What? What happened to him?"

Trianglehead ruffled his feathers in mock indifference.
"Rolled down a zslope," he said. "Klutz."

Fear welling up in her eyes, Berlyn tugged at Camera 12's
reins, trying to get the construct to turn around. Obediently, the
camera slowed, but there wasn't enough room between trees
and buttressed roots to turn.

As the camera came to a slow halt, so did the others behind it.

"What's the holdup?" Calyx's voice sprouted from the back of the group.

Berlyn struggled with the reins, the panic in her stomach becoming a nauseated, hollow feeling in her gut. "Aitchley!" she cried. "He's not with us!"

Calyx waved the young girl forward. "I know that!" he retorted. "Gjuki and Poinqart are with him! Keep going!"

Thunder cracked the night sky.

"But what are—" Berlyn tried to protest.

"Look," Calyx interrupted rudely, "we don't have time for this! The Daeminase could be right on our asses! The kid'll be fine. He'll probably catch up with us by morning. Now *move*!"

Heavy misgivings weighing down her thoughts, Berlyn felt her resolve crumble and reluctantly let Camera 12 resume its westwardly direction. She couldn't help the great feeling of emptiness devouring her insides—it felt worse than when she had left Aitchley behind after being attacked by brown trolls . . . and she remembered all too well what had almost happened then!—but Calyx was right. Going back now could mean their death—they had no idea where the Daeminase were—and Calyx wouldn't leave Aitchley behind to die, would he? If Gjuki and Poinqart were with him, he'd be all right. Gjuki had guided Harris to safety once before; there would be no reason why he couldn't do the same for Aitchley.

Unless the Daeminase had caught up with them and they were already dead.

Still wrestling with her thoughts, Berlyn hardly noticed the heavy rain that began to fall high above in the rainforest canopy, a deep rush of liquid that drowned out the night calls of the tree-dwelling denizens. The humidity of the Bentwoods grew worse—a thickening, solidifying feeling clogging the air—and Berlyn didn't even catch the foul scent of decay that hung suspended in the moistness like a cloud of hovering insects.

Ivylike tendrils of black-thorned plant life unexpectedly launched out of the foliage, coiling and writhing in serpentine grace.

Berlyn let out a single scream, drowned out by the heavy rainfall from above.

* * *

Without even thinking of his own safety, Aitchley dove headfirst through a wall of green, the Cavalier's sword singing above his head. The downpour clogged his ears with an incessant *shhhh* of falling water, but his eyes remained locked on the spot where Gjuki had been pulled into the bush. Whatever moonlight there may have been before was now completely blotted out by dark clouds converging overhead, yet Aitchley pressed on, all but blind in the blackness of the EverDark.

What might have been two figures wrestled through the darkness, lean and plantlike in their profile. Thorny limbs flailed and thrashed through the brambles, and the entire region stank with the warm, fetid odor of decay. The rush of the rain nearly drowned out any sounds of struggle, and Aitchley blinked continuously at the gaunt, vague silhouettes fighting through the pitch.

Steel flashed in the young man's hand, yet uncertainty held his blade. Which one's Gjuki? he wondered. I can't see a Gaal-damned thing!

A faint blossom of misty white light suddenly sparked from atop Aitchley's staff, illuminating the area with an unnatural lambency. Pure illumination—brighter than torchlight or sun— draped the rain forest in undiluted splendor, throwing glittering reflections off the billions of raindrops that spiraled through the canopy. A curt hiss of surprise escaped the Rafflesia's flower- like head as it turned tiny white eyes on the young man, a deadly tentacle snaking out toward his staff.

The Cavalier's sword slashed sideways, severing the approaching limb and spattering the ground with thick, pasty sap. Effortlessly—as if meeting absolutely no resistance in the air— Aitchley directed the sword back around and amputated the creature's other limb, freeing Gjuki from its deadly embrace. Hissing, the Rafflesia turned on the young man, its awkward, plantlike body too slow and clumsy to get out of the way as the Cavalier's sword flashed again.

The Rafflesia crumpled in two pieces, both upper and lower halves still twitching and convulsing.

Gjuki rubbed tenderly at where sharp thorns had pierced his neck; a thin, pale fluid trickled between his leathery fingers. "Many thanks, Master Aitchley," the Rhagana said. "If there is one thing worse than the stink of Rafflesia, it is the deadly touch of their vinelike arms." He threw an urgent look over one shoulder. "Come now. We must hurry. I fear the others may be in like danger."

Dark shrubbery crashed and splintered behind them as Poinqart fought his way through the blackness toward the light of Aitchley's staff, a look of hybrid terror on his crossbred features. "Mister Aitch! Mister Gjuki-plant!" the half troll shouted. "More are coming! Poinqart can stinky-smell them!"

Adrenaline and fear recharging his tired and weary body, Aitchley tossed a quick glance at the Rafflesia dying at his feet. Walls of immense green surrounded him on every side, and the warm, fetid stench of decomposition seemed to permeate the darkness just beyond the halo of his glowing staff. "Then let's get the Pits out of here," he declared.

The rain fell harder.

Sharp thorns dug into the smooth flesh of Berlyn's arm and neck, tightening around her body like ivy pythons. Pain lanced through her system, and she could feel blood instantly well up around the puncture wounds in her skin. Her surprise was so great she wasn't even able to react before the whiplike limbs entwining about her pulled, jerking her off the back of Camera 12 and hurling her headlong into the bushes.

Trianglehead released a frantic squawk as Berlyn's shoulder was pulled out from under him. "Waaaauuuugh!" he exclaimed.

The rain forest did a somersault, and Berlyn landed somewhere in the leaf litter, a tightening noose of vine squeezing the life from her. Blood dribbled down her left arm and across her neck—spotting her dress with red—and she could feel the inhuman grip crushing the air from her windpipe. She made a frenzied attempt to stand, but the limbs kept pulling her forward, throwing her off balance. A vertiginous buzzing started in her ears as she struggled to breathe, and she could feel her hold on consciousness beginning to slip away.

The stranglehold about her throat suddenly ended, and Berlyn took in a strained gasp of air, clutching desperately at her neck. A thick, pasty fluid spattered her face and arm as the vinelike limbs split in two, and it took a moment for Berlyn to get her bearings before she could make sense of what was going on about her.

Aided by the ring around her finger, the impenetrable darkness of the rain forest was not a problem. Stanced before her—

her curved blade of black steel dripping with sap—stood Thiazi BladeWalker, machete in hand. Camera 12 stood immediately behind the Rhagana, a bright light just above its single eye helping to spotlight the EverDark, and the others were quickly pushing their way through the foliage and rain.

Berlyn probed gingerly at the wounds about her throat and arm. "What . . . what was that thing?" she questioned.

"Rafflesia," replied Thiazi. "Without the PathFinder's guidance, we have stumbled across their domain. We must change direction at once."

Despite the blood and sharp stinging encircling her throat, Berlyn felt a pulse of anxiety race through her thoughts. "But what about Aitchley?" she fretted.

Calyx frowned. "Gjuki can track us," he consoled her. He stroked thoughtfully at his salt-and-pepper beard. "Unless they've been attacked already and are dead."

Leathery fingers tightening about her spear, Eyfura gave the jungle an apprehensive scan. "Come," she said. "Where there is one Rafflesia, there will be many others. We must not dawdle."

Even before the SpearWielder was able to complete her sentence, bushes parted before them and on their left, issuing forth a cluster of walking flowers. Vinelike arms snapped and whipped through the air, and the Bentwoods filled with the stink of decaying meat.

Calyx stopped stroking his beard long enough to pull free his warhammer. "Too late," he quipped.

Guided by the silvery mist of light enveloping the head of his staff, Aitchley shoved through the rain-soaked foliage, weaving his reckless way through the maze of dark trees and lianas. Thunder grumbled like an angry behemoth from the canopy-hidden heavens overhead, and moisture spattered and pelted the young farmer as he pushed his way through the tangle of green. Twice he stumbled over some night-cloaked root or vine despite the unwavering glow of his staff—and the second time he nearly wrenched his ankle—but the young man didn't care. All that mattered to him was that there might be more of those murderous flowers out there . . . and so was Berlyn.

If we ever get out of this one, I'm never letting Berlyn out of my sight again, the young man resolved. Even if it means riding tandem on Camera 12, I'm never leaving her side again. Never!

So suddenly that Aitchley almost didn't have time to stop, Gjuki halted in front of him, tiny black eyes peering into the darkness. A grim expression creased the Rhagana's face—and Aitchley knew instantly that *that* was a bad sign—and he held his body tense and rigid as if expecting something unsavory to happen.

Aitchley waited as patiently as he could before his anxiety got the better of him. "What? What?" he whispered impatiently. "What's the matter?"

Gjuki's eyes never left the blackness ahead of them. "There is a large bed of Rafflesia ahead of us," he quietly explained. "We will have to go around."

The apprehension and fear churning through his stomach caused Aitchley's voice to catch in his throat. "Are the others up ahead?" he worried.

Gjuki nodded once. "Yes," he answered. "I fear they are being corralled."

Aitchley blinked his bewilderment. "Corralled?" he echoed. "You mean like horses?"

The fungoid gardener turned his pearl-black eyes on the farmer. "You must remember what I said before, Master Aitchley," he said. "If subterfuge and mimicry do not work, the Rafflesia overwhelm their prey by sheer number. They do this by driving their prey into the waiting arms of other Rafflesia. Then they are torn apart and eaten."

Aitchley's stomach heaved at the thought. "The Pits they are!" he exclaimed. "Come on! Let's—"

Gjuki's gaunt arm held the young man back. "That would be unwise, Master Aitchley," he advised. "We need to formulate a plan."

Something that may have been a human scream or just the cry of a rainforest bird suddenly broke through the rapid-fire chatter of falling rain, sending a mind-numbing surge of adrenaline through Aitchley's brain. Before he was aware of what he was doing, the young man had pushed Gjuki to one side, knocking the Rhagana off his feet, and gone vaulting through the shrubbery, sword in one hand, staff in the other.

Even Gjuki was surprised by the young man's impetuosity. "Master Aitchley!" he warned. "Wait!"

The silver glow of Aitchley's staff was already swallowed
up by the thick press of dark trees.

His face contorted in an unreadable mix of trollish humor
and human concern, Poinqart offered Gjuki a helping hand up.
"Mister Aitch does not listen-hear so good sometimes," the
half troll remarked. "Poinqart has learned this the difficult-hard
way."

Sprinting after the young farmer, Gjuki responded, "Let us
hope this is not one of those times."

Berlyn screamed as the phalanx of giant flowers closed in
around her, filling the rain forest with their foul stink of death.
Deadly vines tipped with barblike thorns slashed the air above
her head, and she scrambled hastily back to her feet, trying to
find her dropped throwing ax in the debris of leaves. One vine
swept perilously close to her left shoulder—its sharp thorns
severing the humid air with a high-pitched whistle—and the
scullery maid let out a half-choked shriek, wildly ducking before the sinuous limb could entwine about her throat.

Thiazi's machete sent the groping tentacle flailing out into
the trees in a sluicing of thick sap.

"There are too many of them," the BladeWalker observed.
"We must retreat."

Mandy clutched tightly in his good hand, Harris threw a look
behind him as a cluster of inhuman figures pushed their way
through the foliage. "Bad news, scout," he said. "They've got
us surrounded."

Gray-green eyes wide, Berlyn gave a fearful look at the ring
of Rafflesia encircling them. "So now what do we do?" she
wanted to know.

A grave expression came to Thiazi's face. "We die," she
said grimly.

Warhammer gripped in both hands, Calyx launched himself
at the line of advancing plants. "The forge we do!" he barked,
his misplaced optimism surfacing. "There's not that many of
'em! And if we were able to fight our way free of the Daeminase, I'm not about to let some walking nosegay do me in!
Come on! Get 'em!"

Three Rafflesia collapsed in a jumbled heap of intertwining
vines, hurled into one another by the force of Calyx's hammer.
The weapon itself did little damage to their plantlike bodies—
only a weapon with a sharp edge held any threat to the carniv-

orous flowers—so Calyx used the floor of the Bentwoods to his advantage. Even as the three he knocked over tried to upright themselves, Calyx brought his hammer down on the vines trailing back along the ground, smashing the black-thorned foliage into a gooey, pulpy mess. A howl went up from the injured Rafflesia as Calyx damaged their root system, and vinelike arms thrashed and flailed in anguish.

"The MetalShaper is right," Eyfura agreed. "We must not let the Rafflesia stop us! Fight!"

Arms draped protectively over her head, Berlyn scurried out of harm's way, barely avoiding Eyfura's daring leap at the front line of advancing Rafflesia. She could hear the struggles going on all about her despite the rain—hear Eyfura's spear plunge into the soft, plantlike fiber of the Rafflesia's body, feel the spatter of thick white sap as Calyx's hammer crushed vine after vine—and yet she could not find her own weapon. Deadly tentacles snapped and cracked over her head, and she was constantly ducking to avoid their black-thorned grasp. The wounds about her arm and throat were slowly beginning to heal—probably from the muted magical tingle radiating from the backpack on her shoulder—and she suddenly remembered the bag of relics Harris had stolen from the cathedral. Maybe there was something in there that could help her in place of her throwing ax, but what? The cloak of invisibility? No, they were too cramped . . . too close together. Turning invisible was almost more dangerous then being visible. So what about the ring of flight? That would help her but none of the others, and she certainly couldn't just leave them all behind. So what was left? Just those vials whose effect they had not yet found out. Should she try one—

A squirming tendril suddenly snaked around her left ankle, feeling its way through the darkness like a blind worm and entwining about her foot. Instant pain lanced up the length of her leg from the sharp thorns cutting into her flesh, and Berlyn made an instinctive leap back, trying to pull herself free of the Rafflesia's grip and slashing her own foot badly as the vine constricted.

Camera 12's steel leg shot out and impaled the giant flower to an enormous fig tree, whitewashing the thick trunk with viscous sap and freeing Berlyn from its deadly grip.

Berlyn sank back to the ground, grabbing at her injured foot. Now I know how they tear people apart, she realized through the agony. They grab you and let you tear yourself apart by trying to pull away!

Warm fluid dribbled over Berlyn's fingers as she tried to stop the flow of blood from her foot, and she tried not to think about the pain arcing throughout her body. She needed to find her ax if she was going to be any help, and as the only one who could see in the dark . . . only she could truly see how very many of the Rafflesia there actually were.

Another probing vine went snaking across the dirt, seeking out warm flesh to entwine, and Berlyn made a wild roll to one side, barely escaping its serpentine strike. She felt something hard and cold protrude beneath her rump, and she eagerly pulled her throwing ax free of the rain-slick leaves, a sense of security filling her breast at the familiar feel of its haft in her hands. Immediately, she jumped back to her feet, hardly feeling the pain anymore in her left ankle, and swung at the horde of carnivorous flowers surrounding her.

"This way! This way!" she could hear Calyx shouting over the chaos of combat and rain. "There's an opening!"

"Calyx! Look out!" Captain d'Ane's voice sounded from the darkness.

"Okay," Calyx's voice shot back, "so there *isn't* an opening!"

Even with the aid of the magical ring around her finger, all Berlyn could see were sticklike plants with giant gaping flowers for heads. Ropy limbs flailed and thrashed through the musty air, and every time Berlyn swung her ax, she was certain to strike plantlike tentacles. An all-too-recognizable fatigue had already started to creep into her shoulders, and—despite the reassuring tickle of the elixir at her back—there remained a stabbing discomfort in her foot, arm, and neck. What little strength she may have gotten from their brief rest quickly evaporated in the thick humidity of the jungle, and she had a growing sense of doom as more and more Rafflesia dominated her magically enhanced sight.

A pair of vines caught in the hem of her skirt, black thorns slashing through the worn material. Fabric tore in great shreds as one tentacle lost its grip—rewarded by only a handful of cloth—but the other vine found its way under her skirt and tried to slip its way around her thigh, ebony thorns pricking at her tender flesh.

With a half grunt, half squeal, Berlyn brought her ax down

on the writhing tentacle of plant fiber, unable to keep the memory of would-be rapists from flashing back into her mind.

A throng of ivylike limbs suddenly grabbed for the diminutive scullery maid, drawn perhaps toward the heat of her body. She felt black thorns tear savagely through the frayed hemline of her skirt, felt another almost catch the back of her hair. A third tried to coil around her right leg, but she managed to jump free with a shriek before it had a chance to tighten. A fourth swung blindly at her face, black thorns slashing dangerously close to her nose, while a fifth made a failed attempt to grab the blade of her swinging ax.

Berlyn tried to scan the rain forest around her but all she could see were groping, grasping tentacles. Maybe Thiazi was right, she mused darkly. Maybe there is no escaping these things.

A sixth tentacle caught the young girl behind the knees, knocking her back and throwing her to the ground. Stars exploded behind her eyelids—and she felt a brief flash of vertigo shoot through her as her head smacked the dirt—before a more nefarious touch of thick vines and creeperlike limbs started to swarm over her like eyeless snakes.

"Aitch—" she started to scream before tentacles coiled about her throat. There was a new noise to add to the cacophony erupting all about her, and Berlyn wasn't quite sure if it wasn't from the dizziness in her own head. Harsh yet muted, a dull, echoing thud of pure force resounded in the young girl's ears, drowning out the sounds of battle and persistent rainfall.

The grip around her neck loosened, and Berlyn cracked open one eye to see the Rafflesia in front of her completely ablaze, its plantlike body engulfed by voracious flames. Thick, acrid smoke polluted the pluvious air as the creature burned, and whiplike limbs writhed and squirmed in fiery anguish as its fibrous body turned to blackened ash.

There was another baritone *poompf* of unrestrained energy and yellow-white fire arced across the trees in a well-aimed explosion, catching another Rafflesia in a sudden volcano of flame.

Blinking the intense flare out of her magically aided eyes, Berlyn struggled to one arm.

Something crashed through the brush behind her.

"*Berlyn!*" Aitchley roared, staff blazing fire above his head.

11

Death in the Bentwoods

Yellow-orange energy exploding above his head, Aitchley leapt over the smoking corpse of a charred and smoldering Rafflesia and raced through the trees to where the conflict raged. Flames filled his line of sight—and the magical silver glow of his staff helped illuminate the jungle—yet he could not see Berlyn. Everywhere he looked, hordes of Rafflesia pushed their clumsy way through the foliage, eager tentacles seeking out soft, fragile flesh to rend, but there was no sign of Berlyn.

Plantlike limbs shot out from the young man's left, black thorns glistening in the flickering light of dancing flames. Even before the Cavalier's shield could swing him around, Aitchley had turned on the attacking Rafflesia, leveling his staff and directing its rounded knob at the scrawny, plantlike body of the giant flower.

Magical forces coalesced in the form of a fireball, leaping from the head of the staff and catching the Rafflesia on its fibrous chest. Light and heat volcanoed in a sudden blossom of sorcery, instantly engulfing the plant in a cocoon of fire, and thick black smoke choked the rain forest. Saplike blood boiled as vines burned, and leathery red petals curled and charred, twisting and blackening in a kind of slow-motion agony.

Not even bothering to launch a fireball at another advancing Rafflesia, Aitchley slammed his staff into the creature's flowerlike face with quarterstafflike agility, taking little satisfaction in the crunch of pulpy fibers.

Gjuki made an attempt to rein in the young man. "Master Aitchley, please!" the Rhagana implored. "Be careful!"

Aitchley shrugged off the gardener's hand. "Berlyn!" he roared again.

Another Rafflesia rose up to threaten the young farmer and was instantly reduced to smoldering ash.

Gjuki flinched as magical fires illuminated the EverDark. "Master Aitchley," he begged once more. "I ask that you reconsider using your staff. Its flames might very well spark a forest fire. One which we would be caught in the middle of."

Aitchley slammed his staff into another Rafflesia and took a step forward. "I don't care!" he shot back angrily. "I need to find Berlyn!"

Poinqart rammed a hamhock fist into a giant flower, spraying white sap. "Missy Berlyn is somewhere-nearby-close," he tried to console the young man. "Looky-see, Mister Aitch. There is Captain-ghostie-d'Ane."

None of his worry or adrenaline-induced rage diminished as Aitchley turned to his right. Flames continued to flicker and feast on the charred remains of many Rafflesia—and the thick black smoke made it harder to see—but there could be no mistaking the faint, ethereal glow of Captain d'Ane's unreal body, floating a few inches above the ground, his silvery outline passing through spinaling wisps of smoke and clusters of leaping flames.

D'Ane offered the young farmer a spectral smile. "Aitchley, lad," he greeted him. "Glad to see you're all right. Looks like you've cleared a way through their rear flanks."

His mind on one thing, Aitchley fixed harsh blue-green eyes on the dead soldier. "Where's Berlyn?" he demanded.

D'Ane looked through his own shoulder. "Toward the front, I suppose," he answered truthfully. "She was riding the camera."

Aitchley went to push his way past the captain and wound up stepping through him. "I have to get to her," he declared.

Without any physical substance, d'Ane knew better than to try to restrain the young man, yet he still made the attempt. "Wait a minute, lad," he said. "Listen to what Gjuki says. Fire's a dangerous thing to be playing with in such close quarters."

Aitchley tried to ignore the ghostly image hovering beside him. "Who cares?" he snapped back. "I need to find Berlyn."

"What good is finding Berlyn going to do if you get us all caught in a forest fire?" d'Ane asked back. "You asked me before about nature's scales. Well, this is part of it. Tinder. Fire. You get a disaster."

Aitchley stopped long enough to give the ghost a cynical stare. "Tinder?" he snidely echoed. "It's raining, for Gaal's sake!"

"And how do you think most fires are started?" d'Ane responded. "Lightning strikes during rainstorms, that's how." The balding soldier looked down at Aitchley with deep concern in his ghostly gaze. "Remember what I told you before, lad," he said in softer tones. "Impetuosity is one of the worst enemies of the soldier. Keep your head or you might very well end up losing it."

Snorting, Aitchley turned away from the ghost, fighting his way through a wall of walking plants. He tried to act unimpressed—tried to pretend that the captain's words held no meaning for him—but he knew better than that. D'Ane was right. Using the staff might very well cause a fire that could spread completely out of control, and then where would he be? More importantly . . . where would Berlyn be?

A door opened somewhere in the young man's subconscious and he heard the droning, inhuman buzz of Tin William's voice fill his thoughts: *There are some things that were not meant to be tampered with, Aitchley Corlaiys. Be wary of nature's scales.*

A sarcastic snort came from his pessimism. Yeah. Right, he grunted. As if it was that easy.

Captain d'Ane watched as the young man moved away from him, dashing through the tangle of foliage with as much determination and bravery as a veteran warrior. It was odd, the dead soldier mused, but the lad had changed so much since those early days back in Solsbury. He was no longer afraid . . . no longer at the mercy of his own self-doubt. He had grown into a true hero. Shown the world that the Cavalier's descendant had as much courage and conviction as the Cavalier himself. A far cry from the frightened little farm boy too scared even to try.

D'Ane felt a smile pull across misty lips. Maybe it wasn't

so odd after all, he concluded proudly. Aitchley's just growing up, that's all.

Still trying to shake the dizziness out of her head, Berlyn clambered to her knees, the throb of her injuries assailing her body. She could feel blood trickle down her neck and between the valley of her breasts, and her skirt was in tatters about her legs. Her left ankle continued to ache despite the sorcerous tingle of pins and needles that emanated from Aitchley's backpack, and flashes of brilliant light exploded over and over behind her eyelids, replaying the sudden eruption of fireball and Rafflesia.

And as she wore Harris's magical ring, the light had been twice as blinding.

Sensing rather than seeing, Berlyn heard someone approach and threw a questioning look upward. She knew from the crunch of shoes on dead leaves that it wasn't one of the shuffling Rafflesia, but she still had to blink in order for her magically heightened vision to adjust.

Crisscrossed by thick sap—a few cuts above his right arm and his right pant leg torn and frayed—Harris Blind-Eye flashed the scullery maid an insincere smirk. "You all right, sweetcheeks?" he queried.

Berlyn pulled herself hastily to her feet, not wanting the southern-city brigand to see her fatigue. "I'm fine," she lied, barely able to find the strength to lift her throwing ax. "Worry about yourself."

Harris slashed at an encroaching tentacle. "I am," he answered. "Why I'm here."

Berlyn's throwing ax gleamed silver gray in the light of burning Rafflesia, her eyebrows narrowing on her brow. "What's that supposed to mean?" she asked.

Harris's grin was not friendly. "You've got the elixir, sweets," he replied, "and I'm fighting one-handed. Something happens to me, I want to be able to get my hands around that elixir as quickly as I can. Figure your boyfriend owes me that much."

"Aitchley doesn't owe you anything," Berlyn shot back, severing a giant flower from off its stemlike neck.

Harris suddenly grabbed her by one arm, pulling her in close to his scarred and bearded face. "And I say he does," he rasped. "Or ain't I the one who helped him get that bunging drink in the first place?"

Berlyn tore her arm out of the bandit's weakened grasp, pivoting around and maiming another groping tentacle. "And Aitchley saved you from falling into the Pits," she retorted, her self-righteous anger offering her a kind of strength. "I'd say that makes you even."

Harris took her by the arm again, and this time Berlyn noticed the growing red stain on the lockpick's bandaged shoulder. "Southern-city don't play by those rules, sweetcheeks," he snarled. "It's because of him I'm on this quest and because of him I might never use this arm again, so I'd say it's because of him I've lost my livelihood. I don't think that makes saving me from the Pits all that much of a favor, now, does it?"

Berlyn tried to pull herself free, but this time there was a kind of unflagging persistence keeping Harris's fingers clamped around her arm. "I don't care what you think," she answered sharply. "Now let go of my—"

Tentacles suddenly whipped out through the shrubbery. One wrapped around Berlyn's right hand, encircling her fingers and rendering her weapon useless. The other entwined around Harris's throat. A look of surprise filled the rogue's blue-black eyes as he tried to bring Mandy up to slice away the constricting limb, but a third coiled around his waist, pinning his arm to his side.

A curt shriek tore from Berlyn's throat as the limb jerked her forward, trying, unsuccessfully, to pull her off her feet and drag her into the undergrowth. Harris wasn't quite so fortunate and pitched forward, landing hard in the leaf litter. A low grunt sounded from the back of his throat as he struggled to free his arm, and black thorns tore across his flesh as he fought, yet Berlyn could see no sign of discomfort or pain in the bandit's lean and hungry features.

Dark steel unexpectedly flashed, severing limbs in a single downward sweep. Caught off balance, Berlyn stumbled back, tripping over Harris and sprawling to the forest floor. Leaves flew as the blonde landed hard on her rear end, and she looked up to see Thiazi's machete chop downward and free Harris from the vine twisting about his neck.

The female Rhagana offered Berlyn a leathery hand up. "Quickly," she advised. "This way. The QuestLeader has made an opening."

Hurriedly, Berlyn sprang to her feet. Her skirt billowed and flapped between her legs like the tattered remains of threadbare curtains, and her right hand and wrist now throbbed with the familiar ache of puncture wounds, yet she took the time to offer Harris a helpful hand up.

"There's another one you owe Aitchley," she mocked.

Face pale and perspiration soaking his forehead, Harris shot the young blonde a venomous glare. "Oh, yeah. Right," he snarled. "I owe him big time."

Sneering, the lockpick followed after Berlyn and Thiazi.

Aitchley spun as a pair of tentacles tried to grab him from behind, black thorns glittering in the fading firelight. The powerful tingle of unearthly magicks flowed up and down his arm from the length of blackened oak in his hand, and he could sense the mental command that directed all the energy arcing out of his body and back through the staff, crackling out the tip of its silver-crafted knob.

Warm, humid air blistered and cracked as the moisture was sucked forcibly out of an attacking Rafflesia and lowered to below freezing, instantly crystallizing all about the giant plant. Blue-white ice formed an almost immediate sheath around the plantlike monster—encasing it in a block of solid ice—and Aitchley slammed the pointed end of his staff into the frozen monster's mouth, shattering its head as easily as if it was a crystal sculpture.

"If you're not careful, kid," a sudden voice said down near his knees, "you're going to get pretty good at that stuff."

Aitchley glanced down at the grumpy-looking dwarf half-lost in the press of thick vegetation. "Just using whatever means possible," he replied matter-of-factly. He swept the surrounding jungle with desperate eyes. "Have you seen Berlyn?"

"Somewhere ahead of us, I suppose," Calyx answered. He gave the Rafflesia-infested rain forest a heavy frown. "Come on, kid. Let's get the forge out of here."

Aitchley moved farther into the jungle. "I'm not going anywhere without Berlyn," he declared.

Calyx sighed heavily. "Aw, knock off the heroics, kid," he suggested. "She's with the camera. We've gotta get out of here while the gettin's good."

Aitchley shook his head vehemently. "I'm not going anywhere without Berlyn," he repeated firmly.

A glimmer of annoyance lit in Calyx's beady eyes as the young man continued deeper into the foliage, but there was a hint of pride at the corners of the dwarf's mouth. "Yeah," he observed, "you're Procursus's descendant, all right. Stupid, stubborn, *and* pigheaded." He stomped off into the jungle after him. "Come on, kid," he added. "Let's go find Berlyn."

Gjuki ducked a writhing coil of vine, feeling the sharp black thorns cut the air above his head. Poinqart caught the flailing tentacle in a powerful, four-fingered grip, crushing it to a white, pulpy mess and flinging the attacking Rafflesia over his shoulder, hurling it through the trees in a spray of white sap.

"Poinqart is worried-scared for the others," the hybrid said, slamming a fist into a Rafflesia that tried to come up from behind. "Poinqart should be helping-assist Mister Aitch rescue-save Missy Berlyn. Mister Calyx-dwarf made Poinqart their protector-friend."

Gjuki dodged another limb, shoving its owner back into the undergrowth. "And a fine job you are doing of it, too, Master Poinqart," the Rhagana replied, "but it is mandatory that we stay where we are. In his desire to find Miss Berlyn, Master Aitchley has broken through the Rafflesia's defenses, and we must leave this passage open for the others. Otherwise we shall all be overwhelmed."

Sharp thorns suddenly dug into Poinqart's arm, an ivylike limb curling about his. With a trollish grimace of discomfort, the half troll rammed an elbow back into the giant flower's face, snapping its slender, vinelike neck in a spatter of ichor.

"Poinqart worry-fears that there are already too-many-hundreds of them," the hybrid admitted. "Evil-bad flowers are many-more-numberous than nasty-bad-brown-trolls. Poinqart wishes-hopes he could just run away from this place."

Gjuki kicked an invading Rafflesia into another. "I agree wholeheartedly, Master Poinqart," he replied.

The dark vegetation suddenly parted and three Rafflesia shuffled toward them. The rains had begun to lessen, and tiny glimmers of moonlight filtered through the dense canopy, glinting evilly off the Rafflesia's tiny white eyes. Their handless arms flailed and swayed like angry cobras, and Gjuki abruptly wished he had a better weapon than his bare hands.

A bright light unexpectedly dissected the darkness, back-lighting the three Rafflesia in blinding white illumination. Curiously, one of the creatures went to turn around, and there was a low *scrunch* as a steel leg went punching through its flowerlike head. A second fell as a black-tipped spear cut through what should have been its spinal column, and a third dropped beneath Poinqart's heavy fist.

Eyfura SpearWielder stepped out of the bushes alongside Camera 12, her dark, leathery skin bespattered by thick sap. Trianglehead sat grumpily on the camera's back.

"SpearWielder." Gjuki nodded his greeting. "Your presence is most welcome."

Eyfura threw a nervous glance over one shoulder as something smelling of death rustled the foliage. "We must not stay here any longer, WorldDweller," she warned. "More Rafflesia approach even as we speak."

Gjuki nodded again. "I know," he said, "yet we leave together or not at all."

A mass of Rafflesia shoved their clumsy way through the jungle, deadly vines slashing and razoring the air.

"Looksz like not at all," Trianglehead said, trying to hide his head under one, bandaged wing.

Shattering into a million, blue-white fragments, another Rafflesia turned to snow and ice. Cold tinged the humid air—an unnatural contrast to the heat and moisture of the Bentwoods—and Aitchley wheeled about to face another plantlike attacker, tingles of powerful energies arcing through his body and out the staff.

Calyx flinched as a Rafflesia limb froze just above his head, cracking and splintering with the sounds of melting ice. "I don't see her, kid," the dwarf remarked, scanning the darkness around them. "We musta missed her."

Aitchley slammed the Cavalier's shield into the face of an ice-bound flower, shattering its leathery petals like glass. "She's got to be here!" the young man insisted. "Keep going!"

"If we keep going, we'll wind up back in Leucos!" Calyx quipped. He brought his hammer down on vinelike legs. "Look, I was just recently lectured on how small distances here can mean life or death. If we keep going, we're gonna get separated from the others for sure. Then what good's that gonna do us?"

Aitchley swung his staff like a club, snapping a giant flower's vinelike body in half. "I don't care!" he shouted. "I have to find Berlyn!"

"All you're gonna find here is an early grave," Calyx retorted, a pessimistic scowl beneath his beard. "Now come on. Do something even your ancestor didn't do and listen to me for once. Berlyn ain't here! She either got away or else there ain't nothing left of her to find! Let's go!"

A horrible sensation of rage and anxiety welled up inside the young man to try to protect him from the truth in Calyx's words, but he could still feel the hollowness start to ache in his heart. Not Berlyn! his thoughts cried. She has to be here! She just has to be! All my life I've never cared about anything like I care about her! She can't be dead! I won't allow it! She's got to be here!

On the verge of tears, Aitchley glared at the rain forest. The rain had finally stopped, and—hidden behind the walls of green—the dim pink light of early morning had begun to tint the eastern skyline. But Aitchley didn't care. As the sun rose higher his fears and anxieties rose with it, and Aitchley could feel the premature emptiness inside his chest threatening to swallow him whole.

A scream of pure anguish ripped through the young farmer. *"Berlyn!"* he howled. *"Where are you?"*

As if in response to the young man's cry, the foliage before him shuddered and rustled. Pink light gradually deepened as early morning filled the heavens, and—staring at the parting greenery—Aitchley felt his apprehensions begin to fade, a tide of relief flushing the anxiety—albeit prematurely—out of his system.

Berlyn! he thought to himself. You're all right. . . .

A horde of Rafflesia came lumbering out of the jungle ahead of him, tentaclelike arms writhing through the leaves. The stink of death hung heavy in the moist, humid air, and the rain forest was filled with the shambling, ungainly shuffle of vines across the leaf litter.

Calyx took a step back, his ruddy complexion waning at the sheer number of giant flowers coming toward them. "Kid," the dwarf remarked, "that ain't Berlyn."

Aitchley blanched. "I can see that!" he sniped back.

More and more creatures pushed their way through the brush, swamping the rain forest with the deep red of their leathery petals. The stench became almost overwhelming as row after row of Rafflesia ambled awkwardly through the undergrowth, and Aitchley could barely blink the shock from his eyes. Hesitation and uncertainty churned within the young man's thoughts, and he found himself unable to retreat, his anxieties rooting him to the spot.

There's too many of them! he grudgingly admitted to himself. Way too many! There's no way I can fight my way through, but . . . What about Berlyn? What if she's on the other side of them? What if they're separating me from her? Then what do I do?

A familiar chuckle of sardonic irony sounded somewhere in the young farmer's brain. Bloody, typical Corlaiys luck . . .

Nervous perspiration joining the bands of heat-slicked sweat, Calyx took another step back, tugging impatiently at Aitchley's sleeve. "Hey . . . uh . . . kid?" he risked asking. "Can we go now?"

Before Aitchley was able to respond, shrubbery suddenly parted behind them. Warily, both dwarf and farmer pivoted to face the new threat, yet a belated sense of relief coupled with another jolt of surprise robbed Aitchley of any reaction.

Backed by the tree-filtered light of the rising sun—her skirt in ragged tatters about her slender legs—Berlyn stepped free of the foliage, gray-green eyes fixed on Aitchley. Her hair was rumpled and splayed about her face—and blood dotted and ringed her neck, arm, and leg—yet she flashed a smile so beautiful Aitchley all but forgot the flowery monsters at his back.

Harris Blind-Eye and Thiazi BladeWalker stood on either side of the young blonde.

"Aitchley?" Berlyn queried his earlier scream.

Aitchley launched himself at the petite scullery maid, hoisting her off the ground in a tight embrace. "Berlyn!" he exclaimed. "Where were you?"

The blonde winced as Aitchley's hug sparked a few sore spots. "Right here," she replied. "You ran right past me when you first showed up."

Aitchley didn't even have any time to feel stupid as a murderous limb unexpectedly lashed out over his head.

"Save the reunion for later," Calyx advised, pushing past the young couple. "We've got to get back to Gjuki and Poinqart. There's no telling how many more of these things are!"

Vines exploded out of the brush on Calyx's right.

Harris smirked gravely. "I'd say a whole lotta 'em."

Tentatively, Gjuki stared out into the dizzying jumble of green, using what little light managed to squeeze through the thick cover of trees high above. A fine white mist roiled through the EverDark—a result of the fading rains and increasing temperature—and the usual calls, hoots, and cackles from the canopy filled the rain forest. The Rhagana had not seen or encountered any of the Rafflesia, for the last few minutes, and that, for some reason, did not sit well with him. He knew the Rafflesia were primarily nocturnal hunters—they were not, as the past few moments had proven, very resourceful, though, against stronger prey—yet Gjuki also knew they would not cease just because the sun had risen. There was food to be found in their domain . . . the Rafflesia would not stop until they had feasted.

Aside from the deafening ruckus of birds, insects, and animals hidden high in the rainforest canopy, the only other sounds were the ocassional *plink-plunk* of raindrops still winding their way through the maze of leaves. Perhaps the Rafflesia *had* given up, but Gjuki could not bring himself to believe that. They were tenacious and bloodthirsty, enjoying the ruthlessness of the hunt. And they would not stop until their hunger was satiated.

All senses trained on the rain forest around him, Gjuki caught the sounds of someone shoving through the brush, the crack and splinter of disturbed foliage barely audible above the cacophony from the treetops.

Eyfura tightened her grip around her spear. "Someone comes," she noted.

He could not understand why, yet the anxiety swirling in his belly intensified as Gjuki stared at the tangle of vegetation before him. What good would all their guarding do if their friends had fallen elsewhere? the Rhagana mused darkly. And what of the Daeminase? Could it be them pushing their way through the jungle before him? Were all their trials for naught? Would things end here . . . caught between Rafflesia and Daeminase?

Bushes parted and saplings bowed as Aitchley and the others came vaulting out of the foliage, a frenzied panic to their pace. The thick sap of Rafflesia blood stained their weapons and clothes, and Gjuki could smell the approaching wave of foul

decomposition, knowing full well that the Rafflesia had not—
as he had hoped—returned to their beds.

Aitchley waved those waiting forward. "Go! Go!" he yelled.

Obediently, Camera 12 moved to the young man's side, followed by Berlyn and Poinqart. Harris and Calyx fought their
way through the undergrowth together, helping one another in
a bizarre moment of comradeship, and Thiazi leapt vines and
flowering plants with the unclothed grace of all Rhagana. Captain d'Ane was a fast-moving glow practically lost amid the
thin, fine mist of the EverDark.

Gjuki held his ground as the others ran past him.

Hurdling a cluster of flowering ginger, Eyfura halted, looking
back at the gardener with a glint of puzzlement in her pearl-
black eyes. "WorldDweller!" she called. "Hurry!"

Gjuki gave a single look over one shoulder, fists clenched at
his sides. "Go, SpearWielder!" he shouted back. "I will buy
us some time."

Uncertainty drawn on her barklike features, Eyfura gave the
rain forest a cursory glance. Ahead, she knew, lay freedom.
Ahead, they would be free of the Rafflesia's domain. Ahead
led back to the Valley of the Diamond Rains. Ahead was safety.

Eyfura tightened her grip on her spear and stepped back purposefully to Gjuki's side. "We leave together or not at all,"
she declared.

On a face usually devoid of emotion, Gjuki smiled a proud,
friendly smile.

The EverDark was a blur of muted greens and browns,
striped by shafts of growing sunlight that managed to slip in
through the leaves. Blindly, Aitchley shoved his way through
the labyrinth of vegetation, letting Camera 12 lead the way.
Branches whipped and snapped almost as cruelly as the Rafflesia's thorny limbs, yet the young man could not hear any
sounds of pursuit . . . not that he could really hear anything
other than his own frantic running. Yet none of that mattered
now. In a few more days they'd get back to the Rhaganas'
mushroom village, and once there, they could pick up their
horses. These days of endless walking would be at an end,
and—more importantly—no more running from creatures like
the Daeminase or Rafflesia. Once they had their horses back,
they could ride all the way to the Dragon's Lair and be done
with it!

The jungle unexpectedly thinned out before the young man, offering him a gloomy gallery of huge trees and a wide stream in his path. The canopy overhead still managed to remain intact—casting only leaf-filtered light down upon the river—and the waters were a deep, rich green, the air above filled with the hovering dance of tiny little midges. Gray-green mosses clung to the trunks of giant trees, and the whole area had an eerie, almost ethereal quality, the green waters of the stream suffusing the gallery with an emerald glow.

Thiazi stepped to the edge of the stream and began to wade across. "We must cross to be safe," the BladeWalker explained, the waters rising only as high as her unclothed thighs. "This stream marks the boundary of the Rafflesia's domain."

Harris gave the green waters a skeptical glance. "What?" he jeered. "Can't they cross moving water or something?"

"The Rafflesia are anchored by their root system," Thiazi answered, climbing out onto the opposite shore. "They cannot thrive in this region because after heavy rains this stream floods the entire gallery. Any Rafflesia rooted here would be drowned." She waved an impatient hand at those on the southern bank. "Quickly now," she urged.

Even before Calyx could voice his dread about water, Aitchley felt a sudden tightening in his gut. He had glanced back casually at those behind him and suddenly realized not everyone was there.

"Gjuki!" the young man exclaimed. "Where is he?"

Calyx watched with a sarcastic frown as the young farmer went dashing back the way they had come. "Oh, for Quin-Tyna's sake!" he grumbled. "Here we go again!"

With all the supple grace of a plant blowing in the wind, Gjuki feinted sideways and dodged, hearing the slice of black thorns hiss dangerously close to his head. The jungle was alive with movement—every bush and shrub infested by the vinelike monstrosities that were the Rafflesia—and ivylike arms flailed and writhed like the thick fronds of some hideous fern. The stink was overpowering—clogging the Rhagana's throat with the stench of rotten meat—and the bodies of dead Rafflesia were beginning to pile up around him, their bloody sap turning the leaf litter to a ichorous swamp.

Eyfura ripped her spear out of another creature's flowerlike head, paying little heed to the white sap that splashed her chest.

"Are adventures such as this a common thing, World-Dweller?" she asked innocently. "Do fights like this occur in the World Outside?"

Gjuki snapped another Rafflesia's head off with a single twist of his powerful hands. "Conflicts like this are rather rare, SpearWielder," he replied emotionlessly. "I spent over twenty years tending garden for Lord Tampenteire and never in that time was I ever attacked. Not even by a single rosebush."

Eyfura's spear drove up and around, punching through the vinelike chest of another flower. "Perhaps I could accompany you on your journey back," she mused. "I feel somewhat jaded now that I have had a taste for such excitement."

Gjuki offered her another—albeit shyer—smile. "Your presence would be most welcome, SpearWielder," he said. "I will discuss your desire with Master Aitchley."

The Rhagana female nodded. "Many thanks, World-Dweller," she said.

Foliage unexpectedly divided behind them, and Aitchley came stumbling free of the green, a look of panic on his youthful features. Sweat streamed down his face from beneath his hat, and there was no mistaking the terror that sparked in his blue-green eyes.

Gjuki turned a cursory eye on the young farmer. "Master Aitchley," he said, a trace of surprise in his voice, "what is wrong? Has something happened?"

Aitchley struggled to find his voice, his own fear and confusion momentarily silencing him. "I . . . uh . . . what . . . you . . ." He finally managed to get his breath back. "What in the Pits are you two doing here?" he shouted at them. "Come on! We've found the way out!"

Gjuki turned his back on the horde of Rafflesia. "Good," he declared. "The smell was becoming unbearable."

Vines suddenly wrapped around the Rhagana's arm, jerking him back and trying to pull him into the brush. More limbs shot up through the greenery, swarming around the Rhagana. Black thorns cut into leathery flesh, and Gjuki was pulled forcibly off his feet, reeled in toward the army of carnivorous flowers.

The Cavalier's sword jumped into Aitchley's hand. "Gjuki!" the young man screamed, leaping forward to help.

Silver sang through the thick, humid air, chopping through plant fiber in a spray of thick sap. Green limbs thrashed and

squirmed on every side, and deadly black thorns gleamed in
the early-morning sun, yet more and more of them slithered
out of the undergrowth. Like a nest of eyeless serpents, the
tentacles squirmed and coiled over Gjuki's body, practically
engulfing him in folds of black-thorned flora.

"Gjuki!" Aitchley screamed again, dismembering inhuman
arms with every swing of his ancestor's blade.

Sputtering—his face covered with pasty blood—Gjuki struggled back to his feet, discarding an amputated limb that still
tried to entwine around his throat. White fluid drenched the
fungoid gardener—and Aitchley was unable to tell which was
Rhagana blood and which was Rafflesia—but Gjuki clambered
upright, a grimace on his face as he favored his right leg.

"My apologies, Master Aitchley," the Rhagana said. "I was
careless."

Aitchley helped the Rhagana limp away from the press of
Rafflesia. "Who cares if you were careless," the young man
retorted. "At least you're not dead."

As more creepers and vines whipped through the walls of
vegetation, Aitchley moved forward, allowing Gjuki to lean
against his shoulder. Thick sap smeared Aitchley's face and
arms, and he could tell the added weight of Gjuki was slowing
him down. It would only be a matter of time before they were
both caught in the Rafflesia's murderous tentacles.

Throwing a glance over one shoulder at the following Rafflesia, Aitchley felt his stomach suddenly knot painfully. He
had thought she was right beside him . . . thought she had
helped pull Gjuki free of the Rafflesia . . . yet Aitchley now saw
that Eyfura had not retreated when he had. Her spear was a
deadly flash of wood and steel, and Rafflesia continued to pile
up around her, unable to get to the young man and injured
gardener.

An imperceptible dread closed in around Aitchley's heart.
"Eyfura!" he shouted. "Come on!"

The SpearWielder turned to look back, what might have been
a faint smile stretching her barklike lips. Thick sap coated the
tip of her spear, and droplets of thick blood spilled down her
slender frame. Tentacles flailed on every side of her, and she
hardly reacted as black thorns encircled her wrist, snatching at
her arm and tearing free her only weapon.

Limbs exploded from the foliage, coiling and wrapping
around the Rhagana in a sudden frenzy of motion. Sharp thorns

ripped and tore through leathery flesh, and ivylike arms groped and pulled at her body. Her legs were jerked out from under her, tugged in opposite directions, and pale blood ran from the innumerable cuts and wounds crisscrossing her frame. Aitchley could only watch in horrified bewilderment as more limbs rose out of the jungle to wrap around her, tearing and pulling like starving xlves at a carcass.

Eyfura managed to catch Aitchley's eye, the vague smile still on her lips. Then she exploded.

White blood spattered the Bentwoods.

12

When a Rhagana Dies

Summer had come to the Dragon's Ridge. Grasses that had once been a verdant green now turned a dull, yellowish brown in the heat of the sun, and the leaves of trees crimped and curled at the edges, burned by unrelenting temperatures. The air was dry and stale, and there was a heaviness to the cloudless blue sky, an invisible weight that dropped down from above and drained the energy out of all living things.

Nicander Tamptenteire stared out at the summertime mountains from the relative coolness of the Dragon's Lair, keeping himself safely concealed in the shadows. The high grasses slowly swayed in a weak breeze—rustling against one another as if exchanging low whispers—and the odd birdcall would sound from either the grasses or a nearby tree. The large boulders and craggy rocks outside the Dragon's Lair entrance seemed to soak in the harsh rays of the sun and reflect them back out, their surfaces becoming hot, brownish-yellow mirrors of concentrated sunlight. The dirt and barren patches of mountainside weren't much better to look at, and Nicander found that if he stared at any spot too long, his eyes would ache and purple and blue spots would dance and caper behind his eyelids.

Reluctantly, the young nobleman ventured out into the heat, sliding almost soundlessly into the ocean of tall grasses. He scratched fitfully at the thick growth of hair spreading like a moss across his face, and no trace of haughtiness or youth remained in his light brown eyes. Now there was only a glint of feral hunger and a kind of frightening instability.

Nicander's fingers flexed and clenched compulsively around the handle of the ornamental dagger in his grasp, as unaware of the action as he was of his obsessive bouts of face scratching. He had found the weapon among the tribute and offerings within the Dragon's Lair itself. It was an incredible knife—undoubtedly dwarven and decorated with enough gems and precious metals to buy a small village—and Nicander could only guess grave robbers had missed it because of its chance concealment under a pile of pottery shards. Amazingly enough, after nearly two hundred years the blade was still sharp and usable—an unspoken testimony to dwarven craftsmanship—and it was keen enough to whittle at wood yet remain unblunted to clean and eviscerate anything Nicander caught. Who knew what other useful items might be farther inside the cave, yet Nicander had not been able to find the courage to descend beyond the first few feet. There were things down there in the darkness—strange shapes and eerie sounds lurking in that amphitheater of pitch—and Nicander had resigned himself to camping just inside the cavern's mammoth entrance, neatly protected from any dangers and inclement weather by the smooth curvature of the enormous rock.

Moving with practiced skill, Nicander slowly dropped to one knee, light brown eyes peering through the tall grass. He could just make out the burrow snare he had rigged up outside the opening of some small animal's home, and he felt his spirits drop when he realized it hadn't been sprung. Perhaps it was his own fault, the nobleman mused bleakly. Perhaps he hadn't built the snare properly, but no . . . he had caught other small animals with similar notched peg snares. All he had to do was be a bit more patient.

Nicander eyed his work critically. The snare hadn't been all that hard to build, and even easier with his dwarven knife. All it had required was some strong cord taken from a fraying piece of tapestry back at the Dragon's Lair, two notched, L-shaped pegs he had carved himself, and the help of a nearby sapling. Staking one peg into the ground, the cord was tied into a noose at one end, attached to the other peg, then looped over the sapling, bending the tree downward to provide tension. Then it was only a matter of hooking the two L-shaped pegs together and waiting. When the animal left its burrow, its head would

pass through the noose and—if Nicander had made the loop
the right size—when it tried to pass the rest of its body through,
its shoulders would jar the cord, detach the pegs, and release
the bent sapling, tightening the noose around the creature's
neck and jerking it up into the air, where it strangled.

At least . . . that's what it was supposed to do.

And to think, Nicander mused arrogantly to himself, I hadn't
really been paying that much attention to Pomeroy when he
had been going on about such rot.

His pride fleeting, Nicander gave the empty snare a frown
and moved through the grass to where he had concealed another
notched peg snare, positioning the noose upright between stalks
of grass in what he hoped was a fairly used trail. He wished
that some of Pomeroy's lessons had stayed with him a little
better than others—all that dung about thatching and building
a shelter didn't do him much good what with the cave so close
at hand—and it probably would have helped to remember more
about what plants were edible and which were not. He had
found clumps of fireweed around the perimeter of the cave and
remembered that the young shoots could be boiled and eaten
like asparagus, but he wasn't sure if the sumac berries he had
discovered were of the poisonous variety or not. Gaal knows
what other kinds of plants he could have added to his meager
diet if he had only been paying a little bit more attention. This
was all Corlaiys's fault!

Nicander felt the rumbling discontent of his belly as he came
across his second snare and found it empty. He could feel the
weakness scurry through his legs and cause a kind of light-
headedness, yet he had grown accustomed to such feelings. He
had learned over the last few weeks how to survive on his own,
and—although he wasn't having much luck now—he had managed to stay alive on whatever he could catch. He also had to
assume the small mountain stream about half a league from his
cavern home helped. If anything, he always had an ample supply of fresh water, but even now, the summer warmth was
shrinking Nicander's life-giving stream to a small brook, and
if the heat continued to intensify . . . he recalled all too vividly
that part of Pomeroy's teachings:

Human beings could not go without water for more than a
few days before dying.

Sudden footsteps broke through the mountain stillness, the
crunch and rustle of heavy feet striding through high grass.

Frantically, Nicander threw a wild-eyed scan at the mountainside, a powerful surge of adrenaline fueling his wasted and weak body. As silently as possible, he loped back to the entrance of the Dragon's Lair, his scratched and dirty fingers curling around his dwarven dagger. He tried to stay low to the ground—tried to see who was coming before they saw him—and fought back the growing hatred and eager anticipation that raged within him.

Corlaiys? his hunger-starved mind wondered. Was it Corlaiys? Had the dung-smeared mudshoveler finally made his way here? Was this to be the moment of Nicander's triumph? Would all his waiting finally be over? Was this to be the day that he, Nicander Tampenteire, brought the Cavalier back to life?

Crouched in the shadows of the great lair, Nicander watched with growing astonishment as a manlike figure crested the rise. Summer sunlight blazed off the man's slender body like the fires from a dwarven forge, and metal flashed and gleamed in the light of midday. The figure seemed to be wearing a full suit of silver armor—an incredible piece of craftsmanship that seemed to mimic the human anatomy—and it stopped at the top of the mountain trail and stepped out toward a rocky ledge, glassy gray eyes sweeping out across the land below.

Nicander struggled with the paranoia and fear ravaging his thoughts. Who was this? the young noble demanded to know. No one had come here in two hundred years! Why was this person here now? And who was he? Was he someone here to see the cave where the great Dragon Myxomycetes once lived, or was he a friend of Corlaiys? Or worse yet . . . was he someone who had the same idea as Nicander? Someone who also planned to ambush the pathetic little farm boy and steal away the elixir for his own purposes? Was that it? Was this person a threat? Did this newcomer dare to stand between Nicander and his rightful heir to the name Tampenteire?

With a single, agonized warcry torn from the very gut of his delusions, Nicander launched himself at the mysterious figure of gleaming silver, slamming hard into the metal of its lower back. Servos whirred and clicked as the man-shaped figure turned to regard the crazed young noble before the mountain ledge was suddenly knocked out from under it, dropping the armored construct off the mountainside and into gravity's cruel, downward grip.

Tin William's videocamera eyes irised wide in what might

have been surprise as it plummeted to the craggy rocks miles below. "Exclamation," the robot exclaimed: "Oh, fuck!"

Butterflies flitted in the streamers of sunlight, and birds called from high above in the canopy. Sunlight danced like diamonds across the surface of the great Mistillteinn River, and Berlyn enjoyed the heady scent of the streaming waters, letting the rush of the river fill her ears. Not as many trees closed about them now—thinned out by the enormous river—yet a great number somehow managed to survive despite constant flooding. Sometimes the river branched off in a number of different directions—separated by vees of black, highly polished rocks—and Gjuki made it a point to crisscross the river as many times as possible since leaving the tangled confines of the EverDark, hoping to make it more difficult for the Daeminase to trail them.

Berlyn couldn't help throwing a wary glance over one shoulder, a familiar feeling of uneasiness twisting at her innards. So far, she mused, we've been lucky. The Daeminase haven't caught up with us . . . yet.

The blonde's concerned gaze shifted to the young man walking ahead of her, his own eyes locked on the rain forest before them. He had hardly spoken a word since that morning in the EverDark, and even though nearly two weeks had passed since the attack, Aitchley showed no signs of pulling free of his depression. He kept his gaze fixed on the jungle ahead as if staring at some far-off point in the distance and said nothing to no one. He ate very little. Slept alone and distanced from the rest. Something eating away at him from the inside.

Berlyn frowned to herself. He couldn't still be blaming himself for Eyfura's death, could he? she wondered.

The young girl looked to her left at the great rushing tide of water, trying not to let Aitchley's depression bring her down as well. She had made her attempts to cheer him up—tried to talk him out of his melancholy—but he just wouldn't listen. Not even Captain d'Ane could say anything that helped, and— after the first week—everybody had just pretty much given up. If Aitchley wanted to be a wartheaded muggwort about it, so be it. There didn't seem to be anything anyone could do to change his mind.

And Gjuki's refusal to let Aitchley use the Elixir of Life had only made matters worse.

"What in the Pits is wrong with you?" Berlyn could remember Aitchley screaming at the gardener. "Liahturetart said there were two doses! We can use one on Eyfura! She doesn't have to die!"

But Gjuki was emotionlessly calm. "It is not the way of the Bentwoods, Master Aitchley," the Rhagana had replied enigmatically. "I will explain later."

But he never did explain, and Aitchley's mood had only gotten worse.

Berlyn pursed her lips. I wish there was something I could do to help pull him out of this, she thought.

A growing rumble began to fill the Bentwoods from the west, and Gjuki guided the group slightly northward, beginning a descent away from the river and through ever-thickening trees and lianas. Berlyn couldn't help flinching every time a vine brushed too close to her body—frightening memories flashing through her mind—yet the tingle of the elixir had long ago healed any wounds caused by the Rafflesia's deadly black thorns. Even Harris was looking a little better.

The rolling thunder of the Mistillteinn Falls grew louder in Berlyn's ears, and the jungle unexpectedly parted to reveal a panoramic view of the lower rainforest basin. A brief flash of vertigo shivered through the young girl's frame—the unexpected drop was dizzying—but she felt a thrill scurry after her abrupt fear. A cool, refreshing breeze—no longer blocked by walls of solid vegetation—billowed through the blonde's platinum hair, and the silver-white spray and roar of the falls crashed and tumbled on her left.

Stretching nearly to the edge of the horizon, deep, rich green filled Berlyn's sight. Huge waves of treetops, clustered so neatly and compact that they looked like one single plant, roiled and dipped like an emerald sea. Billions of leaves interlocked without touching their neighbors—it saved them from disease, Gjuki had told her—and the rain forest suddenly resembled one great big crown of broccoli, interrupted only by the occasional emergent rising higher than its brothers and sisters.

Below them and to the left—half-lost between jungle and cliff wall—hid the Valley of the Diamond Rains, its Rhagana village cloaked in a constant spray of moisture and enduring shade. Even the mushroom houses that Berlyn knew could grow as high as twelve feet looked like tiny little fungi from this height, and she felt the vertiginous excitement offer a boost of strength to her weary and tired body.

She threw an awe-filled glance at Aitchley; his face was stern and his gaze was blank.

Guiding the quest down the sloping hillside back toward the valley, Gjuki picked out a careful trail. The brief respite of fresh, circulating air vanished as Camera 12 followed the Rhagana back into the press of the rainforest trees, and Berlyn felt the humidity close back in around her like a tight fist.

There was a look of certain doom on Calyx's face as he huffed and puffed his way down the sloping terrain. "Don't like it," the dwarf grumbled. "Daeminase are following us for certain. They have to be after all that noise and stink back in the EverDark." He nearly slipped on the plant-choked slope, saving himself by grabbing at a pink-and-white orchid; his look grew even darker. "Deathless bastards are gonna come roaring through here just like they did to the *Kwau*," he went on. "Isn't there another way around?"

As surefooted as a mountain goat, Gjuki stepped lightly down the hillside. "Remember, Master Calyx, there is only one passage over the Mistillteinn Falls and it is in the caves behind the falls themselves," the fungoid gardener said. "We have no choice but to return to my village."

Calyx frowned. "Yeah, but—"

"We have no other alternative," Gjuki interrupted. "We must go through the valley." He gave the dwarf a rare smile. "Your concern is appreciated, but I will make sure my people are well aware of the dangers. They will take certain precautions that the *Kwau* were unable to."

The Rhagana's words hardly reassured the dwarven smith. "Precautions?" he muttered back. "What kind of precautions? Mass suicide?"

As they descended farther into the shadowy valley, Berlyn felt her own anxieties burn at her breast. They had to assume that Daeminase were following them again—no amount of trickery on Baugi's part could have hidden the stink of Rafflesia or the odor of burning wood—and sooner or later the monsters would follow their trail straight through the valley. It might not be all that long before they were leaping and sprinting down this very slope! What manner of precautions could the Rhagana take when those eyeless monstrosities came tearing through their village after the quest?

"You're not going to try and fight them, are you?" worried the blonde.

"Rhagana know better than to fight when the odds are against them, Berlyn GoldenHair," Thiazi replied. "When the Daeminase arrive, we shall simply not be there."

"You're going to evacuate the whole village?" Harris blurted, the lawlessness inside him whispering the criminal possibilities of such an event. "They're gonna tear your homes down around your bunging ears!"

"You forget," Gjuki corrected the thief, "the Daeminase are not out to wantonly destroy. They are after us. More specifically . . . they are after you, Harris Blind-Eye. An empty village should offer them little in the way of temptation."

Harris scowled, the reminder that it was his blood that awoke the Daeminase not sitting well with him. "Sez you, plantman," the southern-city outlaw snarled. "Minute those bungholers leave, you're gonna come back to a village that's nothing but mushroom pâté. You might as well leave a sign that says tear down our homes,'cause that's exactly what they're gonna do."

Neither Rhagana seemed impressed. "And even if they do," Thiazi remarked, "our people will continue. A village—unlike a life—can be rebuilt."

Berlyn was momentarily startled to hear a low mutter come from Aitchley's direction. "Yeah," she heard the young man murmur, "tell that to Eyfura."

They walked the rest of the way in silence, the increasing rumble of the Mistillteinn Falls making further discussion difficult. Berlyn had forgotten how loud the rush of falling water was—like the constant boom of thunder filling the entire valley—and she could already feel the light drizzle of spray as they neared the Rhagana village. A couple of times she was surprised to find other Rhagana swelling their ranks, stepping seamlessly from the rain forest and joining their group, their black-tipped spears held out before them. It was kind of unsettling, she noted. One second they weren't there; the next, they were. If Berlyn didn't know any better, she'd think they had some of those magical cloaks in Harris's backpack. In all, it made her feel better about Gjalk and Baugi.

If Rhagana could hide in plain sight like that, she thought with some conviction, they could probably survive the Daeminase coming through here.

By the time the quest-members reached level ground, a large crowd had gathered at the base of the valley. Escorted by more and more sentinels that seemed to just step right out of the middle of trees, the nine returned to the Valley of the Diamond Rains, a flutter of relief passing through Berlyn. Even though they were still being trailed by the Daeminase, it did the girl good to be back in a populated area . . . to see the familiar sights of houses and streets surrounding her.

Anyway, it sure beat icy columbariums and caverns of volcanic rock.

As soon as they were back in the village, Thiazi and Gjuki began barking out quick orders, the crowd of curious Rhagana dispersing to obey. Sentinels went sprinting back into the surrounding jungle while others went to gather food and prepare the group's horses. Still others hurried down the marshy avenues to inform those that had not turned out for the group's return, alerting the whole village to the coming danger.

Berlyn felt a hand touch her arm through the sudden brush of activity. Questioningly, she looked up into Gjuki's leathery face. "Why don't you and Master Aitchley get some rest," the gardener advised. "My people will handle things from here."

Feeling somewhat overwhelmed by the unexpected bustle, Berlyn nodded dumbly, allowing herself to be lead through the muddy streets of the Rhagana village to the large mushroom house where she and Aitchley had stayed before. All around her, humanoid fungi moved quickly through the town, preparing for whatever dangers might follow the quest, and Berlyn felt a pang of guilt for not helping. The thought of rest had made her suddenly realize how very tired she was, but all the activity made her think that maybe she should do something as well. Thanks to Gjuki's guidance, they had put a day or two between them and the Daeminase—perhaps more if any of Baugi's ploys had worked—and all the hidden sentinels would alert them to the Daeminase's presence, giving them plenty of time to leave before the monsters arrived. Maybe it would be better if she took this opportunity to sleep and just let the Rhagana do what they were doing.

Berlyn had little choice. She was asleep before her head hit the crude pillow of sweetly sour moss.

Spray like a light rain filled the shadow of the immense valley, and Berlyn relished the cool breeze that winged its way through the village. Free of the claustrophobic crowd of trees, the humidity was not nearly as intolerable here, and the constant drizzle from the nearby falls was cool and refreshing rather than stale and stifling. The sun started its slow westward descent as Berlyn sat comfortably in a mushroom-cap chair, a needle and thread and the tattered remains of her dress in her lap. Not having anything else to wear, she had slipped into the scant outfit given to her by the *Kwau* and found the loincloth much cooler and less confining than her dress. Even as she stitched up some of the larger tears in her skirt, the blonde considered the possibility of wearing her *Kwau* garments for the rest of their time in the Bentwoods. She was more comfortable in them, and her self-consciousness was practically gone. After all, the Rhagana ran around naked! Why shouldn't she be as free?

Trying to repair another slash in the frayed fabric—she never had been very handy with a needle—Berlyn glanced up at the mushroom village. Most of the activity had died down and life had returned to normal by the time she had woken up from her nap, but she couldn't help feeling the uneasy rumble in her stomach at the thought that the Daeminase were still out there. Missives from sentinels as far as twenty leagues away reported no signs of the creatures, and Calyx had agreed to spend the night only after a long, heated discussion with Captain d'Ane. Of course, the dwarven smith concluded that the Daeminase would catch up with them while they slept, and eat them all, but Captain d'Ane had persuaded him to let them stay if they promised to leave as soon as the sun rose the next morning. Grudgingly—probably influenced by his own weariness—Calyx had relented.

Berlyn drew in a hiss of air as she accidentally pricked herself with her sewing needle, sticking the injured finger in her mouth. Gray-green eyes narrowed as she inspected her work—it was slipshod and crooked, but at least it resembled a skirt again—and she checked the dress for any other major tears. She had decided to leave a few—she had gotten used to the freedom of movement some of the rips provided—but the more . . . strategic tears had to be fixed. She *would* be returning to civilized areas in a few weeks.

Inspecting the dress for other damage, Berlyn heard footsteps slosh almost soundlessly through the marshy street. She glanced up to see Gjuki approach her, his calm, expressionless face still somehow friendly and amicable. Although he wore clothing, Berlyn thought she could still probably pick him out from among all the other Rhagana if he did not. There was something about his face—a familiarity that Berlyn would never forget. She had no choice but to smile as he neared.

The gardener gave a single nod of greeting as he stopped before her. "Miss Berlyn," he said. "Master Aitchley. Would you come with me, please?"

Setting aside her dress, Berlyn blinked a few times to clear her eyes of surprise. Quiet and brooding, Aitchley had been sitting up against the side of their mushroom cottage, slumped in the mud near her side. He had been so silent, the blonde hadn't even realized he was there.

"I don't want to go anywhere with you," the young farmer growled at the gardener.

Gjuki held out a hand. "Please, Master Aitchley," he said. "I said I would explain, and that is why I am here. Will you not come at least to hear me out?"

With a disbelieving grunt, Aitchley pulled himself to his feet and started after the fungoid gardener, a belligerent, challenging gait to his walk. Berlyn hurried after them, her bare feet sinking in the damp soil. She didn't understand Aitchley's attitude— why be so rude if Gjuki was going to explain himself? Did Aitchley enjoy being depressed?—and there was very little he could do about Eyfura now. If he could accept the fact that Captain d'Ane had wanted to remain dead—and how strange did that sound?—why couldn't he get over the fact that Gjuki believed Eyfura should stay the same? Why was he being so confrontational?

Leading the pair through the small village, Gjuki took them down a muddy road to a corner of the town bordering the rain forest. Dark gray shadows covered the ground like a matting of blackness, and the spray from the falls still sprinkled a light mist around them. A few trees encroached upon the village, and Gjuki weaved his way through them, stepping across a well-worn path. Only a few trees could survive so close to the marshy, saturated soil of the valley, and there were wide stretches of empty, muddy ground between them even though their branches met overhead to form a thin canopy.

Aitchley gave the sporadic clustering of trees a frown. "Yeah? So?" he snorted, scanning the area with a sardonic eye. "You gonna tell another story about ants and the trees they live in?"

What might have been a hurt expression passed briefly across the Rhagana's face. "No, Master Aitchley," Gjuki replied. "I am going to explain why my people need to die.''

A jolt of surprise suddenly arced up Berlyn's spine as Gjuki stepped near an enormous tree trunk, and the young blonde abruptly realized it wasn't a tree trunk at all. A great leathery stalk that mimicked tree bark drove down into the marshy earth, and the deep, gray-brown color had fooled the scullery maid into thinking it was just another tree, but—when her gaze slowly lifted skyward—she caught sight of the huge, umbrellalike pileus that cast them all in shadow. Adnated gills ringed the underside of the umbonated cap high above them, and the smell of the giant mushroom was slightly soapy, filling the tiny copse of trees. Its dark gray cap and pale yellow gills reached almost as high as the treetops, and Berlyn noticed smaller, bracketlike fungi growing up along its massive stalk.

"Daeminase Pits,'' the young girl breathed her awe. "What is this thing?''

Gjuki stepped near a small opening carved into the stalk of the giant mushroom. "It is called the Nidus,'' he answered. "It is where I shall make myself clear.'' He stepped inside. "Please, follow me.''

Wordlessly, Aitchley and Berlyn trailed the Rhagana, not even Aitchley's resentment able to keep the awe off his face. Like the smaller mushrooms of the village, Berlyn could tell this structure was natural, yet she had never seen a toadstool this big. It stood almost as high as the Tridome back in Solsbury, and its stalk had to have been about six to ten feet in diameter.

The humidity inside the great mushroom was worse than anything she had ever felt before, and Berlyn was glad she only wore her biarki-fur loincloth. The soapy stink of its pale, fleshy interior filled the blonde's nostrils, and it seemed even larger inside than it was outside. Great catacombs of yellowish-white hyphae crisscrossed and honeycombed the enormous chamber, creating a kind of alien labyrinth, and Berlyn noticed a few Rhagana tending to strange-looking shoots and bizarrely twisted crops, checking their growth and recording their height, moving from plant to plant like meticulous farmers.

Gjuki looked away from the otherworldly scene and peered down at his two friends. "Till now, no one but Rhagana have entered the Nidus,'' he said emotionlessly. "You should feel honored.''

Berlyn turned perplexed eyes on the weblike chambers inside

the gigantic mushroom. I don't get it, she admitted to herself. How does this help anything? Does Gjuki think feeling honored is going to make Aitchley understand? I thought he was going to explain why he didn't want Aitchley to use the elixir on Eyfura—

The sudden, awed comment from Aitchley shattered the scullery maid's train of thought. "Are those . . . are those baby Rhagana?" the young man wondered.

A faint smile crossed Gjuki's barklike features. "This is our seedbed, Master Aitchley," he replied. "Our Nidus. It is here where we come to reproduce. Where our offspring grow to adulthood in relative safety."

Another shudder of surprise gripped Berlyn's slender frame. Aitchley was right! she suddenly noticed with wide-eyed shock. Those were baby Rhagana! She hadn't noticed it before, but they were miniature versions of the adults, all compacted and hunkered down like a flower that had yet to blossom. A fine, semitransparent sheen of wax seemed to cover each Rhagana spore, and unlike their parents, they had no feet, their stalklike legs actually growing up out of the soft, marshy soil.

Blinking, Berlyn managed to pull her eyes away from the smaller versions of Rhagana sprouting up out of the dirt, but she was unable to find her voice.

Aitchley could only gape as well.

Gjuki's smile grew as he waved a hand out to encompass the interior of the giant mushroom. "Rhagana are fungi, Master Aitchley," the gardener explained. "We grow in damp, shaded places, and unlike true plants, we contain no chlorophyll and are unable to turn the sun's energy into food. We are, in fact, the fruiting bodies of the mycelium you see before you, and as a fungus, we spore to reproduce." Pearl-black eyes fixed intently on the young man. "Have you ever seen a puffball spore?"

Tearing his eyes away from the Nidus of young Rhagana, Aitchley nodded slowly. "I . . . uh . . . Yeah . . . I think so," he sputtered.

"When it is ready, a puffball releases its spores most explosively," Gjuki went on. "Sometimes nothing more than a single raindrop can trigger this eruption of life. For us, it is the same. As we grow older we produce spores in asci. These spore sacs are located at what would be your chest cavity and groin region. When a Rhagana dies, these spores are released to ensure the continuation of our species. We do not need to mate like your kind. Indeed, some of us are exact duplicates of our parent. When we feel the time upon us, we come here . . . to the Nidus. The CareTakers and SporeTenders see to our needs and help us in our last, and greatest, act. However, there are times when we are unable to come here. Times when we die out in the uncertainty of the Bentwoods or beyond. Even still, as our life force leaves us, we will spore just the same. We shall cast out our children and pray to All That Is that some will live to reach maturity and return to the valley of our people's birth. And that is what happened to Eyfura, Master Aitchley. She did not just die . . . she gave birth to a whole new generation of SpearWielders."

All the sudden information had a hard time pushing its way past Aitchley's shock. "But . . . but . . ." he flustered.

Gjuki smiled gently. "I myself was quite fortunate Harris's blade struck me where it did. If not, I would not be here speaking with you." He gave the alien-looking Nidus a cursory scan. "Death is not an end for my people, Master Aitchley," he continued. "It is a beginning." Tiny, black eyes searched the young man's face. "Now do you understand why I did not want you to use the elixir on Eyfura's remains?"

Aitchley still fought for the use of his tongue. "I . . . I . . . I . . ." he stuttered. He finally gave up trying to make any sense, staring in astonishment at the weird, otherworldly farmland-nursery. "I understand," he responded.

Gjuki's smile widened. "Good," the gardener replied, placing a warm hand upon the young man's shoulder. "Now let us leave this place. I would hate for the CareTakers to mistake me as one who is ready."

Berlyn smiled back at the Rhagana, realizing he had made an attempt at humor, but Aitchley was still overwhelmed by the images before his eyes. The way the smaller Rhagana resembled such obvious plant life. The way the adult Rhagana moved about the spores, tilling and cultivating like farmers tending their crops. The way the spores—as they grew to maturity—began to resemble their parents more and more.

And, through it all, the young man couldn't get the droning buzz of Tin William's voice out of his head, its inhuman words suddenly taking on newer—and even greater—meaning.

Life and death are part of the natural order, Aitchley Corlaiys, the construct had said. *When a species interferes, disaster is the only result.*

13

Ambushed

Stars twinkled and glittered in a sky unobstructed by trees. Aitchley Corlaiys hardly noticed as he walked out of the Bentwoods and into the lush, fertile valley between the Mistillteinn and Alsace rivers, his black-and-white stallion following obediently behind him. Tall grasses rustled in a warm, westwardly breeze—tinged by the distant heat of the Molten Dunes—and it felt as if a great weight had suddenly been lifted from the surrounding air. Although the night was still warm, the oppressive humidity of the rain forest was gone, and it was the refreshing circulation of cool air that finally succeeded in pulling the young man free of his thoughts.

Calyx gave the valley a gloomy scowl, his *meion* trailing behind him. With what could have been a weary sigh, the dwarf unslung his heavy bag from his shoulder and slumped down into the grass. "I'm probably going to regret this," he muttered, "but we'll stop here for the night."

Thankfully, Berlyn slid down from off Camera 12's back with the squeak of bare flesh against steel. She still wore her *Kwau* loincloth—and a little tickle of cold caressed her near nakedness—but the young girl relished the chill. Happily, she did a tiny little pirouette through the cool air before settling back in the grass, staring up at the stars. For the last six or so days—ever since leaving the Rhagana village—Calyx had pushed them harder than any retainer or chamberlain had ever worked the Tempenteire kitchen staff, allowing them very little rest and only a few hours of sleep a night. The dwarf hoped that the hidden bridge behind the falls might slow the Daeminase down—maybe even a few of the eyeless bastards would try to cross the river itself and get swept away—but being a dwarf, Calyx had very little faith in whatever optimism he could muster. Worriedly, he had hurried the group along at such a pace that even Harris Blind-Eye no longer had the strength to complain. With their horses behind them, the others had had no choice but to follow, winding their way out of the wetness and tangle of the Bentwoods while the awful humidity sucked the strength right out of them

Grass rustled and Berlyn turned to see Aitchley approach, unslinging his backpack and settling himself down beside her. A faint, weary grin pulled lopsidedly across the young man's face, but Berlyn could tell it was forced. Ever since Gjuki had shown them the Rhagana Nidus, Aitchley had remained enigmatically silent. At first Berlyn thought that Gjuki's explanation had not been enough—that Aitchley was still upset over Eyfura's death—but then she started to notice it was more than that. It was more like the young man was wrestling with something . . . that some troublesome thought—not guilt—roiled and churned about his head.

Berlyn returned the young man's smile, redirecting her gaze to the stars. Crickets chirped and sang softly around them, yet the valley was practically mute compared with the unceasing ruckus they had left behind in the Bentwoods.

His eyes glassy and unfocused, Aitchley lay back, folding his arms behind his head. He felt the cooler temperatures touch his sweat-streaked skin, yet remained vaguely detached from his own feelings. The humidity and claustrophobia of the rain forest had lost its hold upon him, but he had not yet fully realized they were gone. He was lost within his own thoughts . . . mesmerized by the words and warnings of a hundred different people.

Berlyn was slightly surprised when the young man tore his eyes away from the heavens and fixed her with a rigid stare. "Do you think I should use the elixir or not?" he unexpectedly asked her.

Berlyn blinked a few times, the question catching her off guard. "Um . . . what?" she managed to get out.

Aitchley continued staring at her. "The elixir," he repeated. "Do you think I should use it?"

"Of course you should use it," Berlyn replied, her own surprise causing her voice to raise in astonishment. "That's the whole point of this quest, isn't it? To get the elixir and resurrect your ancestor?"

Dropping back into silent introspection, Aitchley returned his gaze to the star-filled night, a confused frown tugging at his lips. Berlyn noticed the look of bewilderment crease the young man's face and knew that if she didn't say something soon, the ensuing silence would mark the end of their sudden conversation.

Propping herself up on one arm, the blonde stared down at Aitchley. "Well?" she asked again. "Isn't it?"

Aitchley's frown deepened. "I'm not so sure anymore," he answered, then proceeded to tell the blonde everything he had learned, including all the warnings given to him by Tin William and how they related to things said by Captain d'Ane, the *Kwau Kirima*, and now Gjuki. Berlyn listened in polite silence, her eyes flicking occasionally to the maroon-colored backpack lying nearby. No wonder Aitchley had gotten so moody lately! the young blonde finally concluded. He had the weight of the whole world upon his shoulders and now wasn't even sure what to do with it!

When Aitchley was done, Berlyn just continued to stare at him, the admiration and awe swelling within her breast. All this time, she marveled to herself, Aitchley had been dealing with his uncertainties all by himself—trying not to let anyone else be burdened by the things he knew—but now he was confiding in her . . . asking her what she thought. She felt her love and respect for the young farmer grow, yet also felt an apprehensive shudder tighten at the pit of her stomach as she became a party to information that could make or break their entire quest.

Feeling Aitchley's eyes upon her, the scullery maid knew she had to say something or else lose the young man's attention. "I . . . um . . . I have to agree with Captain d'Ane," she declared, trying to sound convincing but hearing the uncertain quaver in her own voice. "I don't think the elixir would have been created if it caused something bad to happen."

Aitchley trained his eyes skyward again with a tired sigh. "I thought that, too," he admitted, "but then there was this whole thing with Gjuki and his stupid Nidus. The cycle of life and

death. The growth-and-decay mulch. I thought I had it all figured out, but that's everything Tin William was warning me
about."

Berlyn pursed her lips, staring down at the dirt between
them. "But Gjuki didn't say we *couldn't* use the elixir on Eyfura," she pointed out. "He just said that we shouldn't."

Aitchley grimaced. "What's the difference?" he said.
"Couldn't. Shouldn't. It just goes back to what Tin William
said: 'There are some things that are not meant to be tampered
with. Life and death are part of the natural order.'"

"Yes, but you said yourself why did he help you if he knew
it was going to cause trouble?" Berlyn responded. "This Tin
William person knew you were going after the elixir, right? If
it was so dangerous, why help you at all? Why give you a
warning not to use it? Why didn't he just leave you to die in
the desert? Why give you Camera 12 to catch up with me and
Harris if he didn't want the quest to succeed in the first place?
It just doesn't make sense."

Aitchley felt the frustration pound at the sides of his head.
"Of course it doesn't make sense," he snarled. "If it made
sense, it wouldn't be so damn hard to figure out!"

"Well, then," Berlyn went on, trying to calm the young man
down, "we have to assume that he knew you were going to
use the elixir."

"But he doesn't *want* me to use the elixir!" Aitchley argued.

"We don't know that for certain."

"Well, what in the Pits else could he have meant?" grumbled the young man. "What else has the ability to upset nature's scales? What else has the power to interfere with the
natural order of life and death?"

"Magic," Berlyn responded. "You said you thought Tin
William might have meant some of the other artifacts we
brought back."

"Yeah, but that doesn't make much sense either," the young
man answered sullenly. "He couldn't have known we were
going to bring anything else back. None of us did. I only
grabbed the staff 'cause I wanted to see if something else
popped up in its place."

"And the staff's as powerful as the elixir," Berlyn reminded
him. "Remember, when it was broken, it destroyed a whole
conclave of evil Wizards."

"Or so the stories go," Aitchley grunted. "Even still, it doesn't bring things back to life."

"But it still works outside the laws of nature," Berlyn said. "It freezes things when it's hot out, and gives off light without radiating heat. These could upset the balance of nature if used improperly."

There was a brief moment of silence between the two as Aitchley stared longingly at the night sky. "I don't know." He finally sighed. "It just doesn't make sense to me. I keep thinking about all the things Gjuki said back in the Bentwoods to Sprage. You know? All those things about trees and ants and humidity and rainfall and how they all worked together, and if you bunged up just one thing, the whole Bentwoods might collapse. I keep thinking that might happen if I use the elixir. I keep thinking that's what Tin William was trying to say."

Berlyn shook her head, feeling her own confidence building. "That can't be it," she said. "He must have been trying to warn you about something else. If using the elixir was going to cause that much damage, he would have never have saved your life in the first place."

Aitchley's brow furrowed in perplexity. "But why—" he started.

Berlyn interrupted him. "What did Kirima tell you?"

The young man faltered a moment, having to switch thoughts in midsentence. "I . . . uh . . . She said I should use the elixir," he answered hesitantly.

"And what did Captain d'Ane tell you?"

Aitchley blinked hard. "He said I should use the elixir."

"And what did Lord Tampenteire and Liahturetart tell you?"

"They told me to use the elixir," Aitchley answered, "but—"

Berlyn placed a single finger up against the young man's lips, silencing any protests. "And *I* think you should use the elixir," she said with growing certainty. "Whatever this Tin William was trying to say, we'll just have to figure it out later. Right now there are other things to worry about . . . like getting to the Dragon's Lair in one piece."

Uncertain—throwing an apprehensive glance over his shoulder at the dark line of trees that was the Bentwoods—Aitchley settled down to sleep, gazing up at the night sky. Berlyn was right, he mused, trying to quell some of his own worries. He had already reached many of the conclusions Berlyn had, and they both couldn't be wrong, could they? He just needed to hear his own theories supported by someone else. And Berlyn was right in another way, too. D'Ane, Kirima, Tampenteire, and Liahturetart all said he should use the elixir. What did Tin William know? He wasn't even from this world. And for all his warnings, even Gjuki had said for something truly damaging to happen to the Bentwoods, it had to be of at least a significant size. The return of one tree or the resurrection of one Rhagana wouldn't be significant enough to throw everything else out of balance.

His mind too preoccupied to worry about such trivialities as the Daeminase, Aitchley felt sleep grab him in a tight embrace and succumbed.

Gradually, the unsettling presence of someone hovering over him—and the light, almost inaudible hiss of something being moved beside his head—pulled Aitchley out of his slumber. He hardly felt his right hand leap to his sword, and the Cavalier's weapon slid free of its sheath so quickly that Aitchley had to blink at his own grace and speed.

The dark specter hovering over him mumbled a startled curse, releasing its hold upon the young man's backpack and falling over backward. Blinking, Harris Blind-Eye landed hard on his rump, unable to stop himself with the use of only one hand. An unfriendly scowl spread beneath his ragged beard and mustache, and a glint of the old villainy flickered through the brigand's eyes but quickly dispersed when he caught sight of the sword tip pointing unwaveringly at his throat.

"Hey, hey, hey, scout," the southern-city lockpick said, carefully redirecting the young man's blade away from his neck. "Not to worry. Not to worry. It's just me."

Shaking the last lingering traces of sleep from his mind, Aitchley sat up, his sword still directed toward the ponytailed outlaw. The faint, pinkish-gray illumination of early morning slowly colored the eastern sky and the stars overhead were slowly beginning to wink out one by one. The others of the quest slept deeply around him, and Berlyn looked beautiful and innocent curled against his body in nothing but her loincloth.

"What in the Pits do you think you're doing, Blind-Eye?" Aitchley demanded in a low whisper, trying to sound menacing without sounding tired.

Harris attempted a look of innocence, which didn't sit well

on his scarred and dirty features. "Nothing, scout," he whispered back. "Nothing at all." His blue-black eyes made a quick flick to the backpack resting near Aitchley. "I was just gathering up my things and going on my way."

Aitchley followed the outlaw's hungry glance to the backpack and sat up even further. "You weren't thinking of making some kind of a profit, now, were you?" the young man suddenly growled his suspicion. "Thinking of maybe taking something that doesn't belong to you?"

Ragged eyebrows knitted together on Harris's forehead, his mask of false politeness dropping away like dead foliage. "I wasn't going to take anything that didn't belong to me, puck," he snarled back. "You've got my saddlebag in there, and I was just taking it back. You got a problem with that?"

A brief flicker of the old self-doubt and uncertainty shifted through the young man, and a momentary burst of embarrassment reddened his cheeks. Harris wasn't doing anything wrong, he heard his pessimism chastise him, and even if he was, Camera 12 would have stopped him as it did back on the OceanGrass. You're making yourself look like an idiot in front of Berlyn.

But Berlyn was still asleep, and Aitchley had come too far to listen to that side of himself anymore. Harris Blind-Eye was the most notorious thief in all of Solsbury, he reminded himself vehemently. He had tried to kill Aitchley twice and had made various attempts to sabotage the quest itself. He had stabbed Gjuki and taken Berlyn hostage. There was no way that Aitchley was going to believe that the southern-city bastard wasn't doing anything wrong. It was in his blood.

Propelled by his newfound strength and conviction, Aitchley pulled himself to his feet and glared down at the lockpick. Beyond them, Sprage's golden palomino pawed uneasily at the grass, already saddled and loaded down with supplies. Harris, Aitchley could tell, had been busy. He wouldn't be surprised if he found a few things in Harris's saddlebags that didn't quite belong to him.

Hoisting his backpack by its remaining strap, Aitchley sheathed his sword and stalked over to Sprage's horse, examining the contents of Harris's saddlebags. Food and water taken from the others crammed the outlaw's possessions, including Sprage's *navaja*. How and when the lockpick had lifted it from Aitchley, he wasn't even sure, but there it was, plain as day.

A few trinkets possibly stolen from Calyx's huge sack were shoved in among the food, and there were even a few of the basalt-rock knives and obsidian necklaces from the *Kwau* lodged among the provisions. It was a veritable rat's nest of ill-gotten goods, and Aitchley felt his teeth grind together at the sheer audacity of the southern-city rogue. *I'm surprised the Cavalier's shield isn't strapped to his bloody back!* the young man thought angrily to himself. *Does he really think I'm that stupid?*

"Nothing that doesn't belong to you?" Aitchley repeated, a sneer on his face. He pulled free Sprage's *navaja* and clicked open its ebony blade. "Half this stuff isn't even yours, and you've got enough food here to feed a small army. What are we supposed to eat if you take it all?"

Harris offered a weak—albeit guilty—grin. "Hey," he tried to joke, "I'm a growing boy. I've gotta eat, don't I?"

So quick that even Harris was unprepared for it, Aitchley jerked free a single pouch of food and heaved it at the brigand, catching him squarely on the chest. Harris let out a startled "whoof!" as the bag fell into his lap, and there was a momentary glimmer of murder in his dark eyes as he turned to glare at the young farmer.

Aitchley threw a single flask of water at the outlaw and tied the remaining saddlebags shut. "That'll get you as far as Nylais," he said, "then maybe you can sell one of your magical goodies. If you're lucky, you won't starve."

A feral sneer twisted Harris's upper lip. "That's it?" he growled threateningly. "One bag of food and a flask of water? After all I've done for you?"

Aitchley heaved the saddlebag of magic rings and cloaks at the lockpick, feeling a strengthening anger flow through his veins. "After all the times you tried to have me killed or put Berlyn's life in danger?" he spat back venomously. "You're lucky I let you go at all. I should take you back to Solsbury and throw you into the Abyss myself!"

The thought of returning to Solsbury's most infamous dungeon drew some of the color out of Harris's face. "Now, now, scout," the brigand said, "there's no need for that kind of talk. You're gonna at least let me have the horse, right?"

As if in response, Aitchley took the palomino's reins and patted the horse affectionately on the nose. "Seems to me this horse belongs to Sprage," the young man replied sharply.

"Your horse got killed back in the Bentwoods."

"But you can't leave me on foot!" cried the lockpick. "I'm an injured man, scout!"

Aitchley just sneered at the bandit. "But I thought you said you weren't taking anything that didn't belong to you," he jeered. "This horse doesn't belong to you."

Harris fought back the hatred and rage burning behind his eyes. "But . . . but . . ." he sputtered. "Have a heart, puck."

Aitchley turned around from leading Sprage's horse back to the other mounts, an aquamarine fire blazing in his gaze. "I do have a heart, Blind-Eye," he snarled. "I'm letting you go. Now get out of here."

Struggling with the fury growing inside him, Harris clambered to his feet, fingers twitching at his hidden sheaths. If he hadn't have been able to read the kid—if he didn't know for certain that the little bungholer wasn't fooling in the least—the lockpick might very well have fought for the horse, but no animal was worth dying over. The kid was too strong . . . too sure an opponent. . . . A far cry from the pathetic little farm boy who had been too scared even to try.

Aitchley watched as the southern-city rogue turned and stormed off, his lean and wiry frame slowly vanishing into the tall grass. A volatile mixture of anger, revenge, and gut-wrenching terror churned through the young man's stomach, and he felt as if all the strength had been drained from him once Harris had backed down. I might talk a good fight, the young man knew, but Harris still scares me. I mean . . . this is still Harris Blind-Eye we're talking about! *The* most notorious thief in all Solsbury!

There was a low chuckle from somewhere behind him, and Aitchley turned to see Calyx sitting up behind him, a sardonic smile drawn beneath his salt-and-pepper beard. The flimsy, silver outline of Captain d'Ane hovered in the early-morning light beside the dwarf.

"You handled that well, kid," Calyx remarked. "Harris Blind-Eye with his tail between his legs. Just the kind of thing I like to see when I wake up in the morning."

Aitchley narrowed a suspicious eye at the smith. "How long have you been up?" he wanted to know.

Calyx gave a noncommittal shrug. "For a while," he replied. "The good captain woke me up once Harris started gathering up his supplies. Don't worry. He wouldn't have gotten far if you hadn't have woken up.''

The stark terror of facing down Harris Blind-Eye returned to fill Aitchley's veins with ice-cold fear. ''Well, why didn't you say something?'' he exclaimed. ''I was scared pithless!''

Smirking, Calyx rummaged through his sack, replacing the items pilfered by Harris. ''It's good for you,'' the dwarf remarked. ''Builds character. Puts hair on your chest. Lets you know that Harris is still afraid of you.'' He moved to where his *meion* was tethered and started going through his own supplies. ''Now help me kick the rest of these sleepyheads awake. If we're lucky, maybe we can get to Leucos by noon.''

Through a delirium filled with beautiful women covered in raw, pustulating buboes, and the feel of unfathomable power searing the flesh from his fingers, General Fain awoke to the sound of hooves against dirt. Perspiration drenched his forehead, matting his hair to his head, and the veinlike black rash of the Black Worm's Touch had spread to his right cheek, creating an ebony pattern of dark meshwork and swelling sores. The second-story loft of what used to be a silversmith's shop was fouled by the overpowering fetor of the Patrolman's sweat and urine, and even in his fevered state, the general could tell the rank, sweetly warm stench of his own body marked him as a dying man.

Hoofbeats once again forced their way through the general's delirium and he pulled himself to a nearby window, staring down through broken, yellowed glass at the street below. He had secluded himself along what appeared to be the main thoroughfare of Leucos and had prayed fervently to LoilLan that Corlaiys and his little band would arrive before he died. It had been blind luck that he had found his way out of the Bentwoods alive, yet it only strengthened his belief that LoilLan herself watched over him. She would not let him die. It was his destiny to obtain the Elixir of Life. He was too great a man to succumb like some worthless peasant to the Black Worm's rancid Touch. Not when he was destined for such greatness. Not when he— and he alone—could bring the land of Vedette back to its former splendor and beauty.

A shudder of joy snaked through the Patrolman's plague-stricken body as he spied the five horses pass beneath his window, his bleary, unfocused eyes savoring that little detail. At the head of the group was the gruff little dwarf, straddling his miniature horse in a blurry collage of colors. Behind him was the Rhagana, a tall, misshapen sapling on his own mount, and something shiny and diaphanous floated beside him, manlike in shape but not a man. Behind them rode the farm boy himself, his near-naked little jam tart riding tandem, her arms clasped lovingly about his waist. Lecherously, Fain felt a half-mad shiver of lust creep about his privates and go shooting through his stomach, lascivious thoughts about the young blonde undulating through his fevered brain. Perhaps he would take her as his own when all this was over and he was lord and master of the universe, he mused vilely to himself, the sickness inside him fueling his debauchery. Sitting there naked behind her little mudshoveler. She needed a real man, not a boy. A true hero to slide his sword inside her sheath. To make her beg and scream and grovel and beg some more. Perhaps he would let her kneel at his feet, naked and subservient, when all was said and done. Perhaps he would keep her around to satisfy his every whim, then throw her aside when she no longer amused him. What else were women good for? It was because of the brainless, prattling little slit of human flesh that Fain had contracted the disease in the first place!

As lewd images gave strength to his delusions, Fain tried to shake himself free of his sudden fantasies. The bitch could wait, he told himself. She would be his when the farm boy was dead. What he needed now was to find the elixir.

Fain glanced once at the two supply horses—one of metal, the other of flesh—and at the half troll riding a palomino at the back of the group before returning his gaze to the farm boy. There, the Patrolman concluded, bleary, red-rimmed eyes fixing on the young man's back. That reddish sack. He didn't have it with him when he left on this quest. Did he? Damn this fever! It made it so hard to think! Something had drawn the general's eyes to the maroon-colored backpack slung over Aitchley's shoulder and he knew that that was where the elixir was hidden. It would be just like the pathetic little mudshoveler to try to keep the elixir close to his body. Not that it would do them any good to hide it. The elixir was his. It belonged to Fain and there was no one to stop him from getting it!

The Patrolman felt a sudden scurry of fear go crawling up his back on rodentlike legs. Blind-Eye! he abruptly remembered. Where was Blind-Eye? He threw a frantic scan down

the street, his fist clenching about the silver chain and pendant
on the floor beside him. A trap, then, was it? Oho! Try and
draw me out and let Blind-Eye stick his knives into my back?
I think not, little farm boy! I think not at all! I am General
Ongenhroth Fain, lord and master over all! I shall be your
downfall, little farm boy, and not you or your little band of
bung-ups can stop me! His knuckles whitened around the red-
gold jewel in his grip. I will wait here, little farm boy, he
decided, his delirium growing. I will wait here until the time
is right. And then I shall strike. And then the Elixir of Life will
be mine! *Mine.*

General Fain sank down below the windowsill as the disease
ravaging his body threw him back into a fevered stupor, the
stink of his own sweat heavy in his nostrils. Soon, he thought
as sensibility left him. Soon . . .

Aitchley and the others rode past the silversmith's shop and
headed westward into town.

A breeze helped cool the summer afternoon as Aitchley reclined against his backpack, using it as an impromptu pillow.
His stomach was full of freshly roasted lamb caught and killed
on the empty streets of Leucos, and the mouthwatering aroma
of cooking meat continued to fill the deserted village. It was
strange, the young man mused, but certain animals seemed immune to the Black Worm's Touch. Even after their owners had
died off or moved away, herds of sheep left behind had managed to thrive on their own. They freely roamed the empty
houses and nibbled at the surrounding fields with ovine indifference, making a home for themselves without any human
interference.

A lopsided—yet satisfied—smirk crossed Aitchley's face.
Well, he added sheepishly, without any human interference up
till now.

Lying back against his knapsack, Aitchley noisily licked at
his fingers. His fingers, face, and hands were all sticky with
drying juices, and he gradually became aware of the weeks of
dirt and perspiration caking into his skin as he tried to lick
himself clean. Berlyn had had the right idea to strip down to
nearly nothing, the young man thought, because now he could
feel the unclean heaviness of his clothes, and he began to wonder if the rest of his body was as dirty as his hands. Even
though the odor of roasting lamb continued to waft about the

tiny village, all Aitchley could smell was the sour-sweet stench
of his own underarms, and it suddenly made him feel highly
self-conscious lying there next to Berlyn. Phew! he finally concluded. *I smell about as ripe as a compost heap after the rains!*

With a crooked, slightly embarrassed smile on his lips,
Aitchley pulled himself up and looked down at Berlyn. The
blonde lay contentedly beside him, her arms stretched behind
her head. She seemed to have no reservations about lying there
in nothing but her *Kwau* loincloth, her breasts stretched flat
against her ribs, and her eyes flickered open when she sensed
Aitchley staring down at her.

Not a hint of embarrassment entered her gaze as she looked
back up at the farmer. "What?" she wondered.

Aitchley felt his own cheeks redden at his suggestion. "Uh
. . . I was just wondering," he flustered. He had to pull his eyes
away from her naked chest and glance eastward in order to get
the words out. "I was . . . um . . . thinking about going down to
the river and taking . . . uh . . . you know . . . a bath," he got
out. "Did you want to come?"

Berlyn sat up quickly, a happy sparkle in her gray-green
eyes. "Yes!" she replied. "Gaal knows I need one!"

Wondering how she could be worried about what she
smelled like when he must have overpowered everything within
a twelve-league radius, Aitchley answered with a wider smile
and got to his feet. He took both sword and shield with him—
the last time he had left one behind, Calyx had yelled at him—
and Berlyn brought along her dress, planning on washing it
before wearing it once more. She also rummaged through the
supplies and came across Captain d'Ane's bar of soap, smiling
happily as she turned to join Aitchley.

Before either of the two could step away from the camp,
Calyx threw a questioning glance in their direction. "You two
going down by the river?" he asked.

Aitchley nodded.

Grunting, Calyx turned back to where he and Gjuki were
drying the remaining strips of meat into jerky. "Take the horses
with you," he ordered curtly. "See that they're properly wa-
tered. And fill a couple of flasks while you're at it. We're getting close to the desert again, and I don't want anybody
dropping dead from the heat."

Aitchley felt the smile leave his lips and a twinge of anger
settled in his belly. Wasn't he even allowed to go down to the

river and take a bunging bath without getting yelled at? he muttered angrily to himself. Take the horses. Fill the flasks. Don't forget to bring your shield; Procrusus never went anywhere without that shield. Oh, and while you're at it, why don't you kiss my butt, too?

Just as an angry retort was about to escape Aitchley's mouth, the dwarf flashed them a rare, heartfelt smile. "Oh, and take your time," he said amicably. "Now that Harris is gone, there's no need to rush. Stupid idiot probably didn't realize it when he left, but he took the Daeminase with him. It's his blood they're following. So you kids have some fun. You've earned it."

Left floundering on the border of saying something he might have regretted, and shocked by the dwarf's sudden good cheer, Aitchley stood in dumb silence, gaping wordlessly. Berlyn had to take him by the hand and lead him like the horses, tugging the young man along behind her. Slowly, the shock wore off, and Aitchley felt the pleasant emotions return, smiling as he walked, hand in hand, down the empty streets with the woman he loved.

Winding their way through the deserted roads of Leucos, Aitchley and Berlyn arrived at the western shore of the Alsace River, a steep, plant-choked slope leading down to the waters. A house built on heavily reinforced stilts practically hung out over the river itself, yet the two teenagers moved across a tiny wooden bridge to the more accessible eastern bank. Heavy, drooping reeds and water plants covered the edge of the river like green bath curtains, and Aitchley released the horses' reins to let them wander about the bank. The waters were a strong bluish green, yet the current was gentle—lathering up in a blue-white froth around the bridge's support posts—and a few sheep rested peacefully nearby, watching the newcomers with their strange, horizontally slitted eyes.

There was a splash behind him and Aitchley turned to find Berlyn already in the water, the bluish-green veil of liquid reaching up to her chest. With a whoop, the young man—fully clothed—cannonballed in beside her, the water engulfing him with an electric jolt of cold. The Alsace, he knew, was a smaller river—nowhere near as large as the Uriisa—but it would serve to help wash some of the dirt and grime out of Aitchley's hair and clothes.

Berlyn splashed the young man as he surfaced beside her.

"I can't believe Calyx told us to have a good time," she commented.

Aitchley wiped water from his face. "Yeah," he quipped, "I didn't think dwarves could wish that ill on anybody."

A little-girl giggle escaped Berlyn's throat. "You know what I mean," she scolded. "He's just as tired as the rest of us." Eyelashes grouped together by water, Berlyn fixed concerned eyes on the young man. "And how are you feeling?"

Aitchley moved closer, taking her in his arms. "I'm feeling a lot better," he answered truthfully. "A whole lot better."

They played in the water for over an hour, watching the sky turn from late afternoon to early evening. Crickets began to chirp and sing in the thick wall of foliage as the two splashed and wrestled in youthful exuberance, Aitchley's concerns washing away like the dirt from his body. Diligently, they scrubbed their clothes and one another—tender one moment, rough-and-tumble the next—and dunked and splashed each other with strength they didn't know they had left. Then they clambered onto the eastern bank and stretched themselves out, drying off in the last lingering rays of the sun.

Surrounded by the milling horses, Aitchley lay out at the river's edge, his feet still dangling into the water. Berlyn lay beside him, her naked hip barely touching his. An evening breeze gently rustled the reeds—delicately kissing the droplets of water off their bodies—and Aitchley felt a sense of deep relaxation fill his nerves, a surge of warmth flowing through his weary muscles. *I could stay here forever,* he mused dreamily, staring up at the darkening sky. *Clean and washed. A full meal in my belly. Berlyn right beside me. What more could I want? I don't even care about Tin William and the stupid elixir anymore. Berlyn was right. I should use it and be done with it. That's the whole purpose of the quest . . . to use the elixir. It would be pretty stupid to get all the way back to the Dragon's Lair and then* not *resurrect the Cavalier, wouldn't it?*

Aitchley slipped free of his thoughts to find Berlyn gazing at him, a wistful, happy smile drawn across her lips. "What are you thinking about?"

Aitchley smiled back. "That this is all your fault," he answered her.

Berlyn propped herself up on one arm. "My fault?" she asked back. "How can this be my fault?"

Aitchley's smile grew. "I'm relaxed," he said. "I'm happy. I'm not worried about whatever it was Tin William was trying to say." He lightly touched her nose with his index finger. "And it's all your fault."

Smiling beautifully, Berlyn slid her naked body up onto Aitchley's, both still slick with river water. "My fault, is it?" she teased. She placed a warm kiss on the young man's mouth. "And I suppose this is all my fault, too?"

Before Aitchley could answer, hurried footsteps suddenly shattered the stillness and tranquillity of the deserted village. A growing sense of anxiety pushed its way through Aitchley's contentment, and he sat up to see Poinqart come thundering across the rickety wooden bridge, a hybrid expression of human terror and trollish rage contorting his features. Trianglehead clutched frantically to the half troll's bulky shoulder, his violet-red crest a blaze of feathers as he looked worriedly behind him.

"Mister Aitch! Mister Aitch!" shouted Poinqart, skidding to a clumsy halt near the teenagers and nearly falling into the river himself. "Trouble-calamity, there is, Mister Aitch! Hurry-quickly-come!"

Naked, Aitchley stood up, his right hand clasping his sheathed sword. "Whoa. Whoa. Slow down, Poinqart," he advised. "What's happened? What's the calamity?"

"Ambushed-surprised, we were!" the half troll replied. "Poor Poinqart was snoozing-napping! Lucky-fortunate I am to be here!"

Tugging her damp dress down over her head, Berlyn asked, "Ambushed-surprised by who?"

"Not by who," Trianglehead remarked from Poinqart's shoulder. "By what!"

Aitchley's expression darkened. "What do you mean?" he asked. "You're not making any sense. Ambushed-surprised by what?"

The terror/rage remained bright in Poinqart's yellow-black eyes. "Trolls, Mister Aitch!" the hybrid exclaimed. "Nasty-bad-brown-trolls! Found us, they have!" The half troll raced back across the bridge. "Quickly-come, Mister Aitch! Quickly!"

Struggling to get into his still-damp pants, Aitchley hopped up the slope after the hybrid, his knuckles growing white around his sword sheath. So much for a relaxing afternoon, he muttered grimly to himself. Bloody, bunging typical.

14

Never Listen to an Optimistic Dwarf

Moving as quietly as he could, Aitchley crept through the foliage behind the buildings, trying to find a way, unseen, back to their camp. Poinqart stumbled and tripped through the brush, and—turning to admonish the hybrid—Aitchley saw Berlyn trying to keep up with them, tugging as her damp skirt clung to her legs or got caught on groping branches.

"Berlyn!" Aitchley hissed at the blonde. "Go back and stay with the horses!"

Clumsily, Poinqart practically fell over a bush.

"Poinqart!" Aitchley turned on the half troll. "You go with her!"

Poinqart swung yellow-black eyes on the young man. "But, Mister Aitch . . ." the hybrid started to protest.

"But nothing, Poinqart," Aitchley retorted, his voice low. "You're making enough noise to wake the Daeminase. Now go back and stay with the horses."

Jerking her dress free of a grasping shrub, Berlyn crept to Aitchley's side. "You go back and stay with the horses," she whispered at the young farmer. "I left my throwing ax back there."

Aitchley narrowed blue-green eyes at the girl. "So what?" he answered brusquely. "Our horses are more important than your stupid throwing ax. Now, both of you. Go!"

There was a moment of hesitation from both blonde and half

troll—and Aitchley could read the uncertainty even in Poinqart's hybrid features—before Berlyn finally turned away, staying low as she headed back toward the Alsace.

"Come on, Poinqart," she said sharply. "Aitchley's right. Let's go back and watch the horses. Let him go off and get killed."

Despite the anxiety pumping through his body, Aitchley threw an angry look at the scullery maid. "I'm not going off to get killed," he snapped back in a harsh whisper. "I just want to make sure Gjuki and Calyx are all right. Poinqart said they got separated when the trolls attacked."

"Went the opposite-wrong way, they did," affirmed the half troll. "Poor Poinqart ran to find Mister Aitch and Missy Berlyn, but Mister Calyx-dwarf and Mister Gjuki-plant went the other way. Too many nasty-bad-trolls all over the everyplace. Poor Poinqart didn't know what to do."

Aitchley offered the hybrid a reassuring smile. "You did fine, Poinqart," he said. "Now take Berlyn and go keep an eye on the horses. The trolls are probably looking for them right now."

As the two squeezed their way through the foliage south of Leucos, Aitchley watched and waited, the rustle of disturbed shrubbery slowly fading into the distance. He didn't like the idea of leaving Berlyn behind—swore that after their time in the EverDark he would never let her out of his sight again—but this was different. If brown trolls had attacked, they were looking for one thing and one thing only: the horses. There was nothing a brown troll liked more than fresh horsemeat, and Aitchley had the unsettling feeling that these were the same trolls that had followed them all the way into the Bentwoods after their mounts. If that was the case, it was pretty foolish to leave their horses behind with just Trianglehead to guard them. What could the fledgling do if he was attacked? Throw insults at them? Daeminase Pits! He couldn't even fly anymore!

Waiting until he could no longer hear Poinqart and Berlyn, Aitchley forced himself forward, trying to stay as low to the ground as possible. He used the backs of houses to help prop himself up, duckwalking awkwardly through bushes and shrubs that slowly encroached on the deserted town. He winced every time his boots crunched and crinkled upon fallen leaves, and it sounded like reverberating thunder every time his shirtsleeve or pants got snagged by a branch or bramble.

Squinting through the purple-blue gauze of approaching
night, Aitchley could hear angry growls and hungry snarls from
somewhere up ahead. His heart beat faster in his breast, yet he
forced reluctant legs to move onward, skulking as quietly as he
could toward what used to be their camp.

A sliver of ice-cold fear went coursing through his bloodstream as he peered out around the corner of an abandoned
house and into the once-empty streets of Leucos. Their campfire still flickered and wavered—spreading yellow-orange light
about the area—but the streets were now full of hideous brown
trolls, snarling and slavering at one another as they fought over
the remains of roasted lamb. Sharp yellow fangs glistened in
the firelight, and black talons grabbed and snatched at strips of
cooked meat. The crude rack Gjuki and Calyx had set up to
dry the lamb had been tipped over, a huddle of twisted, gaunt
creatures fighting over the scraps. A few of the beasts sniffed
and snuffled around the empty houses, one inspecting the
throwing ax left behind by Berlyn.

Aitchley grimaced. *Berlyn's upset 'cause she left the ax behind,* he muttered dourly to himself. *I left my stupid staff and
the—*

A sudden hand fell upon Aitchley's shoulder, and it took all
the young man's restraint not to scream out loud. Heart leaping
into his throat, he swung about, the Cavalier's sword a whis-
tling, hissing blur of steel before him.

Gjuki leaned back as the tip of Aitchley's blade severed the
air near his nose. "My apologies, Master Aitchley," whispered
the Rhagana. "I did not mean to frighten you."

Trying to beat back the tide of fear-induced adrenaline
screaming throughout his body, Aitchley forced himself to calm
down. "It's all right," he shot back sarcastically. "Just because
my clothes are clean, there's no reason why I can't piss in 'em
again!" He took in a few deep gulps of air before fixing a
concerned eye on the gardener. "You're all right?"

Moving soundlessly through the brush, Gjuki peered around
the side of the house at their troll-infested camp. "It appeared
the trolls were more interested in our supper than in us," he
replied. "The smell of cooking meat must have made them bold
enough to enter the town."

Aitchley frowned as the gangly monsters snapped and
snarled at one another over strips of roasted meat. The damn

things are everywhere! he mused dismally to himself.

Gjuki pulled his gaze away from the camp. "Come," he advised the young farmer. "The sooner we're away from this place, the better off we will be."

Aitchley couldn't tear himself away from the marauding brown trolls. "Um . . . You didn't happen to grab anything before you left, did you?" he wondered.

Gjuki shook his head. "The trolls' attack was quite sudden," he answered. "We were barely able to escape with our lives. Neither Master Calyx nor myself was prepared for combat. And poor Master Poinqart was roused out of what appeared to be a most peaceful nap."

Aitchley glared at the squabbling trolls, his frown deepening. Typical Corlaiys luck, he grumbled to himself. Absolutely typical . . .

With the low *shunk!* of a raised window sash, something grumbling and cursing clambered out of a house a few doors down and tumbled into the shrubbery. There was a clatter and clink as a large sack followed and more cursing as Calyx pulled himself out of the bushes, testily brushing himself off.

Through the solid wall of the house, Captain d'Ane floated effortlessly through wood and mortar.

Swiftly, Aitchley sprinted to the dwarf's side and helped him to his feet, blue-green eyes flicking nervously toward the troll-filled streets. Too busy fighting over fresh meat, none of the monsters had heard the noise.

His attention divided between Calyx and the trolls, Aitchley tried to help brush dirt and leaves out of the smith's silver-black hair. "Are you okay?" he asked.

Calyx spat dirt. "As happy as a one-eyed snake in the mines of the Solsbury Hills," he quipped irritably. He threw a disgusted look around the side of the house at the trolls. "I can't believe these muggworts are still after us," he murmured to no one in particular. "Don't they ever learn?"

Gjuki helped shoulder the dwarf's heavy sack, a friendly hand touching the smith's arm. "Things could be worse, Master Calyx," the Rhagana said. "The trolls may have seen our horses if Master Aitchley had not taken them with him. As it is, it seems their theft of roasted lamb is keeping them sufficiently preoccupied."

Calyx allowed himself a tiny grin. "Yeah," he grumbled, "I

guess you're right. If those buggers had smelled the horses, we'd be running from them all the way back to Aa.'' He started a brisk stomp back toward the Alsace. ''Oh, well.'' He shrugged. ''So much for stopping here for the night. We might as well move on.''

It was Captain d'Ane who noticed Aitchley's reluctance to leave. ''Aitchley, lad?'' the ghostly soldier queried. ''Is something wrong?''

Aitchley pried his eyes away from where the trolls prowled the darkening streets. ''I . . . uh . . .'' the young man stuttered. ''Um . . . We can't go yet.''

Salt-and-pepper eyebrows knitted over Calyx's beady eyes. ''Well, why the forge not?''

Aitchley felt embarrassment well up in his throat like bile. ''Uh . . . Berlyn left her throwing ax behind,'' he used as an excuse.

Calyx gave an apathetic shrug. ''So what? I'll buy her a new one in Viveca,'' he snorted indifferently. ''Come on.''

Beads of perspiration formed under Aitchley's hat. ''Uh . . .'' he tried again. ''I . . . uh . . . left my staff behind, too.''

Calyx threw a questioning glance over one shoulder, his ruddy complexion darkening momentarily. ''Oh, well,'' he concluded, ''it was too dangerous to be playing around with anyway. Maybe a few of the trolls will blow each other to bits trying to figure the damn thing out.''

Swallowing hard, Aitchley clamped his eyes shut as if afraid of seeing the dwarf's reaction. ''Iforgotmybackpack,'' he announced.

There was a moment of volatile silence as Calyx stared at the young man, his face an unreadable mask. Only a single cocked eyebrow gave any indication of the emotions surging through the dwarf. ''What did you say?''

Aitchley risked cracking open one eye. ''I said I forgot my backpack,'' he repeated, slower this time.

Silence hung—huge and ponderous—over the outskirts of Leucos before Calyx turned back around with a shrug, trudging through the woods toward the Alsace River. ''Well, at least you remembered to bring the Cavalier's shield,'' he remarked, heading off into the dusk.

Aitchley hurried after him. Bloody, bunging typical, was all he could think.

*   *   *

Berlyn's gray-green eyes went wide. "You forgot the *what*?" she all but shrieked.

Aitchley struggled to keep the growing redness from engulfing his face. "I said I forgot the backpack, okay?" he retorted. "I didn't bring it with me! I didn't think we'd need it at a bunging river! I left it back at the camp, where I assumed it would be safe, okay? I bunged up! I'm sorry! How was I to know we were going to get attacked by brown trolls?"

Rummaging through his heavy sack, Calyx didn't even bother to look up at the young man. "You didn't," he answered calmly, a hint of his misplaced optimism tinging his words. "Nobody did. It's not your fault."

Feeling useless and stupid, Aitchley stalked over to the banks of the river and plopped down in the reeds. And the day had been going so well! he grumbled morosely to himself. He was even starting to feel better about himself and what to do with the elixir and then this had to go and happen! Bloody typical Corlaiys luck!

Still half-buried in his giant sack, Calyx paid little attention to the young man's disappointment. "Our best bet is to just wait them out," he decided. "Wait until they finish off what little meat was left and get disinterested. Then the only thing we'll have to worry about is if they come this way. The last thing I want is them smelling our horses. Then we'll never get rid of 'em!"

"But what if they don't leave?" Aitchley muttered pessimistically. "What if they just stay there?"

"Oh, they'll leave, all right," Calyx replied. "A brown troll has an incredibly short attention span. If they can't kill it or they can't eat it, they'll soon lose interest in it. All we have to do is wait them out."

"But what if they find the elixir?" worried Aitchley. "What if they take it with them? I mean . . . I left my backpack just sitting there."

Calyx surfaced from his bag. "So long as there's no food in it, they're not going to care," he said.

Nothing the dwarf said made him feel any better. "But—" Aitchley protested.

Calyx went back to digging through his enormous sack. "Look, kid," he interrupted, "by morning, they'll be gone. We'll just walk in there and pick up anything we might have left behind. It's not the end of the world."

Grimly, Aitchley stared down at the dark river, throwing the occasional rock at the black waters. Not the end of the world, he muttered his despair. I left the bunging Elixir of Life behind and let a bunch of trolls get it! What kind of a dull-pated, addlebrained warthead am I? Even if they don't care what's in it, who's to say they won't take it with them? Brown trolls are notorious scavengers.

Frowning heavily, Aitchley stared at the dark river. Some hero I turned out to be, he grumbled angrily to himself.

The night grew darker.

Aitchley ducked back into the protective cover of shrubbery, a bleak, hopeless expression drawn across his youthful features. Accusingly, he trained blue-green eyes on the dwarf next to him. "I thought you said they'd be gone by morning," he said.

Calyx tightened his grip around his warhammer, giving the noontime sun a rancorous scowl. "So I was wrong," he snarled. "Serves you right listening to an optimistic dwarf."

Aitchley's fingers lightly tapped the hilt of his own weapon, a grave yet thoughtful mien clouding his face. "So what do we do now?" he whispered.

Calyx sneered at the trolls still occupying the empty town. "I'm thinking. I'm thinking," he growled back.

A wispy haze of silver in the bright sunlight, Captain d'Ane trained spectral eyes on the creatures. "I'd go in there myself but I'm not tangible enough to grab the backpack," the soldier said. "The most I'd do is distract them."

"And there is no guarantee that you could do that either, Captain," Gjuki remarked. "The farther west we have gone, the less prominent you have become. In such bright daylight, the trolls might not even be able to see you."

Calyx stroked thoughtfully at his beard. "But they could see us," he mused.

Aitchley narrowed suspicious eyes at the smith, an unsettling feeling starting in his belly. "What do you mean by that?" he asked.

"What I mean is a distraction might be just what we need," the dwarf replied.

Anxiety growing, Aitchley shook his head violently. "No. Oh, no!" the young man argued. "I'm not going out there and getting chased by a bunch of trolls!"

"Who said anything about you, kid?" Calyx retorted. "I was

thinking more of Gjuki or myself. Just something enticing enough to get those trolls off their big brown asses and after us. Then we waltz right in and pick up the backpack.''

Aitchley tried to ignore the warmth filling his cheeks. "And you think it's going to be that easy?" he questioned. "You walk in, the trolls follow you, and everything's all right? How are you supposed to get back? Won't the trolls just follow you back here and find the horses?"

Calyx grinned. "Not if we use your camera," he answered. "The damn thing can fly, right? I'm sure it could outrun a couple of trolls." His grin widened. "We'll be gone before the trolls even know which way we went!"

Apprehensively, Aitchley stared through the leaves at the village. "You're getting awfully optimistic again," he told the dwarf. "Should I stop listening to you now?"

Calyx gave the farmer a frown. "Leave the sarcasm to me, kid," he quipped. "You're losing your edge."

Pearl-black eyes on the village, Gjuki turned to face Calyx. "I must concur with Master Aitchley," the Rhagana said. "A distraction could prove dangerous."

"It's not like we've got a choice," Calyx answered sharply. "Look, these trolls are getting complacent. They've got food. They've got shelter. And they didn't have to fight anybody to get it. Any minute now they're going to start sending out scouts to see if there's anything to eat here beside sheep. If they catch a whiff of our horses, they're gonna be on our butts for the rest of the trip, and I'd rather that not happen. The easiest solution is to grab the backpack while they're not looking and be on our way. If the trolls want to stay here after that, fine. Let 'em. The town's deserted anyway."

"But what if something goes wrong?" Aitchley worried. "Camera 12 was pretty badly damaged by the Daeminase."

"It flew the Canyon Between," Calyx pointed out, "and all I need it for is just a few seconds. Twelve made the good captain look like he was standing still."

D'Ane offered the dwarf a slightly embarrassed smile. "Yes, well . . ." he replied, "I wasn't in the best of health, now, was I?"

Aitchley scratched at his hair beneath his hat. "Yeah, but . . ." He faltered. "It just . . . I don't know. It just seems like there should be an easier solution."

Calyx flashed the young man a wry smile. "The easiest so-

lution would have been the trolls leaving on their own, but I
should've known they wouldn't've done that. Too convenient
for us. A distraction's the only way to get that backpack back
without having to fight our way through forty or fifty trolls.''

The uncertainty continued to swirl in Aitchley's eyes.
''Yeah, but . . .''

Calyx sighed heavily, beady eyes shifting to the village. ''All
right. Look,'' he concluded. ''We'll wait until evening. If they
haven't left by then, we go with my plan, all right?''

Reluctantly, Aitchley gave a feeble nod, the anxiety churning
through his stomach like a cluster of nervous butterflies. Beyond the trees, the horde of trolls roamed the empty streets of
Leucos.

Aitchley spent the rest of the day in quiet worry, sitting at
the edge of the riverbank and staring into the waters. He
couldn't help but feel guilty for his own stupidity, cursing himself over and over again for leaving the backpack behind. All
attempts to console himself—to reassure himself that it wasn't
his fault . . . that the backpack should have been safe at the
camp—crashed hard against the brick wall of the young man's
pessimism, and he could hear the malicious sniggering of his
own self-doubt rising back up out of the recesses of his mind.

Real good, he mused condescendingly to himself. You go all
this way—you actually get the Elixir of Life—and then you
lose it to go off for a little skinny-dip with Berlyn. And for
what? You didn't even *do* anything, for Gaal's sake! It was
just a bath! I should have known better. I should have known
that a bung-up like me couldn't do anything right. Should have
known I'd figure some way to bung this whole thing up. Hah!
All those times Harris tried to sabotage the quest . . . He should
have just waited around. Sooner or later I would have done the
job for him!

Despondently, the young man stared into the river, watching
as the sky reflected the colors of early evening into the waters.
Berlyn must think I'm a real muggwort, he thought morosely.
I bet the Cavalier never did anything stupid like this. No. Only
Aitchley Corlaiys is capable of such a feat. Only Aitchley Corlaiys could bung up a whole quest by leaving the Elixir of Life
behind. Duh! What was I thinking? After all the good stuff
that's happened between me and Berlyn, what was I trying to
do? Ruin everything?

A few frogs began to croak and chirrup along the shallows of the Alsace as Calyx pulled himself to his feet. He gave the darkening sky a sour look as he started toward the rickety bridge back toward Leucos. "We've waited long enough," he declared. "Gjuki and I will be back in a little while."

A barb of guilty surprise lanced through Aitchley's chest, causing him to spring hurriedly to his feet. "Gjuki?" he blurted, anxious eyes flicking from Calyx to Gjuki to Berlyn than back to Calyx. "Since when was Gjuki going?"

Calyx gave the young farmer's protests an unfriendly scowl. "Since it was decided Gjuki's ability to get in and out of places unseen makes him the best suited to retrieve the backpack," the dwarf replied. "As one with the early-morning mist and all that."

Aitchley jogged briskly to the bridge, a weird roiling of worry, surprise, and bewilderment clouding his thoughts. "But I . . . um . . . I mean . . ." he sputtered. "This is my fault," he finally got out. "I should be the one going."

And it's the only way I can show Berlyn I'm not a complete bung-up, he added mentally to himself

Calyx fixed the farmer with a curious eye. "It's nobody's fault," he answered gruffly. "It doesn't matter who gets it back so long as somebody gets it back."

Aitchley's fingers curled anxiously around his sword hilt. "And that somebody is going to be me," he insisted. "I left it behind, I'm going to be the one to get it back."

"It's not a contest, kid," retorted Calyx, exasperation welling in his voice. "I picked Gjuki 'cause—next to Harris—he's the best at getting in and out of places unseen. There's no point in risking anybody else's life."

"But I'm the one who left it behind," Aitchley argued. "I'm not about to have Gjuki risk his life for my stupidity!"

"I can assure you, Master Aitchley," the Rhagana replied solemnly, "I will be all right. Did I not assist you in getting the alchemical necklace back from Archimandrite Sultothal?"

The memory of Gjuki practically fading into the darkness and mist momentarily leapt to the forefront of Aitchley's thoughts. "Yeah, well . . ." The young man faltered. "You were the distraction. *I* went in and got the damn thing."

Calyx let out an impatient huff, stomping across the bridge toward Leucos. "The point is moot, kid," the dwarf declared.

"You stay here and watch the horses. Gjuki and I will be back in a little while."

Aitchley felt his fingers tighten about his weapon. "No," he answered.

Eyebrows lowered over beady eyes. "What did you say?" Calyx growled at the young man.

Boldly, Aitchley stepped across the bridge. "I said no," he repeated. "Either I go or Camera 12 stays here with me."

Calyx's gaze flicked briefly to the metallic construct waiting obediently nearby. "Come on, kid," he pleaded. "This isn't getting us any—"

Aitchley remained indignant. "Either I go or Camera 12 stays," he said again. "Then what are you going to do?"

There was a tense moment of silence broken only by the rush of the river and the high-pitched croaking of little frogs. Even in the diminishing light of early evening, Aitchley could see Calyx's face grow a deeper shade of red, and the smith's knuckles went white around the shaft of his warhammer.

With an abrupt turn, Calyx resumed stomping across the bridge. "All right. Fine," he grunted abrasively. "Aitchley and I will be back in a little while. Gjuki, stay here and watch the horses."

There was a sudden rustle of reeds as Berlyn jumped hastily to her feet. "If Aitchley's going, so am I," she announced.

Before Calyx could reply, Poinqart was immediately behind the young blonde. "Poinqart goes, too! Poinqart goes, too!" cried the half troll. "Did not Mister Calyx-dwarf make Poinqart Mister Aitch's protector-friend? Poinqart must come to see that Mister Aitch comes to no horrible danger-harm."

Calyx threw his hands up into the air. "Why don't we just send an invitation and tell the trolls we're coming?" he exclaimed. He trained an accusing glare on Aitchley. "See what you started?"

Aitchley struggled to keep his stubbornness alive. "I don't care," he replied. "I'm coming and that's that."

Grumbling and muttering, Calyx crossed the bridge back into Leucos. "Now you're getting *too* much like Procursus," he mumbled under his breath. "Next thing you're gonna want to do is take on the Dragon all by your lonesome!"

Kneeling in the bushes just south of what used to be their campsite, it became harder and harder for Aitchley to maintain his stubborn bravery. The sight of gangly brown trolls moving about the empty town—the smell of their foul bodies tainting the wind—chipped and chiseled at the young man's determination, and he began to wonder—albeit a bit late—why he had been so adamant about coming.

What are you going to prove to Berlyn if you get yourself killed? he could hear his pessimism rasping at him. *What are you going to prove if you get ripped apart by brown trolls? That you were right? That you were a complete bung-up? And now she's sitting right behind you, so she can just watch for herself when you fail to get the stupid backpack. Or to get ripped up herself if you bung this up, too!*

Teeth clenched, Aitchley tried to ignore his own dark thoughts. It's not bad enough these were the same thoughts that had gotten him into this predicament in the first place; now they had turned on him. Before they had told him he had no choice, he had to recover the elixir himself; now they told him he didn't have a chance. Sometimes the young man wished he could just turn off the various thoughts scampering about his head and go on about his life without all the commentary going on in his skull.

Soundlessly, Calyx clambered to his feet, warhammer in hand. "All right," he whispered, beady eyes on the village. "I'm gonna go around this way. You go around the other way. Try and find a good vantage point and then stay there. Once they go chasing after me, run in and grab the elixir. I don't care about anything else. Just make sure you get the elixir. We'll meet back by the river. Got that?"

Aitchley's mouth had suddenly gone as dry as the Molten Dunes, so he just nodded mutely.

Shadowed by Camera 12, Calyx pressed into the foliage. "Make sure they're all after me before going in, kid," he advised. "One of 'em catches a whiff of you and we're right back where we started from."

The shrubbery around the town and the darkness of coming night quickly swallowed both dwarf and camera, leaving a warm breeze to rustle the bushes alone. Despite the warmth of the wind, Aitchley felt a cold lump settle rigidly in his belly, and a few beads of nervous perspiration formed at the back of his neck as he started a slow creep through the brush. He hardly heard Berlyn and Poinqart skulking behind him—the crunch and rustle of his own passage resounding in his ears—and he was momentarily relieved when he stepped out of the bushes and onto a small dirt path, ducking hurriedly around an abandoned building.

Berlyn and Poinqart were like twin shadows behind him.

Nervous sweat beading his face and icy fear lodged in his stomach, Aitchley threw an apprehensive glance down the dirt road. Dark, deserted houses blocked his line of sight, yet he knew the trolls were just a few streets away, lounging about in inhuman laziness. He could hear their growls and grunts as they roamed the town, and he hoped he didn't run across any who had strayed from the main pack. The last thing he needed was to bump into a few trollish scouts and blow the whole thing.

A gentle tap landed on the young man's shoulder. "Aitchley," Berlyn whispered into his ear. "What about over there?"

Questioningly, Aitchley followed Berlyn's pointing finger to an abandoned tavern at the end of the block, its western side facing the street where their campsite had once been. It didn't offer much in the way of cover, Aitchley mused, but it made for a good vantage point. From there, he should be able to see the trolls and their camp.

Moving as quickly and as quietly as he could, Aitchley sprinted to the deserted tavern, ducking down behind what used to be a watering trough. What little water remained in the trough was greenish black, and the foul stink of stagnant water filled the young man's nostrils like the cloud of midges and mosquitoes whizzing about its surface. He felt a tiny burst of pride wiggle its way through his rib cage when he realized he could see most of what used to be their campsite, but the arctic cold in his gut intensified to quickly extinguish whatever optimistic thoughts he may have had.

Daeminase Pits! the young man cursed his disbelief. Look at them all!

Like some monstrous festival, hordes of brown trolls filled the street, snarling and slobbering. Some slept on their backs like dogs—hind legs crooked and raised and their arms stretched above their heads—while others nosed around their new surroundings. The bodies of dead sheep fairly littered the road, their blood staining the dirt a liquid black, and slavering trolls gnawed and tore at the remains. There were even some females milling about the males, their distended, pear-shaped breasts dangling from scrawny chests like ponderous, misshapen weights, and two trolls rutted and thrust in animalistic passion in full view of the others. Their lean, skeletal limbs appeared somewhat insectlike in their movement, and the stink of their unwashed bodies reached Aitchley even through the veil of stagnant water.

"Nomion's Halberd," Berlyn whispered under her breath. "There must be a hundred of them!"

Aitchley had to swallow the sudden lump in his throat. "They must have called the whole tribe down," he guessed. "Calyx was right. They do look like they're planning to stay."

"Not for wait-long, Mister Aitch," Poinqart said assuredly. "Mister Calyx-dwarf will soon come-out-appear and chase the nasty-bad-brown-trolls away."

Nonetheless, it felt like an eternity crouching behind the rotting wood of an old watering trough, the stench of foul water and brown troll tainting the air. The sky continued to darken—melting from a purplish blue to a velvety black—and Aitchley had to squint through the approaching night. *I wish Calyx would hurry up and show or else I'm not gonna be able to see a Gaal-damned thing!* the young man muttered. *I should have brought Tin William's lightstick along but . . . dammit! That's in the backpack, too!*

Aitchley felt a concerned hand abruptly land on his shoulder, another hand delicately clasping his. "Here," Berlyn whispered in his ear. "Take this."

There was a momentary flutter of surprise as Aitchley looked down at the brownish-red ring in the palm of his hand, the tickling vibrations of its magic slowly burrowing its way up his arm. "Where'd you get this?" he wondered. "I thought Harris took all his stuff back?"

Berlyn offered the young man a beautiful smile. "I've been wearing it since the Shadow Crags. Guess he just forgot about it." She smiled again. "Quick. Put it on."

Still trying to figure out why Harris would let the blonde keep it, Aitchley slipped the magic ring onto his finger, feeling the painful jolt of sorcery stab at the center of his forehead. He grunted his discomfort—he didn't know why seeing in the dark had to make your head hurt—but, as quickly as it had come, the buzzing began to fade, leaving behind only the unnatural sensation of sorcerous pins and needles.

Blinking his magically enhanced eyes, Aitchley almost missed seeing Calyx pop free of the bushes near the tribe of brown trolls, hooting and prancing before the startled beasts. It

was almost like there was no darkness at all, the young man
noted in awe. He could see Calyx clearly . . . even see the wild,
buggy-eyed expression on the dwarf's face as he spun about
and dropped his pants, exposing his dwarven ass to the entire
town of Leucos. Even the trolls were highlighted by the magic
of the ring's brownish-red stone, and Aitchley could see their
astonished faces as Calyx played a short tattoo on his own butt
cheeks.

"Come on, you ugly, slobbering, motherless bastards!" the
dwarf howled at the bewildered trolls. "Come on! Look! I'm
a dwarf! Come and get me!"

As the surprise slowly left the horde of brown trolls, yellow
fangs and black talons flashed as they charged the lone dwarf,
scrabbling over one another in their eagerness to get to him.
Smirking beneath his beard, Calyx pulled his pants back up and
went dashing down a side street, immediately vanishing around
the side of a building.

"Come on, you bloated sacks of troll dung!" Aitchley could
still hear the dwarf yelling. "I'm right here! Don't let me get
away!"

The streets emptied almost magically as torrents of brown
trolls went rushing after Calyx, disappearing down the dirt road.
Blinking, Aitchley could only gape at how quickly the monsters
departed, their simple, trollish minds set on one thing. Daeminase Pits! the young man couldn't help swearing. Dwarves
and trolls must really hate one another for so many trolls to go
chasing after one little dwarf!

Still trying to blink himself free of the shock, Aitchley hardly
felt Berlyn and Poinqart pushing insistently at his back.

"Aitchley, go!" Berlyn exclaimed. "Go!"

Blinking dumbly, Aitchley leapt to his feet and went sprinting down the dirt road, tugging the Cavalier's shield onto his
left arm as he did. He was still wrestling with how quickly
Leucos had become a ghost town again even as he skidded to
an abrupt halt in what used to be their campsite, magically
enhanced eyes making a brief scan of the streets.

Come on! Come on! he urged himself desperately. It's got
to be around here someplace Calyx said they wouldn't be interested in anything if it wasn't food.

Maybe it was the haste of his frantic searching—or maybe
it was the weird, greenish kind of tint from the ring around his
finger—but Aitchley couldn't find the backpack. The streets

were filled the piles of fresh troll turds and pieces of dead sheep, but the young farmer could find no hint of his backpack, staff, or throwing ax.

A glimmer of steel flickered briefly in the young man's eyes, and he jogged quickly to where Berlyn's throwing ax lay just outside a deserted silversmith's. Urgently, the farmer snatched the weapon up, immediately noticing the teeth marks marring the ax's shaft. So the trolls *had* been poking around in our stuff, the young man concluded. When they found out they couldn't eat it, they threw it away. That means the backpack and staff have to be around here somewhere.

There was a sudden, high-pitched whine that sounded awfully familiar, and Aitchley turned his gaze west toward the surrounding woods. He could hear the clamor and confusion as the trolls chased Calyx through the trees, but the night was suddenly filled with the building crescendo of Camera 12's gimballed rocket.

A tremendous blaze of blue-white fire unexpectedly ignited the western sky, Camera 12 launching itself straight up out of the trees. Blinded, Aitchley let out a single garbled cry, the sudden bright light stabbing into his magically aided eyes. Bright spots as brilliant as a million suns supernovaed behind his eyelids, and the young man dropped dazedly to one knee, trying to blink the sudden eruption of lights and colors out of his eyes.

"Daeminase Pits!" he grumbled out loud. "I'm blind!"

Something suddenly growled at his back, and the young farmer turned clumsily on his heel, trying to focus through the blazing afterimages of Camera 12's rocket. Bleary shapes of muddy brown flesh blurred and wavered before him, and Aitchley rubbed frantically at his aching eyes. He thought he smelled the sour stench of brown troll, and he squinted and strained to see what it was actually confronting him.

Black talons raked the air before the young man's face, and grotesque, swollen breasts swung as the brown troll launched itself forward.

Aitchley made a frenzied attempt to retreat, his eyesight slowly returning. Yram's tits! he cursed vehemently to himself. Not all of the trolls left!

The ring around his finger made sure he saw the mouth full of yellow fangs flash hungrily for his throat.

15

More Returnings and Recoveries

Blue and gold flashed as Aitchley slammed the Cavalier's shield into the leaping troll's face. Fingers, teeth, and claws shattered against the unbreakable *gnaiss,* and the female troll did a twisting backflip, hurled back by its own redirected momentum. Trollish blood splattered the shield, and a startled shriek tore from the monster's throat as it crashed hard to the ground, its hideous face a smear of broken cartilage and splintered teeth.

Still trying to blink the foggy, residual film of near blindness from his eyes, Aitchley squinted, stars and bright lights continuing to disrupt his vision. He could just barely see the troll at his feet—barely able to make out the look of trollish pain and befuddlement on its bloodied features—and he suddenly became aware of further movement ahead of him.

In what was probably pitch darkness—but what looked like shadow to the young man's magically enhanced eyes—Aitchley spotted a gathering of trolls clustered beneath the overhanging porch of a nearby house. All appeared to be monstrous, repulsive females, huddled together as if for protection, and some even clutched grotesque infants to their distended breasts. A brown troll weanling hissed threateningly at the young man from behind its mother's leg.

Blinking the fuzziness out of his eyes, Aitchley took an awkward step back, his fingers curling about the hilt of Berlyn's throwing ax. Afterimages of Camera 12's rocket continued to blur his vision, and he tried to focus on the crowd of females and their offspring, hoping they didn't decide to attack him en masse. He couldn't be sure, but there looked to be as many as twenty or thirty clustered under the porch, and—Cavalier's weaponry or not—Aitchley knew thirty trolls were more than enough to reduce him to troll turds.

Blood dribbling about its shattered teeth, the attacking troll rose into a menacing crouch, yellow-black eyes fixing vindictively on the young man. What talons remained unbroken on its clawlike hands flexed and curled expectantly, and a stream of blood-mingled saliva oozed from its mouth as an unsatiable hunger rumbled in its inhuman belly.

With a catlike screech, the troll launched itself at Aitchley, claws extended. Startled—still disoriented by the blinding flash—Aitchley spun on his heel, his right hand diving for his sword. He was momentarily baffled when he couldn't free the weapon, completely forgetting about the throwing ax already in his hand, and he hastily contemplated dropping one and grabbing the other.

Saliva and blood spraying, the troll leapt. Flinching, Aitchley decided against dropping the ax and dropped into a defensive crouch, whipping the Cavalier's shield about and readying himself for the blow.

The blow never came.

Caught in midair, the female troll released a hellish shriek of surprise and anger, black talons slashing angrily at the powerful green arm clamped about its shoulder. A mingled look of human disgust and trollish rage contorted Poinqart's features, and he flung the brown troll backward, sending it spiraling through the air with a one-armed throw. Screaming, the female crashed through the front of an abandoned tannery, twisting and spinning through rotting wood. Timbers cracked and splintered and debris littered the street, but the troll did not rise up out of the destruction, its skull crushed by the mighty blow.

The other females began to edge out into the streets, menacing snarls directed at the green troll that had invaded their new home.

Berlyn's hand was suddenly on Aitchley's shoulder, drawing his attention from the advancing creatures. "Aitchley, come on!" she urged him. "Let's get out of here!"

Nodding eagerly, Aitchley jumped to his feet and sprinted down the empty street, hastily turning the corner and leaving the campsite. Berlyn ran ahead of him, and the young man could hear Poinqart's heavy footsteps at his back as they rounded a building, ducked between houses, and dove back into the foliage of the surrounding forest.

Brushing leaves and dirt from the top of his hat, Aitchley stayed low in the bushes, blue-green eyes searching the dark streets for any signs of movement. Brown trolls, he knew, chased anything. Any second, he expected to see the horde of females come roaring around the corner—ugly, trollish offspring in tow—but pursuit never came. The town remained deathly quiet, interrupted only by the occasional song of a nearby choir of crickets and the distant clamoring of the males pursuing Calyx.

Straightening his hat, Aitchley stared at the street with magically aided eyes. "Where are they?" he whispered breathlessly. "Why aren't they chasing us?"

Beside him, Poinqart peeked out of the brush with angry, yellow-black eyes. "Funny-silly, Mister Aitch," the half troll chided. "Female-girls do not hunt-pursue people. That is the manly-males job. Female-girls make more ugly-brown-trolls. That is all they do."

Berlyn snorted beside Aitchley. "Some job," she responded.

Anxiously, Aitchley kept a careful eye on the dirt roads around them. "So why'd that one attack me, then?" he wanted to know. "Why didn't they go with the others?"

Poinqart pushed aside an obstructing branch, watching the empty town. "Female-girls do not hunt-pursue, Mister Aitch," the half troll said again. "Poinqart should have realized-remembered this before Mister Aitch went out to find-retrieve the magic-Elixir-of-Life. Nasty-bad-trolls now consider-think this to be their home. When manly-males go out to hunt-pursue, female-girls stay home and tender-care the troll-tadlings. That is why they have stayed-remained, Mister Aitch. They will not leave-depart their new home. They will battle-fight if they have to."

A frown drew across Aitchley's lips. "They won't leave?" he echoed discouragingly. "Well, if they won't leave, how in the Pits are we supposed to get the stupid backpack back?"

Poinqart offered the young man a feeble shrug. "Poinqart does not know, Mister Aitch," he answered honestly. "Only knows female-girls will not leave-depart . . . not even to hunt-pursue Mister Calyx-dwarf."

Aitchley could feel the despair and disappointment well up inside him, slowly devouring any hope he may have had. His fingers tightened unconsciously around the shaft of his throwing ax, and his eyes cut an angry swath through the dark town, a reproachful frustration growing to rival the despair.

I don't believe it! he thought to himself. I bunged up even this! Calyx successfully clears the entire town of male trolls, but the females stay behind! So now what am I supposed to do? I'll never get that backpack at this rate! I might as well just forget about it and head home to Solsbury! Some hero I turned out to be! I get stopped by a bunch of females protecting their young! Bloody typical!

Gray-green eyes narrowed in thought, Berlyn scanned the darkness. "Isn't there some way we can chase them out?" she wondered. "If the females thought there was some danger to their young . . . ?"

Expression contorted, Poinqart shook his head curtly. "Female-girls do not leave for any-no-things," he replied apologetically. "Will battle-fight if they have to, but they will not leave-depart. If they leave-depart, how will manly-males know where to find them? Only way for female-girls to leave is if one of the manly-males comes-back-returns to get them. Then they move to new troll-village-home."

Berlyn bit thoughtfully at her lower lip. "But what if they had to leave?" she pressed. "What if the town caught fire or something?"

A confusion of trollish perplexity and human sadness twisted the half troll's face. "Nasty-bad-trolls are stupid-dumb, Missy Berlyn," the hybrid said. "Even burning-hot-fire will not make them leave-depart. Stupid-dumb-female-girls maybe-might even try to battle-fight the burning-fire. That is how stupid-dumb they are."

"But what—" Berlyn tried again.

"We can't set fire to the town," Aitchley interrupted her, a contemplative look on his otherwise despondent features. "We still don't know where the damn backpack is. We can't risk the elixir getting burned up. Our best bet is to try and sneak back in there and find it."

"But how can we sneak back in?" Berlyn wanted to know. "There are still trolls there!"

Aitchley's frown deepened as he swung a questioning look at Poinqart. "Poinqart," he said, "when I first went in, they didn't attack me right away. It wasn't until I got too close to where they were hiding that they jumped out at me. Do you think I could go back in there and not get attacked if I didn't go anywhere near them?''

A jumble of mixed expressions clouded the half troll's face. ''Poinqart is not certain-sure, Mister Aitch,'' he replied, ''but female-girls know your scent now. Know you are a menace-threat, they do, and they might not let you near-approach now without attacking-kill you.''

''And besides,'' Berlyn added dourly, ''what if the elixir's near them? It wouldn't make any difference if you could go in or not.''

Aitchley scowled. ''Well, it beats setting the town on fire,'' he barked.

''I was just trying to think of a way to get them to leave, that's all,'' Berlyn snapped back.

There was a sudden silence as the two teenagers returned their attention to the streets, an angry frustration crackling between them. They had been so close! At least Calyx's part of the plan had worked. How could the dwarf have known that females were there and that they, unlike the males, never hunted?

A million thoughts and a million unresolved solutions screaming through his head, Aitchley sat and stared at the empty town. If there was no way to get the trolls to leave, how could they get back into the town? And if there was no way to get back into town, how could they find the elixir? And if they didn't find the elixir soon, how long was it going to be before the males lost interest in Calyx and came swarming back into town? Daeminase Pits! Nothing was going right! All Aitchley had to show for almost getting killed was his stupid throwing ax and the inevitable I-told-you-so from Calyx. After all, it was the farmer's fault that the dwarf had postponed the distraction until nightfall. He should have just let the dwarf take the camera when he had wanted to, but no! Aitchley had to be argumentative! Maybe it was best if the young man just kept his stupid mouth shut from now on. All he ever did was get himself into more and more troub—

A hand unexpectedly draped itself across the young man's shoulder and he made a startled spin, half expecting to see Gjuki behind him. He was even more surprised when he stared into the rotting teeth and raggedy beard of Harris Blind-Eye.

The lockpick shifted soundlessly on one knee, a knowing grin stretched across his scarred and ugly features. "Hiya, puck," the southern-city outlaw cheerfully announced. "Got a problem?"

Hooting and hollering, Calyx clung tightly to Camera 12's tungsten-steel reins, the wind screaming past his ears. The night sky was a rush of blue on black—stars no more than brief streaks of light—as the construct rocketed upward, banked sharply, then dove down into the press of trees, shrieking through the dark woods north of Leucos. Cheering, Calyx hung on for dear life, a wild thrill stampeding through his body.

"Whoooooooyah!" the dwarf yelled, rocketing through the dark woods. This was better than the coach races back in Aa, he mused joyously to himself. This was real speed! This was faster than a whole team of *meion*! Hammer and anvil! It was faster than a normal-sized horse! And the sensation! In all his life, Calyx had had no idea flying could be so exhilarating. Why hadn't someone come up with this before? Once he got back, he had to tell the other dwarves about this phenomenon! Surely they could devise something. Maybe copy some of Camera 12's more curious parts? He was sure Aitchley wouldn't mind.

Branches and trees whipped past the dwarf at incredible speeds, the camera weaving unerringly through the darkness. Adrenaline-charged excitement crackled through the smith, and he let out a rousing whoop as the camera unexpectedly dipped, swung sideways, performed a barrel roll, then shot back up into the sky.

Calyx couldn't keep himself from laughing. This is great! he thought merrily. This is absolutely fabulous! Why didn't the kid tell me he had this kind of power at his beck and call? We could've gotten back to Viveca weeks ago! Or at least flown on ahead and replenished our supplies!

Forcing himself to remember that he had a job to do, Calyx turned his head and peered down into the darkness behind him. The night stretched out full and black—the woods a thick carpeting of ebony below—and over the roar of Camera 12's rocket and the glare of its blue-white flame, the dwarf couldn't see any of the trolls pursuing him. He knew the bastards had to be back there—brown trolls couldn't resist the urge to chase anything!—but he had to make sure. Last thing he wanted was the kid walking into their old campsite and getting jumped by a couple of trolls that didn't feel like running!

Applying a little pressure with his left knee, Calyx got Camera 12 to bank, steering the construct the same way he'd direct a horse. How a creature made of metal could feel the dwarf's leg, he didn't know—something he'd have to look into if he wanted to build a Camera 12 of his own—but the machine responded just the same. Stars blurred as the camera turned, arced up high, then went screaming down at an astonishingly steep angle.

Hanging on with both hands, Calyx roared with laughter.

The uniform blackness of the treetops parted like a magical ocean as Camera 12 dropped back into the woods, blazing through the brush at nearly fifty miles an hour. The whip and whistle of passing shrubbery sang in Calyx's ears, and he let out a rollicking howl as the camera zoomed out into a small clearing, slalomed around a large boulder, then zigzagged back on course.

Yellow-black eyes went wide as a dwarf-ridden bulk of metal unexpectedly came shrieking out of the trees in a roar of blue-white flames.

Calyx waved a threatening fist as the horde of pursuing trolls scattered frantically into the underbrush. "Come on, you pithless, sorry excuses for a species!" the dwarf yelled uproariously at them. "Come and get me!"

Camera 12 banked, swerved, then roared back off the way it had come, a hundred bewildered, slightly mystified trolls still chasing after it.

The grin was still on Harris's face as he turned away from the campsite and ducked back down behind the watering trough, blue-black eyes fixing on Aitchley. "So I go away for a few days and everything gets all bunged up, eh?" The lockpick gloated. "Ah, me. Where would you be without me, puck?"

The brigand's teasing did not sit well with Aitchley's already wounded pride. "Right where we are now, Blind-Ass," he growled menacingly. "Except we wouldn't have to sit here and listen to you."

"Why did you come back anyway?" Berlyn asked, gray-green eyes narrowed suspiciously at the thief.

Harris flashed her a knowing, yellowed smirk. "Well," he answered jeeringly, "let's just say I guess I owed the kid."

Aitchley sneered at the dark campsite. "You won't owe me anything if you can get that backpack back," he muttered. He pointed through the blackness at the distant buildings. "Now there's a group of females over there," he instructed. "Near the tannery. Poinqart says they won't attack you unless you get too close, but the backpack might be—"

Harris's grin vanished as quickly as a lightning flash. "Whoa, whoa. Hold on a minute, scout," he interrupted. "What makes you think I'm gonna be the one to voluntarily walk into a group of trolls and poke around for your backpack? *I'm* not the brainless warthead who left it behind."

A flicker of confusion entered Aitchley's gaze. "I . . . uh . . ." he stammered. "Um . . . Well, *I* can't go back in there. Poinqart said they'd see me as a threat now."

Harris shrugged. "So?" he replied. "I'm not going in there. I'm an injured man, scout, remember? If I get attacked, I can only fight one-handed, and I don't owe you that much to throw my own life away."

"Well, what else are you good for?" the young man responded, the frustration starting to well back up inside him. "You're a thief, Gaal damm it! This is what you do best!"

Harris just smirked. "What I do best is look out for my own interests, puck," he replied. "I didn't come back to pull your bung out of the cask."

"Then why did you come back?" Aitchley spat.

Harris lazily stretched out behind the watering trough, reclining back against the side of the tavern. "Who knows?" he mocked. "Maybe I come back 'cause I forgot the ring your little girlfriend there has. Or maybe I just wanted to see this thing through to the end. I'm a complex man, scout. Maybe you'll never know."

Aitchley glared murderously at the lockpick. "Yeah, right," he snarled. "And if dung were a religion, you'd be the high priest!"

A expression of hybrid puzzlement on his face, Poinqart looked first at Harris and then back at Aitchley. "Poinqart does not understand," admitted the half troll. "If sneakthief-Harris isn't going to get the magic-elixir-drink, and Mister Aitch can't get the magic elixir-drink, who is there left to get the magic-elixir-drink?"

Aitchley turned to shrug at the half troll. "I don't—" he started to say.

Berlyn suddenly cut the young man off. "I am," she declared.

Aitchley swung wide eyes on the scullery maid. "What? You?" he blurted. "What are you? Crazy?"

Berlyn offered a nervous smile. "Yes," she replied. She turned toward the relaxing lockpick. "Harris," she abruptly ordered, "give me your supplies."

Cruising high above the Molten Dunes, Camera 12 dipped and rose through the night sky with arobatic expertise. Calyx clung to the construct's back, beady eyes wide at the wonders that met his sight.

Still and dark—like an ocean that did not move—the desert stretched out for leagues beneath the dwarf, engulfing the landscape with a broad emptiness that glimmered an eerie blue in the moonlight. Rocky crags and jutting cliffs were tiny and insignificant from this height, and the shifting, rippling dunes were like frozen waves in an earthy sea. Far beyond—a green speck on the northern horizon—Calyx could just barely make out the thick forest of Karthenn's Weald, and slender ribbons of silver-white radiance were the winding courses of the Alsace and Mistillteinn rivers. He could even see the vast blackness to the east that was the Bentwoods, its thick, lush jungle a solid, ominous wall of darkness.

Calyx stared down at the world. From up here, he mused dreamily to himself, it was beautiful. It was almost as if Procursus had never died . . . that things had never gotten to be as bad as they were. It was strange. Up here, there was little to indicate the famines and plagues that ravaged the land. Little to let one know that the people who inhabited such a beautiful land lived amid squalor and disease. That starvation and sickness made their lives short and miserable, and that nothing they did made anything better. Could even Procursus save the world from that? He was a great man—make no mistake about that—but could even Procursus fight against natural disasters? Drought? Floods? Wildfires? None of these things even existed in Procursus's time, and it made the three-hundred-year-old pessimism rise up inside the dwarven smith.

Probably not, he concluded, but the people could sure use a Cavalier right now.

Gravely—dark thoughts returning to quench the dwarf's amazement—Calyx steered Camera 12 eastward and back toward the town of Leucos. *The kid should have the backpack by now,* he estimated, *and the trolls are chasing phantoms to the north. We shouldn't have anything to fear.*

With a roar of its powerful engine, Camera 12 banked and descended.

Apprehensively—her right hand sweaty around the haft of her throwing ax—Berlyn fumbled with the brocaded clasp about her neck. Dark folds of samite draped her slender body and she could feel the silkenness of Harris's cloak rest heavily upon her shoulders. She wore the brown-red ring on her left hand—its sorcerous tingle coursing up her arm—and it enabled her to see the worried look etched into Aitchley's face as he watched her.

"At least let me go instead," the young man begged, concern furrowing his brow.

Berlyn managed to snap the clasp shut despite the nervous shaking of her hand. "You can't go," she answered. "Poinqart already said they'd see you as a threat."

A look of helplessness crossed the farmer's face. "Yeah, but," he protested, "if I wore the cloak, they wouldn't be *able* to see me!"

Berlyn looked down at the flowing folds of dark material covering her body. "Doesn't matter," she answered curtly. "They'd smell you and still attack. You know that's what Poinqart meant."

Aitchley's mouth worked but no sounds came out. "But—"

Licking dry lips, Berlyn tried to beat back the butterflies that kamikazed through her stomach. "No buts," she replied. "If Harris won't go, I'm the only one left. And we can't send Poinqart in 'cause brown trolls hate green trolls. They'd attack him if he went anywhere near them or not."

Aitchley threw a frantic look eastward. "What about Gjuki?" he insisted. "I'll run back and get Gjuki. He could probably do it without the cloak."

Berlyn moved to drape the oversized hood over her head. "Not enough time," she answered bluntly. "Calyx said he was going to lose the trolls after leading them away. If they don't have anything left to chase, they'll be coming back here any minute. I've got to go."

Searching desperately for excuses, Aitchley lapsed into a helpless silence.

Berlyn tried to offer the young man a reassuring smile. "I'll be all right," she said. "They can't hurt what they can't see."

Nervously, the blonde slipped the hood over her head and disappeared, replaced by a vague, shifting veil of wavering air. Aitchley could just barely see the Berlyn-sized distortion move slowly away from the tavern and toward the troll-infested campsite, her invisible feet skritching and crunching over the dirt of the road.

Grinning, Harris watched where Berlyn used to be. "That's some girl you've got there, puck," he complimented the young man. "She's got some head on her shoulders."

Worry roiled like nausea through the farmer's belly. "Yeah," he grumbled glumly. "Let's just hope it stays there."

Like an infant learning how to walk, Berlyn stepped carefully down the dirt road, muttering a curse as she stumbled and nearly fell. Dirt and pebbles scraped underfoot—and the blonde regained her balance before she fell—but she scowled reprimandingly to herself. This was going to be harder than she thought, she mused grimly. Even though she could feel the dark samite touching her legs—even though the dirt was hard beneath her feet—she could see neither legs nor feet, making the simple task of walking an unusually difficult chore. It was like going down the stairs in the dark. Sometimes—late at night—someone would forget to light one of the many staircases about the sprawling Tampenteire estate, and in the pitch blackness, Berlyn would have to navigate by feel. Sometimes she'd miscount the steps and add or subtract an extra stair, usually resulting in a sudden clumsy lurch. That was what this felt like. Not being able to see her feet beneath her, the young blonde wasn't quite sure where she was going to put them next. She'd probably have less trouble if she shuffled down the road—not bothering to pick her feet up—but then the trolls would hear her for sure. She had to step as quietly—and as carefully—as she could.

So intent on her invisible feet, Berlyn glanced up to discover she had entered their abandoned camp, an abrupt wave of anxiety rushing through her body. She could see the females and their young huddled together for protection under the overhanging porch near the tannery, and she felt a trickle of perspiration wind its way down the back of her neck. Brown, mottled lips drew back in a menacing display of yellow teeth—and for a moment Berlyn was afraid they could see her—but then she realized it must only be her scent. Growling low, the trolls remained where they were, yellow-black eyes scanning the darkness.

Trying to walk without scuffing the dirt, Berlyn looked out across the road, gray-green eyes peering magically through the darkness. She had no trouble seeing through the night—the brown-red ring filling her hand with the tickle of pins and needles—and she surveyed every inch of the town around her, trying to spot the backpack with the least amount of movement. Pieces of dead sheep and clumps of troll shit spotted the square, and she could feel the anxiety growing in her belly.

Where is it? she mused desperately to herself. Come on, where the Pits is it?

A sudden shaft of darkness stood out in her magically aided eyesight, and she made a quick jog to her right, stumbling only once. I'll never get used to this! the young girl cursed, invisible samite billowing about invisible legs. It's just not easy to move when you can't see your own body!

Silken fabric unseeable but rustling about her, Berlyn dropped to one knee outside an abandoned silversmith's, her slender fingers curling around the blackened oak of Aitchley's staff. She felt a smile stretch her lips as the powerful aura of sorcery arced through her arm, and she threw a victorious glance back at where Aitchley was hiding. The staff! She beamed proudly to herself. At least I found something!

There was a sudden scratch of clawed feet behind her, and the blonde whipped about, electric fear coursing through her bloodstream. One of the trolls had left the safety of the porch, slowly making its way out across the street to where the young girl knelt. Its long, pointed nose rose skyward as it sniffed at the air, and its long black talons clicked and glimmered in its inhuman uncertainty.

Berlyn froze. Nomion's Halberd! She panicked. What do I do? What do I do?

As if tasting the sudden fear, the troll halted not more than three feet from her. Its yellow-black eyes seemed to flicker with an evil glow, and it craned its head from one side to the other as it savored the air. It knew there was an unusual scent nearby—could smell the presence of an intruder—but its eyes said otherwise. Despite the unmistakable tang of a human female, there was no one there.

Confused, the troll snarled at the shimmering ripple disturbing the night air.

Berlyn reaffirmed her grasp on the invisible throwing ax in her invisible grasp. She had only been this close to a brown troll once before, and even then, she had had Aitchley's shield between her and the monster. Now there was nothing but empty night separating them, and regardless of the fact that was she invisible, Berlyn couldn't help feeling that the troll knew she was there.

Kill it! she heard her mind unexpectedly rasp at her. Kill it before it kills you!

Invisible perspiration slicked the shaft of Berlyn's ax as her fingers tightened around it. Threateningly, the troll bared its teeth at the distortion of nothingness then started to turn away, no longer interested in a smell that had no body.

With all her strength behind it, Berlyn's invisible ax blade narrowly missed the female troll's scrawny neck, cutting a small gash across the creature's shoulder instead.

Screaming, the troll leapt backward, yellow-black eyes going wide with inhuman astonishment. It felt the sudden pain of steel slicing through flesh—even heard the whistle of a human's weapon shriek close to its ear—but it still saw nothing. Nothing to attack. Nothing to tear at. Only the mysterious scent of human female.

Not expecting the troll to move, Berlyn was unbalanced by her own swing, her diminutive body carried along by the sudden ferocity of her own attack. Cursing, she tumbled forward, smacking the back of her head upon the floorboards of the silversmith's and feeling the throwing ax spill from her grasp. Stars momentarily ignited behind her eyelids, and she put a hand to her forehead, trying to stop the sudden dizziness that had invaded her skull.

The troll suddenly screeched its surprise when a young blonde unexpectedly popped into existence beside it.

Horrified, Aitchley jumped to his feet. "It can see her!" he cried out, hand leaping to his sword.

Harris tried to tug the young man back down. "Keep your head down, puck!" he hissed. "You'll have the whole brood out after us!"

Teeth clenched, Aitchley ignored the outlaw, starting a sud-

den sprint straight for their abandoned camp. "I don't care!"
he shouted. "It can see her!"

Still trying to shake the dizziness from her head, Berlyn re-
focused magical eyes at the troll, immediately noticing the way
it glared directly at her. Daeminase Pits! she cursed. It can see
me! I must have knocked the hood off when I fell!

Contemplating whether or not she should pull the hood back
over her head, Berlyn screamed as the troll lunged, sharp yellow fangs filling her line of sight. She grabbed frantically for
her throwing ax, couldn't find it, and made a clumsy attempt
to scuttle backward on her rear, throwing up the only protection
she had left.

Aitchley's staff exploded in a sudden thunderclap of energy,
blue-white electricity arcing out of the blackened wood and
punching a hole clean through the brown troll's gangly body.

Smoking, the troll's corpse flipped backward, charred skin
and muscle flaking off into the air.

The dizziness in her head accentuated by the sudden overpowering sensation of pins and needles, Berlyn tried to shake
herself free of the abrupt queasiness. Her entire body felt numb
yet alive, and she could taste the magic flowing out of the staff
and into her, diluting her blood with sorcerous energies.

Howling and snarling, the horde of females came scrambling
out onto the street, loping forward as a group.

Berlyn screamed when a hand suddenly grabbed hers, and
she looked up into Aitchley's face with a look of unrestrained
panic in her eyes.

"Come on!" the young man yelled, jerking her hastily to
her feet. "Let's get the Pits out of here!"

Despite the group of trolls rushing toward them, Berlyn held
her ground. "But what about the backpack?" she shouted.
"We still haven't found the backpack!"

"Bung the backpack!" Aitchley screamed. "It's not important! We have to get out of here!"

"But—" Berlyn protested.

Aitchley grabbed at the staff in the young blonde's hand,
trying to pull her along behind him. "I'm not going to lose
you over some stupid elixir!" he howled at her. "Now come
on!"

Stubbornly, Berlyn tugged back on the staff. "But the males
will be coming back soon!" she cried. "If we don't find the
backpack now—"

"I don't care!" Aitchley roared, glancing over his shoulder to see the trolls nearly upon them. "You mean more to me than some stupid quest or some Gaal-damned magic—"

The staff in their mutual grasp unexpectedly erupted, discharging a funnel of pure force that struck the earth and crackled along the ground. Dirt spumed and rock split in its wake as the release of sorcery traveled toward the oncoming trolls, filling the town with a growing thunder before culminating in a deafening roar and blistering wave of apocalyptic heat. Flames nearly twenty feet high suddenly volcanoed up from the ground, instantly incinerating the first line of trolls. Fiery gales tore through the town, bodily lifting Aitchley and Berlyn and hurling them back down the street. One house crumpled in on itself in a sudden upheaval of crumbling timbers and rotting wood, and thick, black smoke swelled through the night sky before billowing up in a mushroomlike cloud and dispersing in an implosion of superheated air.

Blinking—staring in trollish stupefaction at the bony residue and cremains of its kin—the remaining trolls backed slowly away, an inhuman awe and fear gradually building in their eyes. Then—snatching up their offspring—the last of the trolls fled back into the surrounding woods, frightened shrieks and terrified howls splitting the still-sweltering blackness.

Blown backward by the enormous wall of fire, Aitchley tried to shake his head clear of his sudden befuddlement. His face ached as if sunburned, and his ears felt clogged, his hearing dulled. Berlyn slumped across him, gray-green eyes wide with disbelief, and the way she prodded a finger at one ear, the young man could tell she was having the same trouble hearing that he was.

Dazedly, Aitchley gaped at the gray-white ashes of what used to be nearly twenty trolls. "Whoa," he breathed. "What in the Pits was that?"

Berlyn blinked back. "What?" she questioned, the ringing in her ears drowning out the young man's voice.

Strong hands suddenly helped both teenagers to their feet, and Aitchley stared blankly at the half troll beside him, his look of bewilderment mirrored on the hybrid's face. "Powerful-big-boom, Mister Aitch," Poinqart said. "Frighten-scared-away all the nasty-bad-brown-trolls."

Shaken, Aitchley retrieved his hat blown off in the explosion and plopped it back on his head. "Let's hope so, Poinqart," he replied, awed.

Berlyn flashed a timorous smile. "I told you fire might scare them away," she teased.

Somehow Aitchley managed to flash her back a like smile, the reverberating thunder of the wall of fire still ringing in his ears. *Daeminase Pits,* the young man swore to himself. *How powerful is this staff? I thought the fireballs and bolts of ice were something . . . we just destroyed a whole group of trolls with one blast! This thing really is dangerous!*

Slow, purposeful footsteps sounded through the thickness in Aitchley's ears, and he turned to see Harris Blind-Eye, a somber mien on his scarred and dirty face. He held something in his hand, and it took Aitchley's befuddled senses a moment before he recognized the backpack, its zipper undone and its flap hanging open. Much of its contents appeared to be missing, but Aitchley could still see the dark green canvas of the Envirochamber and the cylindrical shape of the thermos.

Harris tossed the open backpack at the young man's feet, a grim scowl crossing his lips. "Looks like the trolls went poking around inside your backpack, scout," he announced darkly. "You have food or something in there?"

Oh, no! Aitchley suddenly remembered. *Tin William's supplies! Those freeze-dried, rehydratable pouches that the construct had said were food! Had the trolls smelled those? Had they gone digging around looking for that? How many other things did they take? What else was missing?*

The anxiety heightening in his breast, Aitchley fixed the lockpick with a rigid stare. "Is the elixir in there?"

Harris shook his head once. "Nope," he answered simply, "but there's some stuff strewn about the street over here. Maybe it's there."

Worriedly—their victory over the trolls quickly forgotten—Aitchley followed the thief to where a few items and fragments of items littered the roadway, immediately dropping to his knees to search. Berlyn and Poinqart searched just as desperately beside him, and the young man could feel the panic growing in his chest.

Oh, isn't this just bloody, bunging typical! he heard his pessimism snort. *We chase away an entire town full of trolls and lose the backpack anyway! Yram's tits! I hope one of the trolls that got fried wasn't carrying it! I'd be the first person in all* recorded history to actually destroy the Elixir of Life!

So caught up in the worry and fear churning through him, Aitchley almost didn't hear the sudden footsteps upon floorboards, looking up at the last minute to see a mysterious figure walk free of the nearby silversmith's. Berlyn gripped his hand in similar surprise, and it took a moment of squinting before the young man recognized the newcomer.

His uniform filthy and in tatters, General Fain stepped down out of the silversmith's and into the street, a cruel, mocking smile on his lips. His gaze was derisive and cold, and Aitchley couldn't help noticing the way he carried himself.

Even though his clothes were mere rags, the Patrolman strode forward like some nobleman dressed in the finest of robes.

The condescending smile stretched Fain's lips as he peered down at the four searching the ground about his feet. "On your knees already," he jeered vilely. "How appropriate."

Aitchley cocked a single eyebrow at the Patrolman, confusion glistening in his gaze. "General . . . Fain?" he questioned.

Fain arched his back, his right hand tightening about a slender, silver chain in his grasp. "*Master* Fain!" he imperiously corrected the young man. He took a threatening step forward, his triumphant smile becoming a malignant sneer. "Well, farm boy," he hissed villainously, "are you ready to die?"

16

Lord and Master

Questions and confusion roiled through Aitchley's brain as he stared at the man stanced outside the abandoned silversmith's. Despite the perplexity clouding his thoughts, Aitchley felt an unsettling sense of dread form in his gut, and he wasn't quite sure why he should feel so disturbed just because of the Patrolman's sudden appearance.

Fain? the young farmer asked himself. What in the Pits is Fain doing here? Has something happened? Is Lord Tampenteire calling off the quest?

A pretentious look on his face, General Fain took a posturing step forward. "Well, Corlaiys," he mocked, "how does it feel to be outdone by your betters? To have had a chance to be something more than just the pathetic little farm boy that you are and to know that you let that chance slip through your fingers?"

Aitchley peered through the darkness at the Patrolman. "What are you talking about?" he asked, nonplussed. "Has something happened? Did Lord Tampenteire send you?"

A grimace of anger twisted Fain's face. "I'm talking about power, you fool," he growled. "Power greater than even Tampenteire's. Absolute power. Absolute mastery over everyone and everything!"

Berlyn leaned in close to Aitchley's ear. "Who is this guy?" she wanted to know.

Aitchley shrugged. "Just some Patrolman," he whispered back. "He took me and Calyx to the Abyss to get Harris. I haven't seen him since."

Berlyn glanced at the general. "So why's he here?" she wondered.

Aitchley shrugged again. "Haven't the foggiest."

Fain's eyes flashed as he glared at the two teenagers. "Are you mocking me?" he screeched with an unexpected ferocity. "I am your lord and master, you worthless little peasants! From this day forward, everyone shall bow down to me!"

There was the nearly inaudible hiss of steel sliding free of concealed sheaths, and twin stilettos were unexpectedly in Harris's hands. "I don't think so, yer generalship," the southern-city outlaw replied. "See, the kid might not remember you, but I do."

Slowly—oozing a confidence that made Aitchley's blood run cold—General Fain turned his attention on the lockpick. "Yes, Blind-Eye," the Patrolman rasped, "and I remember you, too. Your attempt to ambush me has proven unsuccessful."

Harris flipped Mandy in his right hand. "Ambush you?" he echoed. "I didn't have any plans to ambush you." Yellow teeth flashed in a nefarious grin. "But it doesn't mean I won't have just as much fun killing you."

"Bold words from a corpse," Fain spat back. "You see, I'm ready for you, Blind-Eye." His fist closed in about the silver chain in his grasp. "I found something you oh-so-carelessly left behind."

What happened next went so fast that Aitchley was barely able to follow it. Glinting dangerously in the moonlight, the young man caught sight of the red-gold pendant suddenly released from the Patrolman's fist, dangling at the end of its silver chain before being spun in a tight circle. An eerie glow of ruby-red phosphorescence radiated from deep within the jewel as it spun, and there was a low, vibrating hum as chemicals and fluids grew volatile and reacted.

As if moving through treacle, Aitchley turned to look at Harris, immediately noticing the look of surprise and fear that drained the blood from the brigand's face. He brought up his right arm to hurl his knife—and his fingers twitched expectantly around its hilt—but the sudden shock had momentarily frozen him in place. Aitchley felt his own muscles lock, and what must have been seconds felt like long, horrifying hours as General Fain spun the alchemical pendant in a tight circle and brought it down onto the hard-packed dirt of the road.

Harris cocked back an arm, the blue-purple bracelet about his wrist gleaming villainously in the moonlight.

With the sound of glass shattering and a puff of bloodred smoke, the alchemical pendant fragmented against the ground.

Time seemed to return to normal.

Suddenly free of his unexpected paralysis, Aitchley made a frantic dive to one side, throwing himself onto Berlyn to shield her from the ensuing explosion. He didn't know how powerful the blast would be—he half expected bits and pieces of Harris to come showering down around him—but he was surprised by the stillness that came instead. Quizzically, the young man propped himself up on one elbow and swung a bewildered look at the two men behind him.

The shattered necklace still gripped in his hand, Fain could only gape at the southern-city outlaw. Crimson smoke still wafted about the street—and there was a curious, chemicallike smell pervading the air—but there was no explosion. Tiny fragments of red-gold crystal littered the roadway, but the purple-blue bracelet clamped around Harris's wrist remained intact.

The look of surprise swiftly faded from his own features as Harris glanced up from the bracelet glimmering dully around his right wrist. "What do you know?" the lockpick quipped. "It didn't work."

Black steel suddenly screamed from his fingers and tore through Fain's left eye, a spatter of scarlet staining the street.

Mouth still open, the general spilled over backward and lay still, Mandy's ebony hilt protruding from his ruptured eye socket.

Stunned, Aitchley forced himself to clamber to his knees, gawking at the southern-city outlaw. Berlyn had a similar look on her face, and even Poinqart looked trollishly befuddled. Blue-black eyes glinting with muted astonishment, Harris looked away from the defective bracelet to the three staring at him.

"Doesn't that just figure?" the rogue remarked. "The damn thing never worked. I could've ditched the lot of you back in Solsbury!"

Poinqart suddenly scuttled off his knees and loped clumsily past Harris and the Patrolman's corpse, lumbering through the doorway of the empty silversmith's. There was a crossed expression of trollish determination and human joy on his face as he momentarily vanished into the darkness of the doorway before reappearing in the moonlight, a decanter of bluish-green glassware clutched in his hamhock hands.

"Mister Aitch! Missy Berlyn!" the half troll exclaimed happily. "Look! Look what Poinqart has found! Magic-elixir-drink, it is! Poinqart has discover-found it!"

Aitchley jumped eagerly to his feet, moving hurriedly to the hybrid's side and taking the decanter in his hands. He immediately felt the powerful pins-and-needles sensation fill his body, but something, he noted, was wrong. The wax ring around the cork had been broken and much of the elixir was gone, the once-full decanter now less than half-full.

The sense of dread brought icicles to Aitchley's spine. "Um . . ." he sputtered in disbelief. "Someone got into the elixir."

Berlyn was instantly at the young man's side. "What?" she exclaimed. "Did it spill?"

Aitchley narrowed blue-green eyes at what remained of the sorcerously glowing liquid; dots and pinpricks of light continued to swim about the magical potion like liquid fireflies. "I don't know!" he answered sharply. "It's just . . . gone! There's barely any left!"

"Is there enough for the Cavalier?" wondered Berlyn, trying to peer into the jaded sapphire.

"I don't know!" Aitchley repeated, his ignorance making him irritable. "Liahturetart said there might be enough for two doses, but . . . but there's nothing left!"

Berlyn grabbed at the decanter, sloshing what liquid remained. "There's about half," she replied, more calmly than Aitchley. "That might be enough to revive the Cavalier."

"Reviving the Cavalier should be the least of your concerns," a sudden voice said from over their shoulder.

Aitchley and Berlyn both turned to see General Fain get to his feet, Harris's stiletto gripped in his hand. Streams of blood like crimson tears streaked the general's cheek, but both his eyes were turned and focused on the two teenagers, a triumphant smile drawing across his lips. "The elixir wasn't spilled," he jeered. "I drank it. And now I can never die." His smile was odious. "Too bad the same can't be said for you."

* * *

With a low rumble, Camera 12 descended gently to earth, its landing somewhat awkward due to its damaged limbs. Brusquely, Calyx slid off the construct's back and landed in the high grass of the riverbank, sweeping the surrounding area with tiny eyes. The horses snorted and shuffled at his back, and Gjuki was a vague silhouette against a backdrop of dark vegetation, illuminated only by the faint, silvery glow of Captain d'Ane.

A frown drew slowly across Calyx's lips. "Where is everybody?" he wanted to know.

"Master Aitchley, Master Poinqart, and Miss Berlyn have not yet returned," replied Gjuki. "Is there a problem?"

Calyx turned beady eyes on the forest. "None that I had," he answered, stubby fingers tapping anxiously at the head of his warhammer.

Captain d'Ane's diaphanous frame dimly lit the surrounding foliage. "Do you think something's wrong?" he worried.

"I'm a dwarf," Calyx responded darkly. "Of course I think something's wrong." He turned away from the woods and stomped over to the horses, taking his *meion*'s reins in his hands. "I should've expected something like this," he grumbled.

Quickly gathering up their things and taking the reins of the remaining horses, Gjuki followed after the dwarf. "But what could the problem be?" the gardener wondered. "Did you not lead the trolls away from where Master Aitchley was?"

Trudging across the bridge, Calyx nodded curtly. "Of course I did," he tersely answered. "All the kid had to do was walk in there after me and find the elixir."

"What if he couldn't find it?" Captain d'Ane asked, weightlessly floating beside the two. "What if a troll took it with him?"

"Trolls aren't interested in things they can't eat," Calyx said. "The elixir would hold as much interest to a troll as you'd be fascinated by a really big rock." He shook his head grimly. "It just doesn't add up."

Passing intangibly through branches, d'Ane followed the dwarf through the dark woods. "Then what do you think happened?"

Calyx shoved his way through the brush toward Leucos. "I don't know," he answered truthfully. "That's what worries me."

*   *   *

Fear and amazement brimming in his blue-green eyes, Aitchley stared at the Patrolman, a weird feeling of disbelief and detachment burning through his body. This is impossible! his mind screamed at him. This is absolutely impossible! Fain was dead! Harris had slammed a stiletto right through the Patrolman's eye and had killed him! And people just don't get back up after getting killed! I should know! Eyfura hadn't. Archimandrite Sultothal hadn't. Captain d'Ane hadn't. So how in the Great Lifeburst of Karnahkarnanz-Leh-Cuns-Ulterlec had General Fain done it?

Fain's smile was a beacon of arrogance, victory, and pure evil. "You still don't understand, do you?" he mocked, tapping Harris's bloodied stiletto against the palm of his left hand. "No troll spilled the elixir. I drank it. I drank it while I was still alive. A magical artifact powerful enough to bring any corpse back from the dead, and I drank it while I still breathed! And now I am invincible. Now I am unkillable. Nothing you can do—nothing you can even conceive of—can ever possibly harm me. I am your lord and master, and you shall all bow down to—"

A sneer twisted Harris's upper lip. "Ah, shut up," he replied.

Black steel shrieked through the air so suddenly that even Berlyn was unable to stop the squeak of surprise that escaped her lips. Scarlet splashed as Renata drove fatally through Fain's healed eye, a tidal wave of crimson and vitreous humor splattering down his already blood-smeared face. Fain, however, only staggered, a slight grimace of discomfort clouding his bloodied features. Then, as casually as if he were brushing a hair from out of his face, the Patrolman reached up and plucked the razor-sharp length of steel out of his skull, hardly acknowledging the grotesque squelch of tearing tissues and dribbling fluids.

The injured eye began to heal almost as soon as the blade was removed. "You always were a slow learner, Blind-Eye," the general taunted. "The longer the elixir flows through my veins, the more powerful I become. In time, your paltry little attempts to stop me will not even slow me down. Stab at me! Impale me! Tear me limb from limb! You will not be able to stop me! The power of liquid life flows through me, and I will be your god!"

Mandy unexpectedly launched from the Patrolman's hand, and the next thing Aitchley knew, Harris had tumbled over backward into the darkness with a sudden grunt. Overwhelming amazement continued to cloud the young man's mind, and—despite the danger facing him—the farmer was unable to free himself of the disbelief and bewilderment locking his muscles in place.

This is impossible! he repeated to himself. Eternal Guardians and Daeminase are one thing! This is nothing more than a Patrolman! A stupid little Patrolman who doesn't even have the common sense to know when to die!

Aitchley felt his legs go weak as Fain turned wild eyes on him. Maybe it had something to do with the elixir being used on a living person—or maybe it was just something in the general himself—but Fain did not appear to be in full control of his faculties. Aitchley'd seen enough lunatics wandering about the fringes of Solsbury to know the Patrolman was a few turns shy of a fully cranked crossbow, and he also knew that mentally unsound people could be even more dangerous than their sane counterparts. This only made Fain's claim to godhood all the more serious.

Anxiously, Aitchley took a single step back, his grip tightening around the bluish-green decanter in his arms.

As if in response, Fain took a step forward, Renata still in his bloodied grasp. "You have no idea the inconveniences you've caused me, boy," the general snarled. "I've had to put up with imprisonment, the plague-dead, and being saddled with Tampenteire's little snot-nosed brat. All of that just to get close to the fabled Elixir of Life." His smile bordered on the edges of madness. "I suppose I really should thank you for leaving your pack so easily accessible. And the dwarf. I suppose I should thank him as well for getting rid of those troublesome little trolls. Then it was only a matter of time before I was able to take what was rightfully mine." He glanced down at the back of his hand as if expecting to see something. "Now hand the elixir over," he snarled, his eyes lifting to meet Aitchley's. "I believe I haven't quite finished with it."

Aitchley shot a worried glance at the container in his hands. Glimmering, the elixir filled the night with a warm golden aura, and—even though half of it was gone—Aitchley could still feel the revitalizing tingle of its sorcery flow out of the bottle and into his body.

Aitchley swung his attention back to Fain. Aside from being
. . . um . . . immortal, Fain only had Harris's stiletto, the young
man noted. *If we can get away from him, he's not that serious
a threat. I mean . . . if he wants to be lord and master over an
empty town that's gonna be full of trolls again any minute, so
be it! I've got a quest to finish!*

Knowing the ring around her finger enabled Berlyn to see
him through the darkness, Aitchley threw the young blonde a
quick glance then unexpectedly dodged right, bolting for the
safety of the surrounding shadows and night-engulfed forest.
"Run!" the young man shouted to his companions.

Growling like some rabid xlf, Fain leapt as the young man,
blonde, and half troll dashed off in three directions. *It wasn't
enough that the lockpick was dead,* the Patrolman concluded.
*The farm boy and his little band of bung-ups had to be made
to suffer as well. They had to feel what Fain had felt—had to
go through all the pain and suffering he had—and they had to
give him what remained of the Elixir of Life!*

Berlyn emitted a curt shriek as Fain's grasping fingers
snagged the billowing edge of her cloak, reeling her in like a
fisherman's trawling net. Her first response was to spin around
and strike at him with her weapon, but she'd seen how easily
Fain had shrugged off Harris's last attack. Like the Daeminase,
General Fain was becoming impervious to any kind of physical
harm.

Instead, Berlyn grabbed frantically at the hood draped about
her shoulders and quickly jerked it up over her head, popping
instantaneously out of sight.

Startled, Fain stumbled back a step and his grip faltered,
invisible samite slipping through his fingers.

The voice of the farm boy suddenly sounded very close to
the Patrolman's ear: *"Berlyn!"*

Fain turned just in time to see blue-and-gold *gnaiss* slam into
his face, lifting him bodily into the air and hurling him across
the street. The Patrolman heard the cartilage in his nose
crunch—felt the searing agony as bone rammed up inside his
head and actually penetrated his brain—but then the pain faded
and his body swiftly healed. Cracked and broken teeth repaired
themselves, and as quickly as the warm, coppery taste of blood
filled his mouth, the sudden gush of fluids stopped.

Shaking any lingering trace of dizziness out of his head, Fain
pulled himself to his feet, a strand of viscous, blood-mingled

saliva oozing down his lips. "You're only making things worse for yourself, boy," he said. "Hand me the elixir and perhaps I'll let you live. After all . . . you did manage to get it for me."

Silver sparkled in the moonlight as Aitchley withdrew the Cavalier's sword. "Get bunged, Fain," he snapped back. "I didn't get it for you. I got it for the Cavalier. I got it so the world would be a better place to live in."

A cruel smile twisted Fain's bloodied features. "And you think your precious Cavalier can save the world by his mere presence?" he taunted. "A man two hundred years out of date? You think *he* has the ability to right the world when nothing all the scients and scholars have done has made a single, bunging difference? You're a fool, boy! A useless little peasant with a head full of mulch! You actually believed the words of four noblemen? They don't want the world to be a better place! They just want it to be the way it was! They just want to feel important again!" Insanity tainted the curve of his smile. "It's a little hard to be noble when your subjects are too busy worrying about famines and plagues to pay you the proper respect."

"Worth a dogling's teat," that's what Lord Chael had said, Aitchley remembered. All their treasures combined weren't "worth a dogling's teat." Is Fain right? Am I nothing more than some glorified errand boy for the nobles of Solsbury? Is this whole quest nothing more than just an attempt to reaffirm their positions?

Aitchley forced the sudden thoughts out of his head, his fingers tightening around his sword hilt. "Like you'd be any different?" he snarled at the Patrolman. "The Cavalier was at least a hero. You're nothing but some petty little Patrolman who wasn't even good enough to join the army!"

An insane fire ignited in Fain's eyes. *"Nothing?"* he shrieked, his voice cracking in his madness. "I am General Ongenhroth Fain, maggot! I am your lord and master, and I will not be denied!"

Mindlessly, Fain launched himself at the farmer, a berserkerlike rage fogging his eyes. Although he had dropped Renata when Aitchley had struck him, the general charged forward as recklessly and as certain as a man armed with a hundred blades. Momentarily taken aback, Aitchley stumbled backward.

Well, that was good, the young man's pessimism grunted sarcastically. Piss off someone who's already mentally un-

sound. Good. Real good. Maybe I should have just run with
the others. I gave the elixir to Poinqart—what was left of it
anyway—so maybe I should have just gone with him? But,
no . . . ! I have to get all riled up and save Berlyn! Daeminase
Pits! When am I going to learn that half the time she doesn't
even need my help?

Fain unexpectedly screamed as black steel ripped effortlessly
across the backs of both knees, severing the tendons. Ham-
strung, the Patrolman pitched forward, his useless legs crumpling beneath him. Aitchley's eyes went wide as the Patrolman
collapsed practically in front of him, and he jumped involuntarily as a dark silhouette rose up from the ground like a
shadow come to life and drove a sharp blade through the general's spine.

Harris slid Renata back into her sheath and gave the young
man a nefarious grin. "You gonna stand around all night with
your mouth open, scout?" the southern-city lockpick jeered.
"Fain's gonna be back on his feet in a minute."

Gingerly, Aitchley danced over Fain's healing cadaver. "I
. . . I thought you were dead," he told the outlaw.

Harris's smirk grew into a smile. "No such luck, puck," he
said. "Only Fain would try and stab someone in the chest when
they've got saddlebags draped over one shoulder." He threw a
brief frown at the cut made in the thick leather of his supplies.
"I think he punctured my water flask, though."

"I'll be sure to puncture more than just your water flask next
time," Fain suddenly said behind them, getting slowly to his
feet.

Mandy twitched in Harris's hand. "Daeminase Pits," the
outlaw swore, "you just don't know when to stay dead, do
you?"

A flicker of discomfort continued to twist the Patrolman's
face as he took a step forward. "The elixir, Corlaiys," the
general hissed. "Give me what's left of it."

Harris stepped between Fain and the young man, Mandy held
between thumb and forefinger. "It's not yours, Fain," the lockpick said. "Now back off or you're gonna be dead again."

The general threw a contemptuous glare at the rogue. "You
never learn, Blind-Eye." He sighed. "I am unkillable. Unde-
featable. Stab me as many times as you want, I will always
return."

The crooked smile widened beneath Harris's raggedy beard.

"Oh, I wasn't thinking of stabbing you anymore," he jeered. He took a step to one side. "Show him what your staff can do, puck."

A muted sense of triumph cut through the shock and bewilderment numbing Aitchley's reflexes, and he leveled the length of blackened oak at the approaching Patrolman. Fain's eyes momentarily narrowed at the glimmering silver knob atop the stave, but the arrogance never left his face. Purposefully, he strode forward, one hand extended as if expecting to have the elixir handed over to him. The smug certainty remained on his face until he smelled the odor of superheated air around the tip of the staff, and his eyes went wide as a titanic ball of fire materialized out of thin air and slammed into him.

In a thunderous explosion of flames and sorcery, General Fain was flung backward, sparks and smoke filling the night sky.

Harris's smirk grew as the general's corpse crashed through an abandoned house, streams of orange-red flames searing the darkness. Dry tinder caught fire easily, and the stench of burning flesh filled the empty town. Thick, acrid smoke coiled through the flames—curling and writhing like hazy black serpents—and burning timbers and shattered bricks collapsed inward, sending a billowing, spark-lined cloudburst spuming into the air.

Harris smiled. "Slow learner, eh?" he mocked the flames. "Even Harris Blind-Eye knows the best way to fight magic is with more magic."

"Then you've learned nothing at all."

Aitchley felt his jaw drop to the ground as General Fain slowly struggled free of the debris of the burning house. His clothes were completely gone—incinerated by the sorcerous blast of fire—and likewise all the hair had been burned from his body. His skin was a bright red as if he had suffered a serious sunburn, and Aitchley could tell it hurt for him to walk, yet he stepped free of the destruction as if uninjured, the fiery color of his flesh slowly returning to normal.

Little tendrils and wisps of smoke coiled up around his body as General Fain emerged unscathed from the flames. "The elixir, Corlaiys," the Patrolman demanded. "Give it to me or die."

Aitchley swallowed hard.

17

Those That Cannot Die

Aitchley threw a bewildered look at Harris Blind-Eye. "Now what do we do?" he wanted to know.

Harris hurriedly replaced his twin stilettos. "Southern-city rules, puck," he responded. "When all else fails, *run*!"

Near panic, Aitchley spun on his heel and followed after the lockpick, hurrying away from the fires that lit the deserted village. Confidently, General Fain strolled after them, a dark silhouette against the backdrop of fiery destruction.

There was no way to kill this guy! Aitchley thought as he ran, and each failed attempt only heightened the young man's disbelief. It had gotten so bad that his own astonishment had muddled his common sense, and instead of doing something, he had resigned himself to just standing there with his mouth open. Who would have thought that drinking the Elixir of Life while you were still alive would give you godlike—or at least Daeminase-like—abilities? And—while Fain's claim to godhood appeared to be inspired by his lack of mental stability—his desire for what remained of the elixir posed a very real threat. Aitchley had gone through quite a bit to get that damn elixir, and he wasn't about to let some regenerative Patrolman drink the rest of it. Not that there was enough to revive anybody else. . . . Fain had already drunk half of it! Liahturetart said there might be enough for two doses—*might!*—so that meant there were no guarantees, but . . . Daeminase Pits! Aitchley was at least going to bring back what was left of the damn stuff!

But what about those things Fain had said? the young man mused. What about this whole quest being nothing more than a ploy by the lords of Solsbury to gain back their positions? Aitchley had sensed that before—had had difficulty believing such men as Lord Elideri cared for the common man's good— but would Lord Tampenteire and Saradd do something like that? Was the resurrection of the Cavalier solely for their benefit, or would the rest of Vedette benefit as well? Aitchley was no longer certain.

Houses suddenly gave way to dark trees, and Aitchley bolted into the forest south of Leucos. He could hear Harris running somewhere ahead of him, but the young man had lost sight of the bandit the moment they had entered the woods. He briefly entertained the thought of using his staff's ability to cast continual light, but that would give Fain something to follow as well. If he calmed down and tried to think rationally, he should be able to find his way back to the river.

Think rationally? the young man's mind shot back at him. How can I think rationally? There's a Patrolman out there who won't die and wants the rest of the bunging elixir!

Trying to chase such worries out of his thoughts, Aitchley slowed to a brisk jog, blue-green eyes cutting through the darkness. Come on, he urged himself, you've been sneaking back and forth between the river and the town all night long. One more time isn't going to kill you. Just calm down and think! The river should be over this way.

Aitchley pushed his way through dark foliage and suddenly found himself face-to-face with what was left of the brood of female trolls and their offspring. Brown lips pulled back in threatening snarls as the creatures recognized the young man, and yellow fangs glistened with a fine sheen of saliva in the yellow-green glow of the moon.

Aitchley felt his stomach knot. Oh, bung! he cursed. Bloody typical . . .

His pessimism heightening, Calyx led his *meion* through the dark woods, a tangible gloom surrounding his compact frame. Something was wrong, the dwarf concluded. Things had gone too well and now they were paying the price for their optimism. Maybe all the trolls hadn't left. Or maybe the kid couldn't find the elixir. Hammer and anvil! Maybe the kid had just tripped

and broken his damn foot! Whatever it was, something had
seriously delayed the three and that something couldn't possibly be any good.

The low, muffled *poompf!* of an exploding fireball suddenly
resounded through the night, and Calyx swung beady eyes on
the darkness. Orange-red flickers of illumination began to color
the black sky, and curls of smoke twisted and writhed up to
vanish into the darkness.

Calyx felt the darkness inside of him grow. "I knew it," he
grumbled, moving purposefully toward the sudden explosion.
"Something *is* wrong."

"Trollsz?" Trianglehead wondered from Gjuki's shoulder.

Calyx fingered his warhammer. "Can't tell," he replied.
"We'd just better—"

There was a sudden rustle of disturbed shrubbery, and the
three immediately took up defensive postures. Dark leaves fluttered about them as Poinqart charged through the foliage, and
a look of hybrid shock and anxiety momentarily crossed his
face as he all but ran into the others. Large feet skidded to a
clumsy halt in the litter of leaves, and huge, four-fingered hands
clamped protectively about the decanter of blue-green glassware in his grasp.

"Mister-Calyx-dwarf!" the half troll exclaimed, yellow-
black eyes growing wide. "Trouble-calamity, there is! Quickly-
come or Poinqart fears Mister Aitch may very well be
alive-no-more-dead!"

Despite the night surrounding them, Calyx pulled himself
into his *meion*'s saddle. "Trouble-calamity, eh?" he replied.
"What kind of trouble-calamity?"

His face half-lit by the magical elixir in his hands, Poinqart
tugged urgently at the dwarf's boot. "Nasty-bad-soldier-man
tries to make us all alive-no-more-dead," the half troll explained. "Quickly-come!"

A look of question scrawled across Calyx's face.
"Soldier-man?" he repeated. "What soldier-man?"

Poinqart kept tugging at his leg. "Nasty-bad-soldier-man,"
he said again. "Stole the magic-elixir-drink, he did! Mister
Aitch gave elixir-drink to Poinqart for protective-keeping but
Poinqart worry-fears that Mister Aitch may be hurty-bad-
killed."

Clucking his *meion* forward, Calyx ducked a dark branch
and headed in the direction of Aitchley's last fireball, Poinqart

hurrying ahead of him. Soldier-man? the smith wondered gravely to himself. What soldier-man? The only soldier-man Calyx could think of was Sergeant Lael back in Viveca, but what would he be doing here? And why try to steal the elixir after helping them rescue the baroness? It just didn't make sense.

Frowning, Calyx rode farther into the woods. Serves me right for being so damn optimistic, he admonished himself. From now on it's doom and gloom. Doom and gloom!

Eyes narrowed, General Fain pushed his way through the shrubbery, squinting against the darkness and the itch of re-generated eyeballs. There was a strange tingling sensation in his scalp and groin as hair grew back at an amazingly rapid pace, and even in the moonlight he could see the flesh of his body slowly pale from a fiery, burned red back to its normal tone.

Fain halted and stared down at his hand, watching in aston-ishment as the whorls and ridges of fingerprints gradually re-turned to mark his fingertips. Hairs also began sprouting up along his arms and chest, and the slight discomfort of seared lungs finally faded as the elixir flowing through his veins healed him internally as well as externally.

Fain balled his newly healed fingers into a tight fist. I *am* unkillable! he mused triumphantly to himself. Not even flames can destroy me! Not even magic! There is nothing left to stop me! Nothing to stop me from returning to Solsbury and making myself lord and master over all! And nothing they can do, and nothing they can say can make any difference! I am undefeat-able!

Fain turned new eyes on the dark foliage. Only Corlaiys stands in my way, the general concluded. Only Corlaiys would dare try to keep me from what remains of the elixir. Imagine what could happen if I drank it all? Godhood, perhaps? A mas-tery over all things physical? The elixir must be mine and no pathetic little farm boy is going to keep me from it!

As Fain pushed through the bushes, something whistled sharply in his ear, landing with a deft *thwunk* in his neck. Sur-prise momentarily clouded his vision—an abrupt jolt of agony disrupting his senses—and he toppled back into the brush, a warm, cascading release of blood gushing down his naked body from his severed neck. His mouth gulped and gaped like a fish out of water as his trachea was cut, and crimson liquid filled his mouth, tasting foul and metallic on his tongue.

Thrashing convulsively, the Patrolman collapsed, spastic fingers clutching at his neck. A hazy, incorporeal sensation briefly addled the general's mind, and he might have passed out as great spurts of red shot from his throat. Throughout the blood, he could feel the severed arteries and muscles of his neck quickly knitting back together, and—as the pain diminished—he wondered fleetingly how even he could survive decapitation.

But then his body was whole again and it no longer mattered.

Smiling, General Fain rose slowly to his feet, peering intently at the surrounding darkness. Warm blood still stained his naked body, but little remained of the ax wound that had practically sliced through his entire neck.

The Patrolman scanned the dark forest. "A valiant attempt," he said with a sneer, "but you cannot kill those that cannot die." He searched the blackness for any hint of his attacker. "Corlaiys's girl, is it not?" he called out tauntingly. "I applaud your efforts but they are all in vain. I am your lord and master, girl, and there is nothing you or your sorry little mudshoveler of a boyfriend can do about it." His smile grew foul. "Come with me," he hissed conspiratorially. "Leave Corlaiys and join me. Magic obviously does not frighten you. Join with me and I will make you my consort for all eternity."

The forest was silent, marked only by the fires still burning in Leucos.

Fain caught a brief shimmer of distortion move swiftly beyond the trees. "So be it," he said, and his smile was tainted with conceit. "Those who oppose me must die."

Berlyn shrieked when Fain suddenly launched himself right at her, crashing into her invisible body and sending them both to the ground. A muffled grunt came from Fain himself as he half expected to pass through empty air, and he was almost as surprised as the blonde as they slammed into one another and went tumbling through the underbrush.

Not even knowing whether she was visible or not, Berlyn struck the ground hard, landing brutally on her back. Stars exploded behind her eyelids and her teeth clacked painfully, sending a disorienting jolt ringing through her head. Dizzy, she blinked gray-green eyes to see Fain above her, his powerful hands grabbing at her shoulders. His naked body was a grotesque crisscross of pale flesh and bloody wet streaks, and the

scullery maid's mind suddenly flashed back to other memories
. . . memories of unwanted and unprovoked hands stroking and
pressing intimately against her, and ugly bodies surrounding
her, leaving her helpless and powerless.

A wild rage built up inside the young girl's breast, and she
rammed a knee up with all the strength in her petite body.
Yowling, Fain rolled to one side, both hands diving instinctively to his groin as tears of intense agony streamed from his
eyes. Painful groans split the night, and Berlyn drew herself
hurriedly to her feet, unseen samite billowing about her. She
gave the Patrolman curled up in a ball at her feet one last
glance, then went sprinting off into the darkness, careful not to
trip over her own invisible feet.

Grimacing, General Fain managed to pull himself to his
knees, his hands still clutched protectively about his naked
crotch. A hot, nauseous churning roiled in his stomach, and it
felt as if all the muscles in his body had been turned to weak,
rubbery, uncooked noodles. Bile threatened his newly healed
throat, and it took him one full minute before he was even able
to get back to his feet.

Magic bunging elixir, my ass! the Patrolman swore vehemently, the burning sickness still twisting inside him. That hurt!
He trained angry eyes on the surrounding woods. No more
games! he concluded murderously. Corlaiys and his little band
of bung-ups were dead . . . and I'll take a very personal pleasure
in killing Corlaiys's little blonde bunghole myself!

Hands still clutching his naked privates, Fain staggered to
his feet and lurched clumsily after the invisible scullery maid.

Aitchley took an uneasy step back, his left hand tightening
around the length of blackened oak. Eight females confronted
him, growling and snarling, and even their inhuman young had
their lips drawn back in menacing displays of sharp, jagged
fangs. The stink of troll filled the small clearing, and Aitchley
could feel the insectlike skitter of nervous perspiration wind
down the back of his neck and disappear beneath his collar.

Bloody bunging typical! the young man grumbled to himself,
taking another cautious step backward. Only I can run from
one threat and smack right into another! Typical Corlaiys luck!
He flashed the cluster of trolls an apprehensive glance. Maybe
if I don't make any sudden moves, I can get out of this without
having to fight them. It looks as if they don't want to fight me

. . . they're probably afraid I'll do to them what I did to their friends.

Anxiously, Aitchley took another slow step back. The trolls watched him retreat with uncertainty in their yellow-black gaze, and a few females hissed and spat threateningly at each backward step. Talons glinted black in the filtered moonlight, and Aitchley could feel their inhuman eyes boring into him.

Just a little bit more, he mentally coaxed both himself and the trolls. I'm almost out of here. Don't worry. I don't want to fight you, and you don't want to fight me. Probably think I'll blast the rest of you like I did the others. Hah! You wouldn't be so scared of me if you knew that I didn't know how I had done that, would you? Daeminase Pits! I don't even know if *I* did it. Berlyn was holding the staff, too. Maybe it was her. Or maybe it was the both of us.

A sudden scream from Berlyn tore through the darkness, and Aitchley whipped about, his right hand flashing for his sword. A white-hot burst of panic-spawned adrenaline burned through his bloodstream, and his blue-green eyes tried to cut through the blackness in a vain attempt to see where the young blonde was.

Provoked by the young man's sudden movement, the trolls launched forward.

Aitchley barely had enough time to turn his attention back to the mottled creatures.

"Oh, mulch!" he cursed.

Astride his *meion*, Calyx jerked about as he heard a curt shriek from Berlyn come from somewhere on his left. Dark trees flanked him on all sides, and he could see the dark silhouette of houses on his right. An orange-red glow gradually faded to the west, and the smell of smoke slowly wafted through the night toward them.

Impatiently, the dwarf squinted beady eyes through the darkness and scowled heavily. "I can't see a damn thing," he muttered out loud. "Gjuki, light a torch. Poinqart, where did you say this soldierman attacked you?"

Poinqart jabbed a thick finger through the foliage. "Poinqart is no longer for-certain-sure, Mister-Calyx-dwarf. Confused-befuddled he is, but Poinqart thinks it was over there. Toward the burning-hot-fire."

Calyx grunted. "Makes sense," he murmured. "I thought I heard the kid's staff go off."

"But who is this soldier that Master Poinqart has mentioned?" asked Gjuki. "And why has he attacked us?"

Calyx spurred his mount toward the dying fire. "Who cares?" the dwarf replied. "I told you people would be after us once they found out we had the elixir. I'm sure there's a lot of people who'd like to have it for their own." He turned small eyes on the half troll. "You said this guy drank some of it?"

Poinqart nodded enthusiastically. "Drank-consumed it, he did!" the hybrid answered. "Now he won't even stay alive-no-more-dead, and sneakthief Harris kill-stabbed him twice!"

Some of the color drained from Calyx's face. "Whoa! What did you say?" he suddenly interrupted. "Harris is back?"

Poinqart kept nodding. "Poinqart does not like sneakthief Harris, but without sneakthief Harris, Mister Aitch and poor Poinqart would never have discover-found the magic-elixir-drink."

A look of doom creased the dwarf's bearded features. "Doom and gloom," the smith swore darkly. "Harris is back." He suddenly rammed his heels into his *meion*'s flanks. "We'd better find the kid and Berlyn and get the forge out of here!"

A look of confusion was on Captain d'Ane's face as he floated after the dwarf. "Why?" he asked. "Don't you want to find out who this soldier is?"

Calyx's mount thundered off through the brush. "I don't care who this soldier is," he retorted. "Harris is back!"

Questioningly, Captain d'Ane floated after the dwarf, a look of unrestrained bewilderment on his transparent features. *If I ever live to be a hundred years old, I'll never understand dwarves,* he mused somberly to himself. *Too bad I'm already dead!*

Adal's Staff erupted in a blistering white nebula of magic, releasing a frigid stream of sorcery that instantly froze a leaping troll in midair. Ice crystals formed a semitransparent cocoon all around the creature's gangly frame, and its body shattered as it crashed to the forest floor, little pieces of freeze-dried flesh and bone skittering across the leaf litter like snowflakes across a road.

Aitchley swung on another troll, the powerful pins-and-needles sensation numbing his hands and arms. The staff in his grasp belched out another stream of blue-white cold—encasing another troll in a solid block of ice—and a third stumbled back, one side of its face crystallizing as it stood too close to the arctic blast.

Black claws tore viciously at Aitchley's face, narrowly missing the brim of his hat. Dodging, the young man brought up his left arm, catching the troll at the elbow with his shield. Bone snapped as easily as straw, and Aitchley felt a sympathetic twinge spark in his own arm as the monster's limb splintered into two pieces, a jagged shaft of bone punching through mottled brown flesh. Howling, the troll careened backward, only to be replaced by another.

Abrupt claws lashed out and tried to tear the staff from Aitchley's hands, tugging with inhuman strength. Aitchley was almost thrown forward as the troll tried to take the staff away from him, and he was jerked and thrashed about as he fought the troll for possession.

The troll suddenly stiffened, its claws falling away from Aitchley's staff. A look of trollish confusion momentarily scrawled across its ugly face, and its hand went uncertainly to the shaft of black steel that had unexpectedly materialized in its yellow-black eye. Blood dribbled down its wrinkled, mottled flesh, and it released a feeble moan as it pitched over backward and lay still.

Another shaft of ebon steel rocketed from the forest and caught a second troll in the eye, blood and vitreous spattering the trees.

Aitchley turned away from the remaining two trolls and spun on the dark figure behind him. A wry smirk twisted Harris's lips as he enjoyed the young man's surprise, but a sudden finger stabbed at the night beyond them.

"Look out, puck," the southern-city outlaw warned. "There's still two left!"

Aitchley wheeled back around just in time to see yellow fangs lunge for his throat. Blue-and-gold *gnaiss* slammed into one of the attacking creatures—teeth and bone shattering against the dwarven alloy—but he knew he couldn't spin around fast enough to confront the other. Wincing, he expected razor-sharp talons to tear at his face and pointed fangs to gouge his flesh.

Instead, he was splashed by blood as an invisible blade sliced effortlessly through the last troll's neck.

Berlyn popped back into sight as she lowered the hood of Harris's cloak. Her throwing ax was coated with trollish blood. "Are you all right?" she asked the young man.

Aitchley wiped blood from his cheeks. "I'm fine," he replied. "What about you? I thought I heard you scream."

A trace of red flushed the blonde's cheeks. "I had a brief run-in with Fain," she admitted. "I tried to chop his head off but it didn't work."

Wiping his blades clean on the grass, Harris retrieved his stilettos. "No chance there, sweets," he said. "Fain drank your elixir." He smiled mockingly. "I guess this means it actually works, eh?"

Stepping gingerly around fragments of thawing troll, Aitchley took Berlyn by the hand and started to lead her out of the small clearing. "Who cares?" he replied. "I just hope Poinqart got back to the others with whatever's left. If Fain wants to be some kind of immortal god, let him. It's not my concern."

Someone stepped leisurely through the brush behind them. "Oh, but it should be, Corlaiys," the Patrolman said with a victorious sneer, his naked body streaked by fresh rivulets of his own blood. "Once I have what's left of the elixir, there will be no one else in all Vedette who can stand in my way. And I've given you the honor of being the first to die by my hands. Isn't that wonderful?"

Aitchley's hand went instinctively to his sword hilt. "You're mad, Fain," he snarled back.

Dark shrubbery unexpectedly rustled, and Fain turned a triumphant sneer on the murky woods. "Ah, no doubt the rest of your little band has arrived," he jeered at the young farmer. "Good. It saves me the trouble of hunting you all down."

Anxiously, Aitchley turned to where the dark branches parted, half expecting to see Calyx and the others. Worried thoughts about the elixir falling back into the Patrolman's hands raced through Aitchley's head, and that was what made it all the more surprising when something tall and gangly came leaping out of the bushes, scarlet flesh glimmering in the moonlight. Fain screamed as crimson talons ripped across his shoulder—tearing straight to the bone—and thick, viscous streams of saliva oozed from the monster's fang-filled maw as it slashed another hand across the Patrolman's belly, freeing internal organs and coils of intestines out onto the forest floor in a sudden slap of wetness.

Berlyn shrieked as another monster came lunging out of the bushes, its eyeless face fixing on its human prey. Another loped out behind it. And another. And a fifth. Branches cracked and trembled as hordes of ravenous Daeminase came thundering out of the darkness, swarming over the injured Fain like ants over sugar.

Five horses abruptly exploded out of the woods, and Aitchley pivoted to see Calyx peering down at him from atop his *meion*. "Come on, kid!" the dwarf screamed at him. "Let's get the forge out of here!"

The cracking and rustling of disturbed vegetation reverberated through the young man's ears as he swung into his saddle, half expecting vicious red claws to suddenly tear at his back. Berlyn was behind him almost immediately, and he could feel her hands shaking as she clasped him about the waist. More and more Daeminase poured into the clearing, and the color drained from Harris's face as he vaulted on top of Camera 12 and tugged frantically at the construct's reins. Chaos filled the forest as gangly red figures tore through the night, and the moonlight glistened on a frenzy of flashing talons and sharklike teeth.

Trying to shove his own bowels back into his stomach, Fain struggled against the circle of monsters attacking him. "No!" he screeched venomously. "You can't escape me! I am your lord and master! Nothing can kill me! *Nothing!*"

Red claws sliced across the general's face, plucking out one eye and baring his cheek of all flesh. Rivers of blood gushed down Fain's face—bubbling and frothing as they covered his lips—and he screamed in agony as another set of claws severed the tendons and muscles of his left arm, pulling the limb completely out of its socket in a sudden squelch of bloody spray and flailing ligaments.

Aitchley felt his stomach heave as a Daeminase clawed a huge gash down the front of Fain's chest, exposing his rib cage and the magically empowered heart beating beneath.

"No!" Fain screamed again, his voice gurgling with the blood rising in his throat. "I am your lord and master! None may escape me!"

There was a sickening crunch as sharp teeth tore off a large portion of Fain's right thigh, bloody talons ripping at bone and pulling at long, stringy coils of vein. Severed fingers spattered the ground in a rainfall of blood, and scarlet liquid formed an ever-widening pool about the dismembered and disemboweled body.

Flesh and muscles shred like dough pulled too tight as another Daeminase tore Fain's right arm free of his body. "No!" the Patrolman screamed. "I am—"

Blood and bile clogged the general's throat as inhumanly strong arms suddenly ripped his head right off his neck, torn and severed arteries shooting bright red geysers into the night. Ragged flaps of flesh fluttered weakly at the neck as Fain's decapitated body still struggled against the press of Daeminase, and it only toppled to the ground when its last remaining leg was pulled out from beneath it. A look of shock and betrayal was on Fain's face as his head was carried away by the Daeminase to be eaten later, and his mouth still worked although no sounds came out. Blood and bodily fluids bespotted his face, and—without a windpipe—Fain's lingering screams were wordless and silent.

Aitchley jerked his horse around and rammed his heels into its flanks, spurring the beast through the woods and away from the grisly sight. The stench of blood hung heavy in the young man's nostrils, and he could hear the ravenous crunching and slavoring as the Daeminase feasted on a body that continually tried to regenerate itself.

Gradually, it was only distance that silenced the sounds of carnage.

Beads of nervous perspiration lining his brow, Harris Blind-Eye forced an uneasy smile across his lips. "I'd like to see him regenerate his way out of *that* one!" he remarked, voice quavering.

The horses thundered through the darkness.

18

Making a Difference

Aitchley awoke the next morning to sounds of crunching and chewing, his mind instantly assaulted by visions of dismembered limbs flailing and thrashing although no longer attached to their bodies. Blood-drenched memories of decapitated heads with mouths that moved and tried to speak sent a disquieting shudder through the young man, and he had to blink himself completely awake in order to chase the horrible images from his mind.

Noisily munching on a greenish apple, Calyx looked down at the young farmer with a mocking smirk drawn beneath his beard. "Wakey-wakey, Mister Aitchy," the dwarf jeered. "It's time to move on."

Rubbing sleep from his eyes, Aitchley slowly pulled himself into a seated position, Berlyn stirring beside him. Birds sang gaily in the surrounding apple trees, and from the position of the sun, Aitchley could tell Calyx had let them sleep almost till noon. They had ridden until the eastern sky had turned pink with the coming dawn, and had stopped in a wild orchard surrounded by blossoms and ripening fruit. They must have put at least fifteen to twenty leagues between them and the pursuing Daeminase, but no matter how far they went, it was hard for Aitchley to block out the bloody memory of the previous night.

Fain may have been evil, the young man concluded, but did even he deserve to be torn apart by the Daeminase? How did it feel to be ripped apart but not be able to die? It was enough to send another shudder down the young man's spine.

Yawning, Aitchley forced himself to get up and eat something. Poinqart and Calyx had gathered some apples—they weren't quite ripe but it had been a long time since Aitchley had eaten fresh fruit—and the day was already warm with late-summer temperatures.

A small frown creased Aitchley's face as he gathered up his supplies and slipped them into his backpack. Potent tendrils of sorcery still trailed up his arms from the greenish-blue decanter of jaded sapphire, but he couldn't help feeling useless and angry as he stared at what was left of the elixir. *All that way,* the young man grumbled to himself. *All those obstacles. And I lose half the elixir to a crazy Patrolman with dreams of godhood! Bloody typical Corlaiys luck! Well, maybe there's enough for the Cavalier. I guess we'll just have to wait and see. . . .*

The farmer's frown deepened as sudden doubts passed through his mind, and he gave the elixir one last look of frustrated confusion before shoving it into his backpack. The others had mounted up around him, and—despite the abrupt hesitation and uncertainty that had entered his mind—the young man quickly shook himself free of his thoughts and pulled himself into his saddle. Berlyn climbed up behind him, and the seven quest-members continued westward.

Perched comfortably on Gjuki's shoulder, Trianglehead swung milky-blue eyes on the surrounding landscape. "Where we go now?" the fledgling wanted to know.

"Back to Viveca," Calyx said from the front of the group. "Replenish our supplies, then on to the Dragon's Ridge."

"Would it not be faster to go north through Karthenn's Weald and into the mountains straightaway?" Gjuki asked.

"Faster, yes," the dwarf responded, "but not necessarily more prudent." He trained beady eyes on the rolling green hills to the north. "We'll have to go through the weald anyway," he went on, "but I'd like to make sure we've got provisions before we do. Plus, there used to be a small path northeast of Viveca. It's probably not even there anymore, but if it is, it'll cut our travel time up the mountain by half."

Expressionlessly, Aitchley turned blue-green eyes to the north, scanning the green hills that led up to Karthenn's Weald. The weald was a huge stretch of lush forest that encircled the southern base of the Dragon's Ridge like a thick green skirt, stretching as far west as the Uriisa River and as far east as

Malvia Lake. It was supposed to have been haunted back in
the days of the Cavalier, Aitchley recalled, but that was before
learned men and scients dismissed such notions as nothing
more than primitive superstitions. Now it was just a dark woodland ignored by most except the occasional woodsman and a
few rabbits.

They rode the rest of the day in silence, their horses carrying
them at a moderate clip. As the sun gradually lowered in the
sky ahead of them, Berlyn tightened her arms around Aitchley's
waist and drew her lips up to his ear. "Is something wrong?"
she wondered. "You've been quiet all day."

Aitchley offered a weak shrug of feigned indifference. "No,
nothing's wrong," he replied. "I was . . . I was just thinking."

"Thinking about what?" asked Berlyn. "That there isn't
enough elixir left to bring back the Cavalier?"

A fleeting jolt of surprise washed over the farmer as he
turned to look at the blonde riding behind him. Was I always
this obvious, he wondered sardonically to himself, or did Berlyn just put her time with Harris Blind-Eye to good use?

"Well . . . uh . . . yeah," he answered, somewhat reluctantly.
"Actually . . . I was wondering if I should even use the elixir
on the Cavalier."

Berlyn's eyebrows narrowed across her forehead. "Back to
that again, are we?" she teased. "I thought we had resolved
that little problem."

The confusion and doubt rose up all over again in Aitchley's
mind. "Yeah, but . . ." he started then trailed off, staring
blankly at the hills to the north. "Something Fain said made
me start wondering again," he said after a long pause. "He
said that the lords of Solsbury didn't really care about the people . . . they just wanted their positions back."

Berlyn searched the young man's face. "Yes," she innocently replied. "So?"

"So?" Aitchley echoed. "So I'm nothing more than an errand boy for them to regain their prestige. They don't care
about us. I'm doing something that'll make me a peasant again
to their nobility—something that'll put me back in their serv-
ice—and I'm doing it voluntarily. Fain also said something I
had already thought of: who says the Cavalier can even do what
Tampenteire and the others say he can do? I mean . . . he's just
a man. He's not Gaal. Daeminase Pits! I'm his descendant and
look at me! I can't even bring forth a decent harvest! That's

hardly inspiring. That's not going to make people want to get up and work.''

Berlyn's eyes glittered with admiration. "Don't be so sure about that,'' she responded.

Aitchley had to fight to keep the warmth and color out of his cheeks. "You know what I mean,'' he answered. "I mean . . . even if the Cavalier does bring back hope to the people, it won't save the land. It's not going to cure the Black Worm's Touch or bring food when famine hits or rain where a drought is. It's just . . . I don't know! We've done so damn much, it just seems kind of anticlimactic to let it all go back to the way it was with just the Cavalier to show for it. I mean . . . honestly, what kind of difference is he going to make?''

Berlyn's arms tightened around the young man's waist and she drew herself in close on the saddle. "Look at the difference you've made,'' she whispered sweetly in his ear. "I know you've changed my outlook on things—I'm actually looking forward to *my* future—and look at Poinqart or Calyx. Nomion's Halberd! Look at Harris. You've actually given a southern-city rotgrub like Harris something that resembles morals.''

Aitchley snorted. "Oh, I had nothing to do with that,'' he responded. "He just came back 'cause he realized he had a better chance of escaping the Daeminase with us than without us.''

Berlyn smiled warmly. "Are you sure about that?'' she questioned him. She rested her head affectionately upon the farmer's shoulder. "You've made a great deal of difference, Aitchley Corlaiys,'' she told the young man. "And I'm sure your ancestor can make even more. And—even if there isn't enough elixir left—I know I've got my very own Cavalier. I guess I can maybe share him with the rest of the world.''

This time there was no way for Aitchley to keep the embarrassed redness out of his face, and he rode on in a kind of awkward silence, his heart bursting with pride. Any lingering worries about Fain, the elixir, or the Cavalier were gone from his mind.

It took twelve more days riding across the meadows and plains south of Karthenn's Weald to reach Viveca. Aitchley looked forward to staying in a real town—no more of this sleeping on the ground or in the Envirochamber—and he eagerly awaited his first glimpse of the city. He felt better about the whole elixir thing—although resilient doubts continued to creep about the corners of the mind—and he stayed in a relatively cheerful mood the whole way there. There was no denying that Fain's use of the elixir had left them with a questionable amount—and uncertainties about Tin William's enigmatic warning continued to plague the young man—but he ignored most of his pessimism's rasping, enjoying instead the warmth of the late-summer sun and the feel of Berlyn's arms wrapped lovingly around his waist.

The sun rose midway through the sky on the morning of the twelfth day as the horses followed a neglected trail through high grass. It had probably once been a road between Leucos and Viveca, but now it was choked with weeds and obscured by years of erosion.

Berlyn leaned forward expectantly, peering over Aitchley's shoulder at the terrain ahead of them. "I can't wait," she said enthusiastically. "Sleep in a real bed. Eat some real food. Take a real bath."

Aitchley felt a smile pull lopsidedly across his lips. "Yeah," he answered, "I know what you mean."

Calyx directed his *meion* toward a small rise, tossing a gruff look at the teenagers behind him. "We won't be staying long," the dwarf informed them. "Thanks to Harris, we've got the Daeminase back on our butts, and the last thing I want to do is lead 'em right into a heavily populated area." He swung back around to face the west. "A day or two," he added. "No more."

Berlyn released a heavy, overemphasized sigh and slumped back on Aitchley's horse in a mock pout. Aitchley felt his own spirits drop at the smith's words, but Calyx was right. If they overstayed their welcome in Viveca, the Daeminase might do the same damage they did to the *Kwau* or to the Rhagana. They had to get in, get their supplies, and get out. Real rest would have to wait until this whole thing was over.

Calyx's *meion* suddenly stopped at the crest of the rise, and Aitchley could almost feel the abrupt gloom that formed in the air about the dwarf. Questioningly, he strained to see over the small hill even as his horse drew nearer. He didn't know what would suddenly make Calyx so depressed—though the dwarf had been in something of a funk since leaving Fain and the Daeminase behind—but they were heading for a town that— according to Calyx—had food and shelter and a baroness who owed her very life to the quest. Even though he had never been there before, Aitchley was looking forward to his stay in Viveca, so what bothered Calyx so suddenly he could not guess.

A lump of ice lodged in his stomach as Aitchley's horse crested the rise beside Calyx. Viveca lay below them, its farmlands still smoking and smoldering from month-old fires, and curls and spirals of black smoke writhed upward from the city itself. A huge, imposing wall of somber gray stones encircled most of the town, and even from here, Aitchley could see busy figures hard at work at its construction. The western side of the city was completely razed—nothing more than charred timbers and gray-black ashes—and scores of uniformed Patrolmen stood sentry atop the half-built wall and at regular intervals at its base.

Practically invisible in the bright daylight, Captain d'Ane floated to the edge of the knoll. "What . . . what happened here?" he wondered.

Calyx's expression was dark. "They're rebuilding the wall," he grumbled. "I guess they didn't learn anything after all."

Riding Sprage's palomino, Harris drew up alongside the others. "Looks like there was a fight," he noted, blue-black eyes sweeping the ravaged city. "Lost a lot of farmland."

D'Ane swung nearly invisible eyes on Calyx. "Another riot?" he pondered.

The dwarven smith just shrugged as he started his *meion* down the path toward the ruined town. "Sure doesn't look like a party that got out of hand," he quipped bleakly.

The sudden blat of a horn sounded from atop the gray wall, and a heavy portcullis clanked and rumbled open, releasing a wave of Patrolmen on horseback. Swords and lances flared in the morning sunlight as the troop of men charged out of the city, their mounts galloping up the hill toward the quest-members.

Harris flicked twin stilettos into each hand. "Patrolmen," he snarled under his breath. "I'm getting pretty sick of seeing Patrolmen."

Calyx's own fingers tapped the head of his warhammer. "I've got a bad feeling about this," he murmured.

Anxiously, the seven waited as the squad of uniformed men charged up the rise, their scrawny horses thundering the burned and scarred earth beneath their hooves. Aitchley felt his fingers tighten instinctively around the gnarled staff in his left hand,

and he had difficulty forcing down the unease and apprehension
that clogged in his throat. They all looked like Fain, was all
the young man could think. Same uniform. Same guy. Was it
possible that Fain had survived? Had he somehow gotten here
ahead of them and turned the other Patrolmen against them?
Calyx had said that Viveca would welcome them back with
open arms—he and d'Ane had practically saved the town from
self-destruction the last time they were here—so what had happened? Why was the city in ruins and Patrolmen attacking innocent travelers? Had there been another riot? Had one of
Paieon's men taken back control of the city?

The thunder of approaching hooves pulled Aitchley out of
his thoughts and back to the danger at hand. Unexpectedly, the
lead Patrolman reined in his horse—a scrawny-looking mare—
and blinked bewildered eyes at the seven quest-members. For
the first time Aitchley noticed the man's uniform didn't quite
fit—the pants were a little short and the shirt a little too big—
and he didn't appear too comfortable riding while holding a
sword. With something that might have been a sigh of relief,
he held up a restraining hand to the four men behind him and
quickly sheathed his weapon.

"Daeminase Pits!" the Patrolman swore softly under his
breath. "It's them. They've come back." He turned urgently
to the Patrolman nearest him. "Kyne, go inform the Palatine
that we have guests. Important guests. Go! Quickly!"

The Patrolman named Kyne—a kid probably a year or two
younger than Aitchley—obediently turned his horse and galloped back for the city. The other Patrolmen slowly gathered
in about the quest, their weapons put away and a look of wonder on their faces. Now that Aitchley got a good look at them,
none of them looked like Fain . . . in fact, none of them looked
like proper Patrolmen. Their leader was a kindly-looking man
with dark leathery skin that had seen too much sunlight, and
his hands were callused and strong. There was even a girl
among them, her uniform fitting as poorly as the rest. Her pitch-
black hair was tucked in a tight bun, and dirt and grime smeared
what was otherwise a young, attractive face.

Blinking suspiciously, Calyx leaned forward on his *meion*.
"Rymel?" he questioned with some uncertainty.

The lead Patrolman offered an embarrassed grin, lowering
his eyes to avoid the smith's incredulous stare. "Yeah," he
answered sheepishly. "It's me."

A trace of befuddlement glimmered in his beady eyes as Calyx peered at the fisherman. "So what's the joke?" he wanted to know. "What are you dressed up like that for? And what in the forge happened here?"

Rymel tried to keep the smile on his lips. "We'll talk about it at the castle," he said, turning his mare back toward Viveca. "I'm sure the Palatine will be happy to see you."

Scowling, Calyx clucked his *meion* after the fisherman's scrawny mount, a grim look clouding his features. "Yeah, well," he grumbled, "I'm not too sure I'll be happy to see him. You people go through more political upheavals than hogs have teats!" He started down the path toward the ominous grey wall, his expression darkening. "Why can't anything good ever happen to us?" he muttered glumly.

Berlyn was disappointed as they rode through the streets of Viveca, her arms instinctively tightening around Aitchley's waist. From the stories she had heard from Calyx and Gjuki, she had expected the city to be as close to a paradise as was possible in Vedette. A town brimming with artisans and merchants. Fields green with crops, and livestock grazing in verdant pastures. Instead, she was greeted by solemn gray stones and burned-out farmlands. Houses in even worse repair than those abandoned in Leucos lined the cobblestone streets, and charred and blackened remains of what used to be buildings slouched on every corner. The acrid stench of smoldering wood filled the town with its stale perfume, and what looked unsettlingly like a mass grave stood open and ominous in a churchyard beside a burned-out church.

The people of Viveca looked as Calyx had once described them—sad and empty—yet Berlyn saw something light up inside them as the seven quest-members went by. By the time Rymel had led them halfway through the city, crowds had started to gather along the streets. Faces blackened with soot or streaked with dried blood and dirty bandages were suddenly smiling, and grateful cheers started to echo about the broken cobblestones. A number of Patrolmen in ill-fitting uniforms—some nothing more than children, others gnarled old men—saluted with chipped and rusty swords, and other Patrol members on horseback joined the impromptu parade. A celebratory throng of townspeople followed the procession up through the ill-repaired streets to the very gates of the castle, clustering about its walls to catch a last glimpse of the seven before they were ushered inside and the gates were shut behind them.

Dismounting, Berlyn turned wide eyes on Calyx. "What did you do the last time you were here?" she wondered out loud.

Frowning, Calyx slid off his *meion*. "Nothing that appears to have made much of a difference," he mumbled darkly.

Escorted by Rymel, the seven quest-members were led through an enormous hall and up a huge staircase. Elaborate tapestries hung from the cold gray stones, and magnificent paintings adorned the wall alongside the stairs. A twisting, writhing banister of obvious dwarven design decorated the steps with finely wrought iron and gold, and impressive statuary stood at the corner of the grand hall, marble eyes watching the seven as eagerly as those of servants and maids.

A wisp of silvery light, Captain d'Ane turned a wry look on Calyx. "Odd," he said with half a smile, weightlessly ascending the stairs. "I feel as if I've just walked over my own grave."

Calyx gave the bottom of the staircase where the captain had died a curt glance. "Cute, Captain," he remarked. "I'm just surprised no one's noticed you yet."

D'Ane glanced down at his intangible form. "I am rather hard to see," he responded. "Probably not much more than a patch of sunlight to these people. I really don't know how much further I can go."

Looking grumpier than usual, Calyx stomped up the enormous staircase. "Well, it's not much further after this," he answered. "We get whatever supplies they can spare and then head east again into Karthenn's Weald. Then it's just a quick hop up the mountain to the Dragon's Lair. I don't know what happened here, and frankly, I don't really care. Weather's gonna start getting cold, and I want to make sure we're up that mountain and back down long before it starts snowing." He tossed a beady-eyed glare up the stairs. "I just hope this Palatine they keep talking about is Lael. He owes us."

"I take it this ain't how you left it?" Harris asked with a malicious grin.

"Things weren't great, no," d'Ane replied, "but they had a chance to get better. Something obviously happened."

Fairly radiating pessimism, Calyx trailed Rymel down the third-floor landing. "Obviously," he quipped.

Hanging back, Aitchley and Berlyn followed the others as

they were led away from the enormous stairs and down a hall
carpeted with bloodred rugs and tasseled golden fringe. A
golden statuette of the Muse sat on an elegantly carved table
as they passed by, and Aitchley couldn't help feeling the unsettling doubts and worries return to his thoughts.

Look at all this, he thought with an awe mingled with disgust. It's just like Lord Tampenteire's estate. There's so much
stuff here you can't help but gawk! And this is nobility. This
is where all the wealth is. And if Fain was telling the truth,
I'm going to be the one responsible for making them wealthy
again. Right now all their gold and rugs and fancy paintings
aren't worth mulch, but if I get to the Dragon's Lair and bring
back my ancestor, Tampenteire and the others will be rich
again. Craftsmen and farmers won't mean as much anymore,
and it'll be my fault. Is that what Tin William was trying to
tell me? Was he trying to warn me about that? Or what? Gaal
dammit! None of this makes any sense at all! Sometimes I just
wish Fain had drunk all the elixir and we'd be done with it!

Wrestling with persistent doubts, Aitchley shadowed the others into a large room. A highly polished desk was the only
piece of furniture, its surface covered by a jumble of papers
and scrolls. A single man sat behind the desk, looking small
and feeble behind the magnificently carved wood. His hair was
black, closely cropped, and thinning on top, and his mustache
was thick and streaked with gray. Heavy circles formed bags
beneath his eyes, and lines and furrows were etched into his
face as deep as the engravings of the desk he sat at. In one
hand he held a scroll, and his other hand was placed flat on
the desktop as if to keep the other papers from blowing off.
From the strained look of concentration on his face, he appeared to be reading all the parchments at once.

A Patrolman—the first Aitchley had seen whose uniform appeared to fit—was the only other person in the room. He turned
smartly as the eight entered and a friendly smile came instantly
to his face as he spied them.

"Calyx. Gjuki," the soldier greeted them, grasping the
dwarf's hand in a powerful shake. "You can't imagine how
glad I am to see you."

A look of heavy skepticism marred Calyx's face. "Oh, I've
got an idea," he answered sarcastically. He gave the room a
questioning sweep. "What happened here, Lael? We leave you

alone for a few months and look what happens. Where's Desireah?''

A flurry of emotions swiftly erased Lael's smile. "We . . .
uh . . . had some difficulties after you left," he answered hesitantly. "Things got . . . a little out of hand."

"A little?" Calyx echoed. "Half the town's burned down
and you're rebuilding the wall! What happened?''

Releasing a weary sigh, Lael leaned back against the desk.
The man behind him looked apoplectic—as if Lael were going
to scatter all his papers—but the Patrolman paid him little attention. "We were attacked," the sergeant finally answered.
"They burned the farmlands and laid siege to the city before
we were able to muster the first of our men. We didn't even
see it coming." He cast his eyes downward. "Baroness Desireah was killed in the first attack."

Aitchley noticed the flash of surprise that drew some of the
ruddiness out of Calyx's cheeks. "She's dead?" the dwarf exclaimed. "How?"

"I did everything I could," Lael went on, shaking his head
sadly, "but she was insistent on helping put out some of the
fires. She was struck by a crossbow bolt in the chest."

There was a somber stillness in the room as Lael paused, his
eyes fixed sadly on the stone floor. Even though Aitchley had
never met any of these people, he felt a muted sense of loss
spark in his own chest, and he stared down at Calyx with re-
spectful silence.

Overcoming his grief with a sudden scowl, Calyx returned
his attention to the Patrolman. "So who's in charge now?" he
wanted to know. "You? Are you this Palatine everybody keeps
talking about?''

Lael's eyes widened briefly. "Who me?" he blurted. "Nomion's Halberd, no! Ghreler here's the Palatine! He's the only
one who can keep any order around here! I've just gone back
to being plain old Sergeant Lael again. Without the baroness,
I guess there's not much call for a chief adviser."

An angry fire burned in Calyx's small eyes as he glanced at
the dark-haired Ghreler. "So how did this happen?" the dwarf
wanted to know. "Was it another riot?"

A flicker of confusion tinged Lael's features. "Didn't Rymel
tell you?" he asked, somewhat surprised. "I thought it was
obvious."

Calyx shook his head sharply. "Not to me, it isn't."

Lael shrugged and turned away, staring out the window behind Ghreler's desk. "Ilietis," he somberly declared. "It was the priests of Ilietis."

Aitchley felt the sudden cold fist of guilty apprehension clutch about his heart and squeeze.

19

An Overly Developed Sense of Responsibility

Guilt rose like bile in Aitchley's throat. "Ilietis?" he exclaimed. "But they . . . we . . . I mean . . . they shouldn't . . ."

Words failing him—and a heavy culpability crushing down on him—Aitchley lapsed into an uneasy silence. Sardonically, Calyx flashed the young farmer a grim smile then turned his attention back to Sergeant Lael.

"Sergeant," the dwarf said, "meet Aitchley Corlaiys. Kid's got a way with words, don't you think?"

The Patrolman forced a weak smile. "The Cavalier's descendant," he said with a nod. "I can see the likeness from pictures of your ancestor. It's an honor."

Overwhelmed by guilt, Aitchley couldn't even bring himself to shake the sergeant's extended hand. "Honor?" the young man spat. "I'm responsible for what happened here! It's all my fault!"

Lael swung a perplexed look back at Calyx.

"You'll have to excuse the kid," the smith responded dryly. "He's got an overly developed sense of responsibility. When I first met him, he acted like being born was his fault."

"This is different," retorted Aitchley. "I'm the one who killed Sultothal. I'm the reason they attacked Viveca."

Calyx blinked beady eyes. "What? Because Sultothal's dead?" he asked back. "Look, kid, you may have been the one to kill Sultothal, but we're the ones who shut down Paieon's trade. If that makes it anybody's fault, it's ours.''

Aitchley hesitated, the certainty of his guilt disappearing. "But—"

"And I suppose we didn't make things any better when some acolytes came into town looking for Paieon," Sergeant Lael interjected. "Three of them were killed outright by angry townsfolk. We threw the ones that survived in the dungeon, let them know in no simple terms that trade between Viveca and Ilietis was over, and then sent them back to their precious Archimandrite to tell him the news. I guess they took offense at what we had to say."

"And that's my fault!" Aitchley insisted. "Sultothal never attacked you when he was in charge."

"That's because Paieon was still trading with him," Calyx replied. "Now be quiet and let the sergeant finish."

Lael nodded curtly as he continued. "They've attacked us three times since," he said. "The first attack was the worst. They managed to steal almost all our stores of food, burn our fields, and kill the baroness. They tried to take the town— probably wanted us to surrender so they could force us to pay tribute—but the people rallied. We forced them back to the Uriisa River before they finally turned and fled. We put Ghreler in charge since he's the only one left who really knows anything about running a town—after all, he did manage to keep things somewhat orderly even under Paieon's rule—and our first order of business was to rebuild the wall . . . this time around the whole town, not just the inner city.

"We hardly had the foundation laid when the priests attacked again. This time they destroyed the entire western section of town. Lost a lot of Patrolmen and villagers in that battle, but we managed to force them back again. Seems a lot of Ilietis's army is made up of townsfolk—regular people wearing armbands—and they're not one hundred percent loyal to Ilietis. Some turn tail and run the minute the fighting starts; others actually change sides right in the middle of battle. It's not good tactics to coerce other people to fight your war for you."

"Especially the way LoilLan's acolytes treat their townsfolk," Calyx put in. "We've been there, and it's no stroll through the Solsbury Hills, if you know what I mean."

Feeling some of the guilt subside—but not totally retreat—

Aitchley fixed questioning eyes on the Patrolman. ''So what happened the third time?''

Lael smiled proudly. ''We turned them back the third time,'' he announced. ''They didn't even get anywhere near the town. As you can see, the wall is almost complete, and we've got double the amount of guards patrolling the western gate. There's also a few sentries keeping watch at the banks of the Uriisa.''

Calyx nodded his approval. ''Sounds like you know what you're doing,'' he observed. He directed small eyes toward Ghreler. ''Now, any chance we can get some supplies or did the priests take 'em all?''

Later, shown to their rooms by Sergeant Lael—huge, magnificent rooms with beautiful tapestries and enormous beds with silken sheets—Berlyn could feel the anger building up inside the young man beside her. As soon as the door shut behind the sergeant, Aitchley turned abruptly on Calyx, all but exploding into a flurry of angry pacing and accusations.

''I can't believe you actually asked them for supplies!'' the young man barked, stalking back and forth across the cold, gray stones of the castle. ''We're responsible for the town getting attacked, and you actually ask them for favors! Didn't you hear anything that Lael said? They've been attacked three times!''

Folding thick arms across his chest, Calyx looked up at the angry young farmer. ''So?'' he queried sarcastically. ''Stop me if I'm wrong, but isn't the whole reason we came here to get more supplies?''

Aitchley stopped pacing long enough to give the dwarf an incredulous look. ''Yeah, but not from a town that's under siege!'' he retorted. ''You just . . . you can't . . .''

Calyx smirked. ''Can't what, kid?'' he asked. ''Ask for something that we need? It's not like we're going to take all that they have left.''

''Yeah, but it's so . . . so . . . tactless!'' Aitchley argued. ''These people have been attacked, and you just ignore it. You ask for supplies like nothing's happened here!''

Calyx settled himself down on a large bed, salt-and-pepper eyebrows knitting across his brow. ''Listen,'' he growled, ''we've got problems of our own, kid. Trouble with the world is that you can't solve everything all at once. Procursus tried that and it got him killed. I'm real sorry Viveca got attacked by Ilietis—and I'm even more sorry that we were partially to blame—but we've got matters of our own to attend to. We can't go around solving everybody else's problems and ignoring our own. We've got to get up to the Dragon's Lair before winter kicks in, and if that means asking a town that's been attacked for some supplies, then so be it. Whatever happens here is not our concern."

"Not our concern?" Aitchley echoed, disbelief cracking his voice. "I killed Sultothal, and you killed Paieon! Between the two of us, we practically made Ilietis attack Viveca!"

"And I suppose a better solution would have been to leave Paieon in charge? Or to let Sultothal remain Archimandrite?" Calyx snapped back. "We took down Paieon for our own reasons, kid, not because he was hoarding all the goods and selling them to Ilietis. Not because he was taking advantage of the craftsmen and farmers of the town. We took him down because he stood in our way. And you did the same thing with Sultothal. He stood in the way of the quest and you killed him. Whether it had an impact on Ilietis or not, it's not your fault. Whoever took over for Sultothal let you go with your life, remember? Was that his fault? Did he know you'd go on to Viveca and shut down their trade? Wouldn't he be just as much to blame for what happened as we are? And what about Paieon? If he had just given us some supplies, we wouldn't have been forced to do anything. We were too busy trying to catch up to you. It's just the way things worked out. No one's fault. No one's blame. It just happened."

"But we have to do something about it," Aitchley argued. "We just can't leave them! What if Ilietis attacks again?"

"And what if they do?" Calyx replied. "Sergeant Lael and Ghreler seem to have things under control. What are we supposed to do? Stay here and protect them?"

"Yeah," Aitchley concluded. "It's our fault. We should try and make up for it."

A grave smirk slowly spread beneath Calyx's beard. "And let's say we do," he said. "Let's say we wait around here until Ilietis attacks again. What do we do about the Daeminase that are chasing us? Now, *that* would be our fault if *they* attacked the town."

Aitchley felt some of his guilt and anger falter beneath the dwarf's logic. "Yeah, but . . . um . . . ," he sputtered.

"And honestly, kid," the smith went on, "there's just seven

of us, and Captain d'Ane's still dead. What difference can six people and one ghost make?''

Eyes downcast, Aitchley went silent. Angry thoughts and guilty excuses still went whipping through his head, but none of them made enough sense to argue with Calyx's logic. What good *would* I be? the young man wondered, his pessimism and self-doubt resurfacing with dark glee. I can't even bring forth a decent harvest and I'm talking like I can change the tide of a battle! Maybe Berlyn *was* wrong. Maybe the Cavalier couldn't make a difference . . . and neither can I.

Calyx offered what might have been a sympathetic smile. ''You can't solve the world's problems all at once, kid,'' he said again. ''You're starting to sound too much like Procursus.'' He shouldered his heavy sack and moved to a door that connected his room with the others. ''And I don't know if that's a good thing or a bad thing.''

Sitting proudly in the saddle of his scrawny mare, Rymel Donterrian pointed out a dilapidated old structure, its roof singed and blackened by fire. Behind him, Aitchley and Berlyn rode tandem on the young man's black stallion, and Poinqart followed astride Camera 12. Awed townsfolk watched as the fisherman-turned-Patrolman led the three through the cobble-stoned streets of Viveca on an informal tour, and Berlyn could feel staring eyes on her from along the road and from inside houses.

''And here's where Sprage used to work,'' Rymel was saying, indicating the half-burned building. ''I had to trick my way into town with Calyx hiding in the back of my cart. We were hoping Sprage would be able to get to the baroness and get the supplies you needed.''

Even though she knew the story, just to be polite Berlyn asked, ''Did it work?''

Rymel steered his horse down another street. ''Actually, no,'' he said animatedly. ''I mean . . . I snuck Calyx into town, but Sprage didn't have much luck. He wound up using my cart to get Calyx to the castle, and I almost beat him up for it. It was all just a huge mess.''

''But work-succeeded, it did,'' Poinqart replied cheerfully. ''Mister Calyx-dwarf and Mister Rymel triumph-won in the end, yes?''

The fisherman nodded. ''Yes, I suppose we did.''

Carried by their mounts down the narrow streets, Berlyn turned away from the impoverished town and stared at the young man in front of her. He was still brooding, she could see. Ever since his discussion with Calyx, he had returned to the same old dark and guilt-ridden Aitchley she remembered from Solsbury. Nothing she had said had been able to pull him up out of the depths of his depression, and she had thought that—when Rymel had offered to take them on an impromptu tour—it might do the young man good to see the town still functioning. Instead, he remained grimly silent, hardly looking at the goods and crafts that—despite the conditions and impending threat of attack—the workmen and skilled laborers of Viveca continued to produce.

"And over here," Rymel went on, "is the statue of Captain d'Ane. Magnificent, isn't it? There was talk of tearing it down to use the stones to help rebuild the wall, but the people wouldn't allow it."

Forcing her attention off of Aitchley, Berlyn looked at the statue. Standing on a thick gray pedestal, it towered nearly ten feet in height, and—although worked from the same cold, gray stones that built up the wall—it somehow managed to be both regal and beautiful. Great detail had been carved into d'Ane's stone features, and the artist had captured both the captain's bravery and compassion. One great stone hand rested on the stone sword at his side, and the statue looked east toward the baroness's castle, a smiling, benevolent expression on his gray stony features. Beneath the statue, a bronze plaque was set into the rock engraved with the words: CAPTAIN EGARTON D'ANE. HERO OF VIVECA. YEAR OF OXIDYAIS 8356M13.

A sudden gentle tug at the hem of her skirt pulled Berlyn's eyes away from the statue and down to the street. A man had ventured onto the cobblestones and now stood beside Aitchley's stallion, tugging shyly at Berlyn's dress. He kept his head down and his eyes averted as if Berlyn were royalty, but the blonde could see the small smile on his face as he offered her up a shimmering fold of silver material.

"Begging your pardon, milady," the villager said, awkwardly shuffling his feet, "but I wanted you to have this . . . as a sign of my family's appreciation for what you and the Cavalier's descendant have done."

Berlyn caught the startled gasp that came from deep in her throat as she took the offered fabric, unfolding it to reveal a

magnificent gown of brocaded silver. Intricate stitchwork
looped and laced about the front of the garment, which seemed
to glimmer and shine like a million stars. It looked like something a queen would wear, and Berlyn felt a warming redness
fill her cheeks as she looked down at the man standing humbly
below her.

"It's . . . it's beautiful," she stammered. "I . . . I can't take
this."

The man looked up briefly. "Oh, please," he replied. "It's
the least I could do."

Berlyn continued to stare in awe at the elegant gown.
"But—" she tried to protest.

The couturier smiled faintly. "Please," he said again. "Consider it a gift. Far, far less than what you have given me."

Stunned, Berlyn managed a weak nod of acceptance, her
eyes locked on the marvelous gown. Bowing respectfully, the
dressmaker stepped backward off the street and into the hovel
he used as a shop. Berlyn turned her surprise on Aitchley, but
there remained a black look of melancholy and indifference on
the young man's face. Poinqart and Rymel, however, both wore
smiles.

"Lovely-pretty, it is, Missy Berlyn," the half troll remarked.
"Poinqart wishes-thinks it would be nice if townsfolk-people
gave him things."

Rymel's smile widened. "Don't be surprised if they do," he
said. "You and your quest—the things you've done—you've
made a real impact on this town. It's been a long time since
Vedette's had heroes to look up to, and your actions have given
people hope. I know for a fact that what Captain d'Ane and
Calyx did here made me go to the river and actually catch some
fish. I even had my own shop for a while."

"What happened to it?" Berlyn inquired.

Rymel shrugged curtly. "It was burned down in the second
attack," he said. Then quickly added, "But look at me now. I
lead my own squad of Patrolmen. Not bad for a washed-up
fisherman from Zotheca, eh?"

As they talked other townspeople—encouraged by the dressmaker's boldness—approached the three mounts. Sudden hands
were touching tentatively at Berlyn's leg and at Aitchley's
horse. Someone had even brought a carrot for the stallion. Startled, Berlyn could only look down as the press of villagers
increased, the same sad and empty faces she had seen on her

way in suddenly glowing. Gifts and presents were suddenly being offered up from the sea of hands around Aitchley's horse—everything from food to finely crafted candlesticks— and Berlyn could only gape at this outpouring of affection. Look at them, she thought. They hardly have anything for themselves and they want to give us their best wares. This is incredible! I don't see how Aitchley can think we haven't made a difference.

But when the young blonde swung her astonished gaze on the farmer, Aitchley's face was as solemn and as dark as before.

Bleak times, was all the young man could muse. Bleak times, indeed.

That night there was an enormous celebration held in the courtyard of Baroness Desireah's castle. Under the glow of a full moon, the merchants and craftsmen of Viveca gathered to honor the quest, bringing with them their finest leathers, softest blankets, and freshest produce. Streamers of red-gold flowers hung like bunting across the castle parapets, and strings of lanterns helped illuminate the wide courtyard. Music performed by a group of village musicians filled the castle grounds, and the heady smells of an elaborate banquet successfully masked the residual stench of burned wood and mass graves.

Despite the celebration, Aitchley sat glumly at a long, wooden table, one hand around a tankard of ale. It was the best ale he'd had in a long time, but even the drink was unable to chase the gloom from the young man's mind. He had let his pessimism take over, and not even a courtyard full of dancing, laughing people could free him.

What's the point? he muttered gravely to himself. The quest. The Elixir of Life. Everything. How are we supposed to make a difference if we run from the very problems we create? Would the Cavalier leave a town that was under attack? Would he have asked them for supplies? Probably not . . . but then again, he never had problems like these. When he was alive there were no plagues. No famines. Towns didn't have to attack one another because one had food and the other had none. And why was that? Was he the cause? Was it because of the Cavalier that there weren't any plagues or droughts or famines? Most people seem to think so, but I know better. Like Tin William said, he was just a man. He ate, he drank, he slept. He just tried to make a difference, that's all.

Someone stepped out of the ring of lanterns and dancing figures to join Aitchley at the table. Rudely, the farmer barely acknowledged Gjuki standing beside him. "Greetings, Master Aitchley," the Rhagana said. "May I join you?"

Grunting, Aitchley shrugged, taking a gulp of ale so he didn't have to answer.

Undeterred, Gjuki sat down. His tiny pearl-black eyes slowly swept over the courtyard full of people before returning to the young man, a twitch of what might have been concern passing over his usually impassive features. "Is there some reason you are not joining in on the celebration?" the gardener wondered.

Aitchley grunted again. "I don't feel like it."

"But the celebration is in your honor," the Rhagana replied. "I do not understand."

Aitchley took another swig of ale. "I just don't feel like it," he repeated.

Tiny inhuman eyes took in the merriment of the castle again before returning to Aitchley. "Just as you did not understand why I wished for Eyfura to remain dead, I do not understand your mood, Master Aitchley," Gjuki tried again. "I believe— just as you were—I am entitled the common courtesy of an explanation."

Aitchley set his mug of ale down with a loud clank, turning an irate eye on the fungoid gardener. "This is stupid, that's all," he spat venomously. "These people have been attacked— their town has been ransacked—and they're having a party for us. Why? We didn't do anything. We're not even going to stay here and help them if Ilietis attacks again. We're just going to take whatever they give us and leave. Hardly sounds like something you should be celebrating."

A flicker of emotion creased Gjuki's leathery face. "I do not believe that is what they are celebrating, Master Aitchley," the Rhagana replied. "I believe what they celebrate are our accomplishments. And theirs as well. You have become a force for good, and your deeds have inspired others."

"That's bung!" Aitchley retorted. "I'm a lousy farmer who can't grow crops! I don't deserve a party."

"But you have gone beyond Lich Gate and recovered the Elixir of Life," Gjuki reminded him. "That is something that has never been done before. And—if even as you say—a 'lousy farmer' can do something so monumental, then it helps others to believe in themselves and their own abilities."

Aitchley peered gloomily into his drink. "Yeah. Right," he grumbled. "I bet they wouldn't be so impressed if they knew I didn't even know what to do with it."

A glitter of surprise flickered through Gjuki's tiny black eyes. "Is that what troubles you, Master Aitchley?" the gardener asked. "Captain d'Ane confided in me your questions about the elixir, and while understandable, I believe they are unfounded. The elixir would not have been created if it posed a threat to the very balance of nature."

"Oh, I don't care about that now." Aitchley waved an impatient hand through the air. "I'm just not so sure I should use it at all. General Fain said some things about bringing the Cavalier back, and—now that I've been thinking about it—there doesn't seem much even the Cavalier can do. I mean . . . look at us. We can't stop Ilietis from attacking again. We can't bring back the supplies Viveca lost. We can't even stop the spread of the Black Worm's Touch. Why does everyone think the Cavalier can?"

A vague smile stretched Gjuki's barklike countenance. "No one believes the Cavalier can cure all our ills," the gardener said, "but much like you are doing, we hope his presence and his actions will spur others to do well. This is an excellent example. Even as you said, Viveca has been attacked and much of its surplus stores of food stolen, and yet look about you. These people willingly give you what they have. They are celebrating your very presence just as I'm sure they did your ancestor two hundred years ago. This is what we hope to achieve by resurrecting the Cavalier. And as for what General Fain had to say: remember, he was quite mad."

Silent a moment, Aitchley stared into the depths of his mug. Finally, he looked back up at Gjuki, some of the despair gone from his features and only a glimmer of confusion sparkling in his blue-green eyes. "Yeah . . . well . . ." he mused out loud. "What would you think if someone told you there are some things that were not meant to be tampered with? To be wary of nature's scales?"

Gjuki blinked. "Were?" he asked.

Aitchley blinked back. "What?"

"You said 'were,' Master Aitchley," the Rhagana pointed out. "There are some things that *were* not meant to be tampered with. Past tense."

A sudden spear of befuddlement stabbed through the young

farmer's brain. "I . . . uh . . ." he sputtered. "I think that's what he said. . . ."

Someone unexpectedly stepped through the open portcullis of the castle and it was almost as if everything else stood still. Openmouthed, Aitchley turned away from Gjuki and stared at the slim, diminutive figure. Her platinum-blond hair shimmered a starry silvery white as Berlyn took a dainty step outside, an embarrassed smile on her lips. The gown of brocaded silver clung to her petite yet shapely torso, then flared out in a flow of material. Serpentine patterns of raised embroidery curled across the front of the dress, and large, leg-of-mutton sleeves fluffed out at her shoulders. Lacy ruffles ringed the diamond shape of Berlyn's cleavage, and the blonde wore the necklace of polished obsidian and basalt given to her by the *Kwau.* A number of heads turned as the scullery maid made her entrance, and Aitchley felt his eyes glaze over as the beautiful young blonde made her way toward him.

She looked even more beautiful tonight than she did when she became a *Kwau,* the young man thought.

Her cheeks tinged with the faintest traces of crimson, Berlyn stepped up beside Aitchley and smiled. "Would you like to dance?" she asked.

Lost in a daze of sparkling silver fabric and yellow-white hair, Aitchley felt a warm flush fill his own cheeks. "I can't dance," he admitted.

"Neither can I," Berlyn replied. She took the young man by the hand. "Come on," she coaxed. "I won't tell if you won't."

Gjuki watched as the two teenagers made their way to the courtyard, the press of villagers and merchants magically parting to let them through. The musicians continued to play a spritely waltz as the two came together, spinning and twirling to the music. Townsfolk watched with wide smiles as the young couple danced across the courtyard, joined by other dancing couples and soon lost to view.

Smirking knowingly, Calyx pulled up Aitchley's empty chair and sat down beside Gjuki, his beady eyes fixed on the young couple. Faint silvery light half illuminated the dwarf's face as Captain d'Ane floated alongside him.

"So," Calyx directed at Gjuki, "did it work?"

Gjuki allowed a rare smile to cross his lips. "As you said it would, Master Calyx,'' he answered. ''I believe we have cured Master Aitchley of his melancholy.''

''Hey, don't blame me,'' Calyx responded. ''This here was the captain's idea.''

Although he was nearly invisible, a ghostly smile flickered across the soldier's face. ''Young love,'' d'Ane said proudly. ''Even though it's been known to cause quite a few ills on its own, there's nothing it can't cure. That gown's a nice touch.''

Gjuki nodded his agreement. ''It was quite fortunate that dressmaker gave it to Miss Berlyn this afternoon, then, wasn't it?''

''Fortune had nothing to do with it,'' Calyx grunted cynically. ''I had to buy that dress.'' He faced his startled companions with a wry smirk. ''How else do you think it could fit so perfectly?''

The three returned their attention to the two teenagers waltzing under the streamers of lanterns and red-gold flowers. ''Speaking of which,'' Calyx went on, ''I was at the center of town earlier today.'' He swung beady eyes on Captain d'Ane. ''Egarton?''

A glisten of scarlet joined the silver that made up Captain d'Ane's cheeks. ''No one ever bothered to ask,'' the soldier responded with a shrug.

The music played on into the night.

20

Lightning Strikes

Clouds converged over the town of Viveca, making the morning overcast and gray. As he pulled himself into the saddle of his *meion,* Calyx gave the darkening heavens a distrustful scowl, pessimistic thoughts roiling through his brain. Looks like rain, mused the dwarf. Just the kind of thing we need to slow us down even more.

Calyx gazed at the others mounted up around him. Aitchley and Berlyn rode tandem on the young man's stallion, and Poinqart had settled himself comfortably on Camera 12. Harris now rode Sprage's palomino, Gjuki beside him on his own horse. Trianglehead looked grumpy and ruffled perched on the Rhagana's shoulder, and the supply horse snorted and pawed impatiently at the dirt of the castle courtyard. Captain d'Ane was the barest flicker of silver beside Sergeant Lael, and Rymel's small squad of five Patrolmen waited behind to escort the seven out of town.

The dwarf's eyes moved back to Aitchley. The kid looked to be in better spirits, the smith noted, although there appeared to be a thoughtful mien still scrawled across the young man's face. Calyx, however, had gotten used to that expression. It was the same one Procursus used to wear when moving on to their next mission. Whether it was quelling a fight between trolls and dwarves or just making sure the Entamoabae behaved themselves—'cause you never could trust a shapeshifter—Procursus wore this thoughtful, introspective look—as if he pondered some great mystery of life—and while the young farmer was silent astride his stallion, it was a lot better than the gloomy, sullen, guilt-ridden person who had been moping around town since yesterday.

Hammer and anvil! Calyx thought. Sometimes the kid could even outdepress a dwarf!

Lael offered the smith a friendly smile as the horses started out of the castle courtyard. "Any chance you'll reconsider my offer and let me come along?" the sergeant asked.

Calyx allowed himself a small grin. "As much as we'd like to have you, Sergeant, I think you'd better stay here and keep an eye on things," he replied. "I'd hate to have the town overrun with acolytes when I get back."

"Not half as much as I would," Lael agreed good-naturedly. "Ah, well," he added with a sigh, "if it's not an injured side, it's the threat of attack. I guess I'm just not fated to ride with you."

Calyx clucked his *meion* forward. "Lucky you," he quipped.

The castle gates rumbled open, and the seven quest-members rode out into the gray morning. A great cheer went up from the crowds of townspeople flanking either side of the road, and Calyx was surprised to see that the entire city had come to see the quest off. Townsfolk wearing ill-fitting Patrolmen uniforms stood at attention, saluting with chipped and rusty swords, and women threw flowers, leaves, and any other greenery they could find. It reminded Calyx of his youth and how such cheering, adoring crowds used to be commonplace anytime he had Procursus rode into town. Procursus! Hammer and anvil, people used to love him. Men admired and wanted to be like him. And women . . . Hah! Women would do more than throw flowers! Half the time they threw themselves at him! And Procursus was ever the gentleman. Never could turn 'em down. Made it a point to give 'em what they wanted as many times as they wanted it. I'm just surprised Aitchley was the only descendant we could trace!

Under gloomy skies, the quest rode east out of Viveca, the cheers and accolades slowly fading as they followed a small path out of town. The ground gradually swelled upward as they rode, the path cutting between grassy knolls dry and brown from the summer sun, and large oaks and birches dotted the horizon. Snakelike, the dirt path wound toward a clustering of trees that would become Karthenn's Weald. It had been a long

time since he had been in the weald, Calyx mused sourly to
himself. The last time had been with Procursus. It was odd the
way history had a tendency to repeat itself.

Gnarled gray branches twisting and writhing toward the
cloudy heavens, more great oaks grew up around them. A kind
of premature dusk settled over them as the groupings of trees
got thicker and broader, and the seven were thrown into a kind
of shadowy twilight, the canopy of leaves blocking out what
little light there was.

Rymel and his escort of Patrolmen stopped at the entrance
to the weald, wary eyes tracing the path to its darkening interior. "The road cuts straight through the weald and up a pass
through the mountains," the fisherman said. "It's in pretty
good condition for at least the first few leagues. After that . . .
I can't say. No one's gone up the Dragon's Ridge for years."

Calyx gave the towering oaks a grim smirk. "That's all
right," he said. "I know the way."

With Calyx's *meion* in the lead, the seven rode into the
gloom of Karthenn's Weald.

At least it wasn't as bad as the Bentwoods.

That was the only thought Berlyn could come up with as she
rode behind Aitchley. Enormous trees—some older than the
oldest dwarf—stood like ancient sentries on every side of the
road, and jumbles of rocks dotted the weald, warm and comfortable in coats of fuzzy green moss. A thin carpeting of
grasses and seedlings flourished despite the erratic patches of
sunlight, and in one spot, there was an entire thicket of birch
saplings all vying for warmth and sunshine. Jays screamed
avian epithets from the highest branches of the oaks at Trianglehead, and in a clearing created by a fallen oak, the ground
was literally awash with a meadow full of foxgloves, some still
in a deep, purplish bloom.

Despite the beauty, Berlyn was unable to shake the traces of
claustrophobia left over from the Bentwoods. Just the enclosure
of trees was enough to bring a sticky, humidlike feel to the
back of her neck, and the gloom of the weald—accented by
the gray clouds—tended to cast a pall even on blooming flowers.

Gray-green eyes rested on the young man sitting ahead of
her, a glimmer of concern igniting their gaze. Aitchley was
feeling better, she noted with some satisfaction. He'd better be

after the night they had together. It had certainly been the best of Berlyn's life. Dancing and drinking and laughing. Even more fun than the Rhagana celebration and too many glasses of nectarwine. She could tell something still bothered the young man, but whatever it was, it was far less serious than the guilt and depression brought about by that whole Ilietis-Viveca thing.

A rumble of thunder boomed from somewhere above the treetops as the horses wound their way up the dirt path, small knolls and rises sloping the ground in earthen waves. The first droplets of rain were deflected by the clusters of oak leaves, but more began to fall, pelting their way through the canopy and reaching the seven down below.

Calyx swung a hateful eye up at the gray heavens. "Knew it," he grumbled irascibly under his breath. "Knew something was going to slow us down."

Captain d'Ane seemed to sparkle magically as raindrops passed through his ethereal form. "It's only a little rain, Calyx," he chided.

Calyx looked downright malevolent. "It's a delay," he grunted back. "It's gonna slow us down and make the journey harder." Reluctantly, he led his *meion* off the path and under a protective canopy of oaks. "Might as well stop for lunch," he concluded. "Be just my luck to catch my death of cold before we get there."

Regardless of Calyx's mutterings, they stayed relatively dry as they ate, Berlyn savoring the freshness of the supplies given to them by Viveca. Even the water in the flasks had a purity to it . . . not like the stale, wet leather taste of the water they had been drinking. And new thick blankets helped to keep some of the chill of the summer shower off their bodies. Berlyn only wished that the sudden rainfall didn't remind her even more of their time in the Bentwoods.

Thunder cracked across the gray skies as the seven rested beneath the massive oaks, darker clouds moving in from the north. Gradually, what few patches of sunlight touched the floor of the weald slowly evaporated, devoured by the sullen gloom. Varying levels of gray and black played across the woodland floor, and the rain started to fall harder, finding its way through the leaves to spatter the people below.

A flash of lightning briefly illuminated the treetops.

Half-hidden under a woolen blanket, Calyx's eyes flashed with rancor. " 'Only a little rain,' " he mimicked Captain d'Ane, a large frown on his lips. " 'It's not going to slow us down. It's only a little rain, Calyx.' "

D'Ane turned a good-natured smirk on the dwarf. "I never said that," he pointed out. "And, besides, it *is* only a little rain. Enjoy it. You don't know what you're missing. I can't even feel the rain on my face anymore."

"That's 'cause you're dead, Captain," Calyx grumbled irately, "and if one of us gets sick—or if somebody's horse slips and falls off a cliff—we'll be silvery and transparent, too."

Berlyn felt her eyebrows knit together. "Calyx!" she scolded the smith.

D'Ane gave the blonde a reassuring smile. "It's all right," the soldier said. "I've already come to terms with what I am. I was just trying to instill Calyx here with some love of life before it's too late."

"Trying to instill a dwarf with a love of life is like trying to teach a pig how to sing," Calyx retorted. "It's a waste of time and annoys the pig."

Another tremble of thunder shook the treetops.

"The storm grows in intensity," Gjuki noted, pearl-black eyes trained skyward. "The rains will do the woodlands good."

Beside the Rhagana—hiding deep within the woolen security of his own blanket—Poinqart cowered beneath the oaks. "Poinqart no likes such thunder-booming-crash," the half troll whimpered. "Terror-scares him, it does."

There was another flash of blue-white lightning across the heavens.

Calyx gave the storm a vexed glare. "Yeah, well," he replied, "just so long as there's no flash floods or hurricanes or—"

Blue-white flared so brightly Berlyn almost fell over backward, the very air about her filling with an intense, hair-raising prickle. Something that sounded like the sky shattering rocked the weald, and a forking shaft of pure electricity arced out of the heavens and slammed into a nearby oak, showering the woods with a fountain of sparks and embers. Ancient wood cracked and splintered—severed branches spiraling free like amputated limbs—all in an abrupt blaze of flames, the stench of smoke cutting through the falling rain like a razor-sharp dagger.

Calyx was on his feet immediately, lunging for the terrified horses as they tried to bolt. "Doom and gloom!" the dwarf swore vehemently. "I *knew* it!"

As falling sparks ignited smaller fires about them, Harris scrambled frantically to his feet. "Your fault, dwarf!" he shouted. "You jinxed us!"

"Shut your face, Blind-Ass, and mount up," Calyx yelled back over the sudden roar of fire, "or else—"

Whatever else Calyx said, Berlyn did not hear. A blast of thunder so loud as to send a painful ringing through her ears exploded at treetop level, spooking the horses even more. The groan of the lightning-struck oak filled the woodlands as it slowly careened sideways, flames licking and leaping along its ancient bark. Other trees quickly caught fire as their brother fell to its fiery death, branches and leaves brushing against one another in a blazing exchange of red and orange. Dead leaves and dry grass instantly ignited, a wall of fire sweeping purposefully southward toward the seven quest-members. Smoke so thick as to bring tears to her eyes filled the weald with a swiftness that surprised Berlyn, and she had barely struggled to her feet before Aitchley was pulling her urgently toward his horse.

"Come on!" the young man screamed at her. "Go!"

Fairly dragged by Aitchley's insistent hand, the scullery maid had little choice as she half staggered, half ran toward the skitterish stallion. Blazing heat roared through the woods north of them—a startling contrast to the cool spatter of rain—and another streak of lightning momentarily bathed the weald in blue-white illumination.

Through the smoke and confusion, the blonde somehow managed to pull herself onto the saddle behind Aitchley, tears streaming from her eyes. Her chest hurt as she inhaled acrid plumes of smoke, and she could hardly see the trees around her as the farmer jerked hard on his horse's reins and directed the stallion down the winding dirt path.

A nearby oak all but exploded as flames reached its trunk, a shaft of blazing orange-red fire consuming its ancient bark. Branches charred and cindered—many dropping away to start other fires—and leaves curled and withered, becoming blackened ash that joined the falling rain.

Calyx ducked instinctively as sparks and ash fluttered down among the raindrops. "You know," he growled irately, "this kind of crap never happened when the Dragon was around!"

Flames roared menacingly as the seven rode through the burning weald, thick smoke obscuring their vision. The wind whipped and screamed through Berlyn's hair as Aitchley's stallion charged through the trees, and she could feel the heat of the fire growing in intensity. Another crash split the forest as a burned and blackened tree toppled ignobly to its death, and lightning again shattered the sky with blue-white force.

Surrounded by the hiss of rain on flames, the smoke began to thin as the horses sped up the sloping terrain. Thunder rolled across the heavens as Aitchley's stallion galloped wildly up a small hillock and through a maze of birches, slowly leaving the burning woodland behind.

The rain continued to fall.

Sliding gingerly out of the saddle, Berlyn slipped off the back of Aitchley's horse and landed with a soft squelch in the mud. The rain had stopped about an hour ago, yet the seven had continued to push their horses until the clouds started to break up and the first hint of a bloodred afternoon pushed its way through the treetops. Spritely, Berlyn found a relatively dry spot under a massive oak and settled back in a comfortable niche between trunk and roots. She winced as she sat down— the ache of hard riding throbbing through her rear end—and she rubbed gently at her tender backside. I'm out of practice, the young blonde thought to herself. I'm going to have to get used to riding all over again.

Moving slowly out of the saddle himself, Aitchley joined her under the tree, throwing a cautious eye up before relaxing. Rain still dripped from the high branches and leaves, but the weald was quiet save for the *plip-plop* of water falling into puddles. The fire had lost momentum hours ago and had been extinguished by the very storm that had given it life, but that didn't stop Aitchley from watching the lingering clouds with a glimmer of mistrust.

Using tinder he kept dry in a leather pouch, Gjuki started a small campfire, helping to chase some of the chill out of their wet clothes. Questioningly, the Rhagana looked away as the flames flickered to life. "I am curious, Master Calyx," the fungoid gardener said. "Forest fires such as the one we just experienced occur quite frequently in the Bentwoods, yet you implied that they were infrequent while the Dragon lived. Do you know why?"

Settling himself down by the fire to rummage through his sack, Calyx offered a shrug. "No," he answered simply. "I guess it's just that the Dragon burned everything before it got too dry to burn itself."

"But that would be most impossible unless the Dragon burned everything," Gjuki went on. "Surely there must have been some region that the Dragon's flames did not purge?"

Calyx shrugged again. "If there was, I never heard of it," he responded. "In all the time the Dragon was around, I'd never heard of any fires caused by lightning strikes."

A glint of puzzlement twinkled in Gjuki's eyes. "But—"

Calyx shot the gardener an abrupt glare. "Look," he interrupted, "I'm not a scholar. I don't understand these things. It's just the way it was."

After his long silence, Berlyn was somewhat startled when Aitchley interjected, "But what about magic?"

Calyx turned a questioning look on the farmer. "Hmm?"

Berlyn could see the uncertainty that moved across Aitchley's face as he tried to voice his concerns. "What about magic, then?" he asked again.

"Well, what about it?" Calyx asked back.

It was Aitchley's turn to shrug. "I don't know. I was just thinking," he said. "I was using the staff before and . . . and it just got so easy. I mean . . . Berlyn and I wiped out a whole bunch of trolls with one blast. I even killed a few Daeminase with it. I was just wondering . . . why didn't anybody ever think to use magic on the Dragon?"

A look of bemusement lightened Calyx's mien. "You know," he answered, "I don't know. Maybe he was immune to it or something. I really don't know." He smirked proudly to himself. "That's a real good question, kid."

"Perhaps there were attempts but the historical records have been lost," Gjuki suggested. "True magic died out over four hundred years ago."

"Yeah, but you'd think somebody would have tried something," Aitchley argued. "Even this Adal guy. I mean . . . this staff really packs a punch. If nobody had heard about him trying something, why didn't somebody else try?"

"You ask interesting questions, lad," Captain d'Ane put in. "Any reasoning behind them?"

Aitchley shrugged, embarrassed. "No," he replied. "Just curious."

"Well, how about it, Captain?" Calyx asked the ghostly soldier. "I thought you were supposed to be all-knowing now that you're dead. Don't you know why?"

"You remember your place in the world when you die," d'Ane responded amicably. "You're not given a course in history or magic. Maybe you were right. Maybe the Dragon was immune to magic. Or maybe our ancestors just knew something that we don't."

As Calyx went back to rummaging through his bag—and Gjuki set about preparing dinner—Berlyn snuggled in closer to Aitchley, the intimate embrace of her wet clothes bringing goose bumps to her flesh. "Is that what was bothering you?" she asked the young man.

Drawn up out of his thoughts, Aitchley fixed blue-green eyes on the girl. "Hmm? What?" he asked. "Oh, no. I was . . . you know . . . just wondering."

Even though Aitchley's clothes were wet as well, Berlyn felt warmer snuggling up against him. "Then why were you so quiet when we left Viveca this morning?" she asked. "Didn't you have a good time last night?"

Aitchley was unable to keep the lopsided smile off his lips. "I had a great time last night," he answered.

"So what were you thinking about?" Berlyn wanted to know. "You weren't still upset over that whole thing with Ilietis, were you?"

Hesitantly, Aitchley stared out into the gloom of Karthenn's Weald, his face taking on a thoughtful look. "No, it's nothing like that," he replied. "I was just thinking . . . Do you remember what I told you Tin William said? About tampering with nature's scales?"

Berlyn fixed the young man with a rigid eye. "Are we back to that again?" she teased.

"Hear me out," Aitchley interrupted, the urgency in his voice silencing the scullery maid. "Gjuki made me realize something the other night. Tin William said there are some things that were not meant to be tampered with. *Were*. Not are. I remember saying to myself there are some things that *aren't* meant to be tampered with back when we were at the Rhagana village, and I knew it didn't sound right, but I wasn't quite sure why. Now I know. *Were* . . . not *are*. All this time I thought Tin William was talking about me and the elixir, and now I find out he was talking about something else altogether."

Berlyn felt her own eyebrows lower as the questions started to seep into her own thoughts. "So what did he mean?" she queried.

Aitchley frowned. "I don't know," he said. "I've been trying to think of everything else he told me, but I just can't remember it all. I remember something about the cycle of birth and death. Of destruction and creation. And something about interfering with nature causing only disaster, but I don't know what the Pits he meant now. I mean . . . when I thought he was talking about me, it made some kind of sense. But now . . . he could have been talking about anything and I'd never know what it was!"

"Is that why you asked about the Dragon and magic?" wondered Berlyn.

Aitchley shook his head. "That? No. I was just wondering that on my own." He stared off into the trees. "I just wish I could remember everything Tin William told me," he mused out loud. "I know there's something else, and it's probably important. I just wish I wasn't so stupid!"

A burst of anger sparked in Berlyn's gray-green eyes. "You're not stupid, Aitchley Corlaiys," she scolded the young man. "You're very bright. I don't like to hear you talk down about yourself."

"Yeah, but I'm the one walking around thinking Tin William was talking about me," he protested. "What kind of an idiot doesn't even listen to what he's being told?"

"We've had other things on our mind," Berlyn excused the young farmer. "When you met this Tin William, you were lost in the desert, searching for me. And we haven't had much time to think about things since then. Nomion's Halberd, Aitchley! We've been beyond Lich Gate and come back! We've been chased by the Daeminase and by Patrolmen who wouldn't die! It's not like we've had time to just sit back and discuss things!"

Shrugging—some of his depression returning—Aitchley drew a warm blanket around himself and Berlyn. "It's not like it'd make a difference," he muttered moodily to himself. "I probably wouldn't understand it anyway."

They rode eastward for another seven days, passing through galleries of oaks and birches on their way into the Dragon's Ridge. Sometimes they crossed wide stretches of meadows filled with flowering foxgloves and dotted by enormous yellow-brown boulders. Storm clouds continued to swell and roil above the mountain range, and a cooling wind blew down off the ridge as the seven rode through a somewhat level pass in the hills. Great trees continued to surround them, and a small stream babbled down out of the mountains and cut a glittering silver swath through rolling meadows of bluebells and nettles.

Even as she rode behind him Berlyn's concern for Aitchley grew. He tried to be in good spirits—even attempted a few lopsided smiles—but the blonde knew he was still obsessing over whatever it was Tin William had told him. She didn't understand why he felt so stupid for not understanding—maybe this Tin William hadn't said anything important at all. Had Aitchley ever stopped to think about that?—and she had gone out of her way to try to make him feel better. A few days ago the two of them and Poinqart had played an impromptu game of hide-and-seek—and he had actually laughed out loud when Poinqart accidentally rolled down a sloping hillside of wild-flowers—but as soon as they gathered together for supper, he went quiet and brooding again. Because it had taken Gjuki to point out something Aitchley felt he should have discovered for himself, the young man felt stupid and useless, and that had brought back all the old insecurities and pessimism. It was almost as if everything he had accomplished didn't mean anything to the young man, and sometimes Berlyn felt she was talking to that same, self-doubting farmer who had been so rudely thrown out of the scullery door back at the Tampenteire estate. And that bothered her. Aitchley had done things that no one else had ever done—not even his more famous ancestor!—yet he moped about like a pathetic farm boy who couldn't bring forth a decent harvest. Sometimes Aitchley could be so frustrating Berlyn felt like whacking him over the head with her throwing ax!

Through a latticework of dark clouds, the sun began to drop behind the western hills, the sky turning the deep red of dusk. There was a coldness coming down off the mountains that leeched the warmth out of the late-summer evening, and Calyx dismounted at the base of an enormous mountain, beady eyes peering upward. The faint path they followed—sometimes overrun with foliage, sometimes barely visible at all—twisted up the side of the titanic ridge, snaking its way upward before disappearing behind a collection of boulders.

Calyx stared up into the darkening sky. "Well, this is it,

kiddies," he informed the others. "Up there's the Dragon's Lair." He threw a taunting smile at those behind him. "Anyone want to turn back now?"

Head slowly craning upward, Aitchley scanned the path to obscurity. "How far is it?" he wondered.

Calyx turned away from the mountainside with a shrug. "A few leagues."

"A few leagues?" Harris sniped back. "What? Three? Ten? How many's a few?"

Calyx's complexion darkened a little. "A few's a few!" he retorted. "I don't know. Four? Maybe five? The mountain's not that high but the path tends to weave back and forth. It's been a while since I've been here!"

Gjuki watched the sun steadily set behind the mountains. "Might I suggest we begin our journey in the morning?" he said. "We are all tired and irritable, and a good night's sleep will do us good."

"Besides," Calyx added with another shrug, "there's no point in trying to make the climb in the dark." He tethered his *meion* to a nearby tree. "The mountain'll still be here when we wake up."

Without much discussion, the group set up a small camp and ate their dinner in relative silence. Dark clouds continued to roil overhead as Aitchley distanced himself from the others, relaxing against a fallen oak. This is it, the young man told himself, his gaze wandering up the dark side of the mountain. By this time tomorrow we'll be finished. The quest will be over and the Cavalier will be back among the living. I just wish I knew what in the Pits Tin William was trying to tell me. He wrapped his cloak tighter about his throat as a low, mournful wind passed through the valley. Oh, well, he concluded sardonically to himself, I've got a few hours before morning. Maybe I can figure out in one night what I haven't been able to figure out for months.

He shrugged despondently to himself. Bloody, typical Corlaiys luck . . .

Blue-gray breasts bare, round, and firm, crested with gray nipples. Pitch-black hair as glossy as the basalt knife in her hand. Dark snakeskin between supple blue-gray thighs.

"You must use it, and use it wisely, *bheidh* Aitchley," Taci says. "Kirima says in your heart of hearts you will know what to do."

Confused, Aitchley blinks, trying to pull his eyes away from the smooth nakedness of her bosom. No, wait . . . not breasts. Wheels. Gears. Silver gears, tinted gray lenses. Gleaming metal frame. The low whir and hum of hidden mechanisms.

"There is a precarious balance at work in all worlds, Aitchley Corlaiys," Tin William proclaims, and an echo of desperation taints the buzzing, inhuman voice. "A regenerative cycle. Birth and death. Growth and decay. Destruction and creation. But these are forces only nature can control in its myriad ways. No single species must ever cause this balance to lose its integrity."

Shiny, pearl-black eyes look up at the night-cloaked canopy. "There is a fragile equilibrium to the entire world, Master Aitchley," Gjuki concludes, "but nowhere is it more prominently displayed than here in the Bentwoods."

"There is a scheme to all things, Aitchley," Captain d'Ane goes on. "The old make way for the young. . . ."

An echo of desperation taints the buzzing, inhuman voice. "Birth and death, Aitchley Corlaiys . . ."

". . . the sick give way to the healthy . . ."

Desperation taints the voice. "Growth and decay . . ."

". . . It's something so basic you practically forget all about it when you're alive. . . ."

Desperation. "Destruction and creation . . ."

"The overall balance isn't infallible, lad."

Twin triangles that resemble a scale; a detailed picture of the Dragon, wings unfurled and flames zigzagging like lightning from its mouth. Taci lowers herself onto the carpet of moss. "All things have their purpose and influence, *bheidh* Aitchley," Taci says after a brief trade of words with Kirima. "A place in the natural order."

Tin William gives a nervous glance over his shoulder. "Statement: Life and death are part of the natural order. . . ."

Natural order.

"When a species interferes, disaster is the only result."

A cruel smile twists Fain's bloodied features. "You're a fool, boy! They don't want the world to be a better place! They just want it to be the way it was!"

The way it was.

Tin William tilts his head to one side in a questioning, innocuous way. "Did you know, Aitchley Corlaiys, that this world was never once subjected to firestorms, earthquakes, pestilence, or floods?"

Calyx ducks instinctively as sparks and ash flutter down among the raindrops. "You know," he growls irately, "this kind of crap never happened when the Dragon was around!"

Aitchley sighs. "It just doesn't make any sense to me. I keep thinking about all those things Gjuki said back in the Bentwoods to Sprage. You know? All those things about trees and ants and humidity and rainfall and how they all worked together, and if you bunged up just one thing, the whole Bentwoods might collapse. I keep thinking that might happen if I use the elixir. I keep thinking that's what Tin William was trying to say."

There are some things that were not meant to be tampered with, Aitchley Corlaiys. Be wary of Nature's scales.

"They try to adapt the world around them rather than adapt *to* the world around them."

"This kind of crap never happened when the Dragon was around!"

"Death is not an end for my people, Master Aitchley. It is a beginning."

". . . a precarious balance at work in all worlds . . ."

Natural order.

Calyx offers what might be a sympathetic smile. "You can't solve the world's problems all at once, kid."

"You've made a great deal of difference, Aitchley Corlaiys," Berlyn tells the young man. "And I'm sure your ancestor can make even more."

There are some things that were not meant to be tampered with.

"You must use it, and use it wisely, *bheidh* Aitchley. In your heart of hearts you will know what to do."

Be wary of nature's scales.

"This kind of crap never happened when the Dragon was around!"

Something that sounded like a scream ripped Aitchley out of his dreams, startling him awake. He hadn't slept at all well—forcing himself to stay awake while he tried to ponder Tin William's words—and he hadn't even realized he had dozed off. A thin mist had formed around the base of the mountain, and the first hint of pinkish-red light was breaking the eastern horizon. Something large and round stood protectively before the young man—half obscuring his sight—and it wasn't until he rubbed sleepily at his eyes that he recognized Camera 12's bulk.

Another shriek of terror and pain sliced through the misty morning, igniting a hot flash of adrenaline in Aitchley's gut. Other sounds of confusion forced their way through the cobwebs in his brain, and he leapt hurriedly to his feet, the Cavalier's sword in his hands.

Someone shouted something as Aitchley jumped up, a dark figure scrambling frenziedly out of the way. Dim shadows and vague shapes moved throughout the mist, and the unmistakable stench of fresh blood suddenly became an overpowering odor in Aitchley's nostrils.

"Wha—" the young man started to say.

Sudden hands were shoving the young man aside, urgently pushing him toward the waiting mountainside. "Run, kid! Run!" Calyx was shouting. "Go for the mountain!"

His mind still wrestling with the images of his dream and the lack of sleep draining his body, Aitchley blinked at the ensuing chaos. "Calyx!" he yelled. "I don't—"

Another high-pitched, inhuman scream split the early morning, and Aitchley's gaze suddenly fixed on the horses. Waves of bright red splashed the grass and drowned the birch seedlings, two equine corpses already littering the mountainside. Exposed entrails glittered with crimson moisture, and torn flesh were ragged strips of ruby. Other patches of scarlet moved with insectlike grace among the trees, and eyeless faces turned in eager anticipation toward the young man.

Like a tide of blood, the Daeminase came crashing out of the weald.

Aitchley's feet felt rooted to the spot. "Oh, bung!" he swore.

21

Dead Yet?

Mist churned and fragmented as lean, skeletal red figures came scrabbling out of the shadows between trees. All thoughts of Tin William and Taci were banished from Aitchley's mind as he tried to shake himself free of his confusion. He felt his fingers curled tightly around the Cavalier's sword—didn't even remember drawing it from its sheath—and tried to blink some of the uncertainty out of his head. Daeminase! his mind screamed at him. The horses! Where's—look out! Daeminase! Where's Berlyn?

Taloned feet splashed through growing pools of spilled blood, and needlelike fangs gleamed a metallic silver in the early-morning light. Aitchley gaped in a kind of dumb stupefaction as claws and teeth tore huge chunks of flesh and bone from the two fallen horses, and the other mounts screamed and pulled frantically at their tethers as more and more of the inhuman monsters poured out of the woods.

Insistent hands were suddenly pushing at him again. "Up the mountain, kid!" Calyx was yelling. "Go! Go!"

Worriedly, Aitchley turned to where Berlyn had slept beside him, startled to see the area empty and the diminutive blonde already scrambling for the mountainside. Poinqart fled beside her, hybrid terror in his yellow-black eyes. Mist swirled and roiled like troubled waters, and Aitchley almost obeyed the instinctive urge to dash forward and join the scullery maid and half troll, actually feeling the muscles in his legs react almost at the same time as he forced himself to stand his ground.

Spinning about, he snatched up the backpack lying at his feet. Oh, no! he mentally told himself. I'm not leaving this behind again!

A sudden shout went up from behind him, and Aitchley spun around to see Calyx turn a wild eye on the oncoming horde of Daeminase. "Gjuki!" the dwarf all but screamed. "This way! Up the mountain!"

Narrowly avoiding the sweep of scarlet claws, Gjuki fought his way eastward. "The horses, Master Calyx!" the Rhagana yelled back. "I cannot leave the horses to die!"

Calyx's warhammer shattered the sticklike leg of an approaching Daeminase. "Leave 'em!" he shouted. "We've got to get out of here!"

All but lost among the mist, Captain d'Ane floated swiftly toward Gjuki. "Calyx is right!" the soldier said. "We've got to—"

Claws suddenly sliced through d'Ane's diaphanous frame, and the captain released an agonized scream, crumpling to the ground in a semitransparent heap. Instinctively, Aitchley vaulted to the dead soldier's side, the Cavalier's sword lashing out and severing a groping arm from its gaunt, haggard shoulder. Calyx was directly beside the young man, his massive warhammer fracturing ribs and crushing internal organs that continued to unnaturally heal.

Blinking, Captain d'Ane managed to struggle to one arm, ghostly eyes peering down at his own gossamer body. "Wha . . . ?" he sputtered. "That . . . that hurt!"

Calyx tried to help the soldier to his feet but his hands passed through the captain's silvery form. "Of course it hurt, Captain," he grunted cynically. "These are the Daeminase, remember? Beasts of Nowhere? The Evil and the Red? Their very job is the torment of the dead. You're just as real to them as they are to us."

D'Ane flashed a spectral frown at where claws had passed through his ethereal chest. "Ouch," he answered. "It's been a long time since I've felt pain. I . . . I kind of missed it."

"Yeah, well," retorted Calyx, "I don't know if dead people can die again, but you'd better get out of here, too, or else you might be in for a world of pain." The dwarf swung angry eyes about the weald. "Has anyone seen Harris?" he wondered.

Curiously, Aitchley turned to look about him, barely ducking the horselike face that lunged silver-gray teeth at him. Steel flashed in the young man's hands, and the entire lower jaw of the Daeminase separated from its body, spiraling out across the oaks in a sudden trajectory of bloodlessness.

Calyx returned his gaze to the tethered horses. "Gjuki!" he shouted one last time. "Would you forget the horses? Run!"

Pale white Rhagana blood streaking his right shoulder, Gjuki tried to free the panicked mounts. "I cannot leave another creature to die in such a way, Master Calyx," the gardener said apologetically. "I must—"

Talons suddenly swept out through the mist, catching the Rhagana in the face. White fluid and tatters of Gjuki's mosslike hair sprinkled the air, and Aitchley felt a horrible, gut-wrenching sensation drop hot lead into his stomach.

"Gjuki!" the young man roared, pushing his way past Calyx and leaping for the downed Rhagana.

A streak of silver, the Cavalier's sword cut a bloodless path to the downed gardener, leaving dismembered pieces of Daeminase all across the forest floor. Severed fingers still flexed and clawed, and one amputated forearm tried to crawl forward on its own accord, grasping futilely at the young man as he charged past.

Calyx let out a heavy sigh as Aitchley sprang straight for the oncoming Daeminase. "Kid!" he yelled pointlessly. "The mountain's *that* way!"

Blinded by rage and concern, Aitchley ignored the smith's warnings, driving his sword straight through the open mouth of a cadaverous red monster. Reddish-brown fluid splattered the young man's hand, and the Daeminase crumpled to the ground, twitching as it died. Others instantly replaced their fallen comrade, faces glaring without eyes in Aitchley's direction. It was horrifying to be stared at by something without eyes, and Aitchley could feel the preternatural fear spawned by such monstrosities slowly rise in his gut and try and sap him of his strength.

Claws slashed the air, knocking the young man's hat off his head. Swearing, Aitchley threw himself forward, managed an awkward somersault, and leapt to his feet near one of the dead horses. He could see Gjuki lying on the ground nearby, white blood dribbling from a wound at his forehead, his clothes drenched in the crimson wash of the dead supply horse.

"Master Aitchley," the gardener croaked, "you should not have placed yourself in such peril. You lead this quest."

Spinning on his heel, Aitchley rammed his shield into a lunging Daeminase; the creature careened backward into the trees. "Shut up, Gjuki," the young man demanded. "I'm not going anywhere without you. Come on."

A claw unexpectedly caught the side of Aitchley's backpack, snagging the nylon and jerking him backward. Startled, the young man felt his balance shift, yet the magnificent sword in his hand drew his arm back and plunged through the skull of the attacking Daeminase. Brackish fluid splashed the young farmer as he turned once again to Gjuki, offering the Rhagana a helpful hand up.

Clambering to his feet, Gjuki continued to head for the remaining horses.

"Gjuki!" Aitchley screamed at him. "What in the Pits do you think you're doing?"

Purposefully, the gardener untethered Sprage's palomino and let the panicked horse run free through the weald. "I am releasing the horses, Master Aitchley," he declared. "To leave them here would be to sentence them to a most gruesome death."

Pivoting, Aitchley decapitated a leaping Daeminase. "Yeah, but—" he tried to protest.

Angrily—perched on a branch of a nearby oak—Trianglehead ruffled red-violet feathers still wrapped in loose bandages. "Krazy!" the fledgling squawked irritably at the two. "That'sz what you are! Krazy! Zstupid humansz!"

It was one time Aitchley had to agree with the gyrofalc. "Gjuki, come on!" he insisted. "It isn't worth it!"

Red figures seemed to pour endlessly out of the weald.

Gjuki finished untying the reins of Aitchley's stallion and Calyx's *meion;* both horses ran frantically into the surrounding woods. "There," the Rhagana declared, "it is finished." He sprinted quickly toward the mountainside. "Hurry, Master Aitchley," he added. "Let us not linger."

Muttering, Aitchley spun toward the path, fingers tight around his sword. "It's about bloody time," he grumbled.

Unexpectedly, the young man felt his boot slip in the growing river of blood, and he pitched over backward, landing hard in a splash of red. Stars danced behind his eyelids as his head struck the blood-drenched earth, and it took a moment before he was able to reopen them, an incessant ringing sounding somewhere in the back of his skull.

When he did open his eyes, all Aitchley could see were hideous mouths of needle-sharp fangs descending for his throat.

Lumbering up the mountainside, Poinqart suddenly stopped and looked down, the woods below him filled with swarming red figures. A few of the ugly-*Eperythr*-no-faces scuttled insectlike up the hillside, evil-cruel-pointy-fangs gleaming with thick saliva. He could see where Mister-Calyx-dwarf hurried-fled up the mountainside, and Captain-ghostie-d'Ane flutter-floated up behind him. Missy-Berlyn hurry-ran ahead of him—her skirt flutter-flapping about her legs—but Poinqart could not speak-see Mister Aitch. A barb of worry-fear sparked in the half troll's breast, and he swung desperate yellow-black eyes down the sides of the mountain-hill in his search for Mister Aitch.

Some protector-friend Poinqart is! the hybrid admonished himself. Poinqart is supposed to watch out for Mister Aitch, not run-away-panic from him! Poinqart must rescue-save him!

Filled with determination, the half troll reversed his thunderous charge, thick, treetrunklike legs carrying him back down the mountain toward the growing tide of crimson figures. Powerful fists lashed out as he plowed through the first of the Daeminase, four-fingered blows crushing skulls and shattering brittle, inhuman bones. Sometimes the monsters crashed back down the hill to get up again; other times they lay still at the bottom, twisted, mangled heaps of scarlet flesh and eyeless death.

Poinqart swept the base of the mountain with worried yellow-black eyes. "Mister Aitch!" howled the half troll. "Where are you?"

Slavoring, a Daeminase lunged for Poinqart; still searching for his friend, Poinqart hardly looked at the monster as he snapped its neck.

"Poinqart!" Calyx shouted from higher up the mountain. "Hammer and anvil! Doesn't anyone pay attention anymore? I said this way! Not back down!"

"But Mister Aitch!" the hybrid protested. "Mister Aitch is not with us!"

"The kid's all right!" the dwarf responded with misplaced optimism. "Just run!"

Although he didn't like to disobey-be-bad, the half-troll ignored the dwarf's frenzied cries and continued running back down the path. Hordes of Daeminase scrambled out of the trees lining the base of the mountain, but Poinqart could still not find his friend. Had Mister Aitch been eaten-killed? Had the ugly-*Eperythr*-no-faces mangle-crushed him as they had the snort-horses? Poinqart would murder-kill them all if Mister Aitch was alive-no-more-dead!

Snarling, a Daeminase suddenly launched itself from above Poinqart, slamming into his back and sending them both rolling down the rest of the hill. Taken by surprise, the half troll tumbled helplessly down the slope, feeling the razor-sharp claws of the creature tear viciously into his back. A hot, stomach-twisting wrench of pain shot through his spine, and he felt his own blood coat his back and legs as he spilled down the hill and crashed into a treetrunk.

Hurting, Poinqart forced himself to sit up, blinking tears out of his yellow-black eyes. Huge nostrils snuffled and tasted the air as the half troll's blood painted the floor of the weald, and a number of eyeless faces turned eagerly in his direction, strands of gelantinous saliva oozing from around silver teeth.

Poinqart thinks Poinqart is in serious trouble-calamity, the half troll thought bleakly to himself. Maybe Poinqart should have listen-heeded to Mister-Calyx-dwarf. . . .

Struggling up the slope of the mountain, Berlyn rounded an outcropping of rocks and suddenly stopped, something not sitting right with her. Anxiously, gray-green eyes scanned the hillside. Lean, inhuman figures like giant red ants littered the base of the mountain; of anyone in the group, she saw nothing.

A cold, unsettling sensation formed in the young girl's stomach. Where is everybody? she wondered.

Questioningly—the arctic touch of horror rising in her throat—Berlyn moved to an outcropping of boulders. The hillside path ran through level patches of grass and trees with some steeper portions of bare dirt and rock, but it wasn't straight up like the Shadow Crags. Two hundred years ago this path had led worshipers up to the Dragon's Lair to pay their respects to the fallen Cavalier, so it was level enough for horses, but it still startled the blonde to discover how far she had already climbed on her own accord.

The weald was a rolling expanse of trees, covering the

ground like a lush emerald carpet. It looked similar to the way the Bentwoods had from beside the Mistillteinn Falls yet with one exception: the hillside below was awash with red figures. Talons and teeth gleamed beneath the rising sun, and Berlyn felt her apprehension grow as she saw none of her friends hurrying up the winding path after her.

Berlyn tightened her fingers around her throwing ax. Aitchley? she mused fearfully to herself. Where are you?

The cold in her gut slowly spread through her bloodstream, bringing with it a kind of anxious uncertainty. What do I do now? the scullery maid asked herself. Aitchley? Calyx? Gjuki? Should I go back and help them? Help them . . . ? I can't even see them! Oh, Gaal! What am I supposed to do?

Her fingers so tight around her ax that her knuckles turned white, the blonde stared helplessly down the mountainside. Part of her wanted to rush back and help her friends, but another part looked at all those scrabbling, spiderlike beasts advancing on her and instincts told her to flee. There was no way she could fight her way through all those monsters, but . . . if Aitchley was dead, did she really want to go on living herself? What was left? Besides . . . where could she run? Where could she hide? They were on a mountain, for Gaal's sake! Once she reached the summit, there'd be nowhere else to go!

Gnawing thoughtfully on her lower lip, Berlyn pulled herself erect. If there's any chance Aitchley's still alive down there, she suddenly resolved, I'm going to help him!

An unexpected hand fell upon her shoulder, and Berlyn shrieked, whipping about so fast that she almost lost her balance and fell. Her surprise only doubled when she found no one behind her. Her heart beating wildly at her breast, she brought up her throwing ax defensively despite the fact that empty air was all that threatened her.

"Hey! Watch it, sweetcheeks!" an abrupt voice exclaimed. "You nearly hacked off my bung-rod!"

The sound of her own heartbeat thundering in her ears, Berlyn could only gape as Harris lowered the hood of his samite cloak and popped back into existence, a grim smirk stretched across his lips. The grin quickly evaporated as he looked past the blonde at the advancing Daeminase, his right hand clamped tightly about Mandy. Dried blood stained his bandaged left shoulder a brownish red.

The outlaw tossed a cursory glance up the mountain.

"You're going the wrong way, sweets," the lockpick jeered. "We want to go up, not down. There's a lot of nasties down there."

Her body now charged by fear-induced adrenaline, Berlyn swung an anxious glance down the mountain. "But Aitchley's down there," she protested. "We—"

Harris grinned beneath his raggedy beard. "The puck'll be all right," he assured her. "He fights better than any man alive." He offered her his hand. "Now come on. Maybe we can find some place to hide once we reach the lair."

Eyes wide, Berlyn searched the brigand's face. "You . . . you're impressed by him," she discovered.

A scowl chased away Harris's smile. "Yeah, well, it's not everyone who can say they got their ass kicked in by the Cavalier's descendant," the rogue remarked. "Now come on. He'll still get pretty pissed at me if I let anything happen to you."

Taking his hand, Berlyn resumed her trek up the mountain, vanishing alongside the outlaw as he pulled the hood back up over his head.

Eyeless, the Daeminase clambered after them.

Aitchley swung out his sword before him, forcing the crowd of Daeminase to retreat. His head was still fuzzy from his sudden fall, and he could feel blood seeping through his clothes as he sat between the two dead horses. Claws slashed and raked eagerly at him, and the serpentine hissing of the Daeminase filled his ears like the rushing vent of volcanic gas.

Splashing through blood and mud, Aitchley forced himself to his feet, barely holding the Daeminase at bay. A horselike head rammed into his shield—momentarily unbalancing him— but he kept his footing in the slippery pond of life fluid, right arm lashing out and catching another crimson monstrosity across the top of its skull.

Great! the young man swore darkly to himself. There's nothing but Daeminase around me! Where in the Pits did Gjuki go? I can't see a damn—

Another pair of claws slashed at the young man's backpack, attempting to slice through its only remaining strap. Snarling, the Daeminase's head tumbled off its shoulders in a spray of reddish-brown liquid, the Cavalier's sword flickering a brilliant silver. Saliva continued to ooze from the monster's fang-rimmed mouth, and it snapped viciously even as its head rolled past Aitchley's feet.

Even decapitated, these things don't know when to die! grumbled the young man.

An unexpected hiss sounded in Aitchley's ear, and he whipped about to catch sight of a Daeminase leaping directly at him. He tried to dodge—tried to bring the Cavalier's shield about to block the blow—but his feet were still standing in the lake of blood, and his left foot slipped out from under him.

Bung! the young farmer swore. Bloody typical—

Squealing, the Daeminase suddenly lurched back in midleap, its clawed hands shielding its face. Flesh tore in ragged grooves up the monster's eyeless features, and it lost its footing in the blood as well, its legs sliding out from under it and hurling it onto its back.

Aitchley's blade drove through its open mouth and staked its head to the bloody ground beneath.

Ruffling red-violet feathers, Trianglehead settled himself down on Aitchley's shoulder. "Zstupid ugliesz," the bird snorted. "We go now?"

Sword flailing, Aitchley gave the fledgling a sideways glance. "How long have you been able to fly?" he wanted to know.

Trianglehead blinked milky-blue eyes at the farmer, his brilliant crest rising and falling atop his head. "Long time," the bird replied with what might have been an avian shrug. He danced impatiently from foot to foot. "Go now?"

Brackish fluid dotted Aitchley's face as he freed another head from its neck. "If you could fly, why didn't you leave?"

Trianglehead scratched at his head with a taloned foot. "Free food," the bird responded matter-of-factly. "Go now before dead?"

Aitchley's shield caught another Daeminase in midjump. "I'm trying," he said through clenched teeth. "I'm trying!"

Trianglehead flapped his wings, trying to keep his balance on Aitchley's shoulder. "Only one thing to do then, eh?" the fledgling remarked. "Try harder."

More Daeminase came scrabbling out of Karthenn's Weald.

Wincing at the injury-pain, Poinqart pulled himself to his feet, trying to block out the tickle-feel of his own blood trickle-running down his back. He had to find Mister Aitch, the hybrid

resolved. Find Mister Aitch or the journey-quest was no more.
Mister Aitch had the magic-elixir-drink, and Poinqart was his
protector-friend. Mister-Calyx-dwarf had said so. Protect him,
he was supposed to. Poinqart was not a very good protector-
friend to let Mister Aitch out of his vision-sight like that.

Silver teeth snapped dangerously close to his face, sprinkling
the half-troll with thick gobs of spittle. Poinqart hardly acknowledged the inhuman shape in front of him, ramming a
powerful fist into the center of the Daeminase's elongated skull
and crushing bone. With a weak groan, the monster crumpled
back into the trees, its long, gangly legs twitching convulsively.

Slimy-foul the ugly-*Eperythr*-no-faces are, Poinqart thought
with a mixed-breed grimace. Poinqart hopes Mister Aitch has
not been eaten-digested or Poinqart will be sadly-upset. Missy
Berlyn, too. Poinqart must rescue-find Mister Aitch and show
Mister-Calyx-dwarf that he is worthy-entitled to be Mister
Aitch's protector-friend.

Snarling, a red figure launched itself out of the woods. Dodging effortlessly, the half troll grabbed the Daeminase's
outstretched arms and hurled it forward, using the impetus of
its own leap to propel it forcibly into the side of a birch. Red-
brown fluid splattered as the creature slammed hard against the
trunk, bark and bones splintering with an audible crack.

Poinqart suddenly dropped to one knee, a four-fingered hand
wrapping about the length of blackened oak lying on the woodland floor. Mister Aitch's magic-power-stick, the hybrid mused.
Mister Aitch must have dropped-forgotten it. Maybe-perhaps it
can help-assist Poinqart find Mister Aitch?

Feeling the pins-and-needles sensation run up his thick arms,
Poinqart pointed the staff at the swarming horde of Daeminase,
his face scrunched up in a look of trollish determination and
human uncertainty. He didn't know how Mister Aitch work-
activated the magic-power-stick, but maybe if Poinqart concen-
trated-thought real hard, it would take him to the young farmer.
It wasn't one of the magic-power-forms that Poinqart had seen
Mister Aitch use, but one never knew.

As the tingling in his arms grew—helping even to mute some
of the pain in his back—Poinqart directed the staff at the largest
grouping of *Eperythr*. The morning sun had now risen fully
over the eastern mountains, but the clouds gathering overhead
kept the weald in a kind of morose gloom. Nonetheless, the
staff in Poinqart's hand suddenly released a flash of orange-red

light, and a titanic fireball unexpectedly brought bright shining daylight to the dark woods.

Smoke and flames roared as the blast volcanoed into a cluster of Daeminase, reducing many to charred corpses that refused to die. Others went flying backward, hurled through the trees in an eruption of heat and smoke. Even Poinqart fell backward onto his rump, staring in horror-awe at the staff in his hands. Only supposed to lead-direct Poinqart to Mister Aitch, it was! the half troll shouted at himself, stunned. Magic-power-stick was not supposed to do that!

Howling and shrieking, Daeminase fled through the forest, sorcerous flames feasting on their inhuman flesh. Sparks popped and snapped under the gray shade of the weald, and thick black smoke began to obscure the woods as the fire spread to nearby trees and grass, the dry summer foliage bursting easily into flame.

Poinqart blanched as the weald caught fire. Uh, oh, the hybrid mused. Poinqart has done a nasty-bad thing. Run away! Run away!

Flames moved inexorably through the forest.

Something exploded on Aitchley's right, bathing him in a sudden shock wave of heat and smoke and nearly knocking him to the ground. Flames suddenly leapt as high as the tallest oak, and Daeminase went shrieking into the woods, their withered, regenerative flesh burning and healing . . . burning and healing.

Distracted by the sudden eruption, the young man screamed as sharp claws tore across his right arm, dropping him to one knee. Trianglehead released a startled squawk, flapping awkwardly to a nearby tree branch as the Daeminase lashed out again, eager talons grabbing for the young farmer's throat.

Inhumanly long fingers continued to flex and grab even after the Cavalier's sword had detached them from the Daeminase's hand, sending them flying in a bloodless flash of steel. Teeth clenched, Aitchley whipped his sword about and drove it straight through the center of the eyeless monstrosity's face, the sudden, jarring blow triggering an even greater fire across his wounded forearm.

Blinking questioning eyes, Trianglehead looked down at the young man. "You dead yet?" the bird wondered.

Aitchley spun around, hacking viciously at another monster. "No," he retorted, "I'm not dead yet."

The fledgling hopped to another branch as fiery sparks crackled through the air. "We go now?" he asked.

Aitchley shot the gyrofalc a venomous glare. "I could use a little help here," he snapped angrily. "Can you see where Gjuki is? Or any of the others for that matter?"

From his vantage point in the tree, Trianglehead swept a diamond-blue eye out over the mountain range. "No zsee nobody." Milky blue eyes trained back on Aitchley. "We dead yet?"

Aitchley felt the despair rise up to counter the pain in his arm. "Yeah," he grumbled morbidly under his breath. "We're dead now."

Unexpectedly, there was a rumble of thunder on Aitchley's right, and the young man swung about, blue-green eyes narrowing. Daeminase continued to surround him—darting in and out of the smoke and mist that roiled about the mountain's base—and flames spread swiftly through the weald. His right arm throbbed hellishly as he warded off an attacking monster, and he began to suspect the thunder he had heard was just the roar of the nearing fire.

A mahogany-colored horse suddenly launched itself through the flames, its rider's sword scything down into the hordes of Daeminase. Eyeless monsters squealed and hissed as steel cleaved through elongated skulls, and a number of the crimson beasts went crumpling to the grass, reddish-brown fluid dribbling from their split heads. Other horses thundered after the first, their uniformed riders hacking and slashing at the army of Daeminase, and Aitchley tried to blink the astonishment out of his eyes as the lead Patrolman drew his horse up alongside the young man and offered him a knowing smile.

Aitchley could only gape up at the man. "General Fain?" he sputtered.

22

The Dragon's Ridge

Sergeant Lael raised perplexed eyebrows. "Excuse me?"

"Sorry," Aitchley apologized, shaking his head violently. "The uniform made me think of someone else."

Lael's sword streaked down, amputating scarlet fingers that reached for his horse's flanks. "Well, climb on," he told the young man. "We'll get you out of this mess." He squinted through the growing smoke. "Where's the rest of your group?"

Aitchley catapulted into the saddle behind the Patrolman. "Up the mountain, I guess," he answered "I . . . kinda got separated."

Lael turned his horse in the direction of the mountain path. "No fault of yours," he declared.

In a sudden thunder of hooves, the small squad of Patrolmen went charging up the mountain. Black smoke churned and roiled through the weald behind them, and the sun kept ducking behind ominous gray clouds, sending an even greater depth of gloom out over the hillside. Red figures scrabbled and loped throughout the smoke, and the roar and crackle of the forest fire was harsh and threatening in Aitchley's ears.

Bloodlessly severing a crimson arm, Rymel Donterrian stared in a kind of horrified shock at the inhuman creatures around them. "What in the Pits are these things?" the fisherman wanted to know.

Wincing at the wound on his arm, Aitchley struck out with

his own sword. "Daeminase," he answered. "They've been hounding us since Lich Gate."

Kyne—the Patrolman even younger than Aitchley—swept apprehensive eyes over the gaunt, skeletal monsters. "I always thought they'd be bigger," he remarked. "Long tusks. Big ram horns. That sort of thing."

There was a small shriek as the young brunette—the only female of Rymel's little troop—narrowly avoided snapping teeth. "Isn't there some way to kill them?" she wanted to know. "I keep stabbing them but they keep getting back up!"

"Go for their heads," Aitchley instructed the girl. "That seems to be the only way to hurt them!"

Lael threw an authoritative look over one shoulder at the brunette. "Stay with us, Jelena!" he barked his orders. "Quickly, now!"

Hungrily, the fire spread out across the base of the mountain, filling the sky with acrid smoke. Aitchley could feel its overwhelming stink slip through his nostrils and glide down his throat, bringing a stifling, asthmatic ache to his chest and tears to his eyes. It was making it difficult to fight, and he readied himself as a Daeminase came loping out of the smoke toward them.

A glimmer of surprise sparked in Aitchley's eyes as the monster raced past them, hissing and snarling. Other beasts scrabbled up the mountainside, ignoring the small troop of horses, and he even saw two Daeminase race right into one another, meeting with a sudden crash of gangly arms and razor-sharp talons.

What in the Pits is their problem? the young man wondered. Don't they see us?

Galloping up the sloping path, the horses reached a plateau and thundered around a bend in the rocks. Black smoke wafted up after them—only not so dense—and Aitchley could feel some of the heat on his back gradually diminish. Now he only hoped the fire didn't follow them completely up the mountain and leave them trapped at the top.

Lael suddenly jerked his horse to a halt, almost hurling Aitchley from the saddle. Calyx, Poinqart, Gjuki, and d'Ane all turned as the small squad of Patrolmen came thundering up the hill, Camera 12's unblinking eye watching them all.

Smirking, Calyx looked up at the sergeant. "Well," he

quipped, "looks like nobody's paying any attention to what I say nowadays."

An embarrassed smile stretched Lael's lips. "I guess I just couldn't stand to be left behind again," he remarked. "Is everybody all right?"

Calyx threw an irate glance over his shoulder at Camera 12. "Yeah," he replied, "I guess we're all right." Beady eyes trained their concern on Aitchley. "You had us worried for a while there, kid," he continued. "We tried sending your stupid camera down to get you, but the damn thing wouldn't budge. It just sat there looking at us."

Aitchley slid gingerly out of the saddle. "This is the whole reason it's with us," he explained, patting Camera 12's arachnid head like it was a horse. "It's supposed to observe us going into the lair. I guess that means it's not allowed to help us anymore."

Calyx grunted indifferently. "Fat lot of good that does us," he snorted. He returned his gaze to Aitchley. "Brilliant idea starting that fire, though, kid. Absolutely brilliant."

Aitchley felt a spear of bewilderment lance through his chest. "I didn't start it!" he exclaimed, feeling guilty for no reason. "I don't—bung! I left my staff behind!"

Meekly, Poinqart shuffled forward, offering the length of blackened oak to his friend. "Poinqart is apologetic-sorry, Mister Aitch," the half troll said, ashamed. "Poinqart was only trying to help-assist. Rescue-save you, he was trying."

Mutely, Aitchley took back his stave, the powerful feel of its sorcerous pins and needles helping to dampen some of the pain in his arm.

With a good-natured laugh, Calyx clamped a friendly hand across Poinqart's shoulder. "*You* started the fire?" he roared. "Brilliant! Absolutely brilliant!"

Confusion welling up inside him, Aitchley turned indignant eyes on the dwarven smith. "Why's it so bunging brilliant that he started the fire?" he demanded. "All you did was scream at me to be more careful! Would it have been so brilliant if I had started a fire back in the Bentwoods?"

Calyx turned a stern eye on the farmer. "Of course not, kid. Don't be ridiculous," he responded. "What makes this fire so brilliant is that it's got the Daeminase bamboozled. They can't find us. They work on sense of smell alone, and—I don't know about you—but all I can smell right now is smoke!"

As confusion slowly turned to comprehension Aitchley felt a lopsided grin cross his own lips. *That's why those Daeminase ran right by us,* he suddenly understood. *And those other two crashed into one another because—with the smoke obscuring their sense of smell—they can't "see." Calyx is right. The fire was a brilliant idea. Too bad I didn't think of it.*

"Nonetheless, it will not take them long before they are able to ascertain where we have gone," Gjuki solemnly pointed out. "There is only one mountain path."

Calyx shrugged with misplaced optimism. "Yeah, but this gives us a good head start," he answered. "With the sergeant's help, we can keep 'em off our backs, get to the lair, resurrect Procursus, and then let *him* kick their ass!"

A twinge of the familiar uncertainty returned to Aitchley's breast. "*If* there's enough elixir left," he reminded the dwarf gravely.

Moving with optimistic assurance, Calyx resumed up the mountain trail. "Of course there's enough elixir left," he replied. "We haven't come this far just to be stopped by a lack of elixir! Come on, kid! Let's catch up with Harris and Berlyn and finish this thing once and for all!"

Slowly—feeling all the old confusion and anxiety welling back up—Aitchley made his way after the dwarf, his head suddenly full of a million questions. *Was there enough elixir left?* he wondered. *And should he use it on the Cavalier as everybody wanted? Or should he just not use it at all? And what about what Tin William had been trying to tell him? What shouldn't have been tampered with? And where was Berlyn? And why in the Pits was Calyx acting so cheerful? Were things really going that badly that Calyx was in one of his good moods?*

Trudging up the hill, Aitchley felt a graimce pull at his lips. *Bloody bunging typical,* he muttered.

Berlyn managed to grasp a solid lip of rock and pull herself up, jerking her skirt out of the way. The path they followed had all but faded out of existence, and rather than try to find where it resumed, she hoped to come across it somewhere higher up the mountain. She hoped she didn't get lost, but she felt an odd sense of security being with Harris. While in the Molten Dunes, the outlaw had never once gotten lost—or if he had, he had never let on—and Berlyn felt safe knowing he had such a good sense of direction.

Inhaling deeply, Berlyn pulled herself up onto the rock shelf and turned to look out over southern Vedette. The mountain dropped away in varying tiers of level ground and abrupt slopes, decorated here and there by trees and large boulders. The weald was like a carpeting of grass at the base of the mountain, black coils and wisps of snakelike smoke still rising up into the heavens. She could just catch a glimpse of Malvia Lake peeking out from around the eastern edge of the mountain, and the Alsace and Mistillteinn rivers were winding, twisting strands of mirrorlike silver in the distance. Ominously, dark clouds roiled and churned overhead, shrouding the craggy peaks with halos of threatening blackness.

Berlyn threw an apprehensive look down the side of the slope. Where was Aitchley? she wondered, the worry growing at her breast. She and Harris had moved halfway around the mountain—and she was no longer able to see where they had camped that morning—but she hoped the others were still following. Thoughts of gangly red monsters ripping and tearing at human flesh had to be pushed from her mind, and the blonde felt another nudge of anxiety place a kind of invisible pressure on her rib cage.

Striding almost soundlessly across the dry grass and bare dirt, Harris Blind-Eye tossed a glance skyward. "League or two," he mused out loud, staring up at the mountain peak. "Think you can make it?"

Gray-green eyes continued to scan the lower levels of the mountain. "Don't you think we should wait for the others?" Berlyn suggested. "I can't tell if anyone's following us."

Brusquely, Harris stepped to the edge of the cliff and gave a disgruntled look at the uneven, sloping terrain. "Daeminase are," he grumbled under his breath. "Better keep moving."

Berlyn caught sight of distant red figures scrabbling effortlessly up unscalable cliff walls after them. "But what about the others?" she insisted. "They might get cut off."

Harris stalked across the plateau like a caged animal. "Serve 'em right," he muttered vengefully. "I told the dwarf heading east would send us right back into those eyeless bungholes, but did he listen to me? Naw. Nobody ever listens to me. I'm just southern-city scum."

"But we needed to replenish our supplies," Berlyn said.

"For what?" Harris spat back. "For one more week of riding? For seven days through a forest full of rabbit and quail? It wouldn't have even taken seven days if we hadn't gone to Viveca. The plantman was right. It would have been faster just to go straight through the weald."

"But the path," argued Berlyn. "The path was northeast of Viveca. Without it, we would have had to climb up and down the Dragon's Ridge just to get this far."

Blue-black eyes flared angrily as the brigand turned his back on the scullery maid. "Yeah, some path," he growled. "Scrub brush and erosion." He swung his angry gaze up the mountain. "If you want to wait around here, that's your choice," he snarled. "Me? I'm gonna go find someplace safe to hide." He jerked the hood of his cloak over his head and disappeared from sight. "See ya around, sweets."

Listening to the faint footfalls of invisible boots, Berlyn felt her fingers tighten anxiously around her weapon. Part of her wanted to stay and wait for Aitchley, but the distant red figures clambering spiderlike up the steep sides of the mountain caused a lump of cold fear to encase her heart. She knew she couldn't fight the Daeminase by herself—their numbers would overwhelm her even before she had a chance—but the worry burning at her breast kept her rooted to the spot. If she couldn't fight the Daeminase alone, how was Aitchley doing? Was he alone? Had something happened to him and the others? Where was he? And why hadn't she stayed behind and helped? She had thought everybody else had run with her and Poinqart, but when she had turned around, not even the half troll was with her. So where was everybody?

The sudden rumble of hooves pulled Berlyn out of her worried musings, and she turned to see a small squad of mounted Patrolmen ride beneath her ledge. She immediately recognized the young man jogging behind the horses and felt the cold fear melt away.

"Aitchley!" she shouted down at the farmer.

Skidding to a bewildered halt, Aitchley glanced up at the rock shelf. The look of surprise on his face was instantly erased by relief, and he vaulted up the ledge and swept the blonde up in a tight embrace. "Berlyn!" he shouted back happily. "Are you all right?"

Feeling the worry and apprehension drain out of her body,

Berlyn savored the feel of the young man's arms about her. "I'm fine," she answered. "Are you all right?"

Despite the pain in his right arm, Aitchley nodded. "I'm fine," he lied. "Just a scratch."

His face turning a darker shade of red as he struggled to pull himself onto the plateau, Calyx gave the two teenagers a sardonic glance. "Great. Wonderful," he quipped. "Everybody's fine. Where's Blind-Butt?"

Berlyn managed to point without breaking off her embrace with Aitchley. "He went on ahead," she said. "He didn't feel like waiting."

From atop his horse, Rymel looked down the hills at the Daeminase. "Not that I blame him," the fisherman remarked.

Gingerly, Lael dismounted, handing his horse's reins to the youthful Kyne. He swung a disapproving eye at the rock shelf above his head. "Horses'll never make it up this ridge," he mused out loud. "Rymel, you, Kyne, and Dabir take the horses. See if you can find another way around. Jelena, Tudor, you're with me."

Saluting, Rymel and his men led the horses up what remained of the path and around a jumbled outcropping of rocks before disappearing from view. Aitchley watched them go, a queasy kind of dread churning in his stomach. He didn't like losing the added security of Rymel's troop, and—even though Lael, Jelena, and Tudor were staying with them—the young man couldn't stop the shudder of uneasiness that passed through his thoughts. There were just too many Daeminase still after them. . . . Aitchley hoped neither he nor Rymel's group accidentally stumbled across any of them.

Calyx drew beady eyes away from the mountain's peak. "All right, kiddies," he announced, grimly sarcastic, "we've got about two more leagues to go. Let's get this over with."

Reluctantly, Aitchley released Berlyn from his embrace and started up the mountain after Calyx. He tried not to let his misgivings and uncertainties regain their hold in his thoughts, and he held on tightly to Berlyn's hand as if to help ward them off. *Let's get this over with,* he heard Calyx's words resound in his own head.

Yeah, his pessimism snorted back, and then what?

The Elixir of Life felt heavy and burdensome across his shoulder.

There was a burning ache in Aitchley's legs as he clambered up the mountainside, a weariness that seared into his muscles. The uneven ground pulled and tugged at the backs of his legs, and loose dirt sometimes made inclines more treacherous than they looked. His right arm still throbbed with discomfort despite the impromptu bandage he had wrapped around it, and—although he could feel its soothing pins-and-needles sensation seeping through the backpack and into his body—not even his proximity to the elixir could quell his aches and pains. Maybe there just wasn't enough of it left to make a difference, and the young man was forced to just grit his teeth and continue climbing.

Lost in a labyrinth of dark clouds, the sun moved steadily into the heavens, peeking out on rare occasions to whitewash the group in sporadic halos of sunlight. A wind picked up the higher they climbed, and Aitchley wondered if the clouds were going to drench them with another late-summer thunderstorm. It didn't look like it—and there wasn't that unmistakable smell of moisture just before a big rainfall—but you never knew. Aitchley wasn't familiar with the weather this far east of Solsbury and he was surprised—even though dark clouds converged overhead—to still feel the warmth of summertime, causing beads of perspiration to form on his brow as he walked.

Following obediently behind Calyx, the young farmer was grateful when they came to a level ridge, his legs thankful for the even ground. The last time they had come across a plateau it had led to a deadend of stone, and they had been forced to backtrack about half a league down the mountain before Calyx could find another accesible route. This gave the Daeminase scuttling up from below the chance to draw closer, and now every time Aitchley heard the wind blow through some brush or through the branches of some lonely tree, he jerked around half expecting to see eyeless faces full of silver teeth leaping hungrily at him.

Drawing in a deep breath, Berlyn sank to the level ground, reclining wearily against a large rock. "I've got to stop," she announced. "My legs are killing me."

Scowling, Calyx shot the scullery maid an impatient glance. "I guess we can take a short break," he agreed reluctantly. "But just a short one!"

"What other kind would you expect a dwarf to give?" joked

Sergeant Lael, settling himself down beside Jelena and Poinqart.

Feeling some of the ache diminish in his own limbs, Aitchley lowered himself to the ground. He wished he still had his hat to pull down over his eyes—he had lost it at the bottom of the mountain fighting Daeminase—and he was beginning to feel the sleeplessness of the night before gnawing away at his stamina. He wished now he had slept better, and he was tempted to pull out the elixir and set it in his lap. Something about the uniforms of the Patrolmen and memories of General Fain, however, made the young man keep the potion safely in its backpack.

Lightly dozing, Aitchley released an audible groan when Calyx called an end to their brief rest. The soreness in his muscles returned as soon as he got back to his feet, and he felt as if he had even less strength than he did before he sat down. He tried to think of things other than the ache in his legs and at his arm, but every time he tried to take his mind off his discomfort, his thoughts immediately focused on the elixir and what he was supposed to do with it.

Oh, this is bunged, the young man finally concluded. I'm tired. I'm sore. And I'm stupid. Why should I even bother trying to figure this out? I'm never going to understand what it was Tin William was trying to tell me, so why don't I just forget about it? We'll just get up there, resurrect the Cavalier, and who cares if the lords of Solsbury were lying? I'm just too damn tired.

Moving across the plateau, the nine came across the continuation of the mountain path and slowly resumed their trek upward. The terrain had become almost entirely dirt and stone, but Aitchley winced as the occasional burr or nettle reached out and stuck to his pants. The wind continued to moan—sometimes threatening to unbalance the young man as he lurched up the steeper inclines—and Aitchley's natural grace continued to manifest itself by making him slip on loose dirt or tripping him over rocks half-buried in the soil.

If it's not biarki holes, it's just plain old dirt, the farmer grumbled to himself.

A quarter of a league higher, the nine came across another tableland of rock. A few patches of grass grew beside a small mountain stream, and one large oak leaned drunkenly on the slope of the plateau, spreading gray shadows beneath a gray

sky. Rymel and his two Patrolmen relaxed under the shade of
the tree, the horses nibbling contentedly at the grasses nearby.
Large, brownish-yellow boulders ringed the plateau, and the
western wall was a sheer cliff of solid stone. Gurgling, the
brook tumbled and babbled down between boulders before
splashing somewhere out of sight.

Calyx gave the mountainside a backward glance as he
stepped through the naturally formed barricade of stone.
"Hmm," the dwarf mused out loud. "Level ground. Advantage of height. Only one route through." He turned a pleased
eye on the reclining Rymel. "This looks like a great place to
hold off the Daeminase."

Even through his weariness, Aitchley felt a sudden barb of
fear. "Hold off the Daeminase?" he echoed anxiously. "What
do you mean? Aren't you coming to the Dragon's Lair?"

The expression on Calyx's face was grim and dark, but then
again—Aitchley considered—the expression on Calyx's face
was almost always grim and dark. "What for?" the dwarf
asked matter-of-factly. "We're being chased, kid. It doesn't
make sense for all of us to go up to the lair when we've got a
perfect place to hold 'em off down here. And there's no defensive positions like this outside the lair. I know. I've been
there. The lair's just this big opening in the mountainside. Daeminase could come at us from any side they want to up there."

"Well, what's to stop them from coming at us from any side
they want down here?" Aitchley queried.

Calyx pointed out the cliff wall to their left and the ring of
parapetlike boulders encircling the tableland. "There's only
one route through," the smith explained. "Right up the middle
of all these rocks. Means they'll have to move single file . . .
which gives us another advantage."

Aitchley eyed the fence of giant stones. "But what if they
just climb over the rocks?" he wanted to know. "These are
Daeminase we're talking about here . . . not men."

Calyx shrugged. "So we position someone on the rocks to
keep 'em off," he answered. "Look, kid, it makes the most
sense. This place is perfect."

Captain d'Ane swept a trained eye over the plateau. "Well,
not perfect," he contradicted the dwarf, "but probably as good
as we're going to find."

"Dwarven beggars can't be choosers, Captain," Calyx retorted. "It's good enough." He stabbed a pudgy finger at the

relaxing Patrolmen. "All right, Rymel: you and your friend there—what was his name? Kyne? You and Kyne watch the eastern slope. Lael, you and the rest of your men watch the path. Poinqart and I can keep 'em off the rocks. D'Ane, you and Gjuki make sure none of 'em sneak around behind us. That should keep the kid safe till he gets back with Procursus."

The cold grew as Aitchley stared up the mountainside. "So that's it?" he said with heavy disbelief. "You say the word and suddenly I'm going by myself?"

Calyx didn't even bother to look at the young man as he clambered to a vantage point atop one of the boulders. "Naw, of course not," he said simply. "I figured Berlyn would want to go with you. And your camera, too, probably. Isn't that what you said it was here for? To go to the lair with you?"

Aitchley felt his mouth moving but no coherent sounds were coming out. "Me and Berlyn?" he finally sputtered. "Me and Berlyn are supposed to make it up the rest of the mountain by ourselves?"

Calyx directed a small smile at the young farmer. "What are you so worried about?" he asked. "You're just going to the lair. It's not like the Dragon's up there waiting for you! We'll keep the Daeminase off your butts."

"And what if some of them slip through?" the young man protested. "They're all over the mountain!"

"This is the quickest way through, though," Calyx replied. "Even for those eyeless bastards. Any of 'em taking the long way 'round won't reach you till you get back here with the Cavalier. And besides, you'll have your camera along."

The fear and anxiety churning in Aitchley's gut was fast approaching panic. "I told you Camera 12 might not be allowed to help anymore!" he barked. "It's only supposed to observe!"

Calyx shrugged again, and Aitchley was beginning to find the dwarf's misplaced optimism annoying. "So it'll observe you in danger and help out," he said. "Now hurry up and get up there. In the time it's taken you to complain, you could've been up there and back already."

Although arctic fear rushed through Aitchley's veins, he felt some sense of reassurance as Berlyn placed a tender hand on his arm. "Calyx is right, Aitchley," she said softly. "It's only about a league more. So long as they keep the Daeminase off our trail, we should be all right."

Aitchley bit back any snide retort or pessimistic remark that threatened to slip past his lips. "Yeah. Right," was all he said, shouldering the backpack nervously.

Moving to the lip of a steep slope, the Patrolmen named Dabir turned a questioning eye on Lael. "Uh . . . Sergeant?" he asked uneasily.

Lael turned sharply on the man. "What is it, Dabir?"

Dabir scratched quizzically at his head. "Um . . . I'm not quite sure, sir," he replied, redirecting his gaze down the mountain. "It . . . uh . . . looks like a man."

Swiftly, Calyx hopped off his boulder and stomped to the Patrolman's side. "Is it Blind-Butt?" he wanted to know.

Dabir's confusion heightened. "I don't think so, sir."

His own worry and apprehensions momentarily pushed aside, Aitchley took a questioning step forward. He didn't know what he expected to see at the bottom of the cliff, but the tone of uncertainty in the Patrolman's voice had piqued his curiosity.

A look of befuddlement on his face, Sergeant Lael joined Patrolman Dabir at the edge of the steep slope. "What is that?" he wondered out loud. "Is that . . . armor?"

Moving up beside Lael, Aitchley felt his mouth drop open and the cold lump of fear in his stomach suddenly swell to devour him whole. Undiluted horror rushed through his bloodstream—turning his veins to ice—and he had to take a step back as the sudden shock almost made him swoon.

Noting the young man's reaction, the others quickly turned on him.

"Kid," Calyx questioned worriedly, "are you all right?"

Blue-green eyes trying to blink away some of the shock from their gaze, Aitchley turned a pale expression on the dwarf. "I know who that is," he managed to croak.

Calyx swung beady eyes down the angled wall of stone at the crumpled figure at its rocky base. "Who?" he wanted to know.

Aitchley swallowed hard. "Tin William," he answered.

The wind continued to moan mournfully around them.

23

Dragon's Lair

Tentatively, Aitchley made his way down the escarpment, carefully testing each rock before putting his weight upon it. Loose dirt sluiced down the incline like brownish-yellow water—disturbed by the young man's passage—and pebbles and small stones dislodged from chinks and eroding crevices to go bouncing down the slope before spiraling off the edge of the cliff and disappearing from view.

Face pale and lips dry, Patrolman Kyne followed the young farmer down the steep incline, his feet not as sure as Aitchley's. A wall of sheer rock on one side and empty space on the other were all that bordered the young men, and each time Kyne felt his boots stumble across the jagged staircase of rocks, all he could see was the vast expanse of Vedette stretched out below him like some illuminated manuscript.

Nearly fifteen feet above them, the other members of the quest looked on, anxious expressions painted on their faces. The ledge where Tin William's body lay was nothing more than a small protrusion of stone—rocky ravines and jagged cliffs leading down to its almost inaccessible base—and Aitchley and Kyne looked small and fragile among so much rock.

Aitchley made a small hop off a crooked boulder and onto the ledge where Tin William lay. He hardly paid any attention to the dizzying drop clutching eagerly at the heels of his boots, and he moved with urgent purpose to the motionless construct's side, a grim frown already tugging down his lips.

Not quite so agile, Kyne jumped onto the small shelf of stone, his arms windmilling to help keep his balance. Vertigo roiled through his head, and he had to close his eyes in order to fight off his rising nausea. He could feel his body pitch and sway, and he tried to keep his eyes on the solid rock beneath and the young man before him.

His face losing even more color, the young Patrolman looked down at Aitchley. "So is it dead?" he wondered.

All but oblivious to his surroundings, Aitchley inspected the still metal figure. "I don't know," he answered. "I can't tell."

Trying to ignore the vertiginous whirl in his brain, Kyne kept his gaze on the manlike shape of cold gray steel. "Well, what is it?" he wanted to know. "Is there a man in there?"

Aitchley frowned at dented metal. "No," he replied, not really paying attention to the Patrolman. "There's nobody in there."

"Then what is it?" Kyne asked again.

Aitchley's eyes trailed down broken joints and exposed wires. "It told me it was some kind of machine," he answered. "Some sort of mechanical construct."

Kyne's eyes went wide. "You mean it could talk?"

Be wary of Nature's scales.

Aitchley's frown deepened at the memory of the robot's inhumanly buzzing voice. "Oh, yeah," he responded sardonically. "It could talk."

Nervously, Kyne gave the cliff at his back an anxious glance. "So what's it doing here?" he asked.

Staring down at the unmoving husk of steel, Aitchley got slowly to his feet. "I don't know," he muttered grimly again. "He probably came here to tell me something."

"Tell you something?" repeated Kyne. "Tell you what?"

There are some things that were not meant to be tampered with, Aitchley Corlaiys.

Aitchley shrugged. "I don't know," was all he said.

Barely audible over the howl of the wind, Aitchley could hear Calyx's gruff voice echoing down the mountainside. "Hurry it up, kid!" the dwarf shouted. "The Daeminase are gonna be here any second!"

Scowling, Aitchley threw a last, disgusted look at the cadaver of steel twisted and motionless at his feet. So what in the Pits *is* Tin William doing here? he asked himself with angry bafflement. Why come all the way from the Molten Dunes unless he had something more to tell me? Or maybe he knew how stupid I was and was going to explain what he had meant before. So what had happened? Did he fall? Why couldn't he fly like Camera 12? You'd think something as incredible as a man made entirely out of metal could survive something like this. It just doesn't make sense.

"Kid!" Calyx's voice resounded from high above him.

Feeling the frustration and confusion turn slowly into a smoldering rage, Aitchley turned away from the unmoving figure and started back up the escarpment. Nothing was making much sense anymore! he grumbled to himself as he climbed. Nothing Tin William had said! Nothing Fain had said! Nothing even he himself had said! Tin William had been purposefully enigmatic and now Aitchley didn't have a clue as to what he had been trying to say! And now . . . now the damn thing shows up here at the bottom of a ravine in the Dragon's Ridge! Why? What was he doing here? What made him leave the safety of his house in the desert? And what about all that "unable to interfere" mulch? Couldn't coming here be considered interference?

Aitchley felt a sudden jolt of anxiety leech some of the angry strength from his limbs. Was that who killed him? he mused fearfully. Had the people who had built Tin William come back to exact their punishment? And if they had, were they still around? Aitchley had no desire to go up against somebody who could build men out of metal or magic lightsticks or thermoses or flying cameras!

His head full of a million new questions, Aitchley clambered back onto the plateau with the others. He hardly felt the tired ache in his legs or the constant throbbing at his right arm, and he moved purposefully to his supplies and slung Tin William's backpack haphazardly over one shoulder.

"Is there any chance of saving your friend, Master Aitchley?" Gjuki asked.

Aitchley strapped his swordbelt around his waist. "No," he answered, teeth clenched in his frustration. "I guess he's dead."

"He won't be the only one if we don't get ready," Calyx remarked, beady eyes flicking warily to the mountain path. "The Daeminase'll be here any second, and you've already lost the head start we had."

The confusion and uncertainty storming through Aitchley's

head mingled to ignite the young man's anger. "So what?" he snapped, snatching up his oaken staff. "What does it matter? Tin William's dead. Whatever he was going to tell me died with him."

"Now, we don't know that, lad," Captain d'Ane replied calmly. "There might have been a number of reasons this Tin William came up here."

An impotent rage burned blue green in Aitchley's eyes. "Oh, yeah?" he challenged. "Name one?" He didn't even wait for an answer. "Tin William came up here 'cause he knew I was too stupid to understand whatever it was he had told me before. And now he's dead, and we'll never know."

Eyes scanning the hillside for Daeminase, Calyx didn't even bother to face the young man. "Camera 12," he said.

Aitchley swung an angry eye on the smith. "What?" he snarled back.

"Camera 12," Calyx said again with a small shrug. "Camera 12 belonged to this Tin William, right? Maybe he was coming up here to tell Camera 12 that it was all right to help out. You ever think of that?"

The dwarf's logic caused the young man's anger to momentarily falter, but the indignant, frustrated fire of his rage could not be extinguished. "Doesn't make sense," the farmer retorted. "He didn't have to come all the way up here for that. He could have met us north of the Molten Dunes or even back in Leucos. He knew where we were going."

Calyx nodded sharply. "Ah, yes," he replied. "The magic windows. So you said." He turned what could have been a skeptical glance at the young man. "Did you ever think maybe this Tin William wanted to get the elixir for himself? Maybe his coming here was an attempt to steal it from us. You've already said he tried to warn you against using it."

"That's what I *thought* he meant!" Aitchley barked angrily. "But I was wrong! Gjuki pointed that out to me! 'Some things *weren't* meant to be tampered with'! Past tense! He was talking about something that had already happened!"

"Perhaps he was referring to our obtaining the elixir," Gjuki suggested, a tinge of remorse in his voice for causing the young farmer such mental anxiety. "Or journeying beyond Lich Gate itself?"

"But we hadn't done any of that yet!" Aitchley voiced his frustration. "We hadn't done anything at all!" He grabbed his shield and started toward the slope where the mountain path curled up along a rocky ledge. "What difference does it make now, anyway?" he mumbled sadly under his breath. "He's dead."

Calyx turned grim eyes on the hillside. "We will be, too, if we're not careful," he declared. "Get ready. Here they come!"

Freeing his sword from its sheath, Sergeant Lael moved past Aitchley to block the entrance to the plateau. "You'd better hurry," the Patrolman advised the young man. "You don't want to get caught down here with the rest of us."

Knuckles white around the haft of her ax, Berlyn took Aitchley by the hand. "Sergeant Lael's right," she told the farmer. "Come on. Let's get out of here."

Despite the angry confusion rattling his brain, Aitchley could hear the telltale hissing of inhuman monsters rising like steam from down the mountainside. The sounds of sharp claws against hard rock cut through the howl of the wind, and a shiver of preternatural terror managed to crawl its way up the young man's spine.

Declaration: There are some things that were not meant to be tampered with, Aitchley Corlaiys. Be wary of nature's scales.

Aitchley swung questioning eyes down the sheer cliff where Tin William lay twisted and unmoving. Gaal dammit! he cursed his memory. What in the Pits were you trying to tell me?

The insistent tug of Berlyn's hand in his pulled the young man from his thoughts. "Come on, Aitchley," the blonde implored, a hint of fear in her voice. "We've got to get out of here."

The scrabble of talons on stone grew louder.

There is a precarious balance at work in all worlds, Aitchley Corlaiys. No single species must ever cause this balance to lose its integrity.

Aitchley frowned to himself. Balance? Scales? he mused ineffectually. What happened that would have caused nature itself to become unbalanced? What had been tampered with? Think, Gaal dammit! Think!

Moving slowly under the persistent pull of Berlyn's hand, Aitchley turned as Calyx's voice cut through the ever-increasing cacophony of skittering claws and reptilian hissing.

"Oh, and, kid," the dwarf said. "Don't worry about it." A

sincere grin spread beneath the dwarf's salt-and-pepper beard. "You'll do the right thing."

Sneering, Aitchley turned away and stalked up the mountain path, the dwarf's compliment stinging like an insult. Do the right thing? he repeated sarcastically to himself. I don't even know *what* I'm supposed to do! How can it be the right thing?

Unbidden, a small door opened in the young man's subconscious, and he could hear the lilting voice of Taci reverberate through his memory as he climbed. *Kirima says that it is good you have the* dhreglei. *The Elixir of Life. She is certain you will do what is right by it.*

Stomping up the dirt path, Aitchley released a cynical snort. Yeah, right, he grunted pessimistically to himself. You and Calyx both!

The inhuman hissing grew louder.

Someone was coming.

Nicander Tampenteire slipped furtively into the shadows of the great Dragon's Lair, his dirty and abraded fingers curling about the dwarven dagger in his hand. Light brown eyes flickered with an eagerness bordering on insanity, and there was a nervous twitch just beneath the nobleman's left eye. He scratched obsessively at his thick beard, and he heard a wheezing rasp of laughter that startled him before he realized he was the one laughing.

Nicander's eyes sparked malevolently. Corlaiys is coming, he whispered vengefully to himself. It can be no one else. After all these months of waiting—after all these months of torment—he would finally have his revenge. One clean thrust through Corlaiys's breast, and the elixir was his! He could return home a hero. Return to reclaim his birthright. Return as the man who saved Vedette. And, oh, how the people would adore him! He would be hailed the savior of the land. The man who went beyond Lich Gate and returned with the fabled Elixir of Life. The man who brought the legendary Cavalier Procursus Galen back from the dead.

All he had to do was kill Corlaiys.

Nicander's hand tightened about his dagger, a wicked smile pulling across his scabbed and dirty features. That shouldn't be too hard, he mused villainously to himself.

*   *   *

With a solid *thwock*, Calyx's warhammer slammed into the eyeless face of an approaching Daeminase, knocking the gangly red monster off the tier of boulders. Lean limbs flailing, the creature bounced back down the mountainside, taking a number of its eyeless brethren with it in its uncontrolled tumble. Others, however, were quick to replace it, silver fangs snapping and flashing.

"This isn't working," Calyx grumbled out loud to himself. "There's more of them than I thought."

Sword gleaming, Sergeant Lael hacked off withered flesh only to watch it slowly pucker and heal. "Now's a fine time to figure that out," he quipped. He drove his blade through the throat of another scarlet beast. "So what are we supposed to do?"

Calyx's arm reverberated with the sudden blow of his hammer striking inhuman bone. "I've got an idea," he said, hopping quickly off his boulder and hurrying to the center of the plateau. "Gjuki," he barked, "get over here and start a small fire."

Shoving snarling monsters back down the mountain with his bare hands, Gjuki shifted tiny black eyes on the dwarf. "I do not think a fire would be in our best interest right now, Master Calyx," the Rhagana replied. "While it worked at the base of the mountain, it would leave us little possibility of escape at this height. In addition, there is not enough fuel to fan a fire of—"

Rumaging through his large sack, Calyx poked his head up long enough to shoot the gardener a withering glare. "I don't mean a fire fire," he snapped. "I mean a fire. Like a campfire."

Befuddlement sparkled in Gjuki's pearllike eyes. "I do not understand," he admitted.

Calyx went back to searching through his bag. "I don't care if you understand or not," he retorted. "Just do it!"

The flicker of question still in his gaze, Gjuki nodded obediently and moved to the center of the plateau, gathering tinder as he went. The mountain wind tried to blow what few twigs and dry grass the Rhagana found, and he had to turn his back on the Daeminase in order to block out the howling gale.

Rymel glanced uneasily over one shoulder, slashing repeatedly at the tide of crimson monsters. "Whatever you're going to do, you'd better do it now," he said.

Moving as quickly as his short legs would carry him, Calyx

joined Gjuki beside the small campfire, a small bag of herbs in his grasp. Without ceremony, he dumped the entire contents of the pouch onto the fire and stepped back as noxious fumes of blue-gray smoke abruptly billowed into the air.

Jelena made a sour face as the malodorous cloud made its way out across the plateau. "Oh, phew!" she exclaimed. "What in the name of the Twin Sisters is that?"

Calyx grinned through the haze of stink. "*Kalreif* shoots," he declared triumphantly. "Confused 'em once before. Maybe it'll give us an added advantage."

Pounding four-fingered fists into the unending tide of Daeminase, a hybrid look of human joy and trollish rage contorted Poinqart's face. "Mister-Calyx-dwarf is very intelligent-smart," the half troll said. "Ugly-*Eperythr*-no-faces are befuddled-confused. They do not even know Poinqart is right in front of them!"

There was a faint smile on Captain d'Ane's glimmering features as the sulfurous fumes spread out across the hillside. "I've got to hand it to you, Calyx," the dead soldier complimented the dwarf. "That's what I call thinking on your feet."

"Thank you, Captain," Calyx responded, grinning. "You don't live to be as old as I am without learning a thing or two."

Weapon flashing, Patrolman Tudor slashed his sword through the scrawny neck of a Daeminase. "This is great!" he exclaimed. "It's like they can't even see us!"

"Less talk, more mayhem," Calyx remarked, returning to his position atop the ring of boulders. "They still outnumber us a hundred to one!"

Even as he moved to assist in the battle, there was a glint of uncertainty in Gjuki's tiny eyes. "While I concur that the plan has merit," the fungoid gardener said, "I have one question concerning such a ploy."

Calyx's warhammer smashed into an eyeless face. "What's that?"

Gjuki threw an apprehensive glance at the small campfire. "What happens if—"

Shrieking, the winds blew across the tableland, sweeping up the foul-smelling smoke and scattering it westward.

"—the winds pick up again?" Gjuki concluded.

As the haze of fetor dispersed, a look of dire gloom spread

across Calyx's face. "Oh, well," he quipped with a shrug. "Never said we'd get out of this alive."

Eyeless red figures swarmed up the mountainside.

Using his staff like a walking stick, Aitchley Corlaiys trudged up the mountain path, fueling his legs with the impotent anger burning inside him. It hardly mattered where he was going, and he kept his eyes down, glowering at the dirt path beneath his feet. His thoughts were a jumble of wrathful confusion and self-loathing, and he didn't even seem to notice the young girl struggling to keep pace with him.

Worriedly, Berlyn sprinted after Aitchley, one hand hiking up her skirt to allow her legs freer movement. She could practically see the black cloud of despair hovering over the young man's head, and she wondered what she could do to help him. This wasn't something a little wine and a little dancing could cure. This cut straight to Aitchley's self-doubt. This went beyond questioning his own worth and his own abilities, and it gave his debilitating pessimism a chance to rise up and crush any self-respect the young man may have gained during his quest to Lich Gate and beyond.

Berlyn gnawed on her lower lip. What can I do? she mused in her own frustration. I've said everything I can think of to make him see he's not a failure, but he just won't listen to me. Why does he have to doubt everything he does? Why is it that every time he does something right, he can find something bad about it? And why can't he just ignore what this Tin William said and do what he believes in? I wish I could just talk to him about it!

Riding on Camera 12's wire-mesh saddle, Trianglehead had no such reservations. "Why you pout?" the bird asked, cocking his head quizzically at the young man.

Aitchley continued stomping up the hill. "I'm not pouting," he shot back.

Diamond-blue eyes fixed on the farmer. "Zsure you are," Trianglehead replied. "You pout like fledgling that get no grub."

"No, I'm not," Aitchley answered, sneering. He continued up the mountain. "Just leave me alone."

"What krawl up your butt and die?" the gyrofalc queried.

"Nothing crawled up my butt!" Aitchley snapped back. "Leave me alone!"

Trianglehead tilted his head to one side. ''Leave you alone,''
the bird echoed tauntingly. ''Leave you alone. Why zshould I
leave you alone? Almoszt done here, yesz? Almoszt time to go
home, yesz? Zso why you act like zsparrow with no brain?''

Aitchley flung a hateful glare at the fledgling. ''What do you
know about it?'' he spat. ''You're just a stupid bird.''

Trianglehead shrugged. ''May be zstupid bird, but better to
be zstupid bird than zstupid human,'' the red-violet fledgling
said. ''Bird know better than to get mad at what been zsaid.
Moszt birdsz zsmart. Moszt birdsz talk all the time. Only not
to humansz . . . Humansz are zstupid.''

The despair rose up in Aitchley's thoughts and devoured
his rage. ''So we're stupid,'' he agreed glumly. ''So what? I
could've told you that.''

Trianglehead flapped angry wings. ''No, no, no!'' he cawed.
''You no zsupposzed to agree! Zsupposzed to argue. Zsupposzed to zsay, 'Humansz no zstupid. Birdsz isz zstupid!' ''

Leaning on his staff, Aitchley crested a small rise. ''All right.
Fine.'' He sighed. '' 'Humans aren't' stupid. Birds are stupid.' ''

Boastfully, Trianglehead ruffled out his breast feathers. ''But
birdsz not zstupid to get mad over what not be zsaid about
them. Only humansz that zstupid.''

Aitchley gave the bird a confused look. ''What?''

An expression of avian exasperation momentarily flickered
across Trianglehead's face. ''Look,'' the bird explained, ''you
mad kausze you no underzstand what been zsaid. Thought it
about you. Find out it not. Now you mad. That zstupid.''

Fearful of the young man's anger, Berlyn risked a timid response. ''He's right, you know.''

A glint of ire flared in the farmer's eyes. ''What?'' he barked
at the blonde. ''Are you going to start in on me, too?''

A tinge of indignant anger boiled just beneath the surface of
Berlyn's words as she narrowed gray-green eyes. ''You're acting like an idiot, Aitchley,'' she snapped. ''All this time you
thought Tin William was talking about you and the elixir. When
you find out he wasn't, you get even more upset. Why? He
wasn't talking about you!''

The rage quickly left Aitchley's eyes and only the desperation remained. ''But why tell me anything at all?'' he demanded to know. ''You weren't there! You didn't hear it in
his voice! He was trying to tell me something, and now he's

dead! And whatever he was trying to tell me was important enough to bring him here to the Dragon's Ridge!''

''But it wasn't about you,'' Berlyn argued. ''You said that yourself. Past tense. Some things *were* not meant to be!'' Frustration threatened to clog the scullery maid's throat. ''Why are you doing this to yourself, Aitchley?''

''Because Tin William came all the way up here to tell me something, and it killed him!'' the young man responded. ''Even if it's not about me, it was important enough for him to do that!''

On the verge of angry tears, Berlyn went silent, biting her lip in frustration. Unable to think of anything more to say, she followed the young man up the winding path, walking quietly between giant boulders. Gradually, the rocks lining the path fell away, revealing a panoramic view of eastern Vedette. Dark storm clouds still swelled in the heavens—and the wind had taken on an ominous chill, chasing the summery warmth down from the mountaintop—but a moment of dazzling awe suddenly cut through Berlyn's worry and anger.

Rounding a bend in the rock, the two teenagers stopped before immense blackness. The wind shrieked in and around the enormous opening in the rock face, and Berlyn felt her mouth hang open at the sheer size of the Dragon's Lair. Bigger than any castle—bigger than the Tridome—the lair was an abyss of impenetrable darkness carved into the side of the mountain. Huge boulders looked like tiny pebbles next to its vastness, and—even though she had seen crude drawings of it in books from the Tampenteire library—the young girl had no idea that the cavern would be so huge . . . or make her feel so small.

''Daeminase Pits,'' she swore under her breath. ''Myxomycetes must have been bigger than anyone thought!''

Unimpressed, Aitchley stalked away from the titanic cavern and looked out over Vedette. Malvia Lake was a tiny spot of blue under all the dark clouds, and Karthenn's Weald was a uniform patch of green, not much more than a cluster of clover from this height. Screaming, the wind threatened to tear the young man off the ledge and carry him down endless cliffs of stone as, curiously, the farmer leaned out over the edge to see the distant ledge where Tin William's body lay bent and twisted far below.

Turning back toward Berlyn, Aitchley was surprised when the Cavalier's shield all but slid down the length of his left arm and whipped him about. Something flashed murderously silver in the muted light of the afternoon sun, and dwarven steel clanged resoundingly off blue-and-gold *gnaiss,* just barely deflected from the young man's throat.

Caught completely off guard, Aitchley took a bewildered step back, a deadly dagger thrusting repeatedly at his shield. Some leprous-looking beggar had materialized out of nowhere and was attacking him, and a clumsy, hasty retreat was the only defense his abrupt surprise allowed.

"Die, Corlaiys!" the beraggled figure screeched. *"Die!"*

Before he had a chance to react, Aitchley felt dirty, scabbed fingers jerk the backpack off his right shoulder and away from him. Befuddled—still lost in a daze of confusion—Aitchley lurched forward, trying to grab for the backpack and his sword at the same time. He didn't know who this bungholer was—didn't even know where he had come from—but the whoreson had just stolen the Elixir of Life! There was no way Aitchley was going to let him get away with that!

As he lunged forward, a sudden hand slammed forcibly into his chest, knocking the air from his lungs and pushing him back a step. Arms flailing, Aitchley felt his left foot step out into empty air, and all sense of balance deserted him.

Berlyn screamed as Aitchley pitched backward off the mountain.

24

Lightning Strikes Twice

Nicander Tampenteire stood, triumphant, outside the Dragon's Lair, dagger in one hand, Aitchley's backpack in the other. The wind screamed through his tangled and dirty black hair, and a wild fire blazed in his light brown eyes. Victoriously, he raised the backpack up by its remaining strap and flaunted it at the dark clouds overhead.

"Mine!" he jeered the cloudy heavens. "At long last, it's mine!" He glanced down at the ledge beneath his feet with bleary, unfocused eyes. "A pity you could not share in my triumph, Corlaiys," he mocked the empty ground, "but you are undeserving of such praise. Why Father sent you on this quest, I'll never know. But I am truly worthy. I am the one who should use the elixir on the Cavalier, and—when I have brought him back from the dead—it shall be me, and not you, who is hailed the hero of Vedette. And then everything you took from me—everything that rightfully belongs to me—shall be mine again!"

Laughing exultantly, Nicander spun on his heel and sprinted into the unfathomable darkness of the Dragon's Lair, the backpack clutched protectively to his chest.

Unable to stop blinking, Berlyn stared in a kind of suspended horror as the ragged nobleman vanished into the cave, leaving the plateau desolate. A horrible, burning emptiness filled her heart, and—no matter how many times she blinked her eyes—

Berlyn could not believe that Aitchley was gone. One second he was there, the next he had been replaced by some hideous, beggarlike stranger who had spirited away the elixir as easily as any southern-city pickpocket. And still Berlyn could not bring herself to believe what she saw. It's not possible, she could hear herself think. We've come so far. . . . We've done so much. Aitchley can't be dead. He can't be.

A sudden skritch of fingers against rock pulled the young blonde from her daze, and she looked down to see a hand clinging frantically to the lip of the cliff. Without a second thought for her own safety, the scullery maid ran out to the edge of the cliff and dropped to her knees, leaning out over empty space despite the whirl of vertigo that roiled through her head. There—dangling precariously by one hand—was Aitchley. A look of flushed determination was on the young man's face, and his fingers were taut and rigid as he clutched at the rock ledge. Fresh blood stained the bandage on his right arm, and his legs kicked and flailed as he tried to pull himself up with one hand, the other grasping tightly to his staff.

Berlyn grabbed the young man with a burst of adrenaline-induced strength and yanked him back to solid ground, tumbling over backward as she did. Startled, Aitchley all but flew up the cliff, landing on top of Berlyn with a whoof of surprise. His head throbbed with the agitated rush of blood and horror shrieking through his system, and he lay in the blonde's tight embrace with a look of blank shock whitening his features.

Tears of joy blurring her eyes, Berlyn clung to the young farmer on top of her. "You're alive!" she cried, so happy the words caught in her throat. "You're alive!"

Aitchley was limp in the girl's arms. "Yeah, well," he responded, dazed, "I guess I've had enough of falling off cliffs or into pits or off bridges."

They lay like that for a few moments, Aitchley trying to catch his breath, Berlyn trying to quell the maelstrom of adrenaline that still surged through her. The pain in the young man's right arm helped to draw him out of his horrified stupor, and he began to realize that whoever had shoved him off the cliff and probably been the same person who killed Tin William.

Rolling off Berlyn, Aitchley sat and blankly stared out over Vedette, his legs dangling over the same cliff that had nearly claimed his life. "Who . . . who was that guy?" he finally sputtered.

Berlyn shrugged, throwing a glance at the enormous cave. "I don't know," she answered. "It might have been Nicander."

Aitchley's shock shifted its attention. "Nicander?" he exclaimed. "Tampenteire?" He gazed sardonically down the mountainside. "Daeminase Pits! Is everybody from Solsbury following us?"

Some of Berlyn's enthusiasm dimmed as the seriousness of the situation forced its way through her happiness. "Well . . . I'm not sure," she corrected herself. "It *looked* like Nicander . . . if Nicander was a raggedy, southern-city leper."

Nodding with newfound certainty, Aitchley kept his eyes on the land spread out before him. "No," he replied, "you're right. It was Nicander. He made some remark about his father sending me on this quest, remember?"

Berlyn pursed pink lips at the young man. "You'll have to forgive me," she quipped. "I wasn't really paying too much attention to what he said. I thought you were dead."

Dark clouds churned and roiled over the eastern landscape. "No such luck," the young farmer despondently grumbled.

Berlyn pulled herself to her feet, one hand resting tenderly on Aitchley's shoulder. "Can you walk?" she asked.

Aitchley stared out over the distant horizon. "Yeah, I can walk," he mumbled, more and more of his earlier melancholy darkening his voice. "Why?"

"Why?" Berlyn echoed her surprise. "Because if that was Nicander, he just stole the elixir! We have to stop him!"

With a resigned shrug, Aitchley stared at the faraway blue speck that was Malvia Lake. "What for?" he questioned dolefully. "He said he was going to resurrect the Cavalier. Fine. Let him."

Another kind of shock made its way through Berlyn, and she gaped in bewildered confusion at Aitchley. "Let him?" she repeated, horrified. "Just like that? You're going to let him resurrect the Cavalier instead of us? You're going to just let him take all the credit for the quest?"

Aitchley shrugged again, disconsolate. "Why not?" he responded. "What difference does it make who resurrects the Cavalier so long as somebody does. I mean . . . that's what we were going to do, right?"

As if blinking might help her hearing, Berlyn stared hard at the sulking farmer sitting below her. "But this is *our* quest!"

she protested. "We've worked for this, not Nicander! He doesn't have the right to do this!"

Aitchley watched the storm clouds swell over Vedette. "What does it matter?" he said, hopeless. "History's not going to remember who brought the Cavalier back to life. All that matters is that he is brought back. If Nicander wants to be the one who does it, fine. I don't care anymore."

Berlyn pinned a harsh eye on the young man. "Has this got anything to do with what Tin William told you?" she demanded to know.

Aitchley's melancholy reflected the blackness of the clouds. "No," he said simply. "Our quest was to get the Elixir of Life and use it on my ancestor. We've done what we were sent to do."

"I don't believe this," replied Berlyn, a stomach-wrenching despair twisting her innards. "I don't believe you're giving up like this."

"I'm not giving up," Aitchley answered, coldly emotionless. "I'm just . . . I'm just tired, that's all." He pulled his gaze away from the rippling clouds and looked at the petite blonde. "Just . . . sit here with me," he asked bleakly. "Will you?"

Her head a jumble of rampaging emotions, Berlyn slowly lowered herself onto the ledge beside Aitchley, staring vacantly out across Vedette. Her stomach cramped and twisted with a stress-induced nausea, and a horrible, overwhelming shock veiled her thoughts like white noise. The wind shrieked through her long, platinum-blond hair as she stared out into emptiness, stupefied. *All that way. All those dangers. And then Aitchley gives up and lets Nicander Tampenteire bring the Cavalier back to life! It isn't fair!*

Distant black clouds flickered blue white with hidden lightning; thunder rumbled somewhere in the distance.

Taking a hasty step back, Calyx barely avoided the scarlet talons that slashed up at him from below his boulder defense. Red figures ran hungrily up the slopes of the Dragon's Ridge, and the scream of the wind was rent by the reptilian hiss of inhuman monsters. Eyeless faces trained on the small plateau, and—like an army driven by starvation—hordes of gangly, cadaverous creatures scrambled up the mountainside toward them.

Calyx frowned heavily. "Um . . . whose stupid idea was it to stay here and hold the Daeminase off?'' he wondered sarcastically.

Sword swaddled in brownish-red ichor, Sergeant Lael gave the dwarf a somber look. "Sorry to remind you," he said, "but I think it was yours."

Calyx's hammer smashed down on top of a ghoulish skull. "Rhetorical question, Sergeant," retorted the dwarf. "I wasn't looking for an answer!" Beady eyes swept out over the legion of crimson monsters. "For some reason," he added pessimistically, "I thought this line of defense might work."

Captain d'Ane offered the smith a ghostly smile. "Never listen to an optimistic dwarf, eh, Calyx?" he teased.

Calyx grunted. "You're learning, Captain." He threw a look of doom at the mountain path. "We might be forced to retreat," he mused out loud. "Who wants to stay behind with me?"

"You can't stay behind!" Rymel protested, taken aback. "You'll be ripped apart!"

"Well, we can't turn tail and run all at once," Calyx answered sharply. "We'll *all* be ripped apart! Someone's gotta stay behind and keep 'em off your ass."

Grabbing an elongated head and slamming its featureless face down onto the boulders, Gjuki said, "I will stay, Master Calyx."

Salt-and-pepper eyebrows lowered as Calyx surveyed the others. "Anybody else?" he queried.

Taking a moment to wipe sweat from his forehead, Sergeant Lael gave the smith a curt nod. "I'll stay," he announced.

"Poinqart, too!" the half troll suddenly interjected. "Poinqart will not leave his companion-friends!"

"Then I'll stay as well," Rymel declared, although his mien wasn't as confident as his voice.

Calyx shook his head gravely as the other Patrolmen also agreed to stay. "You people are the stupidest lot I've ever had the privilege to fight beside," he said. "Too bad we'll all be dead in an hour."

The hills ran red with Daeminase.

As black and as depressing as the storm clouds moving across the sky, Aitchley Corlaiys sat at the edge of the cliff just outside the Dragon's Lair and stared off into nothingness. His mind was a numbed, vegetative thing—overrun by despair and dark pessismism—and what few thoughts infiltrated his melancholy centered mostly on his self-doubt and ultimate failure.

Only I could be capable of such a bung-up, the young farmer
mused sullenly to himself, staring blankly at the faint blue dot
that was Malvia Lake. Only I can go all the way to Lich Gate
and beyond—actually get the Elixir of Life—and then have it
stolen from me right outside the Dragon's Lair! Bloody typical.
I should have expected as much. I suppose I could do what
Berlyn wants. . . . I suppose I could run down there after Nicander and take the elixir back, but for what? What would be
the point? If General Fain was right and bringing the Cavalier
back is just a ploy on the part of the nobles of Solsbury, maybe
it's fitting that Nicander Tampenteire performs the final act. Or
maybe Lord Tampenteire sent Nicander up here to wait for me
. . . to make sure the Cavalier was brought back in case I should
get wind of his plans? Naw . . . that doesn't sound like Lord
Tampenteire. He's always been honest with me. Still doesn't
explain what in the Pits Nicander's doing up here, but . . . what
does it matter? Let him have the damn elixir. Let him raise the
Cavalier up from the dead. What difference does it make? It
just goes to show what a complete and total bung-up I am.

Feeling hopeless and self-pitying, Aitchley glanced at the
beautiful young girl sitting beside him. More than disappointing
himself, Aitchley felt sorry for Berlyn. After all . . . she had
believed in him. She was what had driven him to complete this
fool quest. It had been her and those gorgeous eyes of hers
inspiring him to do better . . . convincing him that he wasn't
some sorry little muggwort from northern Solsbury. But when
it came down to it—when everything was drawing to a close—
only Aitchley Corlaiys could snatch defeat from the jaws of
victory. Regardless of what Tin William had been trying to
say—regardless of whatever warnings General Fain or Kirima
or Taci or anybody else had been trying to give him—only
Aitchley could have the Elixir of Life stolen right out from
under his nose by a sniveling little ragworm like Nicander Tampenteire. But so what? Let Nicander deal with it. Let Nicander
possibly bung up the entire balance of nature. What did Aitchley care? He was a lousy little mudshoveler from northern Solsbury who deserved nothing more than to go back to his
pointless life of not bringing forth a harvest year after year.
But now . . . now he'd have to go back without Berlyn. Now
that she'd seen what a pithless bung-up he was, there was no
way the young man could win her back. She had seen him for

what he truly was: a nobody. A worthless little peasant farmer who couldn't even grow crops.

Maybe he *should* go to Zotheca and build coffins for a living. . . .

Flickering like a jagged fork of pale fire, lightning drove through the clouds gathering over Malvia Lake. From this distance the lightning looked small—almost harmless—and Aitchley felt a cynical grunt come from somewhere deep inside his head as he watched the zigzag of electricity arc down out of the sky and disappear into distant forest.

Looks like something, the young man mused. Something I've seen before . . .

Like some foul behemoth, Aitchley's pessimism rose up to smother the small spark of curiosity. Oh, what difference does it make? it rasped with dark apathy. Lightning is lighting whether it's far away or not. Maybe it'll start another fire.

A tickle of remembrance festered at the back of Aitchley's mind. Fire? he wondered to himself. Is that what it looks like . . . ?

Unbidden—as unexpected as a religious revelation—a crude carving on dark blue rock came suddenly to mind, superimposed over an even cruder tattoo drawn by wizened, palsied hands. It was an image of the Dragon, wings unfurled as it hovered above some unseen horizon, rock mouth gaping wide as a stream of fire zigzagged as sharply and as crookedly as a shaft of lightning from between its stony fangs. Questioningly, Aitchley turned away from the storm clouds and stared down at his arm where the *Kwau* Kirima had drawn a similar glyph on his flesh. Lightning? His brain flip-flopped its confusion. And the Dragon? What in the Pits is *that* supposed to mean?

The dream from that morning suddenly burst through Aitchley's conscious mind, filling his thoughts with a hundred new epiphanies.

There is a precarious balance at work in all worlds, Aitchley Corlaiys, Tin William's voice resonated throughout the young man's skull. *A regenerative cycle. Birth and death. Growth and decay. Destruction and creation.*

Aitchley blinked.

There is a scheme to all things, Aitchley, Captain d'Ane declared.

Taci's voice resounded through Aitchley's memories: *The rocks above our heads. The dirt beneath our feet. All these things have a purpose. A task. A place in the natural order.*

Statement: Life and death are part of the natural order, Aitchley Corlaiys. When a species interferes, disaster is the only result.

Aitchley stared wordlessly at the distant lightning strikes. *Natural order?* he asked himself, perplexed. Like what Gjuki was saying about lightning causing forest fires? Would that be considered part of the natural order?

Tin William's voice suddenly cut through the young farmer's confusion. *Did you know, Aitchley Corlaiys, that this world was never once subjected to firestorms, earthquakes, pestilence, or floods? For nearly the entire millennium in which I have served as TransWorld Observer, the land of Vedette suffered no known natural catastrophe. And yet—in less than two centuries—this ecosystem has broken down.*

A look of awe slowly made its way across Aitchley's features. Two centuries? he asked himself. Two hundred years . . . ?

Calyx's face was dark and gloomy in Aitchley's mind's eye. *You know,* the dwarf growled, *this sort of crap never happened when the Dragon was around!*

As if burned, Aitchley suddenly leapt to his feet, startling the young blonde beside him. Curiously, Berlyn turned to regard him as Aitchley swung an urgent stare at the Dragon's Lair.

"Aitchley?" the scullery maid asked. "What's wrong?"

Gaping, Aitchley slowly turned on her, a look of astonishment bleaching his youthful features. "We have to stop Nicander," he said as if in a trance.

Despite his words, Berlyn felt a jab of self-righteous anger. "Why?" she snapped back, suddenly harsh. "I thought you gave up."

One foot moving inexorably after the other, Aitchley started toward the massive cave. "No, no," he answered, his voice and actions growing more confident with each step, "you don't understand. We have to stop Nicander."

Berlyn drew herself to her feet, sensing the urgency that had spawned in the young farmer. "You're right," she admitted, her tone still sharp, "I don't understand. One minute you're giving up, and the next you want to resurrect the Cavalier yourself!"

Aitchley's somnambulistic walk became a brisk jog. "No,

not the Cavalier," he replied, his jog now a run. "We're not supposed to resurrect the Cavalier."

Confused—and slightly fearing the young man's mind had snapped—Berlyn started a hurried sprint after Aitchley. "Well, if not the Cavalier, then who?" she wanted to know.

Aitchley ran as fast as his legs would carry him into the impenetrable darkness of the Dragon's Lair. "Myxomycetes!" he shouted fervently. "Tin William wanted us to resurrect the Dragon!"

Mouth opened in astonishment, Berlyn felt her legs lock underneath her, freezing her in place. Determinedly, Aitchley ran into the cave ahead of her and disappeared from view.

Silver teeth snapped shut near Calyx's face, spattering him with thick, gelantinous saliva. Flagging, the dwarf barely kept the ravenous monster at bay, his warhammer shoved against its inhuman breastbone in an attempt to keep its fangs from his throat. The others were too busy fighting their own battles to notice the dwarf's predicament, and Calyx felt an odd sense of true pessimism flourish inside him.

This is it, the smith mused gravely to himself. I'm dead. We're all dead. Dabir's already been knocked out of the fight with an injury, and more and more Daeminase are getting past us and onto the plateau. In another few seconds they're going to completely overrun us and win. Guess it won't matter much to me. . . . I'll be dead by then. Can't . . . hold this . . . bastard off . . . forever . . .

With a perturbed hiss, the Daeminase slashing and clawing at Calyx abruptly lurched to one side as if struck, pitching off the face of the boulder and spilling down the hillside. Surprised, Calyx barely had the chance to get back to his feet before another monster launched itself at him, needlelike teeth gnashing in a murderous display.

On a ledge slightly above and to the right, there was a ripple in the mountain air as Harris lowered the hood of his cloak. "Looks like you got yer hands full there, scout," he mocked the struggling dwarf.

Calyx felt a sneer stretch his lips. "You still alive, Blind-Butt?" the smith shot back testily. "I was hoping the only good thing to come out of this was your death."

"Now, is that any way to talk to the man who just saved

your life?" the southern-city lockpick jeered. "You'd think you were ungrateful or something."

Calyx lashed out with his hammer, but he could feel the fatigue in his arms. "Don't do me any favors, Blind-Ass," he spat. "I thought you ran away."

Smirking, Harris looked down at the monstrous forms scuttling and scrabbling their way up the mountain. "Guess I did," the outlaw replied thoughtfully, "then I got to thinking. These eyeless bungholers are after me, and you and the kid went out of your way to help fight 'em off. Didn't have to, you know? I know how you feel about me. I can read people, remember?"

Calyx barely dodged a vicious sweep of scarlet talons. "Nothing secret about the way I feel about you, Blind-Ass," he snarled. "You're the worst kind of human scum imaginable . . . only thinking of yourself and how to make a profit."

Harris's smirk widened. "Thank you," he quipped, "and you're so downright bloody moral you and the puck make me sick." He waved an exaggerated hand through the air. "Always doing the right thing. Always taking the time to help out . . . even if it meant helping a worthless, no-good rotgrub like myself."

A growing weariness continued to sap the strength from Calyx's limbs. "Get to the point, Blind-Butt," he ground out. "I'm about to get killed here."

Harris hopped down off his ledge and onto the plateau. "That is the point, innit?" he remarked. "You've saved my life from these eyeless bastards, and now I'm in your debt." His smirk vanished and his blue-black eyes went cold. "I *hate* being in debt."

Narrowly avoiding another swipe of deadly claws, Calyx retreated a step. "So what are you gonna do?" he demanded. "Save us all from certain doom?"

A cruel smile spread beneath Harris's raggedy beard. "Yeah. Could say that."

Not even Calyx's grim sense of humor could find anything to chuckle at. "Save your delusions of grandeur, Blind-Butt," the dwarf advised. "Even if the kid does get back here with Procursus in time, not even the fabled Cavalier can fight off *this* many Daeminase!"

Removing his cloak, Harris strode nonchalantly across the tableland. "That's the thing," he said. "I ain't no bloody useless Cavalier."

Out of the corner of his eye, Calyx watched the thief move across the plateau toward the ragged cliff where Tin William's body lay. He didn't know what the brigand was planning, but—from the way he talked and the certainty in his step—Calyx began to wonder if they might just have a chance.

Oh, listen to yourself! his three-hundred-year-old pessimism chided him. Now you're starting to believe in your own misplaced optimism! You know you do that when things are irrefutably bad. Only when someone's about to die do you tell them they're healthy. Only when things have gone completely wrong do you say everything's all right. Why don't you get your head on straight for once? Whatever Harris has in mind isn't going to amount to a hill of *gnaiss* shavings! This is Harris Blind-Eye we're talking about, for QuinTyna's sake!

Stanced at the edge of the cliff, Harris turned to face the army of Daeminase, a humorless expression engraved on his ugly face. He gently unwound the bandage at his left shoulder and exposed the wound that slowly healed on his body. Large, horselike nostrils twitched and quivered expectantly as the scent of the lockpick's blood was carried off on the wind, and a number of blank, empty faces turned their eyeless stares in eager anticipation at the southern-city rogue.

Scowling with sudden uncertainty, Calyx took a step toward the thief. "Harris," he voiced his concern, "what are you—"

Harris took another step closer to the edge of the cliff until the tips of his boots were sticking out over empty space. "Take your friends and get out of here, dwarf," the bandit advised. "Let the Daeminase through."

Sword flashing, Rymel turned astonished eyes on the brigand. "But . . . but that's suicide!" he exclaimed.

Harris ignored the fisherman's protest, a grave smile spreading gradually across his lips. "Just do as I say," he ordered. "Take your men and get out."

Beady eyes locked skeptically on the southern-city lockpick, Calyx was silent only a moment before doing as requested. "You heard the man," he barked at the others. "Fall back. Let the Daeminase through."

Streams of viscous saliva drooling from their mouths, the Daeminase clawed and scrabbled for the cliff's edge, their large nostrils savoring the tiniest hint of blood in the air. Some raked and clawed at one another in their eagerness, and Jelena let out a startled scream as she accidentally stumbled and a horde of monsters were suddenly rushing across the plateau past her . . . all heading directly for Harris Blind-Eye.

A muted sense of admiration growing in his breast, Calyx started up the mountain path as Daeminase ran mindlessly for the southern-city rogue. "Maybe I was wrong about you," the dwarf told the outlaw. "Maybe you do have some sense of what's right."

A malevolent sneer twisted Harris's smile. "Don't get maudlin on me, dwarf," he quipped. "I'm not dead yet."

And so saying, he leapt off the cliff.

Aitchley descended farther into the enormous amphitheater of stone, his way lit by the magical staff of carbonized wood in his left hand. Eerie shadows played across the immense cavern interior—leaping and twisting against a backdrop of jagged rock—and the young man felt a lump of uncertainty clog in the back of his throat. Behind him—running to catch up— Berlyn made her way down the dark, uneven path, gray-green eyes wide with wonder. The magical torchlight played yellow white off her platinum-blond hair, and the unnatural glow of the staff seemed to highlight her features with an aura of luminous bewilderment. Her fingers tightened anxiously around the haft of her throwing ax as she ran, and she tried to quiet the nervous beating of her heart as she caught up with Aitchley and grabbed him by one arm.

"Aitchley, wait!" she begged, struggling to catch her breath. "Are you sure about this?"

Aitchley continued down the sloping passage, blue-green eyes glittering in the silvery light of his staff. "Sure about what?" he whispered back. "Keep your voice down. Nicander's up there somewhere."

Worry and adrenaline burning through her bloodstream, Berlyn pulled the young man to a reluctant stop. "Forget about Nicander for a moment," she hissed. "Are you sure about this? I mean . . . resurrecting the Dragon?"

Despite her desperate grip on his arm, Aitchley resumed walking down the dark path. "Of course I am," he said, although a quaver of doubt tainted his voice. "That's what Tin William was trying to tell me all along."

Apprehensively, Berlyn followed the young man down into the cavern's depths, her hand still clutching to his arm. "But the Dragon?" she queried, aghast. "The Dragon was the most destructive force in all Vedette's history!"

A furrow of determination creased Aitchley's brow. "Exactly," he replied. "And that's what Tin William meant. 'Some things were not meant to be tampered with.' He wasn't talking about me. He was talking about the Dragon. He was talking about how the Cavalier killed it."

The fear churning about her stomach made Berlyn's voice tremble. "How can you be so sure?" she implored. "Think this through. If you bring back the Dragon—"

"If I bring back the Dragon, I restore the balance my ancestor destroyed by killing it," Aitchley interrupted. "Look, even Kirima knew what had to be done. 'All things have their purpose and influence.' That's what she said . . . and I wasn't even really paying all that much attention. It wasn't until Gjuki made that comment about lightning strikes that it suddenly made sense."

Confusion glimmered in gray-green eyes. "What comment?" Berlyn asked. "What are you talking about?"

Aitchley moved slower down the dark, stone path, flanked on all sides by pieces of elaborate pottery and gold-flaked urns of past tributes. "Remember when the lightning hit the weald?" he asked back, not even waiting for Berlyn's answering nod. "Gjuki and Calyx started talking about how lightning never used to cause fires back when the Dragon was around. That's because it didn't have to! That was the Dragon's purpose!"

Berlyn blinked. "What?"

"Tin William told me that—up to about two hundred years ago—Vedette never once suffered from plagues, or fires, or earthquakes, or anything like that. Why? Why was Vedette such a paradise when someplace as near as the Bentwoods or the Shadow Crags dealt with forest fires and volcanoes? It's like something Calyx said back when I first met him. None of these bad things had ever happened before in Vedette, but there had always been the Dragon. That was why!"

Berlyn felt her eyes narrow questioningly as she stared at the young farmer. "Are you trying to say that the Dragon is a force of nature?" she asked. "That Vedette never suffered any natural disasters because that was the Dragon's job?"

Aitchley nodded his head enthusiastically. "Exactly!" he replied. "And when my ancestor killed Myxomycetes, it was just like all those things Gjuki told us about in the Bentwoods. All those trees relying on ants, or bees relying on certain kinds of flowers. When one is removed, the balance is either destroyed or shifted until something else can be found to restore it. That's why the land started suffering two hundred years ago . . . the exact length of time since the Dragon's been dead!''

Regardless of the exuberant certainty resonating through Aitchley's words, Berlyn could only shake her head sadly. "Aitchley," she grimly disagreed, "that . . . that's impossible. There's no way the Dragon's influence could affect all of Vedette."

"That was something else Tin William told me," the farmer insisted. "He said that even though Vedette had depleted its natural resources of magic, there was one form of natural phenomenon that had remained. That natural phenomenon was the Dragon!"

Berlyn turned to look deep into Aitchley's eyes. "Are you saying the Dragon was magic?"

"The Dragon and Vedette were magic!" Aitchley responded excitedly. "When the Dragon died, Vedette's magic was thrown out of balance. That's why nobody ever thought to use magic against the Dragon. Way back then—being in tune with all the magic that was around—they probably knew what a vital importance the Dragon was to the land! Without it, they knew the land could die!"

A trace of skepticism caused Berlyn to gnaw on her lower lip. "But to resurrect the Dragon . . ." she mused out loud. "It caused so much destruction. So much death. People might despise you once they find out what you've done."

"But that's its whole purpose!" Aitchley argued. "What difference is there between the Dragon or a lightning strike starting a forest fire? Both strike without warning. Both destroy and kill. Or an earthquake? Or a flood? All of these things can be harmful and deadly, but at the same time they're also beneficial. Fires make way for new growth. Floods promote healthy soil and better crops. It's a regenerative cycle. Birth and death. Growth and decay. Something Captain d'Ane said was so basic and simple that we all but forget about it while we're alive!"

"But the Dragon . . . ?" Berlyn still doubted.

Grinning lopsidedly, Aitchley squeezed her hand upon his arm. "Trust me," was all he said.

Followed by Camera 12, the two teenagers descended farther

into the titanic cave. Questions continued to roil through Berlyn's mind like angry storm clouds, but there could be no denying the look of absolute certainty on Aitchley's face. It was as if the young man had just solved the world's most frustrating puzzle, but the blonde couldn't bring herself to believe that Myxomycetes was the answer to all their problems. True, what Aitchley said made a kind of perverse sense, but . . . the Dragon? Without the Dragon, Vedette's population had run unchecked and that, in itself, had resulted in plagues and famines. Couple that with drought and floods and severe winters and Vedette had not fared very well without the beast, but that didn't mean they should use the Elixir of Life to revive the Dragon, did it? Or was it like Gjuki had said? Even the Rafflesia of the EverDark played their part, and if they were eradicated—like Harris had suggested—there would be nothing left to keep in check the smaller animals who, in turn, kept in check the insects who kept the plants in check. There *was* a sort of balance to nature. Is that what Aitchley was always going on about when he said to be wary of nature's scales?

The ground began to level out as the two moved toward the center of the great lair. The remains of tributes and offerings continued to litter the hard stone about their feet, and there were even a few blackened and dried flowers in some overturned vases, preserved by the stale air and chill of the mountain cave.

Aitchley heard Berlyn gasp beside him and felt her hand tighten around his arm. Questioningly, the young man drew his attention away from the shards and fragments on the ground and redirected his gaze to the floor of the massive amphitheater. There—at the very center of the enormous cave—rested the Cavalier's Tomb, an impressive, dwarven structure of marble, silver, and stone. The Cavalier himself rested upon a catafalque of gold—its scaffolding encrusted with precious gems and glittering jewels—and crested by a coffin of black onyx and shimmering glass. Even through the gloom and murk of the Dragon's Lair, the Cavalier's armor gleamed a splendid silvery white, and Aitchley took an awed step forward, eyes riveted to the form sealed within its coffin of glass and polished ebony.

Resting nearly four feet off the ground on its stand of gold and silver—surrounded by dwarven-carved pillars of stone and marble—the Cavalier's Tomb looked as resplendent and as beautiful as it probably did two hundred years ago. None of its jewels or inlaid gemstones had been touched by grave robbers—probably fearing some dire misfortune might befall them if they desecrated the actual gravesite of the great Cavalier, Aitchley surmised—and aside from a thin layer of dust, the glass of the elegant coffin still glistened in the sorcerous light of Aitchley's staff.

Within lay the Cavalier himself. Gleaming silver armor seemed to radiate an almost sentient glow, and the Cavalier lay peacefully on his back, the same sword in Aitchley's sheath resting lengthwise down his ancestor's body and held in place by clasped gauntlets across his chest. Here and there, Aitchley could see where the Cavalier's armor showed signs of damage or fusing—spots that Calyx had been unable to fix after the Cavalier's final battle with the Dragon—but they were hardly noticeable. The visor of the Cavalier's helmet was open, its plume of gyrofalc feathers—no doubt replaced after the fiery confrontation with Myxomycetes—still flaming a bright red violet. A momentary burst of horrified surprise rocked the young man's composure as he stared into the face of his ancestor, half expecting to see the same youthful features he had seen on Tin William's wall of magic windows.

Fleshless features of naked bone met Aitchley's gaze instead, empty eye sockets staring eternally at the massive chamber's high ceiling. The Cavalier's lower jaw had become unhinged from the rest of his skull—offering what looked like a skeletal scream of yellowing bone—and the stale, musty smell of decay slowly made its way into the young man's nostrils.

This is it, he told himself with some disbelief. This is the great Cavalier of Vedette. This is my ancestor. But . . . where's Nicander?

Curiously, Aitchley turned toward the rear of the colossal amphitheater and felt an unexpected jolt of amazement swell in his chest. Trying to blink back the shock that blurred his gaze, Aitchley stared through the gloom at where tremblers of magical light played faintly off something huge and ominous. Ahead of him—dimly lit by the pale white light of his staff—coiled an enormous skeleton larger than the largest castle. Great yellowing bones stretched the length of the gigantic amphitheater, forming a grisly panorama of death and decay. A rib cage nearly as large as the Cathderal of Thorns—linked by discolored vertebrae the size of small horses—filled the young man's vision. Cracked and ancient fangs as long as Aitchley's arm protruded from the great beast's skull, and empty eye sockets nearly large enough to climb into stared out into the eternal blackness of the Dragon's Lair.

Aitchley felt his legs go weak beneath him. Myxomycetes! His brain reeled with the shock. This is the creature you want to bring back into the world?

Anxiously, Aitchley peeled his eyes away from the monstrous skeleton and looked at Berlyn. "I don't get it," he managed to croak. "Where's Nicander?"

Someone suddenly materialized out of the darkness behind Berlyn, and a blade of dwarven steel was suddenly pressing against the scullery maid's throat. "I'm right behind you, Corlaiys," Nicander Tampenteire hissed with barely restrained glee. "Now . . . show me how to open your magic bag or your little blond bunghole dies!"

Aitchley grimaced. Bloody, bunging typical . . .

25

A Legend Reborn

itchley Corlaiys wrestled with his disbelief. A zipper! he marveled quietly to himself. All that stood between Nicander Tampenteire and the Elixir of Life was what Tin William had called a zipper!

Impatiently, Nicander pressed his dagger against Berlyn's throat. "Open the bag, Corlaiys," the young nobleman demanded, an anarchy of madness swirling in his eyes. "Open the bag or the whore dies."

Aitchley hesitated, staring down at the maroon-colored backpack forced back into his hands. Even through its thick material, the young man could feel the unnatural tingle and tickle of the Elixir of Life, and he briefly considered ignoring Nicander's demands and using the elixir himself. But then he looked up into those beautiful gray-green eyes and the fear that radiated within, and he knew that he could not do it. Berlyn meant more to him than any stupid elixir or quest ever could, and if Nicander wanted to use the elixir on the Cavalier, there was very little Aitchley could do about it so long as he held Berlyn hostage.

Turning the backpack over in his hands until he found the start of the zipper, Aitchley trained blue-green eyes on the bedraggled noble before him. "Nicander," he said, "listen to me. You can't resurrect the Cavalier. We need—"

"*Silence!*" Veins stood out on Nicander's neck. "Save your lies for someone who cares, Corlaiys!" he screamed. "The

Elixir of Life belongs to me, and I *can* resurrect the Cavalier! All *you* can do is stand by and watch me!''

Aitchley's eyes flicked nervously to the naked blade at Berlyn's throat. "But that's just it," he tried to explain. "We don't want to bring back the Cavalier. We—''

"I said silence!" Nicander shrieked again. A droplet of blood appeared as the dagger's point pricked Berlyn's flesh. "Open the bag and give me the elixir . . . and keep your mouth shut.''

With a faint, almost inaudible "grrrr," Aitchley undid the zipper at the sides of the backpack and slowly withdrew the Elixir of Life. Powerful tendrils of sorcery slithered their way up the young man's arms, filling him with renewed strength and chasing some of the ache from his wounded forearm. Strange shapes and shadows pranced about the massive cave as the elixir's unearthly aura of magic filled the chamber with a macabre flicker of greenish-blue light, and Aitchley managed to throw a helpless look back at the only other two creatures in the lair. Camera 12, however, watched motionlessly—its single glass eye focused on both young men—and Trianglehead perched on the construct's back, observing with avian curiosity. Not that there was anything either one of them could do, Aitchley concluded dourly. Nicander had them all by the short hairs.

The glimmering, emerald-turquoise glow of the elixir flashed off eyes glinting with a fearful mindlessness. "Now," Nicander commanded, "drop your sword and come here."

Scowling, Aitchley did as he was told, his gaze locked on the young blonde in Nicander's dirty grasp. What difference did anything make if he lost Berlyn now? he asked himself honestly. Without Berlyn, nothing mattered. Not the elixir. Not the quest. Not even the answer to Tin William's stupid riddle!

His swordbelt clanking about his feet, Aitchley took a slow step forward. He held the Elixir of Life out before him, yet he couldn't help the nervous raspings at the back of his thoughts. Something, he decided warily, was wrong. There was something in Nicander's eyes . . . something that said he couldn't be trusted. It reminded Aitchley of the way General Fain had looked, and the young man began to consider the possibility that—even if he gave the young lord the elixir—Nicander might not let either one of them leave the lair alive.

Licking eager lips, Nicander took the elixir in his free hand.

"Yes," he hissed triumphantly to himself. "It's mine. The Elixir of Life is mine!"

Taking a cautious step back, Aitchley eyed the nobleman with open defiance. "Now let go of Berlyn," he demanded.

Nicander's gaze drew away from the green-blue decanter and slowly focused on the young man, an insidious sneer twisting his bearded features. "You'd like that, wouldn't you?" he mocked. "I let go of the girl and you try and take back the elixir, eh?" He taunted the young farmer with the vial. "You want it, don't you?" he jeered. "I can tell. You want to be the great Aitchley Corlaiys, the man who brought the Cavalier back to life. The one who went beyond Lich Gate and risked his life for the good of all Vedette. Because if you aren't, you go back to being Aitchley Corlaiys, worthless little farm boy working on a plot of my father's land. A useless little peasant mud-shoveler with his face streaked with dung and his clothes covered in filth. But that isn't what you want, is it? You think you're a hero now, don't you?" He looked down at the girl in his grip. "Think you can save her before I slit her throat?" he taunted malignantly. "Can you move that fast, farm boy?"

A horrible unease began to swell in Aitchley's gut as he watched Nicander wave his dagger menacingly before Berlyn's throat. He isn't kidding, the young man realized with mounting terror. Getting the elixir isn't enough . . . he's thinking of killing Berlyn.

Aitchley's right hand curled into a fist. "If you so much as scratch her, I'll tear your bunging heart out," he snarled at the lord.

A look of brief shock whitened Nicander's face before it was replaced by raucous, insane laughter. "You know"—the young noble guffawed—"for a moment there, I truly believed you! Your time out in the wilderness has done you some good, Corlaiys. You've actually developed something of a backbone."

"What would you know about it?" Aitchley snapped back. "You haven't got the courage to—"

Berlyn stiffened as Nicander's dagger prodded harder at the underside of her jaw. "Aitchley," she implored, "please . . ."

Blanching, the farmer immediately reined in his fury. Getting mad at Nicander isn't going to solve anything, he mused. He's got the elixir *and* Berlyn. What have I got? Nothing. Not even my sword. All I've got is my shield, a bird, a stupid camera that won't get involved, and . . . my staff . . . ?

Nicander pressed his dirtied, bearded face up against Berlyn's. "Yes, Aitchley, *please*," he mocked them both. He traced his dagger threateningly down the front of Berlyn's neck to the valley between her breasts, the razor-sharp blade cutting effortlessly at the threadbare fabric of her dress. "Quickly, farm boy," he jeered. "Make your move or the girl dies anyway."

Trying to tune out Nicander's taunts, Aitchley glanced at the staff glimmering a faint silvery white in the murk of the cave. There was no way he could use it with Berlyn standing in front of Nicander the way she was—no fireball or plume of ice that wouldn't hurt her as well as him—but there had to be something he could do. The staff had to have other powers than the ones he had used. Think! Think, Gaal dammit, think! What was it Calyx had said? What had Adal the Blue been able to do that could help him and Berlyn get out of this situation . . . maybe even steal back the Elixir of Life?

A sudden voice resonated through the young farmer's head, startling him. *Aitchley?*

Aitchley blinked his surprise. *Berlyn?*

There was befuddlement in the girl's tone. *I can hear you,* she realized. *How . . . ?*

The staff must be transmitting our thoughts again, Aitchley understood. *Do you think Nicander can hear us?*

We'd be able to hear him, too, wouldn't we? the blonde pointed out. *What are we going to do?*

Aitchley frowned. *I've got my staff—and Nicander doesn't know what it's capable of—but I don't know what to do with it without hurting you.*

Forget about me, Berlyn replied. *Get the elixir back. That's all that matters.*

No! Aitchley insisted. *You're more important to me then some damn elixir! There's got to be some way to get you and the elixir away from him! Safely!*

The two lapsed into silence, each trying to think desperately of a way out. It was weird to think and hear Berlyn's thoughts as well as his own, Aitchley mused, and sometimes her thoughts were so powerful they seemed to be his. Even through the mental noise of his own contemplation, Aitchley could hear her thoughts racing hurriedly through their entire adventure, trying to come up with some sort of plan that could set them free.

Aitchley sensed Berlyn's idea even before she voiced it.

Aitchley! the young girl mentally projected at him. *The light from your staff! Remember when you first tried to use it? It was too bright to see by. Do you think you can get it to do that again?*

Aitchley glanced skeptically at the oaken staff in his left hand, hoping Berlyn didn't pick up on his pessimistic thoughts. *I . . . don't know,* he answered hesitantly. Then he thought of something else. *Aren't you still wearing your ring?* he asked. *If I make the staff flare up, it'll blind you, too.*

Not if I close my eyes, the scullery maid responded. *I'll be ready for it, Nicander won't be.*

Feeling his self-doubt and insecurities rise, Aitchley fixed his attention on the gnarled staff. He had no idea how he had made the staff flare up the first time—all he had been trying to do was get it to light the lava tunnels around him—but the ancient oak seemed to have a rapport with the young man. Sometimes—just by thinking about it—the staff reacted. Would that be enough to help Berlyn?

White light unexpectedly filled the chamber, erupting with all the intensity of a miniature star. Even though she had closed her eyes, Berlyn still saw the purplish-blue spots and halos that went off behind her eyelids, and she heard Nicander's startled cry as the staff all but exploded in his face. The touch of cold steel at her neck fell away, and she crooked an arm and slammed her elbow into Nicander's nose, taking grim satisfaction in the audible crunch of shattered cartilage.

Blinded and dazed, Nicander staggered back, both hands going to his face. Blood streamed in bright red rivulets from his broken nose, and a million suns supernovaed behind closed eyelids. He hardly felt the sturdy oaken staff crack against the side of his head, and he didn't even hear the dwarven dagger clank noisily out of his grasp. Sightlessly, he lurched to one side, a feeble grunt escaping his lips as heavy wood connected with his stomach and doubled him over.

Tearing the decanter of jadded sapphire out of Nicander's stubborn grip, Aitchley turned to where the enormous skeleton of the Dragon encircled the width of the massive chamber. ''That was easier than I thought,'' he remarked. ''Come on, let's—''

With an agonized warcry, Nicander launched himself blindly toward the sound of Aitchley's voice. Berlyn couldn't stop the curt shriek of surprise that slipped through her lips, and she watched as the young noble ran into the farmer and tackled him about the waist, propelling him backward. Aitchley felt the wind knocked from his lungs in a rush of air as he was slammed against the elegant gold and marble of the Cavalier's Tomb. Wood clattered against stone as the staff slipped free of his fingers, and a few stars buzzed through his cranium as he felt the enormous coffin behind him tip and sway beneath their combined weight.

Berlyn gaped as the two men crashed into the jewel-encrusted catafalque. "Aitchley!" she cried a warning.

With a low groan, Aitchley, Nicander, and the catafalque all toppled to the stone floor, the glass of the Cavalier's coffin shattering into a million pieces. Dry, brittle bones and musty armor rattled and rolled across ancient rock as Aitchley's famous ancestor broke into as many pieces as the coffin's glass. Aitchley barely kept his grip about the Elixir of Life as he landed hard on his back, Nicander above him, while tiny fragments of glass stabbed painfully into his shoulders.

Still trying to blink the flare of the staff from his eyes, Nicander reached out and ripped the elaborate sword from the Cavalier's bony grip. "The elixir, Corlaiys!" the nobleman screeched insanely. "Give it to me or die!"

Steel glimmered in the murk of the Dragon's Lair as the Cavalier's sword swept down for Aitchley's head.

Hissing and snarling, wave after wave of Daeminase poured over the edge of the cliff, eyelessly pursuing the scent of Harris's blood. Forgotten in the mass of gaunt red figures, Calyx hurriedly ushered the others up the mountain path, flinching every time a cadaverous red body passed too close. It seemed, the dwarf mused, that when they set their minds on it, the Daeminase were only interested in one type of person. That was probably why they had primarily attacked Fain back in Leucos. With all that blood all over him, Fain had been the perfect target. And now—once Harris had removed his bandage—the smell of his blood removed any interest the Daeminase may have had in the others and focused it all on Harris himself.

Calyx pushed at Rymel's back. "Come on! Come on!" he shouted. "We haven't got all day!"

Jaw slack, Rymel continued to stare over his shoulder at the cliff where Harris had jumped. "I don't believe it," the fisherman murmured out loud. "He sacrificed himself for the rest of us!"

Calyx shoved Jelena and Lael unceremoniously up the hill before him. "Now, I wouldn't put it that way," the dwarf protested. "He helped us out. Big deal. It's his fault the Daeminase were after us anyway. Now let's take advantage of his distraction and get the forge out of here!"

Jelena's brown eyes were wide. "How can you say that?" she wanted to know. "That man died for us!"

Calyx couldn't help but stick out his tongue and razz the young brunette. "Oh, he did no such thing," he retorted, scrambling up the path behind them. "He's right over there."

Gawking, Jelena and Rymel both turned to look out over the ledge where Harris had so selflessly led the Daeminase. Hordes of crimson figures continued to leap blindly off the cliff in their pursuit of the lockpick's scent—flailing and shrieking as they dropped to the jagged rocks below—yet the outlaw himself stood just a few feet below the very cliff he had left, unaffected by gravity as he hung suspended in midair.

Jelena stopped in her amazement. "Twin Sisters!" she swore softly. "How can he do that?"

Calyx shoved at the girl's backside. "Magic ring," he answered tersely. "Now move!"

Smirking, Harris reclined comfortably in empty space, blue-black eyes trained accusingly on the dwarf. "Couldn't let me have my moment in the sun, eh, scout?" he teased. "Couldn't let 'em think I did the noble thing just once in my life?"

"You couldn't do the noble thing if it had huge breasts and a bunghole," Calyx quipped back. "Now are you gonna float out there all day or come with us?"

Harris turned his smirk on the inhuman beasts that ran right out into empty air in their attempt to catch him. "You go on ahead," he replied. "There's a few more o' these wartheads that want to try their hand at catching me. Maybe one of 'em thinks he'll get lucky and fly, eh?"

"Yeah, well," Calyx answered, "don't be patting yourself on the back quite yet. Fall like that won't kill 'em—'less they land on their heads—so most of 'em are just gonna get back to their feet and start climbing back up after us."

Harris did a lazy backstroke through the air. "Yeah, so?" he said. "It bought you the time you needed, right? Admit it, dwarf, I saved your life. That makes us even."

As phalanx after phalanx of Daeminase stepped blindly off the cliff, a pessimistic frown darkened Calyx's face. "It's not me you owe, Blind-Butt," he said somberly. "It's Aitchley." He jogged urgently up the mountain path. "And I think we'd better get up there and make sure he's all right," he added. "I've got a bad feeling about this."

Harris floated up the side of the mountain. "Oh," he quipped, "like that's a surprise."

Silver-gray steel flashed in the gloom of the Dragon's Lair, and Aitchley fumbled frantically for anything to save him. His fingers sifted desperately through broken old bones and fragments of armor, but his eyes remained locked on the figure poised above him, its dwarven sword cleaving downward for his skull. Pieces of glass bit into the young man's back, and he could hear the stale, musty air of the lair scream as Nicander brought down the Cavalier's blade.

Feeling his fingers close around something thick and metallic, Aitchley wheeled about, blocking Nicander's blow with the armored torso of the Cavalier. Yellowish-brown dust and brittle remnants of bone sprinkled out of the paladin's breastplate and into Aitchley's face, and the resounding clang of dwarven steel against dwarven steel echoed thunderously throughout the massive cavern. Only one limp arm still hung from the breastplate—clad in its dully glistening pauldron— and Aitchley swung the arm up with all his strength, hearing the hollow *thwock!* as the Cavalier's cowter rebounded violently off Nicander's head.

With a howl of pure rage, Nicander fell over backward, tumbling into the splintered remains of the Cavalier's coffin. Blood bubbled from his broken nose—mingling with the rabid spittle streaming down his chin—and he locked vengeful eyes on the young farmer. "The elixir belongs to me, Corlaiys!" he shrieked. "You cannot take from me what is rightfully mine!"

Discarding his ancestor's armored torso, Aitchley slid his shield onto his left arm. "Aw, get bunged," he snarled back, unimpressed.

Screaming, Nicander launched himself forward, sword flailing above his head. Aitchley flinched as dwarven steel rebounded off blue-and-gold *gnaiss,* the sudden shock of the blow reverberating through his arm. No other weapon had ever sent such a threatening shudder through his shield before, and

Aitchley frowned with growing apprehension at the blade in
Nicander's hands.

That's Procursus's sword, he grimly reminded himself. Calyx
made it probably as well as he made his shield. I guess the
only question is which did he make better? Shield or sword?

The young man threw an anxious glance over one shoulder.
And do I really want to wait around here to find out? he added
pessimistically.

Shuffling the Elixir of Life into the crook of his right arm,
Aitchley took a wary step back, blue-green eyes scanning the
surrounding gloom. As if possessed, Nicander kept after the
young man, the Cavalier's sword flashing and glinting in his
hands. The metallic thunder of steel against *gnaiss* echoed
through the enormous cave, and each attack sent a worrisome
tremor through Aitchley's shield. He hadn't felt such blows
since fending off Archimandrite Sultothal, and—like Sultothal—Nicander's attacks were sloppy yet fueled by a murderous rage. An ominous soreness began to ache in the young
man's left arm each time Nicander's sword deflected off his
shield, and every wild blow knocked him back a step, threatening to unbalance him or jar loose the elixir.

Aitchley glanced through the murk. Where in the Pits is my
sword? he wondered desperately. It's got to be around here
someplace!

Tearing through stale, musty air, Nicander's weapon drove
in again, caroming off Aitchley's shield and forcing the young
man to retreat. Something as solid as the trunk of a large tree
unexpectedly pressed against the young farmer's back, and he
realized with abrupt alarm that he had somehow managed to
back himself into a corner. Wondering how he could mistake
the size of a chamber so vast, Aitchley turned his head to look
behind him.

Looming up out of the macabre greenish-blue flicker of the
elixir's aureole, the Dragon's rib cage was a wall of yellowing
pillars, dry and flaking like ancient bark. Each rib was twice
as thick as Aitchley and so tall that the young man couldn't
even see the connecting vertebrae high above him. A bony
forearm lay curled nearby with talons as long and as sharp as
broadswords, and a blackness so dark and so absolute lurked
within the cathedral of the monster's rib cage that not even the
unearthly glimmer of the elixir could pierce it.

Fragments of bone chipped and sprayed like shrapnel as

Aitchley ducked beneath Nicander's sweeping blade and ran between the gigantic ribs, disappearing into the bowels of the skeletal Dragon.

Blood frothing at his lips, Nicander followed.

An unsettling nausea creeping through her, Berlyn watched the two men step into the Dragon's rib cage. With the brown-red ring around her finger, the entire cavern was as well lit as a castle foyer, and the elixir in Aitchley's hands was like a brilliant white pulse of virgin radiance. She picked up the staff lying half-buried in the debris of the Cavalier's coffin and felt her fingers tighten reflexively around the gnarled oak as it instantly flickered to silvery life. The pale light highlighted the worry in her gray-green eyes as she took an apprehensive step forward, gnawing on her lower lip with such dread that she tasted blood.

She tossed a nervous glance at the bird and camera sitting passively behind her. "We've got to do something!" she declared.

Blinking milky-blue eyes, Trianglehead cocked his head to regard her. "What we zsupposzed to do?" he cynically asked back. "That guy krazy!"

"But we just can't stand here and do nothing!" Berlyn protested, strangling the wooden staff in her grasp. "We have to help Aitchley!"

Trianglehead scratched at his head with a taloned foot. "What you do?" he queried sardonically. "Walk between them? Interrupt fight? Maybe disztract Aitchley? Beszt thing for all to zstay here."

Berlyn's eyes narrowed as the clash of steel against *gnaiss* reverberated through the great chamber. With her enhanced vision, the cave was brightly lit, and she had no trouble spotting Aitchley's discarded sword lying behind her. Jogging quickly to the weapon—which was still in its sheath—Berlyn snatched up the blade before turning back to the Dragon's corpse.

"You can stay here if you want," she admonished the fledgling. "I'm going to try to help."

With what might have been a look of avian disdain, Trianglehead watched the scullery maid hurry off into the darkness. "Why I bother?" grumbled the bird. "No one ever liszten to me. Zstupid humansz!" He launched himself into the stale, musty air.

*   *   *

Stumbling in the dark, Aitchley felt rather than saw Nicander's sword rebound off his shield, the murderous impact shuddering through the young man's arm and knocking him in the opposite direction. He tried to find his footing—tried to make some sense of where he was—yet he was surrounded by an impermeable veil of liquid blackness. The elixir in his hands did him little good—its greenish-blue aurora illuminating the young man's midsection but too bright to look past to see the ground at his feet. When he tried, spots and blurs of color flashed behind his eyelids, and the darkness of the cave only seemed to get deeper. For Nicander, however, the elixir was a flashing beacon. Swing at the glow . . . that was all he had to do . . . and Aitchley knew it. He briefly considered throwing the decanter—toyed with the idea of hurling it toward Berlyn and hoping she'd catch it—but with the elixir blazing in his hands, he couldn't see a foot past his own face let alone find Berlyn in all this blackness!

Steel flickered in the light of the elixir, glancing off Aitchley's shield and catching the young man just under his left eye. Abrupt pain like the lash of a white-hot whip tore across the farmer's face, and he could feel the warm dribble of blood start to trickle down the length of his cheek and across his neck.

The small wound only seemed to fuel Nicander's madness. "Die, Corlaiys!" the curly-haired noble screeched. "Just as you have taken everything from me, so, too, shall I leave you with nothing!"

More surprised than hurt, Aitchley wiped away the blood. "What in the Pits are you talking about?" he snapped in angry exasperation. "Did everybody who followed me from Solsbury go crazy or something?"

Instead of answering, Nicander lunged forward again, bringing the Cavalier's sword down in an overhanded sweep. Expertly—despite the ache beneath his left eye—Aitchley caught the blade with his shield and turned it aside, bringing the blue-and-gold *gnaiss* up and slamming it under Nicander's chin. Teeth clacked together painfully as Nicander flipped backward, bright red geysering from his mouth. Steel clattered in the darkness as the Cavalier's sword spiraled out of the nobleman's hand, and Nicander landed in a heap near the far wall of enormous ribs.

Cautiously backing up toward the Dragon's skull, Aitchley

threw a questioning look at the massive ribs arching over his head. He could feel the warming tingle of the elixir flowing through his body and curing the painful throb under his eye, and he wondered fleetingly if he should take this opportunity to run. All that mattered was that Nicander didn't try to use the elixir on the Cavalier—not that that seemed possible now that Aitchley's ancestor was spread out across the lair like so much bony debris—but somehow he didn't think that would dissuade Nicander. Like Fain, something had happened to the young lord, and it was obvious he was no longer in full control of his mental faculties. *What did I take from him anyway?* Aitchley wondered to himself. *I haven't seen the whoreson since he threw me out on my ass in front of Berlyn!*

Drooling blood and spittle—spitting out cracked and broken teeth—Nicander climbed slowly to his feet, light brown eyes piercing the darkness. Aitchley could see the unsteadiness in his stride, but it gave him little reassurance as the young Tampenteire moved totteringly to one side and picked up his lost weapon.

"Not good enough, farm boy," Nicander jeered from around a broken jaw. "You must do better than that if you hope to beat me."

Aitchley firmed his grip around the elixir, feeling its nimbus of sorcerous energy add strength to his bruised and weary body. "You're not using the elixir, Nicander," he growled.

A ghastly, blood-streaked smile stretched painfully beneath Nicander's ragged beard. "And you think you will, farm boy?" he questioned. "You who can't bring forth a decent harvest? You, a seventeen-year-old peasant whose life means nothing? A self-doubting, cowardly little dungspreader from northern Solsbury? You are not worthy, farm boy. Only I am worthy of such greatness. Only I deserve to be hailed as the hero of all Vedette." Nicander cocked his head to one side, his smile growing wider. "Why I'd wager you don't even know *how* to use the elixir!"

Aitchley blanched. *He's right!* the young man suddenly realized, blue-green eyes widening at the decanter glimmering in his hands. *I don't know how to use the elixir! Dead people can't drink, so what am I supposed to do with it? Pour it on them? But there can't possibly be enough left to pour on the entire Dragon! There might not have been enough to begin with! The Dragon's huge! So what am I supposed to do? What* happens if there isn't enough? Will it work at all? I don't know! Nicander's right!

A feral gleam lit Nicander's eyes as he noticed the young man's hesitation. "You see," the nobleman declared, "you *don't* know. You're an unschooled, illegitimate rotgrub. Now give the elixir to me."

A crushing despair rose up in Aitchley's thoughts, filling his head with the despondency of his own debilitating pessimism. He's right, you know, the young man's darker side hissed at him. You're not worthy. You should have just let Nicander go and resurrect the Cavalier. What difference does it make to you, anyway? You're a loser. A worthless little farm boy. If you tried to use the elixir, you'd probably waste it. Spill it. Use it the wrong way. And then what would you be? You'd be the man who went beyond Lich Gate—who faced the Daeminase, journeyed through a volcano, and nearly plunged into the heart of the sun—and all for what? The biggest, most absolute bung-up in all recorded history: the misuse of the fabled Elixir of Life! And only Aitchley Corlaiys could be capable of such a feat. Only Aitchley Corlaiys could bung everything up so close to its completion! Why not just pour the elixir on the ground and save everybody a whole lot of embarrassment? Or just give it to Nicander. *He* probably knows what to do with it.

Nicander took an arrogant step forward, left hand outstretched. "You are not worthy, Corlaiys," he rasped maliciously. "Give it to me."

A sudden shout interrupted Aitchley's thoughts.

"Aitchley!" Berlyn cried. "Here!"

Pulling himself up out of the darkness of his despair, Aitchley turned toward the petite scullery maid, blue-green eyes squinting through the blackness. He heard the whispering hiss of his sheathed sword across stone as the blonde slid it between giant ribs toward his feet, but his eyes remained locked on the young girl herself.

Lit by the silvery aura of Adal's Staff, Berlyn's hair gleamed yellow white as she ran across the monstrous cavern, her torn and tattered skirt billowing around her legs. Her right hand clenched the haft of her throwing ax, and a look of deep concern strained her beautiful features. Yet it was her eyes that held Aitchley's attention: beautiful eyes that drifted from light green to ashen gray, filling with a flurry of emotions as she ran toward him.

Fear, worry, and hope blazed in gray-green eyes.

Like a lightning strike, Aitchley felt those eyes rip through him, tearing a great gaping hole in his despair and freeing him from his pessimism. Berlyn believes in me! he was suddenly forced to realize. And Poinqart! And Calyx! And all the others! They wouldn't have followed me for so long if they didn't think I was capable of doing some good! Even Kirima had faith in me! Why am I always the last person to believe in myself? Because I know how many times I've bunged things up? So what? Everybody makes mistakes. Even the Cavalier made a mistake! No one holds *them* to it. Why should I? *You can't deny the positive.* That's what Captain d'Ane said to me back at the Tridome. And he was right. Just look at all the things I've done! I've faced the Daeminase! Journeyed through a volcano! Survived the Canyon Between! These are things that I not only survived, but that no one had ever done before! I'm the descendant of the bloody Champion of Vedette, for Gaal's sake! Despite everything I might think, I'm *not* a failure! I *can't* be! Not so long as Berlyn believes in me!

Snatching up his scabbard, Aitchley quickly hooked the belt about his waist, glancing again at the enormous ribs arching overhead. Adrenaline and confidence burned through his veins—coupled with the powerful caress of the Elixir of Life—and he felt his self-assurance swell as he stared at the decanter in his hands. There are some things that were not meant to be tampered with, eh? he asked himself cynically. Let's see if this makes any difference.

Nicander's eyes widened as he watched the young man bend forward almost to a crouch, the elixir held out in both hands. "What are you doing?" he demanded.

Without answering, Aitchley snapped back upright, both arms thrown high above his head. Jaded-sapphire sparkled green blue as the decanter spun end over end into the musty air, the luminous fluid within flickering and pulsating with minute pinpricks of life. Weird shapes and odd shadows splayed across the titanic ribs as the jug spiraled upward, ancient glassware striking ancient bone in a sudden reverberation of sorcerous thunder.

Undiluted rage overwhelmed Nicander as the decanter shattered against the ribs high overhead. *"No!"* he howled, charging the young man before him.

With a boom of released energy, the jaded-sapphire broke,

splashing the yellowed bones with liquid life. Flares of pure golden force snapped and popped like meteoric sparks, and incandescent fluid coated the bones of the skeletal Dragon. Powerful tendrils of effulgent white sorcery seeped into dry, semipetrified osseous tissue, saturating the ribs and vertebrae with a sudden infusion of life. Proteins formed from magic; minerals formed out of sorcery. Bone cells awoke from a two-hundred-year-old slumber, magically depositing a compound of calcium and phosphate along the Dragon's yellowed spine.

Like silk and cobwebs, nerve fibers and pia mater began to grow out of nothingness, brought forth by the liquid dripping from the Dragon's vertebrae. Snakelike wisps and streamers of energy coagulated to form arterioles as large as Aitchley's arms, and the first tracing of thick red muscles and gauzy white tendons began to hinge across the Dragon's backbone.

Hardly looking away from the miraculous reconstruction going on above his head, Aitchley could hear the warbling warcry of Nicander Tampenteire drawing near. Steel flashed once in the young farmer's hand—whipping free of his sheath and sweeping out in front of him with a casual grace that defied believability—and Nicander halted, a startled look drawing the color from his face. Blood ran red from the deep gash across his abdomen, and the look of surprise remained on his face even as he stared down at his own disembowelment. Uselessly, the Cavalier's sword clattered from his limp hand, and he took a single step back, staggering slightly as blood pooled about his feet.

The look of surprise was still on his face as Nicander Tampenteire crumpled lifelessly to the floor.

As the pulsing glow of the elixir's magic slowly traveled down the length of the ribs around Aitchley, deep, rich scales—as large as the Cavalier's shield—formed across the Dragon's back. Veins and arteries slithered about muscle, and the brilliant flickers of sorcery crackled and fused as an enormous heart began to form in the empty cathedral of ribs where Aitchley stood.

Sliding his bloodied sword back into its sheath, the young farmer gave a last look at the magical rebirth going on around him. It's working, he breathed his astonishment. The elixir's bringing the Dragon back to life.

Scales moved down the sides of the Dragon's rib cage; ligaments spun like cotton wool out of thin air.

A momentary jolt of panic broke through Aitchley's awe. I'd better get out of here! he abruptly realized.

He moved swiftly toward the gleaming ribs, feeling the now familiar pins-and-needles sensation emanating from the whitening bones. Light filled the great cavern, and there was an ominous rumble of power as more and more of the Dragon's great bulk took on renewed life. Great, spiny black barbs of cartilage rose up along the Dragon's spine, and walls of living cells spread like plaster across the space between bones. Muscles entwined and embraced the skeletal framework—covering bone in a deep red jacket of tissue—and veins and arteries squirmed and coiled like vascular maggots through re-formed flesh.

His ears full of the soft gurgle of regenerating tissue, Aitchley went to step out from between living bone. Unexpectedly, his foot snagged something, pitching him forward onto the ground. Bewildered, he looked back through the Dragon's glowing rib cage to see Nicander Tampenteire's vengeful hand clamped firmly around his foot, a powerful death grip holding the young farmer back.

Weakly grinning through a beard covered with blood, Nicander managed to look up at the young man. "You . . . are not worthy," he hissed, fingers closing tighter around the young farmer's foot.

Frozen in place by the panorama of sorcery coruscating before her, Berlyn stared, transfixed, at the plumes of energy boiling and storming around her. She watched as heavily armored plates moved across the Dragon's serpentine neck, creating jagged whorls and sharp ridges above empty eye sockets. Great black horns glistened in the whirlwind of white sorcery, and she could feel the torrential wind of uncontrolled magicks shrieking through the cavern and penetrating her body, bringing with it the same kind of tickling sensation as the elixir. Any ache or bruise that may have burned her body faded before the sorcerous gale, and the entire Dragon's Lair was filled with an ever-increasing typhoon of life-giving sorcery. Even long-dead flowers turned toward the light, a hint of rosy color returning to their withered and blackened petals.

Wheeling through the darkness, Trianglehead swooped in low and landed on the young blonde's shoulder, staring unblinkingly at the Dragon. "Wasz he zsupposzed to do that?" the fledgling asked.

Berlyn nodded, dumbfounded. "I . . . I think so," she responded hesitantly.

Anxiously, Trianglehead threw a nervous glance behind them. "We go now?" the bird queried. "No want to be around when that thing wakesz up!"

Trying to blink some of the shock out of her eyes, Berlyn managed to look back at the distant cavern opening. "Yes," she said, her voice hushed. "I think you're right."

Struggling with the awe that threatened to overwhelm her, Berlyn returned her attention to the blazing lights and blinding sorcery that infused yellowing bones with magical life. Anxiety growing, her eyes trailed down the dark green scales covering the Dragon's rib cage. Where was Aitchley? she wanted to know. The Dragon was almost wholly reformed. What had happened to Aitchley?

The apprehension mounting, Berlyn stepped forward, her fingers tightening around the staff in her grasp. Aitchley? she asked herself one last time.

Bloodred eyes began to form in empty sockets.

Scrabbling frantically upon his stomach, Aitchley tried to crawl the rest of the way out of the Dragon's interior, his free foot kicking viciously at Nicander's face. As if unfeeling, Nicander's hand remained locked around the young man's foot, his head snapping back and forth each time Aitchley struck at him. Bright red muscle formed out of thin air above Aitchley's head—stretching inexorably across glowing bones to where he lay—and he could feel the growing warmth of the Dragon's innards as intestines and lungs solidified out of scintillating thaumaturgy. It was like the Guardian, the young man mused in a brief moment of lucidity. Substance forming from nothing but white light . . . and if I don't get out of here soon, I'm going to become part of that substance!

Drawing himself up on one elbow, Aitchley slammed his foot into Nicander's face, trying to tear his other foot free. "Let go!" he demanded.

Wordlessly, Nicander hung on, the inferno of magic around them giving his malnourished and wounded body unnatural stamina.

Green scales draped a foot above Aitchley's head, rough and craggy like limestone.

Aitchley rammed his foot against Nicander's head again, the heat of panic starting to sear through his thoughts, his fingers tearing wildly at the stone outside the Dragon's rib cage.

One side of his face swelling with black-and-blue flesh, Nicander offered the young man a mocking smile. "You are not worthy," he rasped accusingly.

Desperately, Aitchley looked out beyond the Dragon's ribs, searching for anything to grab hold of. A rock. A crack in the floor. Anything to give him the leverage he needed to pull his remaining leg free of the Dragon's stomach. Muscles and ligaments draped the bones above him, and he could feel the wormlike crawl of veins and nerve endings as they slithered underneath him to form the Dragon's chest wall. The warm, coppery smell of fresh blood filled the young man's nostrils, and he thought he could feel the thunderous reverberations of a monstrous heart beginning to beat.

Aitchley made another futile kick at Nicander. "Let go of me!" he screamed.

Smiling mindlessly, Nicander clung tighter.

As mottled green flesh moved to cover him Aitchley's fingers suddenly touched something cold and metallic. Without even looking to see what it was, he grabbed what felt like steel and swung on Nicander with all his strength. Armor flashed in the halo of white magic as Aitchley cracked the Cavalier's empty helmet across Nicander's face, taking a grim satisfaction in the sound of dwarven steel shattering bone. With a feeble groan, Nicander's fingers released their hold upon Aitchley's leg, and the young nobleman crumpled forward, rivulets of blood streaming down his crushed temple. Cursing, Aitchley launched himself forward, somersaulting free of the Dragon's rib cage just as thick green scales sealed the gap in the Dragon's chest.

Nicander's unmoving hand was the last thing Aitchley saw before the Dragon's body became whole again.

Still clutching the Cavalier's helmet, Aitchley lurched frenziedly to his feet, trying to run even before he was up. He threw a wild look over one shoulder at the gargantuan skeleton now fully clothed in flesh and scales and stumbled in a blind panic toward the lair's entrance. Thick black smoke began to curl from the reptilian nostrils, and the last trace of bone at the Dragon's tail turned green with re-formed flesh.

"Go! Go!" the young man screamed at Berlyn. *"Run!"*

With the sound of growing thunder, the great Dragon Myxomycetes slowly lifted its head and blinked newly formed eyes; Aitchley and Berlyn ran desperately for the exit.

Grim-faced, Calyx stalked up the mountain path, stomping up dirt trails that looked vaguely familiar. The others followed, filling the air with their merriment. Chuckling, Harris Blind-Eye hovered a foot or so above the path, slowly floating forward as the ten clambered toward the Dragon's Lair. The Patrolmen stared in awe at the levitating lockpick, and Calyx had to force the scowl onto his face or else give in to the growing celebration going on around him.

"I have to admit," Harris was saying, "if those bungholers had had eyes, they would have been buggin' from their sockets!"

Gaping, Jelena reached out and touched the floating brigand. "What's it feel like?" she asked, wide-eyed. "To fly, I mean? What's it like?"

"Kind of a weird tickling sensation in your belly," Harris responded. "Kind of pulls you upward."

"I knew a man who could make sheep's bladders rise into the air if he filled them with hot air," Rymel said. "Or were they goat's bladders? I don't remember. Maybe it's the same kind of thing."

"Powerful-sorcery-magic, it is," Poinqart remarked, yellow-black eyes glittering with a hybrid awe. "Brought back from ugly-slimy-Lich-Gate, it was."

Calyx threw a disapproving look at the nine behind him, beady eyes recognizing an outcropping of stone that hadn't changed in two hundred years. "Would you be quiet?" he snapped gruffly. "We're almost there. I want you all to be on your guard."

Smiling, Sergeant Lael turned a reassuring eye on the dwarf. "What for?" he asked good-naturedly. "You said yourself there shouldn't be anything between us and the lair. Isn't that why you sent Aitchley on ahead?"

Calyx's scowl deepened as he stalked up the hill. "I know. I know," he grumbled back. "I've just got a bad feeling about this."

"So you said," Gjuki noted, "but like Sergeant Lael, I can see no imminent danger."

Calyx glanced up at the dark clouds swelling over the mountain peak. "It's just a feeling I've got," the dwarven smith answered.

Unexpectedly—appearing from around a bend in the rocks—Aitchley and Berlyn came scrambling down the mountainside. Loose dirt spumed up in brownish-yellow clouds beneath their feet, and Calyx could see the look of terror in their eyes even from this distance. Berlyn held both Aitchley's staff and her throwing ax, and the young man clutched what looked to be a dully gleaming helmet. They ran downhill so fast as to be out of control, and as soon as he saw them, Aitchley began waving the helmet in his hands, urging them back down the mountain.

"Run! Run!" the farmer screamed at them.

Confused, all ten stopped, staring up the mountainside at the two teenagers rushing toward them. Abruptly—as if there was a sudden implosion—a great sonic boom tore at the very heart of the Dragon's Ridge, the sound of massive wings flapping in unison. Dark clouds swirled and churned in a sudden fit of disturbance, and Calyx could feel the abrupt rush of air as something so huge and so enormous that it seemed to block out the entire sky launched itself out of the mountain and glided effortlessly into the heavens.

Calyx's ruddy complexion paled as Myxomycetes exploded into the open air and swooped overhead; a grave somberness darkened the dwarf's mien. "Oh, kid," he said softly, slowly shaking his head. "What have you done?"

"Response: He has done what needed to be done. Aitchley Corlaiys has righted the balance his ancestor disrupted one hundred and eighty-seven years ago."

Curiously, Calyx turned to see the humanoid robot Tin William mechanically following them up the hill, his metal feet clanking faintly against the rock. Boots skidding in loose dirt, Aitchley came to a bewildered halt beside the dwarf, blue-green eyes going wide at the gleaming figure of steel coming toward him.

"Tin William!" the young man exclaimed. "You're alive? I thought you were dead!"

Videocamera eyes fixed on the young farmer, gray lenses irising with a faint whir. "Please, Aitchley Corlaiys," the construct answered, "have a little more faith in my builders than that. If one of my cameras can survive being torn apart by creatures as brutal as the Daeminase, a small fall of fifty-seven and a quarter feet should barely dent my chassis.''

Storm clouds roiled and splintered in silent agitation as Aitchley blinked at the silver figure. "But . . . but I saw you," he sputtered. "You looked all broken and damaged."

As if guilty about something, the man-shaped form of metal glanced at the rock beneath its feet. "Explanation: A necessary ruse on my part," the robot replied. "I needed to make you think I had been taken off-line so you would understand the importance of my warning." Videocamera eyes panned to watch the Dragon winging its way through the dark clouds over Vedette. "Conclusion: It would appear as if my ploy was successful."

"But the Dragon?" Calyx all but shrieked at the two. "Do you know what you've done? You've just managed to resurrect the most evil, destructive force this land has ever known!"

Tin William turned to regard Calyx with emotionless eyes. "Statement: As the Rhagana Gjuki once said," the robot replied, " 'Nothing in nature is truly evil.' The land of Vedette is a magical place that exceeds the parameters of most understanding. Yet it was clear there once existed a balance between Vedette and the Dragon. No natural disasters befell this land because the Dragon took the place of such events. As Aitchley Corlaiys can explain to you, no lightning strikes caused fires, no rains fell when they were not wanted, no plagues took the lives of those who lived here. Vedette was a veritable paradise with but one exception: the Dragon Myxomycetes. When the Cavalier Procursus Galen slew the great beast, he left a void in the natural balance of the land. Aitchley Corlaiys has refilled that void."

Berlyn turned admiring eyes on the young man. "You were right," she gasped.

Despite the surge of pride that warmed Aitchley's breast, Calyx kept dark eyes on the figure of gleaming steel. "Yeah, but the *Dragon*?" he repeated his earlier sentiment.

If Tin William could have smiled, he would have. "Declaration: You will see," the construct announced assuredly. "The balance will return to normal. The cycle of life will once again be complete. People will die in Dragon's fire—and homes and lands will be set aflame—yet the plagues will be gone, burned away by the Dragon's rebirth. Fields will yield crops. The seasons will become milder. Everything you remember as a dwarven child will become so again. The land of Vedette will be returned to the greatness it once was.''

Harris couldn't keep the skeptical sneer off his face. ''All because of one giant lizard?'' the ponytailed lockpick questioned. ''I don't understand.''

Tin William turned gray lenses on the rogue. ''Statement: That is because it is magic, Harris Blind-Eye,'' the robot replied. ''It is not for you to understand.''

Banking sharply—with a rushing whoosh like some powerful river—Myxomycetes turned in midair and swooped back over the mountain range, spraying the lower plateaus with blistering streams of liquid fire. Shrieking and screaming, any surviving Daeminase were instantly incinerated, turned to charred ash beneath the sweep of purifying flames. Then—with a single flap of great leathery wings—the Dragon rose up and headed into the sky, punching a huge hole in the row of storm clouds to let streamers of afternoon sunlight come pouring through.

Gjuki flinched as thick plumes of acrid smoke rose up along the mountainside and went spiring into the heavens. ''But what of Lord Tampenteire's initial quest?'' the Rhagana wondered. ''Our task was not to restore the land, but to give the people someone to look up to. What are we to do in that respect?''

A grim frown still on his face, Calyx took the helmet clenched in Aitchley's hand and unceremoniously plopped it on the young man's hatless head. ''I'd say we've got our Cavalier right here,'' the dwarf announced. ''What do you say, kid? You up to the task?''

Despite the abrupt panic and self-doubt that flared in his chest, Aitchley felt a crooked smile pull across his face as he saw the encouragement and love glowing in Berlyn's gray-green eyes. Bloody, typical Corlaiys luck! he thought humorously, one arm entwining about the beautiful girl at his side.

Like some great sailing vessel, Myxomycetes glided through the dark clouds, brilliant patches of sunlight trailing in its wake. The air filled with the faint lingering of pins and needles.

Epilogue

8357M2
YEAR OF VANEUR

Sunlight streamed over the fields in waves of golden brilliance, showering the burgeoning crops with springtime warmth. Tender green shoots reached up out of the dirt in thankful supplication to the sun, and birds chirped and twittered in the nearby orchard of dangleberry trees, searching among the budding flowers for insects and maybe the occasional ripe berry.

Wiping at the perspiration beading beneath the brim of his new hat, Aitchley Corlaiys stopped weeding for a moment and leaned back on his hoe, surveying his fields with a lopsided smile. Uniform rows of green grew all around him, and he felt a thrill of pride ripple through him as he looked out across the farmland. For an acre in every direction, the land was his, stretching across the southeastern edge of northern Solsbury. He even had enough land to raise some sheep if he wanted, although he didn't have the money to buy any yet. But that, Aitchley knew, would change. Incredible as it sounded—as hard as it was for the young man to believe—he was a landowner now. Given the land by Lord Tampenteire as a reward for his services, Aitchley was no longer a simple peasant working someone else's fields. Now these lands—these growing crops—belonged entirely to him. Whatever money he brought in was his as well. He had the makings of a very rich man . . . and things were growing now, too.

When he had first returned to Solsbury, he had been surprised at how simple it had been to convince the four lords that he had done the right thing. With an enthusiastic speech about respecting nature—and with the backing of his friends—Aitchley had explained to the audience seated in the Tridome's vastness everything Tin William had told him. Some weren't happy with the outcome—especially Lord Elideri, whose fields and castle had already been destroyed by the resurrected Dragon—but as Calyx reminded them, they would learn to live with it. It was a small price to pay for Vedette's return to its former glory. The only real difficulty Aitchley had was convincing these people that a ritual sacrifice had never been necessary. Young virgins couldn't stop Myxomycetes's carnage any more than they could stop the spread of the Black Worm's Touch. And for months—since Myxomycetes's return to the skies above Vedette—there hadn't been a reported case of the Black Worm's Touch . . . not even in the squalor of the southern-city. Tin William had been right after all.

Smiling, Aitchley straightened the brim of his new hat and looked down at the growing plants. He was a hero now, he thought with some bemusement. He had lost track of how many parties and celebrations he had attended . . . first in Viveca, then in Solsbury. One even in Zotheca. He felt kind of foolish wearing the Cavalier's helmet at these gatherings, but the people cheered and clamored for him in such a way that his awe overwhelmed his embarrassment. He'd lost count of how many times nubile young girls threw themselves at him and tried to smother him in their kisses. A few times Berlyn had even yanked him out of the room, a hint of jealousy flickering in her gray-green eyes. But she was every bit as much the hero as he was. Young men gathered in huge throngs to catch a glimpse of the scullery maid, and she had numerous propositions from wealthy suitors to join with them and start a family.

Aitchley looked up at the large stone cottage situated at the center of his lands, a warming coil of smoke corkscrewing out of its chimney. Never in his life had he thought he'd live in such a magnificent house, yet there it was. Four rooms. A kitchen and dining area. Built by the finest craftsmen in all Vedette: dwarves from Aa. It had been Calyx's wedding gift to the young couple, and it had taken a group of talented dwarves less than a month to build. Calyx even left the Cavalier's shield as the first of Aitchley's new furnishings, hanging proudly over the young man's fireplace.

The door to Aitchley's house opened and a lumbering, inhuman shape came waddling outside, long gorillalike arms almost touching the ground. A happy expression was carved into the hybrid face, and yellow-black eyes sparkled with a mix of human joy and trollish contentment.

"Mister Aitch! Mister Aitch!" Poinqart called from across the fields. "Missy Berlyn says breakfast is ready! Hurry-come inside to eat!"

Practically materializing from between the trees, Gjuki stepped away from tending the orchard and approached the young farmer, a faint smile on his face. "There is nothing like a good morning's work to make one hungry, Master Aitchley," the Rhagana declared, not quite as emotionless as before. "I, for one, am famished."

Letting his hoe drop between the rows of crops, Aitchley nodded, starting a brisk walk toward his house. "I know what you mean," he replied. He tossed a cursory glance back at the dangleberries. "Trianglehead," he called. "Are you coming?"

There was a sudden explosion of chaos as the starlings, finches, and cowbirds hopping about the orchard abruptly fled in a panic, startled into flight by the gyrofalc that spun out of the trees. A glittering petulance flickered in the bird's diamond-blue eyes as it settled on the young man's shoulder, and it fidgeted from foot to foot as Aitchley fixed it with a reprimanding gaze.

"How many times have I told you to leave the other birds alone?" the young farmer scolded.

Trianglehead ruffled his brilliant crest. "Don't kare," the bird grumbled. "Hungry."

"I told you to look by the grainary if you're hungry," Aitchley replied. "Keep the rodents away."

"No like rodentsz," Trianglehead retorted grumpily, nestling his head under one wing. "Taszte mouszy."

"Just be sure to stay well away from Master Poinqart's chickens," Gjuki reminded the gyrofalc. "I'm afraid he treats them more like pets than livestock."

The smile stayed on Aitchley's face as he sauntered toward the cottage, a bounce in his step that had never been there before. Even with the Dragon, life was a hundred times better.

Seeds that were planted actually grew. Rains fell when they were expected. Even the winter hadn't been as harsh. And so what if the Dragon posed a constant danger? It was no more constant than an earthquake or an erupting volcano. Or even a lightning-struck tree bursting into flames. These were things that happened . . . and there was nothing anybody could do about it. If the Dragon replaced all those things, so be it. That, as Taci had said, was its purpose.

Aitchley's smile widened as he noticed the petite figure step into the doorway beside Poinqart, wringing a dish towel in her slim hands. Gray-green eyes sparkled in the morning sunlight, and a beautiful smile pulled across glossy pink lips. The reddish-pink gown she wore hugged her diminutive frame, flaring out at the middle where her rounded belly stretched the fabric. It seemed, Aitchley reminded himself with a lecherous smirk, that one of the times he and Berlyn had decided to be a little adventurous had resulted in something more, but they hadn't discovered that fact until they had returned to Solsbury and had already been wed. It now looked as if the baby would come sometime during the late spring or early summer, but Aitchley wasn't worried. He knew that in the time of the Dragon, women didn't die in childbirth. The magic of the land forbade it.

Aitchley hummed to himself as he strolled across the fields. How about Procursus if it's a boy, and Taci or Eyfura if it's a girl?

The sudden thunder of hoofbeats rumbled through the stillness of the morning, and Aitchley glanced up to see an impressive-looking coach pulled by a train of three *meion* come rolling down the dirt road toward his farm. Even from this distance he recognized the distasteful frown on the driver's ruddy features, and it never ceased to amaze him how good that scowl made him feel.

Pulling up at the cottage at almost the same time as Aitchley and Gjuki, Calyx clambered down from his seat and brusquely opened the door to his elaborate carriage Silver flashed in the dwarf's hands as he withdrew a magnificent breastplate and glimmering chain mail from the coach, each piece of armor radiating an almost sentient gleam. Smaller pieces of armor lay scattered across the floor of his carriage, and Calyx tried to gather all the various segments into his stumpy arms at once, lumbering awkwardly toward the open door of the cottage.

With a resounding clatter, Calyx dumped the armor at Aitchley's feet, a dark, pessimistic look etched on his face. "Well, kid, what do you think?" the smith wanted to know. "Everything's here but the gauntlets and tassets. They probably won't fit you anyway, but I should have 'em ready in about another month."

Aitchley looked down at the magnificently forged armor at his feet. "I don't know," he murmured. "I think I'll feel pretty stupid wearing a full suit of armor."

Calyx gave the young farmer an unsympathetic look. "You're the new Cavalier, kid," he said bluntly. "Get used to it."

"Splendid-fancy, it is," Poinqart said, holding the breastplate up to his own barrellike chest. "Poinqart thinks Mister Aitch will look most heroic-handsome."

Berlyn draped a loving arm around her young husband's waist. "So do I," she agreed. She turned pleasant eyes on Calyx. "Breakfast is just about ready, Calyx," she added. "You're more than welcome to join us."

"It's probably stuff I'm allergic to," the dwarf remarked, "but I think I will."

A trace of color still flushing his cheeks, Aitchley gathered up the dwarven forged armor and carried it into his house. "I don't know," he muttered a second time. "Do I *have* to wear this stuff?"

"Do you *have* to wear it? Did I *have* to make it?" Calyx sniped back, taking a seat at the table. "Look, you're the Champion of Vedette now," he went on. "As soon as the harvest is over in the fall, we're expected to visit two other towns: Karst and Viveca. And Ilietis wants us to come by to oversee their new political order since ousting LoilLan's acolytes. No lords. No barons. Just townsfolk running the place the same as Viveca. Oh, and speaking of Viveca. I got a message from Sergeant Lael a few weeks ago. It seems Sprage made it back safe and sound. And get this: He brought Taci *and* Gjalk with him!"

Gjuki blinked tiny eyes. "My SporeKin has ventured into the World Outside?" the Rhagana said with a deep chuckle. "That is something I surely must see!"

"Any word on what happened to Harris?" Aitchley asked.

A wry grin split Calyx's beard. "Tampenteire and Saradd were true to their word. Got the bracelet off him and pardoned him for all his crimes. 'Course, I'm sure their lordships didn't like the idea of letting the most notorious thief in all Solsbury go with a cloak of invisibility in his possession, but . . . I have the feeling Harris is going to be a very rich man in a very short amount of time!''

As the others talked among themselves Aitchley moved into the kitchen to help Berlyn with the food. Despite the happiness and optimism flowing through his system, the young man felt a nagging remnant of self-doubt poke tauntingly at his breast, and he stared glassily out the window into the blue sky.

Immediately sensing his impending melancholy, Berlyn moved up alongside the farmer, slim arms encircling his waist. The feel of her warm body and pregnant belly against him successfully pulled the young man from his thoughts, but his smile was only half-sincere as he looked down into her gray-green eyes.

''What's the matter?'' Berlyn asked him gently.

Aitchley glanced back out the window, staring up into the sky. ''I'm not sure,'' he replied hesitantly. ''I . . . I don't know if I can pull this off. I feel awkward pretending to be something I'm not. I wish sometimes Captain d'Ane hadn't left. I mean . . . I know he was dead and all, but . . . I could kind of use his advice right now.''

Snuggling up beside him, Berlyn squeezed the young man affectionately. ''I may not be Captain d'Ane,'' the blonde told the young man, ''but I know this much. You're the Cavalier of Vedette, Aitchley Corlaiys. Don't you forget that.''

Aitchley frowned heavily. ''But I'm not the Cavalier,'' he replied. ''I'm just a farmer.''

Smiling, Berlyn gave him one last hug before picking up a platter full of food. ''Well,'' she answered cheerfully, ''you're *my* Cavalier, and if I have to share you with the rest of the world, then so be it.'' She gave him a quick kiss on the cheek. ''Now come on, your friends are waiting for you.''

Chased away by the simple warmth of her lips upon his cheek, Aitchley felt his self-doubt wither and die. So be it, he repeated thoughtfully, a reassuring smile drawing across his face. If the Dragon has its purpose, maybe even I have mine.

His smile grew as he walked back out to where his friends waited for him. Bloody, bunging typical . . . !